The Pirates Of The Whimsical Winds

Book One

THE PIRATE HORDE

Tianna Blackboot

WELCOME TO THE OUTER ISLES...

Pirates, street thugs, murders and worse? Just another day really. That's life in the outer isles. My home.

Commanding an untrained crew, traveling the world, and sailing a ship I have no right being the captain of—Not too bad for a teenager, right? Of course, add in a past that won't leave me alone and the looming threat of an epic war, and things are about to get interesting. I guess it's time for me to step up.

I just wish I knew what I was stepping into...

The Pirate Horde is a wild, whimsical, and wordy coming of age tale full of adventure, high seas shenanigans, witty repartee, and one very confused and frustrated protagonist who's probably too smart(mouthed) for her own good.

This book touches on several potentially triggering topics including violence, mental and physical abuse, slavery, piracy, racism, classism, sexism, ageism, nationalism, anxiety, alcohol use, black market deals, historical inaccuracies, internally inconsistent linguistic structures, teenagers with far too much independence, and at least one girl who has no idea what she's doing with her life.

If any of these things will cause you undue stress to read, it might be best to sit this one out. Otherwise, enjoy!

~*Tianna*

A NOTE ON TRANSLATION

The stories in the Pirates of the Whimsical Winds, and in fact most of my books, are a narrative retelling of the journals and logs that I kept at various points throughout my life. As such, they were originality written in the common low-Tirican dialect that I grew up with. Since my native language is completely foreign to you here in this world, the stories have, by necessity, been translated into something more readily accessible to the general population. i.e. American English.

You will notice that there are instances where certain words appear untranslated. In most cases, this is because there is no direct correlation or variation in modern English that that fully captures the meaning of the original text. To preserve the nuance of the meaning, I have left it as is. Of course, other times I have left it untranslated for poetic effect. This is a novel after all.

Any subsequent translations from English into other languages of this world will potentially dilute the narrative further. This is always a risk that should be taken into consideration when reading any translated text, of course. Implicit or unconscious bias of the translator will always be a factor. You, as a reader, will have to weigh these risks for yourself.

And before you ask, no. I have no intention of publishing the complete, untranslated Tirican journals. Those are mine alone and have some personal details that don't need to be told.

Whatever language you end up reading this in, I hope you find it an enjoyable experience. *Yat som deshk*, my friends.

~*Tianna*

FOR THE HORDE

YOU KNOW WHAT YOU DID

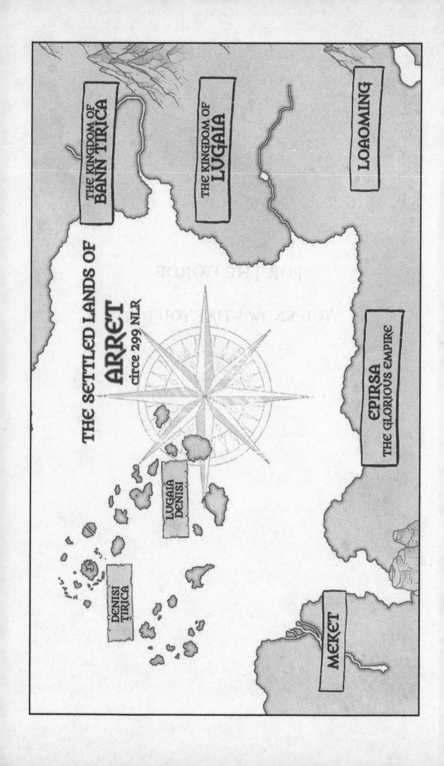

THE SETTLED LANDS OF

ARRET

circe 299 NLR

THE KINGDOM OF
BANN TIRICA

THE KINGDOM OF
LUGAIA

LOAOMING

EPIRSA
THE GLORIOUS EMPIRE

LUGAIA
DENISI

DENISI
TIRICA

MEKET

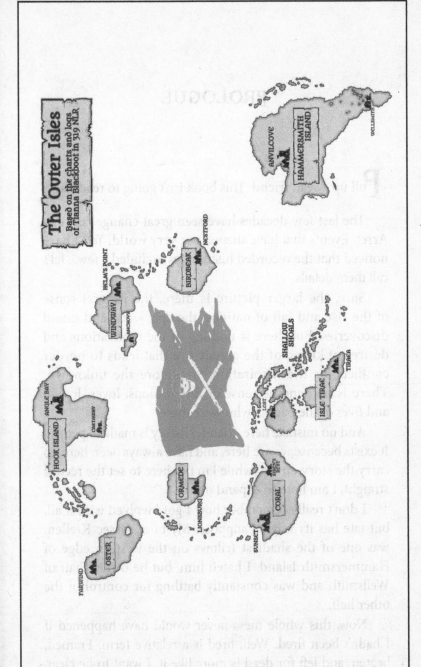

The Outer Isles
Based on the charts and logs
of Tianna Blackboot in 319 NLR

ANVILCOVE

HAMMERSMITH ISLAND

UNCLESMITH

NESTFORD

BIRDBEAK

HELM'S POINT

WINDWAY

ANCHORY

SHALLOW SHOALS

ANGLE BAY

HOOK ISLAND

CANTERBURY

LOST COVE

ISLE TIRAE

TIRAE

ORMEDE

SINGER'S REST

CORAL

LIONSBURG

OSTER

SUNSET

FARWIND

PROLOGUE

Pull up a seat, friend. This book isn't going to read itself.

The last few decades have seen great change come to Arret. Events that have shaped our very world. Yet, I have noticed that the recorded history has excluded a few... let's call them details.

Sure, the larger picture is there, the general sense of the rise and fall of nations, the epic wars, and grand discoveries. But there is nothing of the motivations and desires of kings, of the greedy eye that leads to border conflicts, or the inspiration to explore the unknown. There is no genuine sense of the passions, loves, losses, and *lives* of the people who were there.

And no mistake here, friend. History is made of people. It exists because we are here, and have always been here, to carry the story on. So, while I'm not here to set the record straight, I am here to expand on it.

I don't really remember how I got involved with it all, but fate has its ways, I suppose. My boss, Jassec Krellen, was one of the shadiest fellows on the western edge of Hammersmith Island. I hated him, but he owned half of Wellsmith and was constantly battling for control of the other half.

Now, this whole mess never would have happened if I hadn't been fired. Well, fired is a relative term. Framed, beaten, and left for dead is more like it. I want to be clear, it wasn't exactly my fault. I maintain complete inculpability for bringing a little justice to an otherwise overly blessed shark of a man.

In the years before the Sea Wars swept across all of Denisi, we were a forgotten people. Tiny islands, inhabited by tiny villages that did their best to carve out tiny lives however they could. Territory, shipping rights, land-usage, even laws were open to interpretation. But while the rest of the world may have seen Denisi Tirica as a haven for all manner of pirates, na'er-do-wells, thieves, and marauders, for a girl growing up, it was just home. My home.

I am Tianna Blackboot. Scholar. Storyteller. Pirate. And this is my story.

Well, this begins my story, anyway. I have no intention of untangling nearly thirty years of history in one book. The scope of it is far too broad for a single volume. But, as these events have shaped me as much as I have helped to shape them, I do promise to tell all in the fullness of time. I hope you brought a drink, because this might take a while.

My story doesn't start with my mother's death, or when I coerced the bookseller into teaching me to read, or even with me working as a bookie for a criminal slumlord. My story actually begins the day I woke up, half-drown, on the beach…

THE PIRATE HORDE

CHAPTER ONE

A bright pain shot into my head as I came conscious. Daggers of sunlight stabbed through my eyes, and there was a thundering roar in my head. I considered rolling over, but just then I wasn't sure I could remember how. A shadow crossed my face.

"Ohh, don't move." Whether I was talking to myself or the shade didn't seem important, but both were good advice. I tried to open an eye to see the shadow-caster and instantly regretted moving.

"Maybe you shouldn't move," said a voice from above me.

I groaned and held both eyes shut until the world stopped spinning. I gladly embraced the stillness.

"Hey." The voice was a lilting feminine alto, and I found myself listening to its notes more than its words. "You need help?" A stab in my side jerked me awake again.

"Stop that," I told the stick that kept intruding on my personal space. I batted at it, but it evaded my grip and poked me again.

This time, I opened both eyes. When my eyes focused, it became much clearer that my antagonist was not a stick, at least not directly. It was, in fact, a girl about my age—seventeen or so—wielding said stick. She stood between me and the sun. It was hard to make out her face, but her hair was a dark braid that hung to her waist. Even slightly concussed, I found her appearance striking.

She sat perched on a boulder, one leg tucked under her. The other rested out in front, showing off brown leather boots that fitted closely around her calves. Scarves and wraps decorated her wherever they could fit. She had dark gray ones affixed to each wrist, two at her waist—one blue, one gold—a bright red one holding back her hair, a black one tucked into each boot, and one small scrap of fraying red fabric tied around her left forearm.

But more than the scarves, what caught my attention was the sunlight glinting from the jeweled hilts of what I could only assume were daggers. Three straight sheaths of increasing sizes hung from her belt. Another glittering pommel peaked from the cuff of her boot. I thought I saw one tucked into her wrist wrap as well, but I couldn't have been sure.

I looked up at the girl I could only presume at this point had to be some new breed of beach-dwelling swashbuckler. I really should have been wondering if this was a rescue or something else, but she seemed nice.

She poked me again. "You dead?"

"I hurt too much to be dead."

"Oh good. Death is so messy. What happened to you?"

I watched the clouds shift and change shape. My mind was wandering, which I knew was a bad sign, but I couldn't keep focus. I didn't really feel like talking, anyway. The roar in my ears was deafening. It kept moving up on me then receding, like… waves?

I noticed I was talking. "… murderous idiot. I'll never understand some people." I think I knew what I was talking about, but I couldn't be sure. Guess I should have been paying attention.

"Well, come along, miss. Let's get you dry at least."

"Dry?"

She shrugged and moved to help me stand. It was more of a challenge than either of us was expecting, since it turned out I had both height and weight on her. Being stoutly made was an advantage I was glad of in most cases, but right now, it was proving a hindrance. Still, I found my stumbling way to a sturdy rock.

Now sitting, I at least had a more prominent view of the beach. *Oh, waves,* I thought, mesmerized by my incredible vantage of not lying half-in the surf. *That makes sense.*

Vague memories started coming back to me of the night before. Krellen's face, thinking I'd betrayed him. Fleeing down the dark alleyways of the Rat's Nest. Tavers' barking orders at his two muscled goons.

Running...

Falling...

Nothing.

I didn't recognize the area where I'd landed, but it could have been anywhere south of the harbor. My companion was waiting patiently for me to get my bearings, just watching me. I wasn't sure why she was still around, but I was grateful.

"I'm Tianna." My hand trembled slightly as I held it out to her.

Her grip was firm but friendly. "Kaelyn Féanaro."

"Féanaro?" I repeated, turning it into a question by the end. "Interesting name."

"I'm not from around here," she explained.

I laughed, sort of. My ribs ached and laughing hurt, so I didn't over-do it. It was an odd name, musical and somehow foreign. Southern Lugaian maybe? Or eastern Epirsan? The isles were plenty diverse, and we saw folks from all over, but it didn't stand out as ethnically anything.

"Well, you must be new to Wellsmith, then. We don't care where you're from, so long as you don't plan on staying."

She offered a light chuckle in reply.

I took a second to catch my breath before addressing my new acquaintance again. "So, Kaelyn, do you make it a habit of rescuing scraps of people you find on the beach, or is this an unusual day for you?"

"It's not every day you get a chance to rescue a damsel in distress," she said with a cheeky grin.

I started to object at her epithet. There was very little damsel about me, though it was hard to argue the distress part. I croaked out something vaguely resembling a sound as my throat refused to work, so I just coughed instead.

"Actually," she went on more sincerely, "You looked like you could use the help, and… well, maybe you can help me, too."

I cocked my head, but stopped myself at the last minute for fear it would fall off my neck if I tried. Instead, I closed my eyes and made a roughly inquiring sound. "Uhhuhmmh?" I asked articulately.

"What happened to you?" she asked, almost as if she didn't want to know the answer.

"Ah, well…" I started, but a moment of clarity gave me pause before I answered. Why was I even talking to this person? I mean, she was clearly not a farmer, and I think I've only ever met a less likely priest once. All I knew about this person was that she wasn't an isler like me. Or at least, not one from this island. Yet, somehow, she was eliciting my trust against my will. "That's a long story."

"Well, I've got time," she said. "I really wasn't doing anything when I happened upon your corpse. I just landed, and I don't plan on staying here long, but as luck would have it, I met you first."

"Huh," I said. "Luck. Right." Luck and I have always had a somewhat complicated history. Right then, I wasn't sure I trusted it to be good.

"Come on," she said. "I'm starving and you need to get out of this sun, at least. Let's get you dry and patched up. We can trade long stories over lunch."

I should have just said no and been done with it, but there was a twinkling in her eye that sparked something in me.

Hot pain cut through my shoulder as she hoisted me up off the rock. I wobbled as I stood, but kept my feet.

She walked down the beach, setting a brisk pace. I followed more gingerly, watching the scenery pass in tree- and rock-shaped blurs that refused to register as landscape. She noticed and slowed, waiting for me.

I tried not to think about how hard I must have hit my head. Not that I had many thoughts at all.

If I had any of my mind left, I would have stopped to wonder why this perfect stranger had stopped to help me. I might have asked who she was or where she had come from. I might have been asking myself what it was she wanted from me. Perhaps even, had I been thinking, I would have realized that we were walking back toward the place I was trying to flee just the night before.

But I didn't. I just dutifully followed, wondering if maybe I wasn't still sleeping.

I trailed behind Kaelyn, following her up twisting paths and cluttered walkways until we joined up with the wide, flat roadway of the Wellsmith quay.

This was the main route for anyone coming and going from the narrow inlet that we liberally called a bay. It was little more than a recessed shore, but a heavy coral reef bordered it to the south and was blocked by massive rocks to the north, making it as secluded as any sleepy cove.

Foot traffic was bustling at this time of day, so we made our way up the broad stone steps to the road above the sea wall. This was the Docks Row. It was a part of town I had cause to know well, yet tried to spend as little time in as possible. Warehouses and whorehouses in equal parts lined the streets that overlooked the ships below.

I wasn't sure where we were going, and I was more concerned with making sure my feet were still moving me forward than gawking at sailors. Navigation was secondary to momentum as I stumbled after Kaelyn.

We worked our way to the end of the Row. Here, the main thoroughfare split off into two busy roads, one leading along the north side of the river toward the nicer parts of town, and the other south, up the hill to the part of town I was familiar with–the workhouses and slums known as the Rat's Nest. She led me south.

Finally, we stopped in front of an unassuming inn. She ushered me through a door that was half-hanging off of rotting hinges, with no hope of being fixed soon. I felt a stab of sorrow for its neglect and inevitable collapse, but that may have been the concussion.

The tavern itself was a musky hole-in-the-wall. There was very little atmosphere to speak of, mostly because what little air was available was consumed by the crush of unwashed bodies and wood smoke. Kaelyn didn't even pause as we entered, but waded through the crowd and chatted shortly to the bartender, and then returned just as deftly before I even had a chance to look around.

She led me into a back corner room full of old dishrags, unused mugs, and boxes of soap. "Wait here." She said.

I didn't even have time to ponder what I was doing in a barroom closet before a small nondescript man in a pristine white shirt came in and started poking at me.

"Excuse me?"

"Hmrmmh." he muttered what I think was an agreement that I was, in fact, excused. He continued to lift my arms, check my pulse, and verify my mobility. I took from this that he must be a doctor. If he wasn't, there wasn't much he could do to me just then to make my situation worse, so I went with it.

He wrapped my wrist in some foreign cloth. I didn't recognize it, and he didn't splint it, but the pain receded somewhat. He cleaned and dressed my various scrapes, and gave me an ointment to put on my worst bruises.

"Much pain?" he asked.

"Yes." I nodded, wincing at the truth of my answer. The world ebbed a bit at the edges, and my vision blurred.

He must have seen the color disappear from my face, because he reached out and grabbed my shoulders, keeping me upright while he worked.

I think I was only out for less than a minute, but when I came to, he peered into my eyes and nodded once, gruffly. "Hmmph," he said. Clearly, my passing out offended him, so I did my best to look contrite.

The taciturn doctor reached into his bag, produced an oozing green tonic, uncorked the vial, and poured it into my mouth all in one smooth movement. I watched him move as if he was dancing; all fluid movements and graceful gesture. At least I would have done, except the bitterness of the tonic almost knocked me out again.

He took one more look at me and proclaimed I was as fit as I was going to get. With that, he turned and left.

The tonic had tasted as vile as it looked, but within seconds my head cleared, and the worst of my pain was gone.

To this day, I have no idea what magic he had used or what was in that salve, but gods know I wish I did. There have been plenty of times I could have used it.

I stepped back out into the common room, wondering what I should do next. There was only one safe place for me in the city, but I didn't know if I was ready to tell them what had happened. I had very few people I could rely on, and I certainly wasn't prepared to have three disappointed faces frowning at me.

I had no real reason to assume Kaelyn stuck around. It was just as likely she had been a figment of my addled brain as it was that she was an actual person who wanted my company for lunch. Actually, that first may have been more likely.

Fate had other plans for me, though. She was waiting for me at the bar.

I made my way over to her as a scrawny boy child of eight years or so appeared from behind the bar. Without a word, he led us to a table opposite the cold fireplace. In less than a wink, or perhaps a very long blink, he had disappeared again and returned with two bowls of thick, greasy stew.

It was the most unappealing thing I had ever seen, smelled, or heard of, and I stared at it accusingly.

I turned aside from the sludge and addressed my companion instead. "So–"

"Ready to tell me what happened to you?" she asked before I could speak, not glancing up from the mush she was shoveling into her face.

I shrugged, pleased that I only felt an intense stabbing pain in my shoulder. "I pissed off the wrong people."

"Oh?" She sounded genuinely intrigued.

I sighed and sat back. Launching into my tale gave me a chance to consider many things that had happened in the last few days, but I wasn't sure how much of it to share with my companion. "How much do you know about Wellsmith?" I asked. "About the way things work here?"

She shook her head. "Practically nothing. I landed at the docks with the first tide, went for a walk, found you, and here we are."

I seized the opportunity to buy myself a little time, and gather a little information. "What do you mean 'landed here'? From where?" I asked.

"Nowhere. Everywhere." she answered cryptically, then sighed. "I've been traveling with my parents for the last couple of years. They are merchant liaisons, and spend a lot of time migrating between various places."

My eyes flew open wide. "Consortium?" I asked, for the first time worried about being alone with a stranger.

"No, no! We're free merchants. My parents are more like business consultants. They travel around and help shipping companies establish new business practices, get warehouses up and running. We have had as much reason to avoid the Merchant Consortium as anyone else."

She paused, eyeing me quietly. "I didn't mean to alarm you," she eventually said. "I wasn't aware the Consortium had much of a presence out here."

"Oh, they do," I told her. "Harassing local ships, imposing accepting payoffs they call tariffs, taking whatever–and whomever–they want. The Outer Isles are still officially in Tirica Denisi, so the Lugaians have no authority, but that matters to exactly no one."

She nodded, then veered the conversation into warmer waters. "We traveled a lot while I was growing up. I've been to Lugaia, Bann Tirica, most of the Epirsan provinces, and just about everywhere else with a coastline. This is my first time this far into Denisi, though."

"Wow," I said. "I haven't ever been anywhere but here. And by here, I mean this city. This half of this city, really. It would take a major upheaval to get me to cross the river."

"Why?"

I laughed, then noticed she wasn't joking. "Why else?" I answered honestly. "Politics."

Her expression darkened. "I guess I'm familiar with that."

"Oh? Lot of differing ideologies in your hometown?" I half-joked.

She scoffed and looked uncomfortable. "I wouldn't say that, no. Especially where anyone could hear me." She leveled her dark brown eyes at me, full of meaning.

"Where are you from?" I asked.

"Tecre." She spoke quietly but firmly.

"You're Meketian?" I tried not to sound shocked, but I couldn't blame her for speaking low.

"Is that a problem?" She met me stare for stare.

I know it must have taken a lot to admit to Meketian heritage anywhere north of the continent, but I was never one to judge someone based on their past, and she had done nothing for me to assume she was either a flesh peddler or a religious zealot, so I didn't take the bait.

I gave an indifferent shrug. "In that case, you probably know other places like here. It's a port town. Corrupt, volatile, and libertine. This whole town is run by money and fear. Our politics are more about maintaining a balance between two terrible choices."

"As opposed to being forced into The One Correct terrible choice?"

"That's the world," I said bitterly.

She smiled and sat back in her chair, relaxing for the first time since we started talking. "I haven't seen much of that. So far, the people all seem nice and friendly."

"The people are nice. The citizens try to make the best life they can, but everyone here is caught between Mitsuni's thugs and Krellen's pirates. And that doesn't even account for Consortium corruption and the occasional slaver raids.

There's not a lot most people can do. We're larger than most shanty towns, but at our heart, that's what we are. Not important enough to be on a map, not small enough to pass by, and not dangerous enough to wipe out or clean up. We just… are what we are. New people come in from anywhere, and we just do our best not to get killed."

A solemn look came across her face. "Is it like that on all the outer islands?"

I shook my head, more in uncertainty than denial. "In some places, I'm sure it is, but I've only known Wellsmith."

She rested her elbow on the table and propped her chin in her hand. "What about the Governor? I thought Hammersmith Island was a Tirican holding?"

"It was. Still is, I suppose. The Governor is mostly useless. Anvilcove is a few days north with good wind and a sturdy boat. And the road is so overgrown with jungle and wild animals that no one, stupid or brave, would take it." I shook my head. "Out here, we're so far away from Tirican justice that we could dance naked in the streets and sacrifice people to old gods and the king would never know or care."

"But what about the war?" She asked.

"What war?"

She stared at me. For a moment, I wondered if there was some epic battle waging just off the shores of my little island that I didn't know about, but that seemed absurd.

One of us was terribly confused, and at that moment, I honestly didn't know which of us it was. So, I just moved on with my tale. "We do have the magistrate's guards here, but they're either bought by the Consortium or completely ineffectual. At best, they ignore any crimes that happen right in front of them. At worst, they help commit them." I shook my head again. "No, we take care of ourselves, and help each other when we can."

"You said you pissed off the wrong people? Who was that? What did you do?"

Where did I even start? The events of my life to that point were all part of some intricately woven and incredibly boring cord, spliced together by the whims of this wretched backwater I'd been born on. Did I begin from when my mother died? I've never remembered her, so there wasn't much to tell. The orphanage that offered me regular meals, a dry place to sleep, and little else? That month I had spent following that acting troupe around? Up until I joined with Krellen, my story hardly felt real, let alone worth telling.

I sighed, and launched in somewhere in the middle. "You need to understand, on this island, you either work for one of the gangs, or you keep a sharp knife on you at all times. The smart ones do both. I started working for Krellen two years ago and did my best to keep my head down. It's just…"

Kaelyn nodded as if she understood. "It's just that it wasn't the life you wanted to be living."

I looked at her, as my thoughts ordered themselves. I chewed on my bottom lip as I considered the girl across the table from me. Eventually, I nodded. "I suppose that's as close to the truth as anything else," I said, then sighed. "Well, like I said, Krellen and Mitsuni each control about half the town, and they both run things their own way.

"Mitsuni relies on more structured enterprises. Gambling dens, opium houses, brothels. Businesses he can buy and run that keep people coming to him. My boss—ex boss, now, I suppose—controls the docks and the slums through intimidation. Do things his way or move along. It's all protection rackets, questionable loans, and taking bets on just about everything. That's what I did."

"You were a bookie?"

"I prefer the term bookkeeper, but yes. It was a simple job. I'd offer bets on every shipment coming through the port. What cargo a ship might carry, the distance they traveled to get here, how long they were staying, how many crew aboard, the captain's favorite color. Didn't matter what. So long as someone could guess at it, we'd place a bet. Then, of course, we'd take the good people's money when they were wrong. Or lie about the results and take their money, anyway."

She coughed, but I saw the corners of her mouth twitch. I found it reassuring, actually. I didn't need to find out the hard way that my lunch companion was a rigorous moralist.

"I don't know about how you were raised, but sometimes the idea of working for someone powerful can be appealing. Especially when you have nothing to start with. It's not that I didn't know Krellen is a glorified thug. I just needed to do something."

I didn't like to admit that working for Krellen gave me a purpose. It wasn't a great, or lucrative, or even enjoyable one, but with Krellen, I was more than just another body crowding the streets. I wasn't about to share those particular insecurities with Kaelyn, though.

"But you still haven't answered my question." Amusement colored the edges of her voice. "What happened?"

I shrugged. "I got bored."

That wasn't entirely the truth. What happened was I got bored with doing Krellen's dirty work. I grew tired of seeing regular people who were just trying to live their lives get squashed under the boot of someone who had no more right to play god than the rodents his home was named for did. I was done playing their game.

"I started questioning some of the orders I was given, especially those from Krellen's nephew," I admitted.

I dropped my gaze away from her for a moment, fighting back the shudder that came every time I thought of him. "Anyway, to cut this already too-long story shorter, someone used my position against me. They planted some coins in my stuff that were definitely not mine and told Krellen that I'd been skimming."

"Oh, no!" she said. "What did he do?"

I smirked at her. "At first, nothing. He didn't believe them. They tried to convince him I was stealing, but I showed him the books that had everything accounted for. Whoever the idiots were, they used their own coin to frame me, instead of his."

She snorted, then let loose a laugh.

I shook my head again, fighting a grin.

"You almost sound like you're fond of him," she said.

I chewed on the inside of my cheek while I thought about that. "No, I think respect is a better word for it. He's a natural leader, something I've never been, and I admire the way he deals with people he considers his equals. But he's not a good man, not even close. He wouldn't blink at destroying people he considers beneath him. When it comes down to it, he's just a bully with too much power, and I couldn't ever be fond of that."

She nodded, seeming to like my answer. "I'm guessing whoever tried to frame you didn't try it again?"

I frowned, remembering the last couple of days. "No, but it sowed a seed of doubt. Krellen believed me at first. And when something else went missing, it was easy to turn suspicion on me."

"What went missing?" she half-whispered, engrossed in my story.

"That's the thing, I don't know," I said. "I just know it was more important to Krellen than a little money."

"That's amazing." She shook her head. "Who would even do that? Why?"

"I can think of a few people who might," I muttered. "I'm not really a people person."

She laughed again, and I felt myself smile back.

I let out a sigh and decided to wrap up this tale. "Krellen wanted to interrogate me, but his nephew wanted me to suffer first, and they fought over what to do with me. While they were arguing, I slipped out. The guards saw me get away and ran after me.

"They chased me to the edge of the city, where they caught up with me. I fought back, of course, which is why..." I gestured at my face, and winced. "The bank there is steep, and I thought it better to take my chances with the tide rather than let them take me. So, I jumped. Then this morning, I was awakened by a stick poking me in the rib and an inquisitive woman asking me questions."

She grinned mischievously at that last bit. It felt a tad recursive, telling her a story that she was a part of, but it reminded me of something I should have asked as soon as we sat down.

"So, Kaelyn?" I said, "What is it you need from me? You said something about helping you out."

She didn't seem the least bit put off by my question. In fact, she almost seemed as if she expected it. Her rejoinder had the earmarks of a rehearsed a reply.

"You have no reason to trust me, I suppose," she said. "You don't know me, and you've been through more than enough to be wary of anyone. It would be foolish to trust someone who just happens to show up at the right moment. Especially someone who looks like they come offering help." She paused. "For all you know, I could very well be trying to trick you into some nefarious scheme."

I nodded. She said exactly what I had been thinking. It's true that I didn't have very many friends, and I didn't trust easily. That wasn't just me, though. All the people of Wellsmith have a well-developed cynicism.

Everything she said sounded true to me, or at least correct. But somehow, hearing her say it out loud laid a lot of my fears to rest. Maybe it was because friends were in short supply for me just then, or perhaps she was just a kindred spirit, but I wanted to trust her.

"Well, I am," she said.

I paused my mental diatribe. Taken aback, all I could do what repeat her last words. "Am what?"

"Trying to involve you in some nefarious scheme. Oh, don't look at me like that. It will be fun!"

"What?" I asked again. Alarm and confusion warred within me as slumped forward. I leaned forward and rested my aching head in my hands.

She laughed out loud and patted me on the back. "Calm down, I'm kidding," she said. "Nefarious doesn't even come close. But while you were talking, it made me think… I mean, I'm wondering if…" Her laughter gave way to hesitation, then wariness, until she was eyeing me with a thoughtful expression on her face. "Do you have anywhere to go? Anyone in this town who will help you out? By your own admission, one of the most powerful men in town wants you dead. So where will you go?"

My stomach dropped, and I felt my fingertips grow cold. That was not a question I had an answer to. Yes, I technically had somewhere I could go, but she wasn't wrong. Krellen was going to hunt me down. I wasn't safe here anymore.

The orphanage stopped being an option as soon as I left. The matron had nearly shoved me out and bolted the door behind me. I wasn't close with any of the workers, innkeepers, or sailors in town. And I sure as hells wasn't willing to run to Mitsuni and beg for him to take me in. With as angry as Krellen was last night, I couldn't even guarantee he wouldn't start a war just to get me back if I did.

That only left Three Brothers, and I wouldn't—I couldn't—bring Krellen to their door. It was the only promise I made to myself when I started working for him and I would hold to it even if it killed me. Of course, that didn't leave me with any options, except…

I looked at the girl sitting next to me. "What are you suggesting?"

Her smiled was effervescent, and she beamed at me like she'd already had me convinced. "We leave," she said simply.

I let the thought float around in my head, not quite grasping what she meant. "Leave… the tavern?"

She chuckled. "Leave… the island?" she mimicked me. "Look, I don't have a plan, but neither do you, right? You've never left Wellsmith. I've never been to the Outer Isles. Why don't we just go see what's out there?"

Her suggestion felt weighted with every hope I had never dared to have. Leave Wellsmith? Could I just do that? Just go and get away from all this? It seemed so simple. Why had I never thought to do that before? It felt like the sun was rising, pushing back the darkness that had always clouded any dreams of my future.

"We could… leave?" I said. "Why?"

"Why not?" she asked.

"Oh, come on! Why are you hesitating?" She placed her hands on the table and leaned in. "How about this? I'll sweeten the deal with a proposition."

"You're not really my type," I quipped automatically, my mind still reeling from her assertion that I could just leave if I wanted to.

"Har har," she replied drolly. "What if I tell you I am on a quest? Would you be interested if I had an objective in mind?"

I paused, considering. "Maybe, but if you do, why didn't you lead with that?"

"It didn't occur to me."

I shook my head, starting to feel like we were going round and round in circles. "What do you want with me?" I asked her again.

She grinned. "I told you. I need help with a quest. It's a minor pursuit of some insignificant iniquity that—"

"Kaelyn," I growled her name, not realizing how that was going to become the common way of addressing her. "What is it you want from me?"

She laughed, clearly enjoying the exchange.

I admit, I was too, though I wasn't about to let her know how long it had been since I'd enjoyed a conversation this much. She was being intentionally obtuse, and her goading was a bit aggravating, but I enjoy good banter more than almost anything.

"I want to come with you," she said.

"With me?" I asked. "This is your plan, isn't it? I'm not going anywhere."

"Aren't you? From what you've told me, you aren't heading back to Krellen's or wherever. You don't have any friends in town, you're trapped. So, we leave. You let me tag along." She paused and bit her lip, like she was trying to keep a smirk off her face. Her gaze danced away, but then came back to land on me. "I have a map."

"A map?" I repeated, surprised. "Like a treasure map?"

She grinned, dancing in her seat. "Exactly. Yes. A treasure map! I got it off a guy I met in Calipi. Lugaian sea trader, Gaston or Gaspert... or something. I can't recall."

I laughed. I couldn't help it. "Kaelyn, first of all, I'm pretty sure Gaspert isn't a name. Second of all–"

"Gaspar! That was it." she interjected. "Very serious type. Good guy though."

"Second of all," I continued, "Pirates don't bury their treasure. That's a myth. Treasure maps aren't real outside of children's games. It's all fireside stories and fishwife tales to add to the mystique of the sailor's life. I promise you, there's nothing romantic about pirates."

To my surprise, she grinned even bigger. "I *know*."

Puzzled, I searched her face. "If you know, then why do you look so excited?" I asked skeptically.

She just laughed. "Exactly."

"Kaelyn," I growled again in warning.

She held up her hands, warding me off with another laugh. "Okay, okay. It's… well, I don't know. I *think* it's a treasure map. It is a map. That much I'm sure of."

"Alright." I heaved an enormous sigh, hiding the fact that it intrigued me. "Tell me more."

Her eyes sparkled. She knew she had me hooked. "I told you I'm from Tecre, but I'm not Meketian exactly. My father is Tirican and my mother is Kurkurani."

"Kurkurani?" I asked, genuinely surprised. I'd never met anyone from that far away.

She waved a hand dismissively. "Not directly. Something like three generations removed? I'm a melting pot, so my cultural heritage is a little hard to pin down. And since we're merchants, as I mentioned, we've developed a few of our own traditions."

I nodded along, mostly following.

"One such tradition," she continued, "Involves leaving the family for a time."

I leaned forward, listening intently. "Go on."

"When you turn sixteen, your parents drop you off in a place you've never been with just a few basic supplies and a map. You're not told anything. You're just supposed to figure out what to do. Sort of a 'find your own path' thing. After you've made your own way for a while, you're free to come back to the family or not."

I sat bewildered. "Why?" I asked. "I mean, I've never heard of anything like that before. And I read a lot. A *lot*. Are there cultures that do this sort of… rite of passage?"

She shrugged. "I don't know. It's just how it's been in my family for as long as anyone can remember."

"Huh."

"Well, we got this map from Gaspar just before we left Calipi. It was the last place I saw my parents. I guess in a weird sense, I traded my mother for this map, which sounds terrible now that I've said it." She blinked and shook the frown from her brow before continuing. "Whatever, it's fine. The point is, this map has led me here."

"Why? What's it a map of?"

She shrugged. "I have no idea. It's the Outer Isles, but it's blank. Here, look." She twisted and reached into a thin cylindrical case at her hip. She pushed aside our bowls and unrolled a small piece of parchment.

I cocked my head, looking at it. It was the Outer Isles, I recognized the shape of the land masses, but there were no markings, no course directions, not even names. It was, as she had said, a blank map.

I sat back in my chair and looked at her. Across from me sat this strange girl, with strange ideals, strange customs, and a blank map. I'm not sure how it happened, but gods help me, I wanted to go with her. I wanted to find something interesting to do with myself now that I couldn't go back to Krellen. I wanted to fill in this map.

"Well..." I looked past the crowded room to the door, as if I could see past it all the way to horizons unknown. "I'm still hungry, so maybe we can find some actual food and talk about it."

"Yes!" She laughed triumphantly, and swallowed the last bite of her stew before standing up. "Are you ready for an adventure?"

"Uhh…" I stalled, trying to formulate a reply. Slowly, I stood. "I suppose so. I can't just leave the island, though. At the very least, I need to go see my uncles."

"Your uncles?" Confusion was written on Kaelyn's face. "I thought you said you don't have any family."

I nodded. My turn to be cryptic. "I don't," I said, and turned toward the door.

Kaelyn followed, clearly wanting to ask more. We pushed our way through the crowd and stepped out into the street.

I blinked several times as my eyes watered from the suddenly overwhelming sunlight. The transition from the dark hovel to the summer day temporarily blinded me. I couldn't see a thing, which was why I walked right into the back of the last person I ever wanted to see again.

Darl Tavers. Jassec Krellen's nephew.

There were a few parts of my story that I hadn't told Kaelyn. Most of them involving the bastard that had spent the last two years tormenting me, abusing me, using me, and most recently framing me. All she knew was that he had tried to kill me.

I fought down a moment of panic as I tried to think of how to get away again.

So much for the luck I'd had yesterday.

CHAPTER TWO

This was clearly the wrong part of town for me to be hanging out in. I probably would have known that if I had stopped to think about where we were. Even if I had never been on this particular street before, we were right in the middle of the Rat's Nest. Krellen's men were everywhere, probably even listening to that entire conversation.

"Well, what have we 'ere, lads?" Tavers' cronies weren't much to remark upon, except I remember them as being different, well-muscled, idiotic goons than the ones I'd run into before.

"Looks like Jassec's little birdie 'as flown back to us after all," one of them whistled from between a gap in his teeth.

"Is a shame Vik. Didn't we do for her the other day? Guess we didn' finish 'er like she deserves."

"No worries, Nate, no worries. We can do it now, ya?"

"Shut up, both of you. You sound moronic," I recognized Tavers' drawl, even as my vision cleared on his clean-shaven, angular face. "How are you, Tianna? It's been a while." His tone was so pleasant it sent shivers down my spine and my vision blurred under the onslaught of terrible memories.

"You seem to be in a jovial way today, Tavers. Have things been going well?" I managed to crack wit, despite the rising gorge in my throat.

He grinned—an honest grin with no hint of irony or ire. I was almost sick.

"Oh quite," he said. "Uncle Jassec has been on a tear trying to find the person who stole from him. Any chance you know where we could find her?"

"Uh, boss, isn't she–" one of his men started before being cut off by the other one. "Shh, you moron. Would he be askin' if it's her?" He was obviously the brains of the pairing.

I shrugged, ignoring the geniuses. "Not a clue, I'm sorry to say. I heard she ran afoul of some of the wilder elements in town and suffered a bit for it. Didn't she drown?"

Tavers nodded sagely. "A rumor, sadly. Doesn't seem to be true after all. I do hope to get my hands on her soon."

"You'd have to let go of your manly organ long enough to grab anything else."

There it was. That glint in his eye that told me I had been standing here just a fraction too long. Too bad I wasn't smart enough to use the time to escape.

He reached out a hand and casually slapped me across the cheek. "I think that's quite enough out of you, motherless worm," he said pleasantly. "Luckily for me, you're not entirely useless. Uncle Jassec will be glad to see you." He leaned in close. His voice dropped low, almost seductively, as he purred, "Maybe he'll even let me have some fun with you when he's done."

I recoiled as far as I could, but his hand lashed out faster than I could see, snaking around my injured wrist.

"Let go!" I screamed, knowing how useless it was. I was feeding into his game, well aware that he enjoyed the pain of others, but it didn't stop me from reacting.

"Don't worry, Tianna," he cooed gently, "I'll take good care of–"

A dagger bloomed out of his right eye, cutting off the rest of that thought. He released me and stumbled back with a cry as a second blade followed. It landed in the shoulder of the goon to Tavers' left.

"Here!" Kaelyn shouted. She tossed me a wicked-looking blade as the second brute came toward me.

While it stands to reason that someone who carries that many blades must have at least a passing knowledge of how to use them, it never occurred to me she might actually, you know... use them. But I didn't have time to wonder at this newly discovered trait of my comrade as the goons closed in on us.

The thug called Nate grabbed for my arm and missed, snagging a handful of cloth instead. I struggled to free myself, but my shirt was firmly in his grasp. Twisting, I dropped to the ground and slipped out of my garment. Now, in my less cumbersome undershirt, I was free to maneuver quickly.

He held up the loose shirt and blinked at it in surprise. I used his momentary confusion to wrap his arm up in the fabric, twisting it around his other wrist.

He struggled with the cloth, unable to free himself. He grunted in frustration and then simply threw him weight forward, hands still tied. He slammed into me, knocking me to the ground. I cried out as I landed on my strained wrist, but I didn't have any time to stop.

I glanced around. Tavers was gone, having fled at the first opportunity. The other hoodlum, Vik, lay in the street, bleeding from one leg, both arms, and his stomach. He wasn't going anywhere. Two more men that I hadn't noticed before surrounded Kaelyn, but she had a wicked grin on her face. She had the situation under control.

I turned back to Nate, slipping sideways and tangling him in the rag he was still trying to free himself from. As he fought to free his hands, I jabbed the curved knife Kaelyn had given me into the soft flesh at the back of his knee. He went down in a splash of blood with an arresting scream.

I punched out with the hilt. It struck him in the face, knocking him backward another step. He stumbled and then surged forward again. As he came back toward me, I slid my sword into the soft tissue just above his belt.

It was easy. So easy. Such little resistance. Just a small amount of pressure was all it took for me to pierce his stomach. My blade slid into his flesh like my pen dipping into fresh ink as I drafted a new tale or sketched a market scene. Only, I knew in the instant that it was done, that I wasn't here to create. My art was destruction, and this... this was nothing like playing pretend.

I withdrew my dagger and looked in horror at the warm blood dripping onto the dirty cobblestone street. Transfixed, I watched the red puddle growing underneath his still twitching body. I was going to be sick.

The sounds of steel clanged nearby, and I looked up to see Kaelyn fighting off the last two. Almost as soon as I saw what was happening, one went down with a knife across his throat. The other tripped backward. Eyes wide in terror, he looked up from where he'd fallen and dropped his blade. He looked like he was going to be sick, too.

Before I could quip about not having the stomach for a fight like this, he spun and raced off down the street. Kaelyn started after him, but I grabbed her sleeve.

"Let him go."

She looked at me, then back to his fleeing form, then back to me. "Are you sure? What if he gets help?"

I shrugged, or at least thought I tried to. My mind was foggier now than when I'd woken on the beach. Adrenaline made me aware of everything and unable process anything that was happening.

"We'd better be gone before he gets back then," I said. "Tavers got away, too."

She hesitated another moment, and then nodded. She quickly bent and cleaned her blade off on the shirt of the man at my feet. Then when she saw I wasn't moving, grabbed the still dripping one from my hand and did the same. She sheathed both and then turned to inspect me.

She examined me closely for injuries. "Are you alright?"

Until that very moment, I had thought I was alright. I was sure that I had been processing my emotions and wisely dealing with the ramifications of all I had been through. And yet, all at once, the last few day's events came crashing down around me. As if with that one question, the dam built up around my eddy of irrationality crumbled, sweeping away any cogent thought.

Rather than break down crying—which was a real possibility just then—I went on reflex. I shook my head, both to tell her no and to clear it of the cobwebs crowding out my thoughts. I cradled my re-injured right wrist against my chest and shook my head again. "Let's get out of here."

She offered me a faint smile. "Know somewhere safe?"

I nodded once and spun around, trusting her to follow me as I ran off up the hill.

I led her down a few back alleys, and around the only church left in town before we paused. Every turn we took, and every road further away from the mess we'd left behind us, was like a balm. I breathed more deeply and soon my mind calmed enough that I could think.

"Do you even know where we're going?" Kaelyn asked between heavy breaths.

I looked around, hoping the answer was obvious. I had been moving on instinct, looking for a safe haven. But there was only one place I would naturally go. I glanced down the street toward the river.

"You've never been to Wellsmith before, right?"

She shook her head and shrugged. "Nope. We mostly traveled around Lugaia Denisi. This is the first I've ever been this far west."

"Then you just need to follow me. I know exactly where I'm going."

She raised an eyebrow. "Great. My trustworthy guide."

I laughed and lifted my chin in the direction of the market. "C'mon. I'll show you the best part of town."

Down another back alley, around a row of houses, and through an archway that didn't seem to hold anything up, we came to an open intersection where several of the smaller roads met. The press of the ramshackle buildings eased, and the hill descended into a full view of the city center.

On the far side of town, lights were just winking into life as bawdy houses and rum runners prepared for the night ahead. Around us, tanners and artisans shouted at one another as they rushed to wrap things up for the day. But there, in the middle of everything, was a perfect little island, covered in every type of brightly colored market stall and shop imaginable.

Kaelyn gaped and I grinned.

"There's an island in the middle of your river," she said after a moment.

"Yep."

"Huh," she said.

I pointed down the hill to the north end of the market island. "See that small building with the green shudders? Not the wagon stall, but the two-story one behind it? That's where we're going. That's Albert's shop."

"Who is Albert?" She asked as we set off down the hill.

"He's… my uncle? Sort of. One of them anyway. Well, I mean… wow, it's been a long time since I've had to explain this. It's fine, trust me. They're good people. The best."

"Okay." I tried not to welter in my awkwardness as she eyed me. She said nothing else and just walked next to me.

We crossed over a sturdy stone bridge to the island. I led her past all the usual market chaos to the far side of the main square. We came to a row of weathered old buildings and stopped by one that was in slightly better condition than its neighbors. Its green roof and neatly maintained window boxes made me grin. It looked more like a middle-class home than a bookshop, but the dusty smell of parchment and vellum gave it away. Well, that and the big sign out front that read, *Three Brothers Books.*

Kaelyn saw it and commented. "A bookstore?"

"Can you think of some place safer?"

"I guess not, no. Do you know these brothers?"

I tilted my head and she gestured at the sign.

"Oh." I shook my head as I headed for the door. "That's just the name of the shop. It's owned by Albert Gardner, and run by his two best friends, Adwin and Jun."

She looked confused. "They're not brothers, then?"

I snorted, stifling an outright laugh. "I really hope not."

The iron door handle was warm from the afternoon sunlight, and I rested my hand on it a moment, enjoying the sensation of coming home—even if it wasn't technically my home. I lifted the latch and pulled. The door rattled in its frame and didn't budge. I stared at it, uncomprehending of the situation. I tried again.

"I think it's locked," Kaelyn said.

"It can't be. Albert is always here this time of day." I rattled the handle again, then knocked. When no answer came, I stepped back, my brow thoroughly furrowed. I looked at the shuttered windows, trying to peer through the slats for a glint of light or movement, but found only stillness.

"Huh," I said. "It's locked."

Kaelyn looked around the street, surveying the other buildings. "We don't have much money, but we could try that road by the river, right? I thought I saw some boarding houses there."

"No need. It's fine. Wait here." Before she could respond, I ducked around the corner into the narrow alley between the bookshop and florist. There, about ten paces back, hidden in the shadows, were three medium-sized crates.

I took one and placed it on top of the other two, and climbed atop them. Then, reaching above my head, I felt along the underside of the eve on the florist shop until I found two small indents, just big enough to fit my fingertips into. I hoisted myself up and braced my feet on the outer wall of the bookshop.

My wrist hurt like nothing I'd felt before, reminding me it had been injured not once, but twice in as many days. It throbbed but held, so I ignored it, pushing down the pain to deal with later.

Quickly shimming my way up the wall, I made my way onto the roof of the shorter building. Then, I turned and half-leaped to a small overhang on the second floor of the bookshop. I grabbed hold of the windowsill to balance myself and then pulled open the shutter. The window was open a hand's width.

I smiled, knowing my faith was well placed. He never would let me down. I slid the pane open enough to squeeze through. Closing the shutter behind me, I then hurried downstairs to unbolt the door for Kaelyn.

With a cheesy, aren't-I-so-impressive grin, I opened the front door onto a wide-eyed Kaelyn.

"Do I want to know?" she asked.

"Probably." I swept an arm open in invitation.

She laughed as she joined me inside.

"I've spent a lot of time here. Albert is something like my guardian," I explained as she followed me into the main room. "Adwin and Jun, too. They're the only reason I wasn't sent off from the orphanage to a workhouse or wed to some mudflat fisherman. They taught me things, looked out for me, helped as best they could–basically raised me. As much as anyone did, anyway."

She paused just inside the foyer. I loved it when new people would come to the shop. I would watch as they scan the rows and rows of shelves overflowing with cloth- and leather-bound tomes. Their eyes invariably travel down to the stacks of books piled in every corner, between shelves, and on counter tops.

There were a few chairs placed almost randomly in and among the shelves for shoppers to read and peruse. At the back of the shop, along the outer wall, was a door that led to a small kitchen, and stairs up to the second floor, where the purveyors lived.

"This is… amazing," Kaelyn said breathlessly. "I've never seen so many books! Where did they even get all of these?"

I grinned as if it were me she was praising. "Salvaging forgotten literature is something of a mission for Albert. He was an ambassador or a royal tutor or something when he was younger and so he has an absurd love of knowledge in general."

She wandered the room a bit, and I smiled as she scanned titles. It was my favorite pastime, too. "This place is amazing! What was it like to grow up here, surrounded by so many books?"

I picked up a random book, flipping through its pages without reading them. "I didn't exactly grow up here. I lived in the orphanage until I was fourteen."

"Oh," she said. "I thought you said they raised you."

I shrugged. "Yeah, in a way. There's not really an easy way to describe it. They were more like teachers? They looked after me, kept me out of trouble most of the time, and taught me everything I know. Reading, writing, figures, fighting, even a bit of cooking…" I shrugged again. "They are the closest thing to family I have."

"Hence why you called them your uncles." A pensive look spread across her face. After a moment, she asked, "Why didn't they just adopt you? It sounds like they care for you. Why leave you at the orphanage?"

I shifted uncomfortably. "It's… complicated. Three men raising a young girl alone, even out here. And Jun is… Hey, do you play chess?" I rose from my seat and walked toward the stairs, not waiting to see if she would follow.

She set her book down with a gentle thunk and rushed to catch up to me. "I'm sorry," she said. "I didn't mean to ask uncomfortable questions. It's not really my business."

I shook my head. "No, it's okay. I just don't like to talk about them when they aren't around. They had their reasons, and it never bothered me. I didn't have a conventional childhood, but I turned out fine."

She fell silent as I led her down a short hallway and into a small parlor. The room was dark, and growing colder as the sun set. I went to the firebox and set to work building a fire in the hearth. Before long, a cheery glow lit the space.

The room was furnished for comfort with mismatched styles. An ornate Loaomineese lounging sofa and two more simple armchairs took up most of the space. There was a small writing desk along the far wall under the window, next to a decorative rack of small foreign weapons in various styles. Directly opposite the hearth, along one wall, was a simple wooden chessboard on a table-height pedestal.

Kaelyn hovered near the door, unsure where to be.

I gestured to one of the chairs. "You can relax here. We're safe."

She hesitated a bit longer. "Are you sure? I still feel weird breaking into someone's home."

"It's not breaking in," I said. "Okay, well, yes. It kind of is, but it's fine. They know I come here."

She still looked uncomfortable, but took a seat in a chair by the fire.

Before the silence could stretch back into awkwardness, I leaped to my feet. "How about some tea?" I disappeared back downstairs without waiting for her answer. I needed a moment to collect my thoughts, and the steeping tea offered a good excuse.

I needed to find Albert and figure out what to do next. Krellen wouldn't give up now that he knew I was alive. He would send someone to drag me back, and I did *not* want to end up in Tavers' hands. I could still feel the ghost of his soft leather gloves brush against burned skin. The sound of his knife on a sharpening stone… I shuddered and pushed aside memories.

Moving automatically, I returned to the parlor with two steaming mugs and a small plate of cakes I had found in the breadbox. Kaelyn accepted her cup with a smile, but didn't try to restart the conversation. My thoughts continued to drift while I sipped my tea, and we sat quietly together.

Sometime later, I sat back in my chair and looked around. Kaelyn was staring at the chess table in the corner.

"Still want to travel with me?" I asked quietly.

She lifted her head to look at me and raised an eyebrow in question.

"I mean, being my associate comes with risks," I told her, feigning lightness. "You knew me only a few hours before I walked you into danger."

Kaelyn smirked. "I hardly think you masterminded all that. And if you did, I'm impressed."

I breathed out something between a laugh and a sigh. "It will happen again." I told her. "Trouble's always been good at finding me."

She shrugged, looking into her teacup.

"So," I asked again. "Still want to travel with me?"

"More than ever." Her grin was infectious and I laughed along with her. "You aren't afraid of fighting for what you believe in, are you?"

I shrugged. "I will fight to protect myself and those I care about, if that's what you mean."

"No, I mean your beliefs, your values. You know what matters to you, and I think that's amazing."

I scoffed. "Don't let my stubbornness fool you. I've never been a woman of conviction."

A thoughtful, yet dark, look came into Kaelyn's eyes. "Sometimes stubbornness is better than conviction."

I was about to ask her what she meant when a yawn overtook me. It was followed by another, and I had to blink the water out of my eyes when I could finally speak again. "Well," I said. "I guess maybe I'm a little tired."

She laughed, stifling her own yawn. "Its been a day. Is it alright if we sleep here?"

I nodded and waved for her to follow me. I walked down the short hallway to the room at the end that I had climbed into a few hours earlier. As I handed Kaelyn a warm blanket and settled onto a woven pallet under the open window.

Taking in the dark room, I spared one more thought for Albert. It really wasn't like him to disappear overnight. At least, I didn't think it was. Adwin or Jun either. For all three of them to be missing at once filled me with a worry that I didn't want to look to closely at.

I knew it was likely nothing. A hunting trip into the mountains, or one of Albert's visits to the farmlands on the north end of the island. Still, I couldn't quite shake the feeling that something was off.

Once more before letting sleep claim me, I wondered where they could have gotten off to.

I awoke with a start. The sky was just lightening in a pre-dawn haze when a clattering downstairs launched me from my bed. Kaelyn was already sitting up, staring at the door. She had a blade to hand, and I nodded silent gratitude for her preparedness.

I slowly crept forward, down the stairs. Voices, urgent but hushed, came from the main room. A light blossomed as someone lit a candle.

"Get him over here," a smooth male voice commanded. It was one I knew better than almost any other. The rough bass grumble in reply told me everything I needed to know. I stood from my crouch and rushed into the room.

Adwin was helping ease Jun down onto a chair near the kitchen door, while Albert grabbed a box off a tall shelf and began rummaging through it. Jun's normally gracile frame looked fragile in Adwin's stout arms. His face was ghastly pale and his bright eyes were creased in pain as he tried to keep his breathing even.

Albert nodded when he saw me. His lean face was tight with worry and his mouth was set in a grim line. "Tianna, get the bottle from the chest in my closet. The green one."

I hurried to the room on the far side of the house, quickly found what he needed, and raced back. I didn't know what had happened to Jun, but I was familiar with this poultice. Albert had used it on me more than once to stave off infection after Tavers' had gotten to me.

He took the bottle from me without a word and drizzled the clear, viscous liquid onto a clean cloth. I knelt in front of Jun, taking one of his delicate hands in mine and squeezed gently, letting him know I was here. His answering smile was tight, but grateful.

Adwin was busy cutting away part of Jun's trousers, uncovering his leg to the thigh. As he pulled the fabric away, I could see a deep gash in Jun's leg, slowly oozing. Much slower than it should have been from a cut this fresh.

Alarm raced through me. Whatever had cut Jun was slowing his heart rate and keeping the blood from cleaning out the wound. I swallowed hard and tried to remain quietly supportive while Adwin and Albert worked.

"Poison." All three men whipped their heads about to look at the girl standing over my shoulder. "I've seen it before. It's Epirsan. An extract from a snake toxin and slows the blood but keeps it from clotting. He'll bleed out if we don't stop it."

Jun turned his head to meet my gaze. He smiled weakly and gave what I think was supposed to be a wink, but came out more as a grimace. "Not to worry, *nisháe*," he told me. His musical Loaomineese accent was thick with suppressed pain. "These are good hands."

Albert finished whatever he was doing with the rag and bent forward, pressing it to the wound. Jun gasped.

"What do you need?" I asked.

"Honey, soft bread, and clean linens. And hot water. A lot of it." He didn't look up, trusting me to fetch what he needed. I hurried into the kitchen. I returned a moment later with everything he'd requested. Then, I stepped back, just hoping not to be in the way.

Albert scooped out the softest part of the bread and mashed it between his fingers before rolling it around in the honey. When he had a sticky wet paste, he slathered it onto the gash in Jun's leg.

Jun jerked at the touch, and bit back a cry.

Adwin moved to stand behind the chair and rested both his hands on Jun's shoulders. "It's a'right, *wodái*, I'm here. I'm right here. You're goin' be fine."

He gave Adwin a faint smile and nodded, trust and love mixed with pain in his eyes.

"Cut this into wide strips." Albert handed Kaelyn a clean sheet, while he folded another. He held the sheet against the wound, pressing firmly.

He took the strips from Kaelyn and soaked them in the large pot of boiling water I had brought him.

He used one to carefully clean around the cut, then bent to examine his makeshift poultice.

I peered over his shoulder. The bread paste was starting to dry at the edges, crusting and flaking away. But in the center, where it nestled against his raw flesh, it was turning a pale, sickly yellow color. I blanched and bit back the bile that rose in my throat.

Albert deftly cleaned it and reapplied a fresh dab of paste. Then, taking the soaking rag, he wrapped the wound.

I looked up at Jun, resting in Adwin's arms. He looked faint, pale and sweating, but less panicked. Albert sat back on his heels and nodded, looking down at the mess of bloody gauze and ichor paste on the floor. "I think that will do it," he said. "We will know more by morning."

"Thanke, Bertie," Adwin muttered breathlessly. His square jaw was locked like he was fighting any expression from taking root on his face, but I could see the gratitude in his eyes. And the fear. "You too, lass. Both of ya."

Kaelyn smiled weakly, and I turned toward Albert, ready for him to take control of the situation and reassure us that everything would be alright. We all needed his soothing, calm demeanor after the stress of the last few moments. It would be alright now.

He stood and dropped the remaining supplies into a pile on the floor before turning slowly. His snapping blue gaze pierced me with a fiery stare.

I sputtered, stunned by the sudden shift in my reality. "Albert, I–"

"What are you doing here?" he roared.

My mind raced as I tried to think of what I had done wrong and came up empty. Albert never raised his voice.

"What do you mean? I… I needed a place to sleep. What the hells happened to you guys? Why is Jun hurt?"

He took a step forward menacingly. I took a step back, and he recoiled. He ran his hands through his hair, tugging on the ends in frustration. When he dropped his arms and faced me again, I noticed the red patch on his shirt, just below the elbow.

"Damn it, Albert, you're hurt, too!"

I dragged him over into a chair and pulled his arm out of his sleeve. The cut wasn't deep, but it was bleeding. I dressed the wound as he continued to scold me.

"I'm fine, child. Quit fussing over me." He grumbled angrily, but he was gentle as pushed me away. He stood and turned toward the stairs without looking at any of us.

I finally took a moment to study each of them. Adwin had always looked every bit the burly man-at-arms. His blonde hair was cropped short, close to his scalp, giving him a severe look but now he seemed hunched, weary and aching with worry as he watched Jun closely. Far more vulnerable than severe.

Jun was one of the most beautiful people I had ever seen. Long-limbed and graceful with softly foreign features that drew the eye to his unusual eyes. But right now he looked like even Death had given him up as a lost cause. His milky skin was sallow and tinged with gray. He leaned back into Adwin's arms, eyes pinched shut, shaking.

And Albert—studious, neat, and careful Albert—seemed shattered. He normally kept his brown hair brushed back, but now it was disheveled and sweaty, drooping into his face. Deep lines that he was still far too young to have were carved into the set of his jaw and the lines around his eyes.

I had never seen anything rattle them like this before.

"Wait a second." I trailed after Albert. "What happened tonight? Are you really alright? Were you attacked?"

He continued walking.

"Albert, talk to me!"

He stopped. A weighted pause settled over him before he sighed heavily. He turned on his heel and spun to face me. "What happened here is what always happens here, Tianna. The slavers, the cutthroats, Mitsuni, Krellen–" he stopped, taking in my face as if he was seeing the last few days written out in bruises. His shoulders drooped hopelessly and he reached out, gently gripping my chin. He turned my head so he could see the dark patches along my jaw. "Did Krellen do this to you?"

I shook my head.

"Tavers?"

I nodded.

He inhaled a sharp breath, concern being replaced by anger again. "Damn it, Tianna!"

I flinched and felt tears welling from the back and forth of his volatile emotions.

"This can't go on. You aren't safe with them!"

"I know, but I'm done. I left."

"And got this for your trouble?" he said snidely. "Men like Krellen don't just let people go."

I glared at him. "I'm safe here, aren't I?"

"I am no longer certain that you will be safe anywhere! Not with us. Not anywhere in Wellsmith."

I stood there in stunned silence, trying to understand exactly what he was telling me. "You... you want me to go?"

He paused and locked eyes with Adwin for a moment. Something passed between them, and I realized this wasn't a spur-of-the-moment decision. He wasn't just lashing out because Tavers had hurt me again. They had discussed this before. They wanted me to go. They wanted me to leave.

"Lass," Adwin said from where he still stood next to Jun's chair. "He's right. Tavers has been getting worse, hasn't he? If you're on the outs with Krellen, you won't be safe here na'more."

I looked at him, trying to keep the tears out of my eyes, and said nothing.

"You know th' three of us would fight th' whole damn city off for ye, if we had to, but..." He trailed off, at a loss for words and turned to Albert, the light in his eyes turning both resigned and determined. "We can't keep going like this, Bertie-boy, and you well know it."

"I know," Albert growled. "But we cannot act hastily."

"Oh aye, wouldn't want to do anything rash." The bitter sarcasm in Adwin's voice was like a gut punch, and it wasn't even directed at me. This haughty stare was so much closer to his usual biting wit that it was almost a relief. Almost.

"You know it isn't that simple!" Albert shouted.

"I know you're afraid of losing everything again, Bert, but how long can we keep this from boiling over? Look around you! It's too late already."

Albert shook his head and stalked off, heading for the front of the shop. He stopped halfway across the room, hesitating, before turning back to me. A dark look came into his eyes. "You don't belong here, Tianna."

I felt as if a bucket of bilge water had just poured over me from a great height. Never in fourteen years of knowing this man has he ever addressed me so bitterly. It took me a moment to understand what he said. "What?"

"It isn't safe for you here. Not any more. If Krellen is looking for you, they will come here eventually."

"W-what?" I stammered, looking for any words. "But this is no-man's-land. If they come here, they'll be picking a fight with Mitsuni."

"That fight is already coming. Don't be their excuse."

The frost in his voice squeezed my heart. I watched him push me out. He raised a wall between us that had never been there before. Some part of me could see that he was trying to protect everyone in the market, not just me, but all I could hear was that he wanted me to go.

"Tianna, child, this is no simple matter. You know what is happening here. You can't possibly be blind to it. Gods, you're part of it!" He took a step forward, his pale face growing redder with each word. "Did you honestly think working for Krellen wouldn't come back to haunt you? You were treading on shaking ground already!"

I blinked back tears, my voice rising before I could control it. "You think I don't know that? Isn't it what you've always taught me? That we need to stand together, to protect each other if we are to survive?"

"Krellen isn't how you survive. Krellen is how you lose yourself in hedonistic mediocrity. You are better than him. You are better than this!"

I shook my head, tears flowing freely now. "Am I?"

Out of the corner of my eye, I saw Kaelyn walking quietly down the stairs. I hadn't seen her leave, but at some point she must have seen how this was going and gone to fetch her bag. I noticed she was holding my boots. She was trying to stay inconspicuous, but the worried look on her face let me know she was here for me.

Albert took a deep breath, forcing himself to calm. "We all must make choices, Tianna. Yours have led you here. I'm afraid you have no other options now."

I felt the ground under me crack from the pressure of his resolute gaze. I balled my hands into fists, digging my nails into the palms of my hands, trying to break through the haze of rage that was threatening to blind me. "So, that's it? All the years of looking after me, teaching me, caring for me, and now you're done? It got hard, so I'm out?"

Albert was silent.

I choked on a sob and nodded. "So, that is it. I'm not wanted here any more." A bitter gasp that was almost a laugh tore through my chest. "Maybe I never was."

Adwin's larger frame came from behind Albert and folded me into thick, strong arms. "Lass, take a breath," he said into my hair.

I stood there, leaning into him, just gasping and sobbing until my breath calmed. One deep breath. Another. A third, and then I took a step back. Looking at all three of the men who had helped raise me. "Where am I supposed to go?"

"North," Kaelyn said.

We all turned to look at the guest on the staircase.

She half-smiled apologetically, but looked confident. "I still have that map, and a few contacts in Anvilcove."

I shook my head. "I've never left Wellsmith," I said under my breath. I knew I sounded like a child, but just then, I felt more like one than I had in my whole life.

Adwin patted my shoulder comfortingly. "Never too late to try something new, aye?" he said quietly.

I looked at Jun, still curled into the hard kitchen chair. "When I was a *nishie*, I had not even left the inner court. Leaving a city should be no trouble." He smiled, his eyes crinkling in joy the way only years of laughter could show. "You are strong for this."

A shuddering sigh escaped me. I wasn't used to them all being in agreement. All my life, I was used to being ignored or unwanted, but this was the first time I could remember being rejected. They wanted me to leave. They didn't want me here.

A warm hand landed gently on my shoulder. Then another. I looked up as Albert held me in front of him. "You are more precious than you can ever know, Tianna. I promised your mother I would care for you, and I meant it. But I cannot protect you here. Not between Krellen out for your blood and Mitsuni after mine. You must go. For all our sakes."

I sobbed. Albert never talked about my mother. I had asked him not to, and he had never felt the need to challenge me. I didn't remember her, but it was enough that I knew he did. I looked up into the steel-blue eyes that had watched over me from a distance my whole life, following me, protecting me, and in them, I saw his heart breaking.

"You didn't fail her." My voice came out almost in a whisper. "I will be alright, Albert. I promise."

He nodded, wetness forming in his eyes that matched my own. He swallowed back his tears, and opened his mouth to speak, but couldn't find the words. Giving up, he shook his head and pulled me close. Holding me in the warmest and rarest hug I'd ever received.

But it didn't last.

I leaned back to say something, but my words were drowned out by the sound of breaking glass. Spinning around, I braced myself to leap into action or away from it. I wasn't sure which. From outside, shouts of anger mixed with cries of alarm as the market erupted into chaos.

"Stay here," Albert ordered. Although it wasn't clear who he was talking to, Kaelyn, Jun, and I stayed put, while Adwin stepped with him to the front door and the broken windowpane next to it.

The taller man glanced out the broken window. "Damn."

"They followed us?" Adwin asked, standing beside him.

Albert nodded, then turned back to face the rest of us. "Looks like we have no time for long goodbyes." He pointed to the kitchen door in a silent order.

I stood there, shock rooting my feet in place. What was happening? They were attacking the market? But... why? This was neutral ground. This was safe from both Krellen and Mitsuni. Who would dare break that fragile peace? What did they gain from it? Every question was written on my face, underscored in fear.

Albert strode across the small distance between us and took both my shoulders in his hands once more. He shook me slightly, and I looked up into his terrified face. He didn't have the answers either.

"Tianna, you must go. Now. I can't keep this from happening, but I can keep you out of it."

"I... I-" I stammered, not sure what happened to my tongue. As I fought for words, another loud crash came from next door, followed by the acrid smell of smoke.

Adwin cursed and pulled what I had always thought was a decorative sword off the wall. He raced out the door as Jun struggled to his feet and hobbled to the kitchen, gathering the medical kit.

Kaelyn silently handed me my boots, and I bent to yank them on. When I stood, Albert cradled my face gently in his hands. One more sorrowful look crossed his face.

"Do you have any contacts at the docks?" he asked.

"The docks?"

"Captains, sailors, anyone who can get you on a boat today?"

I struggled through the haze of emotions, trying to form any useful thought. "I think so."

He nodded once, grim determination creasing his brow. "Then go. And don't you dare come back here." His words were harsh, but I saw the barest gleaming of heartbreak in his eyes. He turned me toward the kitchen and pushed. "Go." The front door burst open as armed men poured in, shouting in a language I didn't try to recognize. "Now!"

His final shout broke through my fog. I grabbed Kaelyn's hand, and we raced out the back door, into the alley.

Swords clashed, followed by cries of pain. Everywhere, screams of confusion and fear rang out. I didn't bother to hide the tears that flowed down my cheeks as we ran. Half the market was burning as we raced down the hill, away from the only place I had ever felt safe.

CHAPTER THREE

It is two-thousand and twelve steps from The Three
Brothers Bookshop to the orphanage, and another three-
thousand six hundred and ninety-seven to the North Dock.
I know these steps inside, backward, in the dark, and in
my sleep. I've walked these steps in the rain, the scorching
sun, injured, sick... and never in my life had they ever been
so long.

I let my feet guide us while I forced myself to think.

I ran through a constant list in my head of who would
be in port now, where they might be headed, and, gods help
me, who would even be willing to take on two runaways
with no sailing experience against Krellen's wishes. The list
was painfully short, and I prayed Kaelyn would chock the
worry on my face up to the riot behind us.

I never did care for the docks. It was noisy. It was smelly.
Everything was busy. People pushed other people about as if
every bit of business they had was strictly urgent.

There was cargo being loaded and unloaded, passengers
waiting to board. Out in the harbor, there were even more
ships, sloops, and brigs waiting for docking space. It was a
cacophony of life that was far beyond me. Especially this
early in the morning.

Kaelyn was right at home. She strolled through the
crowd, as comfortable here as in an empty hallway. I let
her lead along the boardwalk while I looked at ships.

We slowly worked our way up the docks, looking for any familiar faces. I asked after passenger freighters from passersby and about local charters at shipping companies. As the early morning crept on toward day, I was about ready to give up.

Kaelyn paused at the edge of the seawall, waving for me to follow her. "This way," she said.

I watched her maneuver between two people arguing over a manifest. She slipped around a large crate, through a group of people, and hopped over a barrel before I lost sight of her.

She was gone.

For a moment, I just stood there stunned, torn between screaming in frustration and collapsing into a sodden mess of tears. Doing neither, I made my way as best I could over to the side of the road and looked out over the water while I tried to catch my breath. I briefly wondered if she would come back for me, but for that space of half a heartbeat, I didn't care.

Go. Now! Albert's last words to me vibrated in every corner of my body. Find a ship, get out of Wellsmith. It was only the beginning of a plan, but it was all I had. Steeling myself with a deep breath, I pushed myself upright and began down the boardwalk once more.

About twenty minutes passed, and I kept walking. I came to the end of the wall where the road became stairs, leading down to the quays with the warehouses and docks proper. I took the stairs down, avoiding eye contact with workmen loading and unloading goods.

I pushed aside my lingering annoyance with Kaelyn. Her disappearing act—and coincidental letting me take care of everything—was not a good way to start a journey. She was all I had left, and I needed to trust her.

Or did I still have her? I stopped. Had she left me, too? If she was gone, I was left to whatever fate or whim I wished to explore, but... what? A wave of loneliness washed over me and I sat down on an abandoned box to contemplate my next move. I really was alone now.

I thought about circling back East and heading inland. I was sure those stories of monsters and cannibals in the forest are just exaggerated to keep kids in line. There wasn't a proper road to Anvilcove, and I don't know if I'd ever heard of merchants coming overland, but I'm sure I could make it work if I was dedicated...

I pushed the thoughts away and looked out to sea.

"What are you doing?" I looked up to see Kaelyn waving from the other side of a pile of crates. "Come on!"

I choked out a loud bark of laughter. It wasn't a joyful sound, but rather one borne of desperation and exhaustion. I sucked in a ragged lungful of air while I regained my composure. Then, I stood and trotted down the lane until I had caught up with her.

"Where did you go?" she asked me.

"Where did I–"

"Did you find one?"

"No! I was looking for you!" I ground my teeth together to keep from shouting. Kaelyn didn't even seem to notice that I was annoyed.

"That's all right. We'll find someone." Her condescending tone did nothing to appease my irritation. "Let's go try the–"

"Let's not," I interrupted.

She looked taken aback, then abashed. She opened her mouth to apologize, but I was all done letting her lead by random action, and I certainly wasn't about to get into an emotional bloodletting just then. I cut her off before she could speak, and focused on our task at hand.

"I know of two ships that will willingly, if not gladly, take us North. But, they are not in the taverns and they are not along the Dock Row. They should be in port either now or within a day, but I am going to continue searching along the quays. If you want to come with me, great. If not, please stop getting in my way."

"I–"

"Kaelyn, if you're serious about getting out of here, we need to be systematic about it. We can't just go running off into the wilderness." *As much as we might want to,* I added silently to myself.

"Yes. But–"

"Would you rather go deal with whatever the hells that was in the market?"

"No... but–"

"I need you to watch my back. I–" My voice hitched in my throat as a tear nearly escaped. Her gaze met mine, and I took a step back. I breathed deeply, letting go of all the emotions choking me. *Vasta!* I hated crying. What a mess. "I can't do this without you," I finished.

Kaelyn looked chastised, but nodded.

I slapped both my cheeks, bringing myself back under control, and turned toward the nearest pier. "Okay," I said. "Let's go."

We started off down the docks again. I explained what ships I was looking for and she was happy to help. As we walked, I looked at the nameplates of ships, and she asked passersby if they knew anything. It wasn't the fastest tact we could have taken, but it was efficient.

We neared the end of the dock without hearing or seeing anything. My spirits sank. This voyage was doomed to fail before it began. The morning sun was ever upward and I couldn't fight the feeling that we were running out of time.

I had very little left to offer to this plan. My energy was flagging and my aches were multiplying. I paused and leaned against a rough wooden lamppost.

I missed.

As my luck would have it, I slipped and fell backward into a pile of crates being staged for loading, spilling barrels and boxes of ribbon, buttons, and beads everywhere.

"Hey! What're ye doin' there!" A voice shouted from the other side of the mess I just made. I looked up as he came around the corner. The black mop of hair and warm green eyes that I saw made me blink and look again.

"Hank?" I said. "I've been looking for you!"

The sturdy man in front of me had a pleasantly deep laugh. I nearly wept in relief and found myself grinning back at him from amid a pile of bric-à-brac. He offered me a hand up. "You know, lass, you 'ave the most uncanny ability t' fall backward into what you want."

"Clumsy and lucky. That's me."

"Friend of yours?" Kaelyn asked.

"You could say that." I turned to look at her with a wry expression. "He used to work with Krellen."

"Before I gained some sense," Hank added. He offered another of his trademark grins and then reached out to haul me upright once more.

"Sorry about the mess." I said, gesturing at the spillage.

He waved me off. "Eh, not a worry. We'll find som'un t' clean it up." He waved to someone standing further down the dock, a tall, skinny fellow, who turned and ran off. Presumably to find someone to clean it up.

"Listen, Hank, do you still run the Outer Island circuit?"

"That I do, lass. We be headed t' Anvilcove next."

Kaelyn let out a squeal of excitement as I grinned and said, "I was hoping you'd say that."

He paused and looked at my disheveled appearance, knowing it had nothing to do with my tumble into the beads. He frowned slightly and leaned in, murmuring, "You a'right, lass? You look like ye've been through the straits without a scull."

I nodded, fighting back tears again. "It's been a long couple of days."

What followed next was the usual exchange concerning payment, luggage, and the usual necessities. The deal made, we followed Captain Hank further down the docks. So far down the docks, in fact, that I wondered where we were.

He led us up to the rocky beach to the northernmost end of anything that looked like civilization. We rounded several decent-sized boulders before coming to a planked pathway leading back up toward the cliffs. Whatever had been hastily built here was intended to be some sort of addition to the docks, but only for those foolish enough— or poor enough—to want to navigate the rocks to reach the beach.

"Well m'friends, there she be." Hank waved his hand in the general direction of the makeshift docks. "Meet the Naked Chicken."

"The Nake–what?" Kaelyn asked, laughing outright.

"Best ship in these waters, missy. Make no mistake."

Her laughter carried until the precise moment she turned to look. A full-rigged and sturdy bark floated merrily where it was tied to the floating dock. It had a broad, flat bow and a square stern. I guessed it was about thirty meters from one end of the deck to the other, and the whole thing had kind of a boxy appearance. Her broad belly was deep, and I could only imagine how much she could carry in both crew and cargo. Though, room for the two of us was really all I needed.

The gunwales were painted a bright, almost garish yellow, which stood out against the dark, natural finish of the bulwark. Everything was well-appointed and much cared for. This was not a poor-man's ship, and Kaelyn's open jaw told me she knew it, too.

I grinned and clapped her on the back as I walked past her with Hank at my side. It seemed to snap her out of her embarrassment and she hurried after us.

"And here be me crew. Jasen, say hello." Hank waved a tall, muscled sailor over to us.

The man dropped down from the ship, nearly leaping over the gangway to get to us.

"He's your crew?" she asked, baffled. "Not like the whole crew, right? There are others?" She whipped her head around from side to side, trying to see any other living souls.

Hank let out a heavy, rolling laugh. "O'course, o'course. Ye' can't sail a ship with only two people after all!" he said with another chuckle. He seemed to think that was all the conversation needed, and turned to walk back up the road toward the main dock.

"Hank!" I shouted after him. "How long do we have?"

Hank ignored me and kept walking.

"We cast off just after midday," a deep baritone voice boomed from behind me. Jasen, I assumed, since he was the only other person around besides me and Kaelyn.

I turned and did the only thing left to me at that point. I introduced myself. "I... I'm Tianna. Pleased to meet you."

"Our other passengers, is it? Have ye any baggage?"

Kaelyn and I both shook our heads.

"Excellent. Well then, lasses, this way, this way." He gestured up the gangplank, waving for Kaelyn and me to proceed him. "Welcome aboard."

"Is this for real?" I asked Kaelyn under my breath.

She just grinned and said, "As real as it gets, m'dear. We're getting out of here."

The sea breeze felt amazing as we made our way up the coast. The day had turned out bright and clear, which I took as a good omen for my first ever sea voyage. I wasn't even too sea sick.

The City of Wellsmith waved goodbye as we bobbed up and down on the water. I wasn't sad, exactly. It was overwhelming, and I still hadn't collected my thoughts. Wellsmith wasn't a big city, but there were still parts of it I'd never seen.

The idea of there being more beyond the city, beyond the island, beyond the ocean? It felt like a someday dream. Like a story that I would tell myself could be if I were someone else, not a reality I was living. The idea of leaving it far behind, exploring the world I'd only ever read about, was... a lot.

The further we got from the Rat's Nest, the more my fears and grief settled. I was too well read to think that the world began and ended at Krellen's doorstep, but knowing it and seeing it were entirely different things. With every mile that passed, my heart lightened until I stopped looking backward to what I'd left behind, and started looking forward.

We were off to Anvilcove! It was still the same island, I'll grant you, but it was the whole other side of the island. And the home of the Governor of the Outer Isles, too!

I had seen Krellen's form of rule, and a bit of Mitsuni's, but I did not know what to expect from Governor Jenkiss. Jengiss? Jenson? I couldn't remember, but it didn't matter.

What kind of man was he? What was his city like? I couldn't imagine it. People and ships and buildings and... I don't know what. It was a *real* city, though. The thought gave me a little thrill, and I danced with excitement.

I gazed north along the coastline toward Anvilcove. Then, in my mind's eye, I looked ever further. What else was out there in the world?

I had read of something called the Counsel of Five that lived in Boarstown, wherever that was. Somewhere north. According to my history books, they were supposedly the seat of power in Tirica Denisi, appointed by the King of the Scarlet Throne to oversee the interests of the isles, blah blah blah. I'd read it, but it was nothing but academic so long as I was on Wellsmith. They didn't want us. We didn't need them.

It never concerned me. Not really. Staying abreast of politics meant keeping an eye out for who belonged to which gang and watching my back when I walked down a dark alley on the wrong side of the river. If the Counsel were so far away in the North, did the Governor have power here? Was he a better ruler than the Wellsmith magistrate who hid in his mansion year-round? This, all of this, was simply new.

I sighed, breathing deeply of the rich salt spray. It had been three days since I decided that I wanted something else for my life. Just over two days since I was picked off the beach by an aimless wanderer. And a mere day since I left my home behind.

Given my options, I didn't regret that decision, nor have I ever since, but I allowed myself a solemn moment to wonder what was left of the market. To wonder if they were still alive. I sighed again, this time tinged with a bit of sorrow.

There was no way of knowing what I was sailing into. What if it wasn't any better out here? What if the rest of the world was just as corrupt and dangerous as Wellsmith and all of the stable government, long life, happy families stuff was propaganda? Were there actually righteous kings in the world or was that fairytales to make people hope for better?

Well, it didn't matter. Hope was a good thing, after all. Like as not, I would still have made the choices that led me here, but maybe I would have made them more decisively. I just wish–

"Ooph!" The bundle of rope hit my stomach while I was mid-thought. "Here." Jasen said at the same time.

I looked in bewilderment at the rope coil in my hands. It was a good stout rope, about the width of my thumb. "What am I supposed to do with this?" I called after him as he scurried up the rigging.

He shouted after himself, "Make yerself useful!"

"Make myself useful... Okay," I muttered, mostly to myself. "And how am I supposed to do that? Am I an end-table?" I stood there for a moment looking at the rope, wondering if anyone would notice if I just threw it overboard.

"Psst..." a voice whispered from across the deck. I looked up, scanning the port rail to see who was lurking there. "Hey, Tianna!" I spotted Kaelyn. She was crouched, half-secluded, between two barrels, and looking lost. She motioned me over.

As I cautiously approached, she looked up at me with a vaguely sheepish expression on her face, then looked down at her lap. The bundle of rope in her hands was a tangled mess worse than the one I held.

"Got you too, did he?" I took a seat next to her.

"What is–I mean... How do you…" She waggled the length of rope hopelessly, then looked at me. "Do you know what to do with this?"

"I don't know. Tie things down? Fasten things to other things? Make… uh, rigging, I suppose?"

She shook her head. "You're as clueless as I am!"

"About this?" I gestured at her with my own coil. "Yes. But I'll have you know that I know plenty about plenty."

She cracked a smile. "Yes, I'm sure you're very smart." A jovial twinkle winked to life in her dark brown eyes. "But that doesn't help either of us right now. What do they expect from us?"

"You mean the captain and mate?" I shrugged. "Maybe they just want us to pull our weight on this trip. We didn't exactly pay them much." *Or anything at all, really,* I thought.

I traded our passage mostly on the memory of past camaraderie and a shared hatred of Krellen. The only thing of value we had to give was one of Kaelyn's jeweled daggers and my favorite book of Farréan poetry. The binding was still solid, too. I miss that book. I'm still sorry I gave it away.

"But I've never sailed before," Kaelyn said. She grew red-faced as her jaw tightened and her frustration grew.

"What? Seriously?" I laughed again. "Your parents are traveling merchants. You've been all over Mervast, you said so. You don't sail, does that mean you can fly, then?"

She looked more irritated than amused at my quips. "I've been on boats before, sure. I've been around sailors, but I've never had to sail one myself. My family always hired a crew."

"This was your idea!" This joke was quickly becoming unfunny. "Do you know how to navigate? How to care for a ship? Where to buy supplies?" I said, the pitch of my voice rising on each sentence until it cracked on the last word.

"Not really, but I could probably fake my way through it if I had to."

My eyes were nearly bulging out of my head. "Then what are we supposed to do? We can't book passage every time we want to travel. We don't have any money!"

She looked away sheepishly and muttered. "I never said it was a perfect plan."

"Clearly," I muttered.

Kaelyn held up the quarrelsome rope, changing the subject. "So... Think we can figure out how this works?"

"Don't look at me," I grumbled. "I don't know what it's supposed to do. It's rope." I fell silent, looking between the coil Jasen had handed me and the knotted mess in Kaelyn's lap. I met her gaze for a still heartbeat, and we burst into laughter.

A sweet feminine chuckle joined our guffaws a moment later. I perked up and glanced around. A short brunette woman, a little older than either Kaelyn or myself, stood about half-way out of the cargo hold. She had bright green eyes that danced when she smiled, and an easy, confident air that reminded me of Jun. She held a pitcher of some mysteriously foaming gray liquid, and a platter of meat that smelled deliciously like roast duck in the other.

"Umm... Hi," I said intelligently.

"Hold this." Still chuckling, she thrust the foodstuffs at the two of us. Since not taking them wasn't an option, Kaelyn and I soon found ourselves holding someone's lunch while the Naked Chicken's mystery woman took up our abandoned rope and proceeded to show us how to tie various knots.

"Like this," she said.

My eyes opened wide. "You mean there are different types of knots?"

She laughed and reclaimed her platter and pitcher. "You're kind of clueless, aren't ya? Cute, though."

"Thanks, uh... Miss." I was incredibly articulate that day.

She pointed at the rope in my hand. "Tie that knot at even intervals, every full arms-length till you reach the end." She turned to Kaelyn. "You do the opposite."

Kaelyn blinked up at her. "Untie them?"

The woman shook her head, still smiling. She pointed at the pile in Kaelyn's lap. "Untangle that mess, recoil it, then get it back to the quartermaster or mate."

"Oh! Thank you," Kaelyn said, suddenly looking like she felt as foolish as I did.

"Wench!" Captain Hank shouted as he emerged from below-decks. "Where's that food?"

"I told you not to call me that, you drunken mulefish!" she shouted back. She winked at us and smiled. "I'm Yiri," she said. "The captain's wife. And you're welcome."

She walked off to feed her apparently starving husband. Kaelyn and I watched her until she disappeared into the cabin. With a shrug, I set myself to tying and untying something called sheepshank knots until my eyes watered.

I looked up from what was probably the seventeenth knot I'd tied flawlessly to see Kaelyn staring off at the horizon. The mostly untangled rope rested idle in her lap. I just watched her as she let her thoughts drift.

It had been a busy couple of days. So much had happened that we hadn't really talked since the night before we left Wellsmith. *The day we met,* I reminded myself.

I didn't really know what to make of her. She seemed intelligent, charming, and excitable—traits I always liked in myself—but these quiet moments threw me off. I'm not saying I didn't trust her. I did. Instinctively. But what if my instincts were wrong? Or worse, what if they were right?

"I'm sorry," I said eventually.

She looked at me with a faraway look in her eyes.

"For all of it. The bookshop, and the riot. For dragging you onto this ship and taking you away from everything. I know it's–"

Kaelyn blinked. She cocked her head to the side and looked at me like I was reading the back page of a Tirican mining guide—equal parts *what are you doing?* and *why are you doing that?*.

"What?"

She held up a hand at the same time she shook her head. "Tianna, I don't know what you're apologizing for. I'm the one who dragged you away from your home. I'm sorry. For the bookshop, and the riot, and everything."

I looked down at my lap, unable to think of anything to say. For the first time since I left, I felt the prickle of tears at the corners of my eyes.

"I'm sorry," she whispered again and turned to look back out to sea.

With a soft sigh, I sat up and shook the morose feelings from where they were trying to settle in my shoulders. I lifted my head and looked out across the deck, then beyond the island passing by on our starboard side, out to the endlessly sparkling waves. Further up and out until my gaze found that perfect line between the real and the possible. In that horizon I saw only promise.

"I'm not," I said.

Kaelyn turned to look at me again, but said nothing.

"I am worried about Albert, and there is no way that riot ended well for anyone, but I'm really sure neither of us need to apologize for it. I'm not actually sure what even caused it." I gave her a tiny smile. "I'm not sorry I left. And I'm definitely not sorry I met you."

She grinned to fight off the blush creeping into her tanned face. "Fine then. I'm not sorry either."

I leaned over to bump her with my shoulder trying to lighten the mood. "So, we know why I fled the only place I've ever called home, but why are you doing this?" I asked, trying to keep my tone light.

I breathed a little easier when her grin stayed in place. "Aside from the family tradition of abandoning us to the whims of fate, you mean?"

"Yeah. Aside from that," I said. "What's your reason? What are you after?"

She shrugged. "It's not a fancy goal or anything, I just have to do something with my life. I've been living with my family, moving from place to place every few years, and I need to do something for myself. I think they're right about letting me see what's out here."

"You've already seen more of Arret than I probably ever will," I told her. "If you don't know what's out there, I don't know who would."

She shifted uncomfortably. "I haven't, not really. I almost never travel past the merchant districts. I've seen shops, and docks, and inns, but it's all been through my parent's eyes. Their world, not the world."

"They're not part of the world?" I teased.

She stuck out her tongue at me, but continued. "I don't know what I want to do, but I know if I stay there, with them, I'll go mad. Become something that isn't right for me. Maybe this," she waved at everything around us, "Is a chance to find out what is right for me. A chance to do something... I don't know. Something great? Gods, that sounds pretentious, but I'm not going to pass it up."

That earnest look was back in her eyes, but this time, it was tinged with conspiratorial excitement. "Are you?"

I nodded. Then I shook my head. Did I want to pass it up? A chance for adventure? Her words seemed like the reasonable answer. Go forth into the world, see what mischief we could get into, explore the cultures I'd only ever heard about, speak the languages I've only ever read, see the world outside of Wellsmith... Thoughts of the last few days warred with fantasy images of far-off places for space in my mind again.

I looked at Kaelyn and remembered the inexplicable sense of relief I felt when she woke me on that beach. It was already too late to make that choice. I made it the moment I followed her.

"You can't pass up something that's already happened," I said philosophically. "Why turn back now?"

She grinned, and we both went back to watching the horizon, and the rope still splayed across our laps.

"How's that look?" I asked, holding up my latest knot.

She screwed up her face as if smelling something foul. Her lips pursed in a thoughtful frown. "You really haven't sailed before, have you?"

"Neither have you!" I threw the half-tied knot at her head and laughed along with her.

Any existential dread that lingered slowly evaporated. Here we were. Two wayward girls, barely old enough for workman's gloves, let alone world travel, yet, somehow that was only a detail. We hardly knew each other, and we had no apparent goal or destination in mind, no plan for our future, or even an idea of what a future might hold for us. Yet we set our course to the extraordinary. No money, no means, and apparently no skills.

No matter. We were doomed to fail in every possible way, and we both knew it. There was only one solution; we laughed.

We let ourselves bask in the ridiculous uncertainty of it all, as our peals of laughter broke out across the open sea like birds flighting from a gunshot. Before long, we were both rolling on the deck in hideous displays of mirth. For several minutes, every time we looked at each other we erupted into gales of laughter, no words needed.

"What's all this now?" Jasen came sauntering over into a maelstrom of giggles. "An' what are ye lasses up to?"

"Oh, sure 'nough, we're havin' a tea party," Kaelyn said in an over-exaggerated Tirican accent, then broke down giggling again.

"So I see. And what have ye been sippin', then? Mayhap I should check th' Cap'n's whiskey stores, eh?" Jasen said.

Kaelyn seemed to regain herself enough to speak. She sat up straight, a serious expression on her face. "Hey, Jasen, what do pirates knit their sweaters out of?"

He knew it for a trap, but it was too late. "What?"

"Yarrrrn." Giggles spewed forth onto the deck like ale at the end of shore leave.

He rolled his eyes, but I saw a quirk of a hidden smile.

"Hey," I piped up. "Do you know why pirates say 'Arrr'?"

Kaelyn raised an eyebrow and shook her head.

"Because 'Fffff' isn't very scary!" We both lost our composure again.

Jasen shook his head and walked away. "Dinner is soon, lasses. If ye can find where ye left yer sanity, yer welcome enough to join us."

Kaelyn and I lied there laughing about nothing for another few minutes, simply enjoying the manic release that comes with bad jokes. We finally regained ourselves enough to breathe normally, and I noticed it was actually getting dark. "Maybe we should go find the others."

"Probably," she said, and sighed.

We stood, and I stretched. I must have been sitting there longer than I thought.

I looked around, trying to get my bearings. Land was far behind us now, only a thin sliver of island left drifting further and further away. I shook my head to make sure I was seeing correctly. "Where are we?" I asked.

Kaelyn looked around just as I had, and came up just as confused as I was. "I thought we were sailing to Anvilcove. Isn't it just the north end of Hammersmith?"

I nodded. "It is."

"Then where are we going?"

"I don't know." I bit my lip, furrowing my brow. I had no idea where we were. We were surrounded by deep blue ocean. Sometime during our giggle fit, we had turned away from the shore and were headed out to sea.

The sounds of laughter and conversation came from within the captain's cabin. I nodded that direction. "Maybe the captain will tell us," I suggested. We both dropped our rope on the deck and made our way aft. As we neared, the smell of roasted meat hit us both, and my stomach growled in a welcoming reply. "And I guess dinner wouldn't be a bad idea, either."

Kaelyn laughed.

We joined Captain Hank, Yiri, and two other people I had briefly met but don't remember well enough to describe to you without lying. Jasen was on deck tending to something. As we tucked into a hearty meal. The conversation flowed, and I was happy to just eat and soak in the camaraderie.

I jumped into the first pause in conversation I found.

"So, Captain," I said. "Not questioning your wisdom or anything, but aren't we headed to Anvilcove?"

He set down his tankard and looked at me with a raised brow. "Aye. Why th' doubt, lass?"

"I just noticed earlier, we were headed north along the coast but now we're headed westward. Was there are change in plans?"

"Not as such, lass. All's well 'n fine. Tell me, ye know somat about currents and wind patterns 'round here?" he asked.

I shook my head.

He flashed me a crooked smile. "We hafta take these things into account when sailin', ya know? Head west to get further north. Faster into the shipping lanes, aye? Tack into th' windward way where there's more traffic abye."

I scrunched my brow. "More traffic? As in other ships? Why would that matter?"

He shared a quick glance with Yiri. "It's safer."

"Ah," I said and sat back. I couldn't really see how that made much sense, but I had to bow to their experience here. There was so much I still had to learn if I was going to be out here.

"Is that a fiddle?" Kaelyn asked, changing the subject. She pointed across the table, behind Yiri.

The captain's wife smiled brightly and tucked it against her shoulder. In answer to the question, she simply pulled the bow along the strings and launched into a lively tune.

I didn't realize how my face had lit up at the music until Hank leaned over and thumped his fist against the meat of my shoulder. "She's good, eh?"

I nodded, my teeth all showing from my grin. "It's been a long time since I heard the fiddle. No one in the Rats Nest could afford one."

Hank laughed, knowing firsthand what kind of hobbies passed for culture in certain parts of Wellsmith. He gave me an impish look. "Do you still play?" he asked just loudly enough that the entire room could clearly hear him.

Everyone turned to look at me.

"Do you play?" Yiri paused her song to ask me. Her face lit up with excitement or a fellow musician.

"No!" I held up my hands as if to fend off the idea. "No, I mean, not the fiddle. I've never even held one. It's a beautiful instrument, though, you play it so well." I stumbled over my words, rushing to change the subject before she could ask the inevitable question that I wanted to avoid. It didn't work, of course.

She held out the fiddle and bow toward me. "Would you like to play?"

Yes! I screamed internally. *Gimme!* The blood drained from my face and I swallowed hard as I fought the impulse to reach for it. "I couldn't!" I must have looked the very image of panic as everyone in the room—officers, mates, and even Kaelyn—all began to laugh.

I took a deep breath, sighing out heavily. Letting go of what was left of my pride, I leaned back in my chair and pasted a cocky grin on my face. I brought my right foot up and rested it on the table, then reach inside the cuff and pulled out a small flute. The room quieted. "How about I accompany you instead?"

Yiri grinned, and Kaelyn looked at me as if I'd just grown a second head that spoke six languages. "You play the flute?" she said, joy lighting up her face. "So do I!"

"Really? Great." I handed her the pipe. "You play then."

She looked at me sideways. "You first."

I laughed, and raised the mouthpiece to my lips.

I was never a great player. I could carry a tune, but I was self-taught, and certainly nothing like an expert or experienced performer, and I could never read music very well. But this was not a concert hall, and there was no set list or program. I simply picked out a little ditty and let the whistling notes dance lightly around the cabin.

Yiri listened for my rhythm and melody, then picked up her fiddle again and joined in. After a few minutes, Hank began beating out a rhythm on the table. Knives and plates jumped wildly as the tempo increased, and we all broke out in jolly laughter again.

After a few songs, I passed the flute the Kaelyn, who played a slow mournful song, followed by a lively, silly one. When she finished, the cook stood and sang a shanty, and we all joined in. And so the night continued for a time.

Eventually, Hank declared it 'later than the watch's tits' and shooed us all away. As the officers dispersed to their racks or duties, I sneaked away for a little peace and quiet.

I made my way to the foredeck, where Jasen was cursing to himself as he steered the ship. "Sounds like quite th' party," he said, nodding in the direction of the cabin.

"That it is." I said. "Who knew so few people could make so much noise?"

"If cap'n be in his cups, as I suspect he might, noise is t' be expected."

I smiled in return, and found a place to sit, then too late to be polite, I asked, "Mind if I join you?"

He simply nodded.

For a while, we stayed there quietly, listening to the sounds of the night and the lingering joviality coming from the corners of the ship. I wasn't tired, even after everything. So, I just sat there, letting my attention wander.

I stared at the stars for a while. I'd heard that sailors used them to guide by, but I couldn't see how. The wind had a bite to it, and I realized it must be turning toward autumn soon. That was just fine. Summer had brought me too many problems. Maybe the falling leaves would take my troubles with them. I sighed and leaned back on the rail, feeling discontented. I wasn't sure what was wrong with me.

I didn't think I had spoken out loud until Jasen asked, "What was that, lass?"

"Oh," I said. "I was just thinking. If anyone had told me yesterday that I would be on a ship on my way to who-knows-where, I would have laughed myself silly."

"Ye did plenty of that earlier, aye?" He chuckled with a pointed stare.

"Aye." I felt my cheeks heat and was grateful for the dark. "I guess we did."

The conversation lapsed into silence again. I coughed, shifting uncomfortably.

"Hey, where are we, anyway? I asked the captain about it, but I didn't really understand his answer. I thought we were headed to Anvilcove?"

"Oh aye," he said lightly. "We are. After a fashion."

"'After a fashion'?" I repeated. "That's ambiguous."

His teeth flashed in the lamplight as he smiled coyly. "I suppose it is."

I half-growled a small sigh. "And I don't suppose you will clarify?"

He laughed and waved me over. "Ye've never sailed, right? Lemme show ye how t' work th' helm."

"Are you sure?" I asked. "I've never done anything like this! I don't want to run us aground or anything."

He laughed again. I seemed to have that effect on him. "S'ok lass." He waved out toward the ocean. "Nothin' out here for leagues. If ye hit something 't will be the firs' time anyone ran aground in the middle o' th' ocean."

I stuck out my tongue at him, but it did secretly make me feel better. "So, what do I do?"

"Place you hands here, and here. Like so. Feel that pull? I'm about to let go, so brace yourself." He lifted his hands, and I slipped sideways, falling to the deck.

He roared with laughter as he regained the wheel. I got up and dusted myself off. Glaring at him, I said, "You knew that would happen."

He shrugged. "Course I did. It always happens th' first time. Now ye know how much pressure t' expect. Come, try it again."

I did eventually get the hang of it and I sailed for most of an hour before all that sleeplessness caught up with me. I yawned once, fighting hard to contain it, and then again almost immediately.

On my third consecutive yawn so large that my jaw cracked, Jasen shooed me off to bed. I would have argued, but it hardly seemed worth the fight, so instead, I turned the wheel back over to him and headed off to find a place to sleep.

CHAPTER FOUR

Sleeping aboard a ship is unlike anything I can describe to you, my friend. If you have had the fortune to try it, then you know what I mean. And if not, I hope you will try to bear with my attempts to do it justice.

At first, the waves were gentle. They softly rocked me back-and-forth in the hammock I had managed to claim for myself. The hammock itself wasn't much more than an old canvas sheet tied at both ends, which left me feeling like so many potatoes safely stored away from rot. It doesn't sound too appealing, but with a pillow beneath my head and my feet propped up, it was surprisingly comfortable.

As the night went on, every creak, groan, and sigh the ship made in the water echoed three-fold belowdecks. The men on watch traipsed back and forth over my head, their boots tapping out a slow, steady beat on the deck above. Not steady enough for me to fall into the hypnotic rhythm of it, just enough to be ever present.

Boxes and crates shifted in the night, casting strange shadows on curved walls. I shouldn't have been able to sleep at all, but at least with the rats constantly scurrying about and the guttural snoring of several sailors, it felt a bit like home.

I did eventually drift off into a dreamless sleep and sooner than I'd wish, I awoke sore and groggy. I stretched away the stiffness I still felt from my run-in with Krellen's goons. My right shoulder released with a low popping noise, and I sighed as the muscle relaxed.

Relief and determination intermixed as I psyched myself up for the day ahead. I was going to make this new life a success. Even if I didn't know what that life was yet.

One step at a time, I told myself. First off, as long as I was on this ship, I was going to learn to sail it. Then, at least, I would have more skills to rely on than just knowing how to add columns of numbers and aggravate local slum lords.

I nodded to myself, stretched again, and headed off to find Jasen for another lesson in… something ship related. I didn't know what. So, I still had a long way to go, but I was itching to get started.

Of course, as I stepped out onto the main deck, he was nowhere to be seen. Just wandering the ship waiting for him to find me seemed a sure way to foul things up for the people who did know what they were doing, so instead I milled around uselessly, waiting for inspiration to strike.

A sailor near the foredeck stood splicing lines together. He glanced up at me just long enough to make eye contact, so I walked up to him.

"Morning," I said.

He nodded in a half greeting, half acknowledgment of my presence.

"I was hoping you could help me a bit?"

He grumbled without looking up from where his hands busily spun a length of rope. "I have my own duties. Can't be doin' yers, too."

I blinked, then realized my error. "Oh, I'm not shirking. In fact, I'm not actually even a crewman. I just meant, can you teach me how to do what you're doing? I want to help if I can."

"Why?" he asked, finally meeting my gaze.

"I want to help," I said again. "Feel useful somehow. I just need to stay occupied."

"And better this than dice or drink, eh?" He flashed me a quick smile, showing straight but yellowing teeth.

I shrugged again, waving my arms in exaggeration. "I suppose it is. So? Will you do the honorable thing and help keep me away from such vices?"

He smirked and waved me over. I approached and peered over his shoulder, watching him work. He showed me a basic splice. Stripping and splaying the rope, then expertly winding it back together. Within moments, the two pieces were one whole, sturdy length. I nodded along, sure that after my hours and hours of knot-tying experience that, I would have no problem with this.

I was wrong. Of course I was wrong. I had less than one afternoon's worth of experience with ropework, after all. But he was a patient teacher and by the time we stopped for lunch, I knew how to make a strong splice, tie three more types of knots, and fashion a basic net.

With a wink, he thanked me for my help and wandered off to his next task. I wasted no time and went in search of another hapless sailor to teach me anything I could learn.

It was well into the afternoon before I spotted Kaelyn doing similarly. The gunner's mate had seemed to take a liking to her and was drilling her on cannon etiquette and fire safety. I left her to it.

Over the next two days, this was my routine. I would wake up, see if Jasen had any tasks for me, and seek out the nearest potential teacher. If any turned me away, I simply looked for another. As much as we had joked about it just being Hank and Jasen, the Naked Chicken boasted a company of nearly eighty hands, so I never had trouble finding someone for me to bother.

Kaelyn caught up to me early the second day and tagged along. Together we learned the simplest of knots, how to belay in a heavy wind, how to read the horizon, and the best ways to clean the boards without leaving the deck too slick. I even got to impress the boatswain with my even stitching on the sailcloth.

It was the first time in my short life that I had ever done a job I was truly proud of. A job that others could be proud of. Sure, I was a terrible hand at knots still, and Kaelyn put me to shame on all things aloft, but I refused to be outdone for long, and I learned.

Before too long, I was taking regular duties on the ship, without supervision. I would do whatever task assigned me throughout the course of the day, and I would join the sailors on deck in the evenings for music and dancing.

Even after all the long years that have passed since, this remains one of my most cherished memories. My time aboard the Naked Chicken was short, but it was my first taste of happiness. Of belonging. We chatted and told stories to the other sailors and morale improved. I was of use. And I was happy. It was almost enough to help me forget why I left in the first place.

One night, late into the first watch, I lay in the hammock dozing. For some time—I couldn't say how long—I just listened to the sounds of the ship. The hull settling and resettling. The rats arguing over a scrap of bread on the floor. The crew on watch gently pacing back and forth.

The rhythmic footsteps were the most hypnotic. I listened to them overhead like the steady ticking of a clock.

Thump, thump, thump, thump, pause.

Then back again the way they came.

Thump, thump, thump, thump. Pause.

Over and over again until it faded into the ambient soundtrack of the night, and I wasn't sure I still heard it.

Thump, thump, thump, thumpthumpthump-

"Cleave spot'ed! Comin' 'bout port!"

What? I sat up and I looked around, trying to get my bearings as I snapped from my reverie. I was on my feet in seconds and heading up the ladder to the main deck.

I lifted the hatch into the cool darkness of the night. Lights flickered everywhere from lanterns passing by. Sailors scurried about tending to duties with a fury and a life I had yet to see on this voyage.

I found the captain and mate standing at the railing, the latter with a small brass spyglass up to his eye. "What do we have?" I heard Hank ask as I joined them.

"Epirsan carrack," Jasen told him. "Heavy one, too."

"Storm wrecked?"

Jasen shook his head. "Like fouled on th' substrate," he said, lowering the glass. He turned and grinned at his captain. "Fools forgot t' check for rocks."

Hank matched his grin and nodded. "Lively?"

"Not terribly. Recommend twenty strong."

"Our luck, then." Hank clapped his hands together and nodded. "Let's get a move on, then."

"Aye Cap'n!" Jasen spun on his heel and started shouting orders. I watched the crew split off to their duties with a speed and determination I hadn't seen before. A spirited excitement was weaving its way through all of them as they hurried through the night.

The captain turned to me. "Lass, why don't ye sit back for this one? Yer my guests, after all." His tone was so jovial I found myself agreeing before I knew what I was agreeing to. I watched him walk off as I nodded dumbly.

He joined a group of a dozen or more sailors, readying the small boats. It wasn't until they started to put into the sea that I noticed they were all armed.

"What is happening?" Kaelyn asked over my shoulder. Her voice was barely more than a whisper.

I shook my head, trying to piece it all together. "Not fully sure."

With a gentle splash, the two dory boats hit the dark ocean, and the crewmen immediately set to their oars. I stood at the rail, watching them slip through the night toward the wrecked ship.

We just watched. My brain spun furiously, trying to piece together what was happening. When the boats pulled alongside the larger wreck, I got my answer.

The away crew of the Naked Chicken swarmed up the sides of the carrack and across its decks. From as far away as we were, I could only make out the shadows of sailors facing off against other, less determined, shadows.

"Are they looking for survivors?" I said quietly to Kaelyn. I tried to sound hopeful, but kept my voice low, afraid to admit what we were both seeing.

"No…" she trailed off. "They're… No."

Sounds floated across the water to me. Metal clanging. Shouts. The occasional scream. My jaw dropped. gaping at the massacre I was witnessing. I turned to Jasen, who was standing next to me, watching it all through a long, brass spyglass. He was grinning.

"You're pirates!" My voice squeaked awkwardly on the last word.

Jasen grinned from ear to ear. Any wider and the top of his head would have come off. He winked at me. "Ye say tha' like it's a bad thing."

As he addressed me, the sounds of fighting on the other ship died out and a figure on the deck waved his arms, a bright red handkerchief in his fist. A single musket shot cracked upward into the sky, and Jasen grinned again. He turned and ran off down the deck, leaving me standing there, gaping after him.

I followed, stunned silent by the mirthful atmosphere around me. Jasen addressed the master of the deck briefly and the two began loading sailors into another boat. The boat lowered into the dark sea, and they began to row. I stood at the rail again and watched as they sped across the expanse toward the carrack. Across the way, sailors were bringing crates and barrels up from belowdecks and loading them into the skiffs.

Kaelyn's whole body was tense and thrumming with an odd energy. I looked at her, trying to figure out what she was thinking. Was she as confused as I was? As scared? As excited? Her eyes darted from me to the wreck and back nervously. Our gazes locked for just a moment. Eyes wide, I shook my head very slowly.

A dark chuckle started low in her belly and slogged its way up into her throat before erupting into a great guffaw. Infected by the absurdity of it all, I joined in her hysterics.

My eyes were wet, but from the laughter or fear, I couldn't tell you which. It was still the middle of the night. I still hadn't slept much, and with the latest revelation that I had inadvertently hooked myself to a pirate ship, I broke. I doubled over, clutching the rail, letting my conflicting emotions roll over me.

Pirates, I thought. *Of course they're pirates.*

What else did I expect from someone who used to work with Krellen? Had I really thought that I would find passage on a safe, quiet merchantman? Were there even safe, quiet merchantmen to be found in the Outer Isles? Lawlessness was the only order out here. I had always known it. There was no getting out of this life.

"Well," I told Kaelyn when I could finally breathe again. I looked at her. The mirth dancing in her eyes was still tinged with a bit of uncertainty. "I guess we're pirates now."

Worry washed through me as the hesitation in her eyes was replaced with a gleeful malice. She laughed again, grinning wide enough to show all her teeth. Had I given her permission to act on some dark impulse? What kind of monster had I just unleashed on the world?

As the first of the boats returned to the Chicken, I gently thumped Kaelyn on the arm. "Come on. Let's go lend a hand."

We spent nearly an hour unloading and securing the cargo before the last of the skiffs came in with the captain. He looked over our work with a smile.

"Couldn't stay out of it, eh, Tianna?" He clasped a friendly hand on my shoulder.

"I like to stay busy."

He nodded as if it were the most obvious thing about me and walked off to survey the rest of the crew.

I looked at Kaelyn, who was waiting to follow my lead. She cocked her head in a clear 'what now' gesture. I glanced around, looking for our next task, when a deep yawn overwhelmed me.

"Oh," I said. "I guess maybe it's time to get some sle–"

A shout from above us interrupted me. "Ship off the bow! Coming in fast!"

I looked up at the crow's nest, and then back down and toward the front of the Chicken, before turning my wide eyes on Kaelyn. We both spun and raced toward the bow of the ship.

We hurried over to where Hank and Jasen stood, peering into the night.

"What's happening?" I squeaked, barely audible above the noise around us.

"Pirates." Jasen replied gruffly.

"What do you mean, 'pirates'?" I asked incredulously.

The mate turned to me, trying not to laugh. "What do you think I mean? Y'know where ye are, right lass? They don't call them the Pirate Isles for nothing!"

"King's Men?" the captain asked.

"Not sure…" Jasen scanned the horizon for the form emerging from the blackness. He raised his glass, then quickly lowered it again and smirked. "Non-aff."

Hank looked relieved, then nodded once and said, "beat to quarters." before walking off toward his cabin.

"Beat to quarters!" Jasen called out at the top of his considerable lungs. He turned and looked at me. "Best get below decks, miss. It's going to get messy up here."

"Wait. What? Are we being chased by pirates? I thought you were pirates." I'd never been at sea before, but I'd heard endless accounts of pirate battles from sailors in Wellsmith. I knew that if we were boarded, we would have to defend ourselves.

"Aye," Jasen replied. "But we're in saturated waters. Th' prizes 're rarer than th' competition here. We 'ave t' fight for what we want."

"Wait. What?" I said again, slower than before. "You mean they're coming after us because of that other ship?"

He turned to me, putting the spyglass away. "Likely they were after the carrack, but we got there first."

"No honor among thieves, then?" I muttered dryly.

"Look, lass, ye've been too insulated in that town of yers, if ye don't know this yet. So, here's yer first lesson. There're four types of people sailing these waters, aye?" He held up his fingers to emphasize his point.

"One. Consortium merchants. They're Lugaian prize fighters masquerading as tradesmen."

He looked at me flatly, and I bit back the bitter taste of bile. I knew all too-well what sort of people sailed under Consortium colors.

"Two. Meketian slavers. Call themselves 'market runners', but everyone knows they trade in isler flesh."

I nodded again. I'd been lucky enough to avoid them, but I had heard more than my share of horror stories.

"Three." He ticked off another finger. "King's Men. Pirates by another name. They're politicos. Freedom fighters of a sort. Trying t' gain support for their King. They do all th' same things pirates do, but like t' claim it's righteous."

"Pirates have Kings?" I asked slowly.

"Nay, lass," he said, "Not usually. But these 'King's Men' sail under unified colors, seeking legitimacy for themselves. People like a cause, Tianna."

That was true enough. Wasn't that the very reason I joined up with Krellen in the first place? To feel like I belonged to something bigger than myself? "Huh." I said, mulling over his words. "And the fourth?"

"People like us." He grinned.

"And we... are *not* pirates?"

He smiled wickedly. "We're non-affs. Not affiliated with any nation, flag, or cause. We simply... are."

I shook my head. It wasn't a denial, more like recognition of something uncomfortable. I felt a stirring of kinship deep in my soul at his words. There was virtue in simply living your life without the constraint of overlords, laws, political machinations, and corruption. To exist in such freedom was a bit of paradise I could only dream of.

"We aren't without a purpose," he mused. "There're some non-affs, like us, that do their best t' protect th' waterways. Pirates have a nasty reputation, but don't matter if you have a King supporting you or not. Actions speak, aye? You don't need a black flag t' pillage and plunder."

"Truer words, my friend." I sighed and considered him. These were good people. If he said they were in the right, then I wasn't in a place to judge. But I still did.

"I just want to clarify," I said. "You go looking for these 'pillagers'?"

"Aye."

"And you fight them, kill them, take their ships and whatever valuable goods they have on board?" I pressed.

"Aye."

"And you occasionally stop and salvage a wreck or two along the way?"

The corners of his lips twitched. "Aye."

"And what, exactly, makes you different from the other factions out here?"

He nodded like I'd finally figured out the answer to a riddle. "Freedom."

It was too romantic a notion, and I had no response to it. I simply stood at stared at him.

"Sorry, lass. We've jabbered too long. Ye really should get below." He tapped my shoulder and pointed to the hatch, then turned sharply to return to his tasks.

Pirates. Consortium, King's Men.

I was raised to believe that pirates were best avoided. If you had to travel, you stayed off the seas or made your hastiest way to the continent. If you sailed further than the sight lines of your home dock, you were susceptible to whatever depravity fate inflicted upon you. It seemed almost fortuitous that I would find out firsthand on my first ever sea voyage.

A thrill of something I hadn't felt in a long time ran through me. It wasn't fear. I'd lived with tha long enough to know how it felt. This was more like... anticipation? I didn't know what was about to happen. I was completely out of my depth, and I couldn't wait to swim.

I stood and watched the other ship floating like a cork without its bottle. Their flag was too far out to be seen in the deep blue of midnight, but their sails were pure white and cleaner than those on any ship I'd seen.

All around me, sailors were rushing around the deck, focused on their tasks. Some of the work was things I had been seeing all week. Trimming the sails, setting the braces, and the like. But others were positioning the cannons and hauling out crates of guns and powder and swords.

The approaching ship slowly started to turn and I waited for the inevitable boom from their broadsides. But it never came. They veered to port, giving up their pursuit of us.

"All clear!" came a cry from somewhere overhead.

"Damn," Hank said. He stood with Jasen, laughing. "I was spoiling for a good fight."

"All good for you, Cap'n," Jasen said, then nodded at me. "But I think our charges're grateful for th' reprieve."

"Damn right," I muttered, drawing another laugh from the two men.

He walked over and rested a hand on top of my head. I found the gesture oddly reassuring. "Don't fret none, lass. We'll get ye t' Anvilcove, safe as a baby's bath."

I tried to take comfort in the sentiment behind his words, and not get hung up by how easy it actually was for a baby to drown in a bathtub. "Sure," I told him with false cheer. "Thanks."

The rest of the trip to Anvilcove was—as Hank had said, it would be—safe and easy. We arrived safe and sound two days later.

I heard a cheerful laugh and turned to see Kaelyn and Jasen making their way over to where I stood, looking out over the vast expanse of buildings and stonework.

"Is this Anvilcove?" I asked as they joined me.

Kaelyn bubbled with excitement, practically dancing where she stood. "Aye. If it's like last time I was here, we're still about an hour out." She pointed to where ships were coming and going from a small set of docks near the far shore. "What you see here is the outer harbor and the industrial district. After we come around this next bend, you can see more of the city."

I blinked and looked again. "There's more of this city?" The harbor I was looking at was easily the size of all of Krellen's holdings in the Rat's Nest, plus several of the taverns and gambling houses in Wellsmith City proper. I was to believe this was only the *outer* harbor? "What does the inner harbor look like?"

"More of the same," she replied. "But the bay here is deeper. So the larger cargo ships port here."

I stood, just taking it all in for a long, uninterrupted moment. Not thinking, just observing. I sure hoped Kaelyn knew her way around. I wasn't at all confident I would be able to find my own feet after wandering the twisting streets laid out before me.

We slowly neared the docks, making our way through the sudden traffic of ships in the bay. I watched the city loom ever larger in my view. Everywhere, people rushed about, conducting daily business, and getting ready for the day. I thought the Wellsmith quays were active, but this was beyond my imagination. I could have stared at the bustling docks all afternoon.

"Ready to learn how to put into port?" Jasen asked us both with a grin.

We answered in the affirmative, and he quickly set us to our tasks. It was hard work, but I wouldn't have expected anything less.

Soon, we were settled and safely ashore. I bad a quick goodbye to Yiri and Hank before finding Kaelyn and Jasen waiting on the docks.

"Thanks again," Kaelyn told him as I joined them.

"My pleasure, ladies. Jus' take good care of yerselves, and each other, a'right?"

"No promises," I said with a wink.

He laughed and shook his head, then hopped back up the gangway onto the Chicken, leaving us to our own devices.

"Alright, miss Féanaro," I tried to affect a tone of severity and mostly failed. "What's next? You said you had contacts in the city. Do any of them have a bed I might fall into for a few hours?"

"Ah," she said, looking away from me.

"Kaelyn?" I asked warily. "You do have friends here, right? Someone who can help us out, point us in the right direction, or give up a place to sleep while we figure out what to do next at least?"

She looked sidelong at me, trying not to show her sheepishness, then grinned. "I don't actually know."

I opened my mouth to yell at her, only to realize I wasn't actually mad. I blew out my breath in a heavy sigh and realized I should have seen this coming. Instead of shouting, I rolled my eyes and shifted my weight to my heels while I waited for her to continue.

"I have one good friend. He's a blacksmith and a jeweler, so if he's here, he's got to be hanging around one of the merchant districts. If not there, then…" she looked around thoughtfully for a moment. "Don't worry, he always turns up sooner or later."

"*One* of the merchant districts?" I said in a careful tone. "How many are there?"

"Only three."

"Holy Gods!" I did shout this time. I threw up my hands. "How big is this city?"

Kaelyn laughed at me, but smiled. "Anvilcove is tiny. You should see Merlaeone in Lugaia sometime! There are nine merchant districts there."

"Lugaians never do things by halves, do they?" I ended with a weak laugh.

"C'mon, it won't take long. We'll find him."

I looked at her shrewdly, scrutinizing her for what could only be lies. "Fine," I said, "Let's go see if we can find him before I turn to begging for food and shelter."

"Is that an option?" she asked.

"I'm not above it." I started off down the street. "But it would be the first time I tried without knowing at least someone in town."

Kaelyn laughed and followed me. "If anyone could manage it, it would be you, Tianna."

I grinned and strutted cockily. "People just naturally love me. What can I say?"

She laughed again, and we headed into the merchant district. And so it was, with a mania born of hubris and uncertainty, that we began our stay in Anvilcove.

CHAPTER FIVE

Three days.

Three days I followed her around town, working small jobs for whoever would toss me a few coins. Packing fish at the docks, hawking dress-goods, selling stale bread crusts to laborers, whatever kept me busy and earned me some capital to fund our next adventure. Three days I spent convincing myself it was worth it.

Three days I pretended I wasn't wasting time.

I spent a fair amount of my days simply wandering around the city, exploring the taverns and boarding houses for work and trying to get a general feel for the place, until I was sure we had no hope of finding anything to help us on our journey.

Thank the gods for Kaelyn, who had almost immediately gone to work for a grocer to earn us a little coin. It was at least enough to land us somewhere dry to sleep that we didn't have to beg or steal to get. She didn't seem concerned by our lack of a plan, so I kept my mouth shut, followed her, and waited to see what would happen next. I had nothing better to do after all.

The morning of our fourth day in Anvilcove dawned dreary, a reminder that Autumn was fast approaching the isles. Kaelyn and I were staying at a small inn on the far northern end of the textile district. Downwind of the tanners, unfortunately, which is how we could afford it.

When I awoke, Kaelyn was already downstairs. She was happily chatting with a man who had average features in that nondescript way that somehow came together to be attractive. I chuckled in faint surprise that Kaelyn was awake for any portion of the morning, let alone chatting with someone before breakfast.

I quietly grabbed a mug of hot tea and went to join them. Kaelyn's visitor handed her something, smiled, and left as I approached the hearth where they were standing. Under other circumstances, I would have questioned this shady hand-off, but things like this had been happening nearly since the moment we arrived.

"Your new friend not staying?" I tried for a hint of teasing, but given my groggy state probably came out gruff.

"Huh? A friend? He was just delivering a message."

I raised an eyebrow at her. "So I didn't see you flirting with him just now?"

She blushed as her eyes opened wide. "What? No!" She laughed nervously. "Why would you even think that?"

I chuckled and stared into the fire next to her. "He just seemed very happy to deliver whatever the message was. So either you just inherited a country estate, or he was interested in you."

She laughed again and punched my arm playfully. "You've gone mad."

I smiled into my tea cup as I took a long sip. It was nice to just shoot the breeze with Kaelyn this way. Being around her was so easy, and we got along as if we'd known each other for years, not days. It was the only part of the last week that had been no problem at all. I liked Kaelyn, and I had no trouble seeing this grow into a real friendship.

As I drank my tea, quietly waking up, I took a closer look at my friend. This morning, much like every other day, she was dressed in simple garb of a loose open-collared shirt over tight leggings and tall boots. The ensemble decorated with more scarves than I could count, of course, but that was Kaelyn. Simple, comfortable, and stylish all at once.

It was only because I was looking that I noticed the mischievous glint in her eye.

With a heavy sigh, I set my cup down. "Alright, out with it."

"What?" she asked innocently.

I fixed her with a pointed stare. "Whatever it is that you're plotting over there in you head." I was curious, sure, but it was also a matter of self-preservation. Three days of looking for something to do and following her suggestions about work were getting old. If she was up to something, I needed in on it.

"Oh, it's nothing," she said, brushing me off again.

I sighed, still too tired to play games. A conversation was coming. Soon, but not this morning. I got up and went in search of more tea.

I never did find out what was in the small satchel she had received that morning, or what was in the following bundles she received over the next few days. She evaded any questions I had on the subject. As long as she didn't want to talk, she was slipperier than a jellyfish in a coconut. It seemed that a real conversation would have to keep waiting.

And so here I was seven days after landing in a new town, sitting in yet another tavern, in yet another part of the city, watching Kaelyn gleefully dance about over her latest endeavor. And all I could do was trust she would get around to including me at some point.

"So what now?" I asked when she joined me at my table. It was nearing lunchtime, and the room was full of the typical bunch of dock-side ruffians trading insults and ale with equal fervor.

Smoke of various kinds permeated the air, and the whole place smelled disturbingly like old fish and fresh mint. Luckily, we found a table out of the way which offered relative privacy.

"This hopeful wandering is great and all, but if I wanted to idle about, I could have done that in Wellsmith."

"All while waiting to run into that Tavers guy again? Good plan," she said.

I tried to laugh at her joke, but all I managed to do was fidget awkwardly and make a disgusted grunt in the back of my throat. "Alright, point made," I said. "But all the same, I would like something to do that isn't one of your 'general scouting and fact gathering excursions' into the city, or whatever it is you're calling them. I mean, come on, Kaelyn! What are we even doing?"

She raised an eyebrow at me. "We're waiting."

I slumped forward onto the table dramatically. "I'm sick of waiting!" I wailed plaintively.

"What?" She raised her voice, nearly shouting to be heard over the increasing noise. Naturally, a quieter tavern would have been inappropriate. We were only discussing our futures, nothing important.

"What are we even waiting fo–"

A thunk next to my head made me jump as a heavy, rough leather pack landed inches from my nose. As I sat back to get a better look, the chair next to me slid out from the table, then back in again as a young man joined us.

He was sturdy but not bulky, with broad set shoulders defined by years of use, and he sat with a relaxed posture. His open, clean-cut features made him look very young, too old to be a child, too young to be fully a man, but his green-gray eyes were weary and told of a history longer than his age and expression would imply.

I was about to decide he was just the serious type, but then he smiled a wacky, self-assured smirk that made me question I'd ever seen that lingering sorrow at all. He was a perfect blend of honest amiability and unaffected cynicism.

One look and I felt like I'd known him forever. This man, whoever he was, was the closest thing I'd ever come across to a kindred spirit.

"Took you long enough," Kaelyn said.

His eyes danced as he looked at her. "And how was I supposed to know you were in town, hmm? I only just got your letter. And you don't exactly stay in one place long."

She grinned. "At least I have places to go."

"Look, *miss*," he started, but trailed off in a laugh, and Kaelyn returned his smile.

"You're Kaelyn's friend?" I asked.

"Tianna," he replied, turning to look at me.

His merriment was catching, and I felt my spirits rising just from being near him. "No, I'm Tianna. You're Merrik?"

He laughed, a low melodic baritone chuckle that brought an answering smile to my face.

"I suppose I am. And I *suppose* I'm Kaelyn's friend, too. Though sometimes I wonder about that. Ouch!" he laughed again as she kicked him under the table. "Fine, fine, I'm Kaelyn's friend," he conceded. He winked at me conspiratorially. "It's safer that way."

We both laughed as Kaelyn made indignant protests.

"Hungry?" Merrik asked, rising to his feet again.

Kaelyn nodded emphatically. "Very."

I turned to Kaelyn as he went to the bar. "So…?" I asked, trying to steer the conversation back to the point.

She ignored me as she watched Merrik make his way across the room.

"Kaelyn," I said a little louder.

She turned back to me, realizing I had been talking. "What?"

"I said, 'what now'?"

"Now, we wait for Merrik to come back with lunch."

"Not that!" I shouted. Although I was hungry, I was much more concerned with my immediate irritation. "What are we doing now? As in, what's the plan?"

She shrugged. "Now we wait and see."

I had had just about had it with her cryptic nonsense. I slammed my mug down on the table. Its contents sloshed over onto my hand. Shaking loose the droplets, I stared her down. "That's it. Ambiguity is one thing. This obtuse refusal to discuss anything with me is another."

She looked at me like I had just grown a third eye somewhere between my nose and my ear.

"I have spent the last week being dragged all over town on pointless errands, talking to an endless stream of people, none of whom seem to have anything to say. I left my home, changed my life, all on your word! Now, I know we never really said we had a plan with this whole 'hey, let's travel the world' thing, but you're carrying on as if you do. So, just tell me. What. Is. Going. On?"

By the end of my tirade, I was standing and boring into her skull with my gaze. Kaelyn laughed, which may very well have been the worst thing she could have done just then.

I screamed and grabbed for the nearest thing I could reach to throw at her, but she beat me to it. With a hand on the tankard I had grabbed, she said to me, "Relax, would you? And sit down."

I sat.

"There isn't a plan. Not really," Kaelyn said.

I raised my hand, ready to slap it on the table again.

She held up both of hers in order to placate me. "I know how you feel about plans and 'doing stuff' and all, so I have been asking around about potential jobs."

A groan escaped me before I could check it. "Not more jobs." I begged her. "I can't handle another day of promoting Miss Stilbury's Latest, Most Fashionable, Grandest Creation. I don't even like hats that much"

"Not day labor. I mean, a proper job. Scouting, trading, transport, something like that."

"You found us a crew to trade with?" I asked., excited for the first time in days.

She examined the table closely rather than meet my eye. I sighed, just about the time she finally said, "Well, no."

I slumped into my chair. "Damn it, Kaelyn! What have I been saying? You've got all these grand ideas about doing something, but you won't sit down with me long enough to figure out what that something is! Half a plan is as bad as no plan!"

Merrik paused at the side of the table. He was juggling three bowls of fish stew and looking back and forth between me and Kaelyn. "What's all this now? I'm gone two minutes and you're fighting again?"

"We're not fighting," we both said at the same time.

Merrik raised an eyebrow, but said nothing. He deftly slid the bowls onto the table in front of us and took a seat.

We all dug into our lunch. I glared at my food, still thrumming under the surface. I had no intention of letting her off the hook this time. If Merrik was as good a friend as she claimed he was, she would just have to deal with him witnessing this.

"Kaelyn," I started.

She looked up at me nervously, then bent over her bowl and kept eating.

After a few moments, I tried again. Calmly this time. "I left my home. I know it wasn't safe there anymore, and I know I had to leave. But, Kaelyn, you promised me we would make this work. I don't do well when I'm left to my own devices. That's why I joined with Krellen. I need something to do. I need a goal, an occupation, *some*thing."

She looked quietly resigned as she said, "I'm sorry." She met my gaze and scrunched up her lips into a wry smile. "Not too late, though, right?" she said. "I have put out feelers. I am looking for a job for us. Something that will take us away from the island."

I watched her growing more excited the more she spoke and felt a little of it myself. But that wasn't a solution.

"There is so much world out there, Tianna. Don't you want to see it? We just need to get off this island, find a ship to crew with for a while, maybe get our own boat one day. We aren't beholden to anyone's rules any more. No more scrounging for food, or working for shady men doing questionable things. We can do whatever we want."

"Isn't that all we've been doing since we got here?" I said. "Taking odd jobs here and there to keep a roof over our heads isn't exactly what I want."

"It's not forever," she said. "Just until we can find a way off this island."

"Oh, damn, that reminds me," Merrik piped up suddenly.

Kaelyn and I both whipped our heads around. He was grinning like a festival mask as he started rifling around in his satchel for something.

"I picked this up near the smelter's road yesterday. Wasn't going to do anything with it, but it seems like you might." He produced a small scrap of paper along with a leather chit and dropped both in front of Kaelyn.

Kaelyn raised an eyebrow in question and picked up the paper. I watched with curiosity as she unfolded it and read. I couldn't see what was written there, but her eyes slowly widened, getting bigger and bigger, until I thought for sure they would burst under the pressure. She didn't seem to be breathing, and after a moment, her hand started to shake.

It was just on the edge of alarming when she finally shuddered. She took a deep gasping breath and jerked her head up to stare at Merrik.

"What is it?" I asked.

"T-this isn't real," she stammered.

He shrugged. "Dunno. Guy I got it off seemed to think it wasn't worth much."

"Not worth much?" she squeaked.

"What is it?" I asked again. When no one answered me, I reached out and snatched it from Kaelyn's loose grip. She remained where she was, unmoving, as her gaze slowly drifted from Merrik to me.

The note read:

Whosoever is th holder of this marker
Herefor now owns The Siren, brig of Tirica,
Mess of a wreck that she is.
The lady be waiting on th bay
at the low dock—pier three, slip twelve.
G'luck to ye. She's yer problem now.

"What is this?" I asked again, this time with bewildered amazement. "A ship? You own a ship?" I looked at Merrik, my eyes now nearly as wide as Kaelyn's were. "But… How? Why? How?"

Merrik shrugged again, just as unaffected as before. "Hard to say. Might be nothing."

"That grammar is atrocious," I commented to myself, then turned to Merrik. "Where did you get this?"

He looked completely unbothered by my questions and answered simply. "Picked it up off a guy, like I said."

"Did you steal it, or what? Like a bet?"

Kaelyn seemed to come out of her daze. "That's true," she said slowly, ignoring me and speaking to Merrik. "It might be nothing. Even if this marker is real, we don't know that the offer is. Who trades a ship this way? Like it's a... a loaf of bread. 'Oh, that's for the cup of sugar you loaned me. Here's a boat in return.'"

"Dunno," Merrik said again. "He didn't seem too broken up about its loss. So, maybe it's a fake. Or maybe–"

"Maybe it's worth looking into," I breathed. I turned to Kaelyn, excitement burning at the edges of my awareness. "Isn't this just what we've been talking about? We want a way off this island, a way to seek adventure. To sail the horizons and find where we're meant to be? Because I don't know about you, but I sure as shit don't want to stay in Anvilcove waiting for life to find me."

Neither person answered, so I pressed on.

"We owe it to ourselves to go see, don't we? I owe it to Albert, and Adwin and Jun, and the other orphans, and hells, even Krellen. I owe it to everyone who ever thought I was worth more but stuck in the mud I was born in." I waved the paper at her. "On the far-flung, offhand chance that this could be real, shouldn't we at least check it out?"

She stared at me, silent and unmoving, for just long enough that I wondered if I broke her. Then a slow, nervous laugh bubbled out of her. It was chased by a grin the size of the Tecre chasm, and I knew I had her.

"But it might not be real," she said. "This could be a fake or a swindle, or something. How do we know it's real?"

Merrik stood and scooped our empty bowls into a pile before brushing his hands off on his trousers. Then he grabbed up his satchel and slung it over his shoulder. "Let's go find out, eh?"

With an excited laugh of my own, we all raced off to the docks.

"Well, I think I know why he let it go so easily," I said as we looked down at the docks.

The road where we stood led down a short hill that ended at a long wooden walkway reaching out over the water. The pier split off into several slips, where small boats were bobbing happily in the tide. Beyond that, its long side tied off to the end of the pier, was a larger ship, maybe two or three times the size of the personal craft in the slips in front of it.

I had little doubt that this was the ship we were here to see. Even with my limited experience, I could see that the others were far too small for open ocean sailing. I had read a great deal about Tirican small brigs, with their double masts and long, narrow hulls. A hundred years ago, they were primarily scout ships used to patrol the kingdom's coastline, but the race for naval supremacy between Lugaia and Epirsa soon made them more or less obsolete.

This one clearly had seen every day of those hundred years. The paint had long since chipped and faded away, leaving raw boards exposed along on the nineteen-meter deck. An uneven coat of whitewash had been hurriedly splashed over it, but it didn't do much more than make it look like the palate of a bored artist. One who was too poor or unbothered to buy new colors.

Several of its sheets were torn ragged, a few held more patches than sailcloth. Many of the beams didn't even have that much, being left bare instead. It was impossible to tell how many sails were supposed to belong to this ship. The rigging was too much of a mess to leave any clues.

The figurehead was that of a warrior woman. The kind you might find in ancient Anaxian tales of female demigod tribes. She was strongly built with a baker's forearms, but she had a slim waist. She wore a flowing dress around her hips that smoothed into the outer hull of the ship, and her long tresses barely covered the naked expanse of her breasts. Her arms were raised above her head, and in both hands she held a skull out in offering. Her face was carved into a permanent glower, making the overall effect formidable.

Nearly the only thing working in the ship's favor was the hull, which—despite the weather-scarred appearance—seemed solid and tight. The forgotten pile of planks gently bobbed and rocked against the pier, ignorant of its sad state.

Kaelyn glanced at me dubiously. It was the shabbiest excuse for a vessel I had ever laid eyes on, and I had serious doubts if it could even sail out of the bay in one piece.

It suited us perfectly.

"I love it," I whispered on an exhaled breath.

Kaelyn laughed, a hoarse, weak sound that was about as unsure as any sound could be. "It's sure… something."

Merrik stepped between us and threw his arms over both our shoulders. "Won't know 'til we look at it, right?" He steered us both down the road to the docks.

With each step, my feet picked up speed until I was practically skipping excitedly down the lane. The pier creaked under my feet as I walked up to the faded, rickety gangplank that dropped from the Siren's deck down to the pier.

"This is a bad idea," Kaelyn said.

I turned to face her. "Kaelyn, my dearest, sweet friend. What part of any of what we've done so far has been a *good* idea?" She looked alarmed until I grinned. Whether she thought I was kidding or knew I was just goading her, it didn't matter. It had the desired effect.

She weakly punched my shoulder and shook her head. "Fine. Let's go." She turned to make the short hop up to the ship and hesitated.

Merrik wasted no time. He just strolled up the loose boards as if they were a concrete walk, the very picture of tranquility. "You coming?" he asked from above us as he turned to look over the railing at where Kaelyn and I both still stood.

Kaelyn took a deep breath, steeling herself, and just as she set her foot on the plank, I pushed her forward.

She spun around, glaring at me, and I grinned again. "Heya! What's got ya lot sufflin' there?"

We turned toward the sharp, masculine voice shouting us down from the roadside-end of the docks. A young man with bright red hair came running toward us. He wore a simple green baldric with a white hound's paw on it over a plain wool tunic. The uniform of a city guard. It seemed someone took exception to our new acquisition.

"Something wrong, sir?" I asked cheerfully, as he caught up to us.

Up close, I could see that he was quite young, maybe only a year or two older than myself. The word 'green' barely even applied, and I wouldn't be the least bit surprised to learn this was his first assignment. Dock duty, of all things, poor kid.

His satiny red hair fell forward into his face as he shook his head, and his green eyes gazed at me suspiciously. "Not as such, unless ya've got a trick in th' nip," he said.

"A… what?" I asked. His accent was unlike any I had ever heard before. It was clearly Tirican—I think—but with a lilting quality that sounded almost like music as it rolled off his tongue. The colloquial twist on the vocabulary left me with a rash of mixed mental images and struggling to understand him.

"Ya ballyin' round th' tough n' tumble, or d'ya have game drudgery with yon Lady?" He nodded to the ship behind me, then looked up at Merrik with concern.

After I was sure I knew what he meant, I said, "No, no business precisely. That is, no trade or barter planned. We were taking stock of her current state."

That did nothing to lessen his look of misgiving. "What's her stockshape t' ya, with no call or cause t' be, then?"

"Well, sir. It's… uh, ours now?" I didn't mean for it to come out as a question, but I couldn't hold back my slight pause. I didn't actually know if this was legitimate or not. After all, I only had Merrik's word that any of this was plausible, and I'd really only known him for about two hours. Kaelyn was right. This was a bad idea.

The guardling seemed to be chewing over his words as another guard approach from behind him. He had an easy, rolling gait as he walked up and rested his hand on the smaller man's shoulder.

This one was taller, broader, and a little more self-assured than the one I'd been talking to, though he didn't seem much older. His confidence was both reassuring and worrisome.

"There a problem here?" he asked.

I almost breathed a sigh of relief when I heard his familiar accent. Not that I had a problem with the other one, but I could think faster in my own language and dialect. "No, sir. I was just explaining that we've come to take possession of our new ship."

He raised an eyebrow and sucked in his bottom lip, which disappeared into his bushy beard. He looked from me to Kaelyn, to Merrik, and finally to the Siren, his frown deepening further with each new subject.

"New ship?" he asked.

I let loose a nervous chuckle that I tried to pass off as exasperated, and shrugged. "Well, not *new* new, obviously. But new to us. We acquired her… last night?" I looked up at Merrik for confirmation, and he nodded. "Last night," I said again, turning back to the guards in front of me. "We just came to get a good look at what it is we own."

"You 'acquired' her?" he asked, and I could practically hear the quotation marks. "Legally, I assume?"

"Absolutely," I nodded quickly. "I wouldn't dream of trying to pilfer something as grandiose as a ship, would you? That's just foolish. Merrik?" I turned back to look at him again. "This was on the up and up, right?"

"Sure," he replied easily.

"There, see?" I told the guard. I flashed him my most winning smile, the same one I reserved for calming the murderous ire of the angry 'investors' that had just been screwed over by Krellen again.

The guard looked uncertain and his companion watched him expectantly. "I don't suppose…" His warm, deep voice trailed off as he thought. He looked at each of us in turn again, and sighed.

Finally, he shrugged and relaxed his stance. "Look, I don't really care. Far as I'm concerned, ye want this wreck you can have her, but we're just tryin' to do our job here, aye? Do you have papers for it? A title? Bill of sale? Anything like that?"

"Of course!" I nodded again as I reached into my pocket. My empty pocket.

I searched again. "One second," I said. "I know it's here."

Still nothing. I gave Kaelyn a panicked look, and she started patting her own pockets. Merrik whistled and we looked up as he reached into his pack. He tossed me down the marker just as Kaelyn produced the letter.

I handed both over to the taller guard. He quickly scanned the note, then looked at the chit before handing both back to me.

"Like I said," he uttered with another sigh. "I don't much care what you do. This ship's been resting here, unwanted, for quite a while. I'm sure th' bosses at the dockmaster's office will be happier with it gone, but you really should get a deed or something, yeah?" He offered me half a smile, then turned back toward the road. "C'mon Iain, let's patrol th' warehouses again."

I watched the two of them until they were all the way back up the road and around a corner. Only after they were well gone did I breathe easier. I turned back to Kaelyn and Merrik, who were wearing matching grins. "Well," I said. "That could have gone worse."

"Yeah," Kaelyn said. "Except, apparently we need a deed. How the hells are we supposed to get that?"

Merrik, now that the coast was clear, dropped onto the pier and joined us. "I can try to track down the guy I got this off of, but I don't know how helpful that'll be."

I nodded, suspecting as much.

"Good luck with that," Kaelyn said. "If I just unloaded a broken down vessel that wouldn't even sell at auction, I'd make myself scarce."

Merrik chuckled. "Aye, but my luck isn't all that bad. Mayhap he stuck around," he said.

"Maybe," I agreed. "But maybe there's another way."

"What're you thinking, boss?" Merrik asked.

I shrugged one shoulder. "I was just thinking about the dockmaster back in Wellsmith. A nasty little man with way too much of a wandering eye. He spent as much time in the whorehouses as I spent in the bookstore. With such expensive habits, you could always be assured that he needed financing. I wonder if the one here is similar."

"You think we can bribe him?" Kaelyn said.

"Maybe..." I chewed on my bottom lip absently as I let the idea roll around in my head. It tumbled around with memories of less than legal work, people and property trades that shouldn't have happened, and two years of learning how to skirt the law. Finally, I looked at my two friends.

Kaelyn looked almost hopeful as she said, "You have an idea."

I felt myself slip back into the knowing grin, which I seemed to be wearing a lot lately. "I might have an idea," I corrected her. "Hopefully, I'm not without a little luck of my own."

CHAPTER SIX

I have always been more comfortable in the seedy parts of town. It's a fact I shouldn't be proud of, yet if I'm being honest, I am rather proud. While other girls my age were afraid to walk alone at night, I could march into an underground gambling house and sit down at a table with a gruff, scowling fiend or three.

Well, not confidently, but I could fake that part.

And so, that night I ditched my companions in order to follow my instincts. With the help of a couple haggard working women, I made my way further inland to an unnamed and unmarked barroom in the basement of a shipping office. It wasn't hard to find the place where the thieves, gamblers, cutthroats, and pirates hung out. These were my people, after all, and I spoke their language.

The room was large but cramped. Mismatched tables and chairs were pushed so close together that it was hard to move even before the addition of people. Yet people there were. Old, young, large, small, high-born, gutter trash—there didn't seem to be much distinction. One man's coin was just as good as another's here.

I watched a woman in a fashionable blue-silk dress roll a set of dice, while a leather-clad man with a large scar down the side of his face cheered her on. Everyone was at least a little inebriated and the energy in the room was almost overwhelmingly merry.

I would have liked to pretend it was just like home, but it was all just slightly off what I expected. In Wellsmith, the gambling houses were owned and operated by Mitsuni's men. They were large, sprawling affairs, with separate rooms for various types of games—dice in the main room, cards in the back parlors, animal races and cock fights out back, that sort of thing. It was organized, guided, and guarded. Debauchery with a purpose.

Here, only passion and enjoyment mattered. These people all seemed to mingle quietly with one another, as if there was an unspoken agreement that it could end at any moment and that nothing that happened within the walls would be shared or discussed outside. The manic urgency worked its way into the atmosphere here, and swept me along with it.

"I'm sorry, what?" I asked, pulling my attention back to the burly man in front of me.

He glowered. "I's askin' why a young'n like you'd be needin' an ink-spotter."

I shrugged noncommittally. "Does it matter? I'd think that if I couldn't keep my mouth shut, you'd already be in trouble." I gestured around us. I didn't know if this operation was illegal, or just frowned upon by society. Either way, he caught my drift.

He choked back a gurgling noise, which I realized was supposed to be a laugh, and then waved for me to follow him. "This way, young'n."

I followed him through the crowd as best I could, bumping into people, pushing others out of the way. I soon realized it would be easiest to follow closely in his wake as people parted in front of him.

He led me to a small table that was sandwiched between two groups of shouting patrons. As I tried to pass, a buxom red-head bumped into me with a drunken giggle.

"Oh, excuse me beautiful," she slurred, draping herself across me with a flirtatious smile.

I grabbed her shoulders to turn her into the arms of a dark man standing next to her, who welcomed the burden enthusiastically. With a chuckle, I turned my attention to the person waiting for me.

She was young. Not much older than me. She had crisp, clean features, and a no-nonsense look. A simple braid hung plaited down her back, and she dressed simply in a linen shirt with a pale blue vest and dark trousers. She sat calmly as her dark eyes scanned the room, seeming to miss nothing, and the amiable smile on her face held mistrust and wariness as much as humor. I would wager she didn't miss much.

"This one's for ya, Annie," my ogre escort said. He jammed a thumb in my direction, then just as abruptly, turned and pushed his way back through the crowd.

Annie looked up at me. I could feel her analyzing me, as if she could measure my quality in the way I held myself or the way I moved. Whatever she was looking for, she found me worthy, and smiled more broadly. She kicked out the seat across from her and gestured at it. "What can I do for you?"

I sat, awkwardly trying not to catch an elbow to the back of the head from the flailing patron behind me. "I need some papers," I said, not wasting time with minced words or small talk.

She raised an eyebrow, and the gesture alone was bored and dismissive.

I cleared my throat and started again. "I'm Tianna. Annie, was it?"

"Anne," she replied immediately. "Hate it when people call me 'Annie.'"

"Ah, sorry. Anne, then." That earned me a small, but genuine smile, so I continued. "I find myself in need of ship's papers. Rather urgently."

She scoffed, but turned it into a laugh. "Any particular ship? There's a few nice merchantmen in the north harbor. Though they are likely guarded, so take that into account."

I shook my head. "I'm sure they're lovely," I said, "But I have a very specific ship in mind already."

"Hmm," she said, that smile still playing on her lips. "Is this a collateral thing? There are easier ways to fence someone else's property. Though, I don't know anyone that's tried to fence a ship before. Could be a fun challenge for someone." She lowered her head, gazing at me from under hooded brows. That dark, measuring look came over her again. "Are you a pirate?"

I choked back my surprise and laughed. "No." *Though amateur volunteer crew for one isn't too far off,* I thought.

She raised an eyebrow again and sat back. The smirk on her face made me wonder if she'd heard my thought. "Oh?" she said.

I chewed on my bottom lip, thinking. "We aren't pirates. But we did encounter pirates on our way here, to Anvilcove. We, my friend and I, aren't really sailors at all. We…well, we found ourselves in possession of a sloop. By rights, it's ours, I think. But we lack the proof."

"You 'found yourself in possession of a sloop'…" she slowly repeated, as if she were trying to parse the words.

"A brig actually. I've recently learned that they're not the same thing, so I really should get in the habit of not mixing those up."

She laughed and shook her head so hard her loose braid swung over her shoulder. When she looked up at me again, she was almost grinning. "Well, now you have to explain."

She reached over and grabbed an empty glass from the table behind her as well as an already open bottle in front of her. Then, she poured a measure of some dark, carmine liquid into the goblet and slid it over to me before refilling her own.

I accepted the glass, and let it rest in front of me while I launched into my tale. I'm not sure if it was the company, the wine, or the relative comfort of an illicit dark and smoky room, but I recounted the events of the last few weeks with simple ease.

Anne seemed caught up in my tale, though I couldn't imagine why. When I got to the part where Merrik dropped the answer to our problem almost literally in our laps, she laughed out loud. It was no quiet laugh either, but a rolling, throaty guffaw that sounded like concert hall music from her light alto voice.

I laughed along with her, having so much fun just chatting with her that I almost forgot why I was revealing my ineptitude.

"So, we finally got the guards to drop the issue, but they said to take the deed to the harbormaster. Though I'm not really sure why, unless it's just a registration issue." I took the last sip of my wine as I finished my story.

"Most likely just squaring away mooring details," she said dismissively. "Dennet doesn't care who owns a ship, so long as the paperwork is in order."

I looked at her. "You know the harbormaster?"

"I know many people." She shrugged. "And those I don't know, I know *of*."

That made sense. Hadn't I been much the same in Wellsmith? Maybe I had found the right person after all.

"I am curious, Tianna," she said at length. "What do you plan to do with this ship once you rightly have her?"

I paused. It was the question most on my mind this last week. What did I even want to do? Everything was new to me and I had no purpose. I couldn't just sail around from place to place, hoping to find something worthy of my time and attention. Could I? I still had such a hazy vision of the future. No wonder I kept feeling lost.

"I guess I will get a crew, find some trading or escort jobs, and... uh, sail?" I said eventually.

"Hmm," was all she said. She sat back in her chair and emptied the remains of the bottle into her glass. She took a careful sip before finally saying, "I think I can help you get your ship."

A wave of relief flushed through me. I hadn't realized I was holding my shoulders too tightly until that burden had been set down. My ship. *My* ship! With papers, that would prove it. It was almost too much to believe.

"Sacred shitting gods!" I practically squealed. "I'm still having trouble believing this is real. Thank you."

"Don't thank me," she said, holding up a hand. "I don't work for free."

I slumped in my chair. "Oh, well no. Of course not. I don't have much in the way of coin, but I will do what I can to come up with it. How much will this cost me?"

She pondered her words for a moment and then said, "I don't want your coin. At least, not for this."

I hesitated. "For what then?"

She smiled, but I noticed it was the same as that first smile, both wary and measuring. "A simple barter. Work for work."

My thoughts raced, and I let them loose. What could I offer her that might be of value? I told her about my work with Krellen, but she didn't seem like she needed an accountant, nor a scribe.

My work taking bets was more up her alley, but I hadn't told her about that, and there were bet-tenders galore in nearly every corner of this room, if that's what she was after. So, what did I have to offer, except coin? Or my blade.

I blanched at the thought. I got lucky the last time I was forced to raise it, and that was in self-defense. The next time? Would I put my life on the line for any reason less than my own life? And faced with it, would I be able to sink the killing blow again, or would I freeze?

Afraid to ask the only question I had, I looked at her squarely, with as much resolve as I could muster. "What do you want me to do?"

My thoughts must have been clear on my face, because she laughed again.

"You can relax. I have no intention of asking you to kill anyone. I'm not even sure why you would think I'd consider asking that."

I breathed out a sigh of relief so strong it nearly turned my stomach from the change in tension. I slumped over the table, a laugh that was borderline hysteria escaping from me. Now that she mentioned it, I don't actually know why I assumed she was after a hit, either. I hoped she wasn't offended.

"I want a job," she said as I sat up again.

"So do I," I countered.

She looked at me, her jaw set tightly. "I can't tell if you're being dense or intentionally evasive. I want to sail with you."

"Oh." It took another heartbeat or two before the words hit my consciousness. "Oh!" I said again. It certainly wasn't murder, but I can't say I expected her to trade me something I needed for something else I needed. "Can you sail?"

"I have some experience, but I'm no professional, if that's what you're asking," she said. "Can you?"

I felt my lips twitch as I fought to hold back a laugh. "Not really, but I'm learning."

She gave a thoughtful nod. "This should be a fairly simple transaction then, Tianna. The papers you need won't even have to be forged, not really. Since we're not copying an existing document, we only need to establish ownership, not provenance. I can have them for you by the end of the week. You only need to agree to my terms."

"Are you fine with being a general crew member? Or are you looking for something more illustrous?"

"I can't really sail, but I can read charts, keep detailed logs, and deal with personnel better than anyone else you're likely to find. I'm not sure where I can be of most use to you, but if you want the document, I come with it."

I fiddled with my empty glass as I weighed my options. Or pretended to weigh my options. When it came down to it, this was a really simple decision. "Alright. It's a deal."

I held out my hand, and she shook it, rising to her feet.

"You won't regret this, Tianna," she said. "Meet me in a few days, and I'll have what you need."

I thanked her and hurried out into the misty afternoon air before she could take it all back. Taking a deep breath, I grinned and mentally patted myself on the back for a job well done. I couldn't wait to tell Kaelyn and Merrik.

"You did *what!*?" Kaelyn shrieked at me. This was maybe the third time in as many minutes she had raised her voice. I had raced back to the inn we were staying at to share the good fortune, but now I was regretting my hurry.

It turns out that hiring new crew members with little to no sailing experience without consulting my shipmates first was a problem.

"She's nice," I said. "And she can solve our problem."

Kaelyn threw up her hands as she paced the floor of the small room we were renting.

"What was her name, again?" Merrik asked.

I glanced over to where he was reclining against the hearth, whittling at a small piece of wood. "Anne."

"What kind of name is 'Anne'?" Kaelyn demanded.

"Uh, Lugaian, I think. Or maybe Tirican. One of those cultural crossover names."

She growled at me. "I mean, what kind of name is that for a forger! What do we even know about her? She's good with a pen, so that gets her a spot on our ship?"

I stood and faced down Kaelyn. "I'm good with a pen, too. Should I leave?"

She shook her head, shaking loose the scarf around her head. She tore it off and looked at me. "That's not what I meant." Her tone was apologetic, but her eyes still snapped with fire.

"I know, but the fact is that none of us knows what we're doing. She can help us and I like her. We can all learn together. And let's not forget she can get us our ship. We won't have any luck at all finding someone to refit her unless we can prove the Siren is ours."

"That's another issue," Merrik said. "We still need coin for repairs."

Kaelyn sighed, the embers in her gaze, banking to a more moderate glow. "Right. I have a plan." She muttered something else that I didn't catch, and turned away from me to contemplate the wall.

I cocked my head, waiting for the rest. "And?"

When she didn't answer or turn to acknowledge that she'd left me hanging, I threw my hands up and turned to examine something on the far wall. I didn't know what. Anything would do as long as I wasn't looking at her.

"So, I've been thinking," Merrik said.

I grumbled, cutting him off. "Kaelyn says she has a plan." The wall was not proving interesting enough to distract me from my irritation.

"So I've been thinking," he repeated without answering me or looking up from his wood block. "What we need is–"

"We?" I asked. "Are you a part of this, then? Last I heard, you sounded like you wanted to pass the ship off to us."

He looked at me like I was slow. "Of course I'm in. Just had to finish up my work first. Since I'll be done tomorrow, there's nothing holding me here."

He raised his head and looked at Kaelyn. When neither of us interrupted him again, he said, "What we need is our own crew and a proper job."

I shook my head in frustrated agreement. "That's what I've been saying."

Kaelyn turned and glanced at me, but answered Merrik. "We're supposed to be meeting someone who has need of a ship, a crew. Or access to a job. Or something. I was a little unclear about the translation. But I'm sure it will be fine."

"We are? Who? And what do you mean, translation?" I asked, surprised. "Translation from what? You do know I can read like four languages, right?"

Merrik raised an eyebrow that I hoped meant that he was impressed and not that he thought I was a braggart.

Kaelyn waved me off. "It's not a problem of a language barrier or anything, not specifically, but the information traveled through more than a few channels before it got to me."

"Kaelyn, I swear–" To her gain, and my increased frustration, a knock on the door interrupted us.

Merrik stood and brushed off the wood chips that clung to his shirt. He then made his way over to the door and opened it to a tired man waiting in the hallway. He wore the livery of the local guard and had a large pack slung across his chest. This courier looked about as comfortable in this inn as a catfish would in an armory.

"Miss Féanaro?" He said, more statement than question.

Merrik waved him inside and pointed him toward my friend by the fire.

Bowing before her, he handed her a folded piece of paper. With no further interaction with us, he turned and fled, ready to be free of this place as soon as possible.

"What is it?" I asked.

She shrugged and broke the seal.

> Milady Féanaro,
>
> We and ours kindly request the presence of thee and thy companions on the first of Moontide, Even Morning. We wish to parley on a matter of peculiarity, and pray that it may lead to acquiescence upon our request. We are desirous of more immediate discourse of the proposition at hand. With due alacrity, make fit to present thyself upon the instance.
>
> ~From our Hand and Pen
> HL A. Jenness

"I see what you mean about the language." I muttered. "We're supposed to go there?"

"It looks that way," Kaelyn replied slowly, still perusing the archaic missive.

"Who's A. Jenness?" I wasn't quite appeased, but I let my irritation go by the wayside. Yelling at Kaelyn never seemed to change anything and rarely made me feel better.

"She's the Governor's daughter," Merrik said around a mouthful of cheese. I blinked and looked again, wondering when he had found food. "Well, one of them. There are five I think? Three of them have names with A, though, so..." he shrugged.

"Well, we have a couple of days before she wants to see us." I said, instead. "Let's see what Merrik comes up with."

"What am I doing?" he asked.

"Looking for 'proper jobs', I think you called them. So far, Kaelyn has been the only one looking. Wouldn't it be better if we all did, now that we have a goal?"

Kaelyn looked at me. "What about you?"

I cocked my head. "What about me?"

It was her turn to shake her head in irritation. "You may not be from this city, but you know port towns and docks better than anyone else I know. Surely you know where to start asking."

"Oh, uh... yeah. I guess that's true." I had been so wrapped up in trying to figure out what Kaelyn was up to, that I didn't even bother to look into answers myself. I tried to appease my guilt by reminding myself that I had gotten us the paperwork for our ship, but I silently kicked myself, and promised to do better on the job front. We were all in this together.

Merrik nodded along with the conversation. "We may as well all pitch in. Oh, and I have a place to stay, if you want it. Save what little coin we do have."

The look I gave him must surely have proclaimed him the benevolent god I thought him to be just then, because he laughed.

"It isn't much, just a small room I've been renting near the smithy, but it's warm and dry, and a lot quieter than this place," he said. "Let's get some dinner, then we can grab your things and I'll take you over there."

I nodded emphatically. "A good meal, a place to sleep, and help finding a job? No wonder you keep him around," I joked to Kaelyn. To my surprise, she blushed. I looked back and forth from Merrik to Kaelyn and changed the subject. "Maybe we can do some shopping, too."

"Shopping?" Kaelyn asked, surprised.

I raised an eyebrow in her direction. I trailed my gaze up and down her clothing, then pointedly turned to look at Merrik, giving him the same treatment. His loose vest and stained cotton shirt were not in much better shape than the garments we had on.

"Look at us, Kaelyn. Do you really want to present yourself to the Governor and his daughter looking like you just washed up with the flotsam?"

"Washed up? I thought that was you?" she joked, and then looked at her raveling scarves and stained vest. She chuckled sheepishly. "You may have a point."

"Great, while you ladies go shopping, I'll start–"

"Oh, no. You too," Kaelyn said, staring him down.

Merrik looked affronted. "But I'm comfortable."

"Sorry, *kashi*," I patted his shoulder in consolation. "We're going to have to do a little better than our usual if we want people to take us seriously. Not sure comfort is the order of the day anymore. At least not this day."

He sighed and grumbled, for the first time looking less than placid. "Fine," he said. "But nothing too flashy."

"Sure," I told him. "Whatever you want."

CHAPTER SEVEN

I am, on occasion, vain enough to preen. As I strutted up the rough stone pathway to the Governor's mansion, I spared a moment of gratitude for our shopping excursion. Now that I wasn't still running around town in salt-worn, badly patched hand-me-downs that never fit quite right, I was feeling a bit more like myself again. Or possibly like myself for the first time. That's a difficult line to pin down.

My new black linen trousers were so soft I couldn't even hear them whisper when I walked. I had a white cotton shirt under a matching black vest that was probably the finest thing I'd ever put on my body.

When I had looked at myself in the tall glass, I remember feeling that I finally looked like myself. Better than myself, even. Like the self I always knew was in there, not the orphan bookkeeper paid in blankets and stew.

Kaelyn's ensemble had changed very little. I'm not sure how she managed it, but from her bright red, loose-fitting pants, to her multi-layered cacophony of scarves, to her short-cut vest over a sleeveless undershirt, she looked the same. Cleaner, maybe, and sharper.

Not sharper in the literal sense, of course. I had to bully her into only bringing two knives into the governor's house. Yet, with even this much, that there was a difference in her that was so subtle I couldn't quite place it. If I didn't know better, I would say she seemed relaxed.

Merrik kept fussing with his sand-colored curls, tying the mass back with a leather strap, releasing it, then retying it. I would have thought it a nervous habit, but Merrik never seemed to get nervous.

His undyed linen shirt was tight across his shoulders. He paired it with a slate blue-green vest, almost the same color as his eyes. Whoever had chosen his outfit had put care into it. He looked like a well-tailored merchant's son, not a blacksmith and would-be sailor. It certainly wasn't flashy, as requested, though the way it fitted to his frame was eye-catching.

We paused at the Governor's door, suddenly unsure of protocol. Etiquette was never something I took an interest in. When would I ever need to know how to bow or give proper address to a noble?

The one time Albert tried to teach me, I overwhelmed him with my questions of 'why' and 'who cares' in regards to which dignitary receives which honorific. He stalked off and I remember overhearing him mutter about the isler aristocracy, at least that of Denisi Tirica, being 'actors in fine hats'. I wasn't sure what he meant, and it wasn't until many years later that I started to understand.

At this point, I wasn't anywhere close to understanding. I still didn't know what all was out there in the wide open world, but from what little I had already seen, titles didn't make a difference. What use was there in calling a lord a lord if they only used that power to make sure they kept being called a lord? I'm sure the continent was the same old mud trussed up in a fancier collar, despite Albert's romantic visions to the contrary.

Small governments always made more sense to me than empires or kingdoms. Flags don't keep people fed. People do. What good was a king an ocean away who didn't care how his people got by?

Albert used to bristle about islers who would pretend they were 'proper Tiricans' but had no interest in ever setting foot on the continent. For the first time, I wondered if maybe he meant the governor, and not the rabble, like I'd always assumed.

Personally, I liked the freedoms the isles brought. Or at least the idea of them. Of course, that same freedom and variety is what had us standing on the governor's doorstep, unsure of what awaited us inside.

I glanced at my companions, hoping that someone knew what to do. Merrik seemed bored and distracted. This was nothing new for him, but also very little help. Kaelyn looked calm, but made no move to approach the door. I wondered if maybe she was more nervous than she let on.

It might be odd that my friend's perceived discomfort made me feel more in control—though I'll concede it might have simply been my increased comfort at finally being attired in clean, well-fitting clothes for the first time in… I don't want to think about how long—but it did. If no one else would step up, I had to. Else we'd be out here all day.

Bracing myself for the unknown, I marched up the front steps and rapped firmly on the immense door. When no answer immediately came, I opened the door and peered in. Walking into the grand foyer, I immediately felt out of place. So much for my confidence.

The polished marble floor looked like it was worth more than the entire Lugaian throne room. Carved statues were interspersed at even intervals down the hall, and shimmering crystalline chandeliers hung overhead.

Even with my vast imagination, I could never have dreamed something like this existed anywhere in the isles. Anywhere outside of the Imperial Palace, for that matter.

The conspicuous wealth was so overwhelming that I couldn't help but whisper, afraid to upset the delicate perfection of the place with my unpolished tongue.

As soon as we crossed the threshold, an attendant clad in the increasingly familiar green and white colors of the Governor's house rushed up to us.

"May I help you?" he asked in a way that clearly hoped our answer would be 'no'.

"Please inform the Governor and Her Ladyship that Kaelyn Féanaro and her party have arrived," I said, trying for something official-sounding.

"Very good, ma'am," he said, bowed, and left.

"Ma'am?" Merrik said, choking back his amusement. "You're about as ma'am-ish as a Meketian pig."

I stuck out my tongue, formulating a biting reply, but luckily for Merrik, the messenger quickly returned and led us down the hall into a study.

The Governor of the Outer Isles and his daughter were waiting for us when we entered. He was short and bland, with an affected air of scholarly superiority but with none of the cool intelligence that goes along with it.

He struck me as pretentious and ineffectual, and I was bored with him already. He waited by the fire, wearing much the same look that Merrik had earlier, as if we were just taking up his time.

His daughter was another matter. It was her we were here to see, after all. She was a tall, dark-haired beauty with the kind of grace that could only be enhanced by a keen mind and intelligent wit. Her dress was tight through the bodice, with wide flowing sleeves, and a full skirt that looked heavy enough that I had to wonder how she walked.

"Miss Féanaro, welcome."

I finally turned to look at her face and gaped.

Her warm alto voice, laced with amusement. "I am so glad you could come."

"Anne?" I squawked before I could stop myself.

She turned to look at me imperiously. "It's Lady Annelia Jenness, if you please. I am happy to make your acquaintance, but let's not lose all formalities."

I continued to gape after her, completely at a loss. This was the same girl I had met earlier, I was sure of it. Her voice, her face, even the cool and calculating way she scanned the room were the same. My forger is the governor's daughter? I couldn't keep my eyes from going wide at the thought, and I fumbled for my words.

"Wh- uh, but..."

"Please, sit," Lady Annelia said, and gestured at a sofa behind her. She gracefully took a seat in a chair opposite us and smiled sweetly.

Kaelyn and I sat, while Merrik stood in an easy and unthreatening posture behind the couch. If I didn't know better, I'd say he looked like our chaperone, but I knew he simply didn't want to be caught sitting if we should have to make a run for it.

"Miss Féanaro, it was kind of you to respond so quickly to my invitation. I wasn't sure the messenger would find you," Lady Annelia continued.

"It was no problem," Kaelyn said uncertainly.

"Who are your friends?"

She glanced at us curiously, not suspiciously, so I took that as a good sign.

"Uh..." Kaelyn eloquently replied to our hostess.

I did my best not to trip over any plan Kaelyn may have had in place, but I couldn't just sit there and let the silence stretch on. Forger or no, liar or no, and despite whatever game this lady was about, I had to intervene.

With a silent head-shake, and a promise to give Kaelyn a long lecture on the importance of planning, I took a breath and called upon the skills I learned from dealing with thugs and murderers all day.

"It is a pleasure to formally meet you, My Lady. I'm Tianna Blackboot." I offered a slight bow from my seated position. "I think you haven't yet met Kaelyn Féanaro. It's her you've been in contact with." Kaelyn nodded as I gestured at her, then waved behind us. "And this is our associate, Merrik Blackhand."

Lady Annelia smiled. "Wonderful to meet you all, I am sure," she said, pouring a cup of tea. She was the very image of ladylike elegance, though I couldn't help but see an overlay of the girl from last night. She poured the tea with the same deliberate care as she had the wine. I noticed she wasn't actually looking at any of us while she talked, but instead kept glancing at her father, still standing by the window. "How do you all know each other?" she asked lightly.

I sat on the sofa watching her movements for a moment more before I remembered I was the one having this conversation. My mute friends were no help. "Kaelyn and I met in Wellsmith, before coming to Anvilcove. Merrik only recently joined us."

She nodded, but said nothing more. She took her time, appearing more invested with the tea service in front of her than in the conversation. After a moment, she handed me a small porcelain cup, and I accepted it with a murmur of gratitude as Kaelyn cut in. "Excuse me, maybe we can cut out the small-talk?"

Lady Annelia smiled, with a look mixed with hesitation and intentional patience. "I understand you wish to discuss business. Of course. I have wasted too much of your time as it is. Forgive my rudeness."

I shot Kaelyn a quick glare. "Of course not, my lady. We are simply eager. We don't want to be any bother for you or your family. If you wish to enjoy a cup of tea and simply talk, that will suit us just fine."

She looked at me, calculating something in my face, though I couldn't tell you what. "No, that's quite all right. On to business," she said as she sat back in her chair. "I have discussed your position with my father, and we have agreed you might do. However, before we can go any further, we would need assurances that if we financed your vessel, we will see quick and safe delivery."

So, that's what Kaelyn had been talking to them about. Financing. I was actually impressed, though I wished Kaelyn had said something to me before walking in here. Still, one riddle solved, I turned to the next. "Forgive me, I am a little behind on learning the details of your agreement with my friend. What, exactly, has she asked of you?"

Lady Annelia looked surprised. "Only that we finance a trade excursion around the Outer Isles and back."

"Ah," I said. "I see. So you are looking for a crew, then?"

Lady Annelia looked at me blankly. "You do have a crew, do you not? I suppose that can be arranged as well. I expected a few amendments to the agreement. It shouldn't be hard to add provisions for the hiring of a crew."

"Add provisions for the..." I shook my head, totally lost. "I'm sorry, but what is it that Kaelyn has offered of us? I'm afraid I'm somewhat in the dark. If you are not hiring a crew, why are we here?"

"I just told you that I would hire a crew," she explained slowly, as if I were a particularly dense and distracted child.

"Yes, but why do you need us?" I waved between Kaelyn and myself as if that would make it clearer who I meant.

"Why, for your ship, of course," the Lady said.

I fought to keep my grimace to a polite glare. "We don't have a ship."

I tried to glare a hole through Kaelyn's skull. I had no idea what she had been telling strangers all over town about our situation, but she only met my gaze with a lazy grin.

"Though we are working on acquiring one," I added, turning back to Anne. I gave her a pointed look, because I was sure she already knew this, but she didn't so much as twitch at my scrutiny.

I shook my head wearily, looking between Lady Annelia and Kaelyn, still trying to piece together what exactly was on offer on either side of this bargain.

"Forgive me, but I'm still trying to understand. You want to hire us to sail a trade excursion around the Outer Isles? You will hire a crew, outfit the same, and even finance the entire voyage?"

"That's right."

"And what do you get out of this?" I asked as flatly as I could.

"Twenty percent of your take and a personal delivery to an acquaintance in Sunset." The Lady informed me.

"A delivery? That's all?"

"That's all. One package to Windhaven Manor on the Isle of Coral, and the rest of your time is yours to do with as you will." She looked far too pleased with herself and I thought I noted a sly glint to her eye that I both liked and mistrusted. She hadn't told me everything, and she obviously wasn't above keeping secrets.

Lady Annelia took another careful sip of her tea, still watching us eagerly.

"What's in-" I started at the same moment her father cut in.

"It's a fool's bargain."

"Excuse me?" Kaelyn said to him, offended.

I choked back a gasp, at her tone. Kaelyn clearly wasn't used to dealing with authority. I didn't know if this was the kind of man who would blacklist our names or the kind that would slit our throats and feed the bodies to his hounds. Either way, I didn't want to find out, and I didn't want to see this deal fall apart before I even knew what it entailed.

"What my father means is that since we are assuming the risk financially, it makes sense that we would ask for collateral or equal exchange of value."

"What kind of collateral?" Merrik asked.

"Well–" Annelia started.

"An outer island excursion is the same as handing out money to pirates and ruffians. This whole endeavor is a fool's bargain," her father grumbled again. "This is on you, Anna. I will have none of it."

She smiled, more warmly this time, and I heard a small grunt of derision from the window. Annelia stood and walked over to her father. I watched her place a small, gloved hand on his forearm and gaze up at him sweetly.

"Father, I know you have much to do. Since we've already agreed in principle, why don't I take over? I am quite capable of handling the details if you wish to tend to other matters."

He sighed heavily and patted her head. With a quick, measuring glance over at us, he nodded. "Very well. Thank you, my dear. I will return should you need anything."

She smiled brightly as he kissed her forehead and hurried out a side door. As it shut behind him, she spun and walked back over to her chair.

She sunk down into it with more ease than she had before, and I noticed an open relief on her face. "Forgive my father. He's not used to letting me make decisions. But this one I took a special interest in."

"My Lady, I can't make any assurances," I told her honestly. "We aren't experienced sailors. We don't even have a full crew. I can't help but think we're getting the better end of this bargain." Kaelyn started to object to that, but I had a question that I needed and answer to before I went any further. "What is it you really want from us?"

She leaned forward and picked up her tea, sipping it carefully. "As I said before, I have discussed your position with my father, and we have agreed to finance your vessel–"

"We don't have a–" I started to object, but she cut me off.

"Including refitting, full cargo, and crew, pay for your maiden voyage as a merchantman."

I eyed her cautiously. "And?" I knew she was still holding back. I was still trying to figure out her game.

"And a crew, and cargo. As I've said." She peered closely at me. "Don't tell me I've made a mistake in my choice. You can't really be that slow-witted, can you?"

I couldn't seem to find my voice for several moments. "You'll have to forgive me, my lady, but–"

"Call me Anne," she waved her hand in a blasé manner.

"Is this for real?"

She nodded. "It would be a very odd joke, wouldn't it?" she asked with a twinkle in her eye.

"That is very generous, Lady Annelia."

She shook her head. "Anne. Please. My title is much too formal for everyday use."

"Are we free to speak, then, Anne?" I asked, hoping she would catch my full meaning.

She glanced toward the firmly closed door her father had exited through and beamed. Turning a sly smile on me, she nodded. "Of course." She reached into a small bag at her side and drew out a hard leather scroll case, which she handed to me. "As promised."

I opened it and fished out a small roll of high-quality vellum. I unrolled it and scanned the contents quickly, before grinning like a madwoman.

"This is perfect," I breathed. Excitedly, I handed the whole bundle to Kaelyn.

She looked it over and her eyes went wide. "Is this real? A deed, a letter of credit, and… what's this?" She held up one of the last pieces of paper. Its ornate scrawl was a little harder to read, but I had seen something similar once before when dealing with a Lugaian merchanteer.

"It's a letter of marque?" I asked, more surprised than anything. That wasn't part of our original deal.

"More like… travel papers." Anne laughed and leaned forward, lifting one slender finger to tap on the pages Kaelyn was gripping tightly. "These will grant you free access to all Bann Tirican-held ports. the Outer Isles, The Reefs, even the mainland should you want to go that far."

With a smile, she sat back and lifted her teacup again. "The letter of credit is good at any Tirican-held bank— should you need further financing on your voyage—and the deed is… well, as promised."

"I… uh…. What?" Kaelyn stammered, looking at me for guidance. She looked down at the stack of papers again and frowned. "These aren't signed."

Anne waved her hand again, unbothered. "Just a small assurance for my part. I wanted to make sure we had an accord before I handed over everything."

"But aren't letters of marque supposed to have a royal seal…" Kaelyn asked, still not quite following.

I sat quietly, tying all the pieces together in my mind and watching Anne.

"I think that's only true for valid copies, Kaelyn," I told her carefully.

"What? These aren't valid?" She glared at Anne. "Is this some kind of setup."

Anne shook her well-coifed head gently. "I assure you, this is no trick. I need someone to make this run. Preferably someone not already in my father's employ. These papers are everything I promise you they are. You won't have any trouble with them."

"But–" Kaelyn started.

"They're fakes," Merrik stated.

Anne, finally looking up at our silent shadow, smiled. "Are they?" She said the words innocently, but her smile spoke volumes.

Kaelyn's head popped up and her gaze bounced back and forth between me and Anne. "Wait, Anne. Like, Anne? *Forger* Anne?"

I chuckled darkly. "She's much more than that, it seems, but yes. Kaelyn, this is the woman I met with yesterday." I turned my focus back to the Lady in question, even as I kept speaking to Kaelyn. "Though I admit, I didn't expect to find her here."

It was Anne's turn to grin. "I apologize for my little joke. I did not realize until part way through our conversation that you two were working together. Once I heard your story, though, it felt too much like destiny to ignore."

I scoffed and pulled a face, making an unladylike noise, but let her continue.

"I am Lady Annelia Jenness, fourth daughter of the Governor of the Outer Islands who is Lord Magistrate of Hammersmith Island. I am also a student of the Invisible Pen, more from curiosity than necessity. As you have guessed, I drafted those Letters, but I assure you, they are entirely indistinguishable from the real thing. I am a nobleworman, a scholar, and it would seem, your benefactor."

Kaelyn went absolutely still, clutching our seemingly authentic documents in her hands. I pretended not to see the slight tremor that went through her.

"No," I said, catching her line of thought. "We aren't owned by anyone. We can't be. And you seem to forget that we haven't agreed to sign on with you yet."

"Not for the financing, perhaps." Anne shook her head. "But you will. You weren't planning on staying in Anvilcove, were you? I was under the impression you were looking to get away from Hammersmith Island With those you can. And our other agreement still stands. Unless you've changed your mind, that is." She reached for the bundle in Kaeyn's hand, and paused pointedly.

I fell silent again, unable to argue with her logic. She had me, and she knew it. I looked at Kaelyn's wary but hopeful expression, then I turned to look at Merrik. He gripped the couch tightly, waiting to see what I would do. I held in my sigh, knowing that there was only one answer left that would get us what we all wanted.

I turned to Anne. "If our deal from the other night still stands, you are our navigator."

She laughed and clapped her hands together merrily. "Oh, this is going to be wonderful!"

I shook my head at this polished lady sitting demurely in front of us. She looked as likely a sailor as the mocking bird sleeping quietly in its cage.

"Lady Ana–Anne," I said, "This is just a trade excursion, right? This isn't... I'm not sure what romantic notions you have of sailing the high seas, but it isn't like in the tales. Believe me, I've read most of them. Life aboard a ship isn't anything like that. I'm not sure you know what you're asking. Vasta, I'm not even sure I know what I'm getting into, but this can't be the life you want for yourself."

I looked over at Kaelyn to see what she made of all this. I mean, how could this ever be a good idea? But, oddly enough, she didn't seem shocked, annoyed, or even amused. She was solemn, with an oddly intense, and pleading look in her eyes.

"Tianna," Kaelyn said quietly. "We can't say no. She can back us fully and help us get the ship on the ocean. Even if Merrik comes with us, we're only three people. We'll hire more, but we need to know who has our back, right? I..." she shrugged. "I trust her."

Kaelyn held my gaze. Her grin slowly grew until it was an overconfident smirk. "Besides," she waved the vellum in my face. "You kind of already promised."

I sat silent for a moment, thinking. I didn't have any kind of argument to get us out of this.

"In answer to your question," Anne broke in. "Those are real, more real than a simple forgery, anyway. I may have written them myself, but that is the magistrate's seal. The Siren is legally yours."

So it was real. Or, real enough. I looked down at the ownership papers to the first real property I'd ever been able to call 'mine'. My hand shook slightly, but suddenly I could see it. Striding the open waters in bountiful freedom; me on the wheel, Kaelyn manning sails, Merrik handling supplies, and Anne, well actually, I still had a hard time picturing her on board a ship, but I was sure we could find something for her to do, because it meant we could have our ship! The Siren, our unchained carriage to anywhere.

Our ship.

I smiled and received answering grins from my mates. That clinched it. Dropping my gaze to the papers one more time, I shook my head. No point in arguing further. We were in. For better or for worse, this was happening.

I went to bed early that night, more exhausted than I had been after that first day of walking all over the city. I snuggled up in the quilt I'd stolen off Merrik. We were back in the small room that was our temporary home, and as I laid there, wide awake, I did my best to forget the strangeness of the last couple of weeks.

If I tried, I could pretend I was back at the orphanage in Wellsmith with the other lost waifs. I could pretend the noise from the street outside was the chatter of a dozen children and their caretakers, that the aromas drifting through the room was the smell from the apothecary outside wafting in my open window, and that the excitement thudding in my chest was just another outing to the shore tomorrow.

But I wasn't eight years old anymore. By all rights I was a woman grown, though I hardly knew what that meant. I wasn't sure if we were doing the right thing. In honesty, I wasn't sure I knew what we were doing at all, but somehow I had to think this was the right thing.

The right thing? How could it be the right thing? At this point, I was barely sure it qualified as a 'thing' at all. My thoughts swirled relentlessly.

Kaelyn had her fascination with just being together and having fun, but I needed to do something. Well, this was something. The isles were notorious as being the worst stretch of sea for anyone who wasn't a pirate. Yet, here we were, a grand total of eight days of sailing experience between us, and a glorious plan to 'go'.

Then again, my treacherous thoughts reminded me, *isn't that where we started? Working for pirates, running from pirates, and now...?*

No. I wasn't really considering piracy as a valid life choice. Even growing up in a city where piracy, and much worse, was a pastime for much of the population, I had to believe that it wasn't the only choice. That if we tried hard enough and looked out for each other, it was possible to live a happy life without hurting anyone else. Piracy couldn't be the only answer. I just needed to find another one.

A trade run. What was wrong with that idea? Our lack of knowledge and experience came to mind again, but I pushed it away. Ugh, this was all so complicated. I tried again to turn my thoughts from Kaelyn, and ships, and this crazy scheme. Eventually, other things dripped into my mind, and I almost managed to pretend I was back at home. Almost.

"Tianna?" Kaelyn said in the quiet room. "You awake?"

"More or less." I half sat up and turned to look at her.

She crossed the room and sat at the foot of my bed.

"What the hells are we doing?" Her laugh emphasized her bewildered expression. It was weird to hear her mimic my thoughts so closely. Weirder still to see her so unsure. "I mean, is this… a good thing? What we're doing?"

"Yes, I think so." I told her, willing myself to believe it too.

"But you're not really sure?"

I shook my head. Of course, I wasn't sure. I still didn't entirely know what was happening, let alone whether or not it was the right course.

"Well." I said blithely. "Even if we fail miserably, lose the ship, cargo, and any chance we have of getting away from the Outer Isles, it's still better than staying in Wellsmith. Following you around blindly beats living on the streets, working for Krellen, or worse. Isn't that what you've been telling me?"

She smiled weakly. "Good point. I guess."

"Something else is bothering you. This isn't about sailing a ship into parts unknown without a crew, cargo, or even navigational skill, is it?"

She chuckled halfheartedly. "No. It's just..." She took a deep breath and fell silent.

I nodded, but wanted to wait for her to confide in me.

At length she spoke again. "It's just, I know I told you that this, me going off on my own, was a family thing, but that's only mostly true. Actually, when my father left to find work in the eastern kingdoms, I was supportive, but I wouldn't go. I refused to let his work get in the way of my life again. So when my mother went to join him, I didn't. I ran off."

She had never talked about her parents before, not really. Certainly not like this. "Then this isn't a family tradition, self-discovery thing?" I asked.

"Oh, it is. I mean, it kind of is. I know I led you to believe that they let me go, but that was only half of the truth. They only let me go after I was already gone." She looked down, bashful.

I wasn't sure what to say. Never having had any of my own that I recall, I didn't know if there was a protocol to homesickness or not.

"It's not loneliness. I mean, I do miss them, but..." she said, making me wonder for a moment if I had spoken out loud. "I promised myself I would make my own life. That the world wouldn't shape me, I would shape it. And... what if I was wrong? What if we fail and lose everything?"

I nodded. That was true enough. Fear of the unknown had kept me at the orphanage longer than it should have and glued to Krellen's side despite seeing him for what he was. I had been afraid to do something different.

I was still afraid.

"What if we fail?" I repeated her question. "What if we don't make enough money to stay supplied? What if we can't sail out of port? What if we're attacked by pirates and killed?"

She sputtered.

"Sorry." I shook my head. "I'm not trying to step on your feelings, but we can lose ourselves in 'what-if' long before we ever step foot outside this door. I don't have much confidence either."

I paused and took a breath, searching her face for the answers that would assuage her fears. "This is all just as new to me as it is to you," I told her. "But questioning this and talking ourselves out of it isn't the right answer. I'm very sure of that. It can't be."

She smiled weakly.

When she didn't reply, I continued. "Stopping to regret the decisions that brought us here would be a complete waste of our time, and given our histories, it like would leave us catatonic."

She laughed. "Yeah, you're probably right."

"Look, Kaelyn, it's going to be great. If the worst happens, we find a new hobby and start a whole new crazy scheme, but we'll do it together."

"What if the worst is we die?" she said.

"Then we won't much care either way, will we?"

She laughed and took a shuddering breath.

"Come on, Kaelyn," I said. "Try to get some sleep. We have a ship to crew and refit tomorrow."

That's all there was to it. Worries aside, we were doing this thing, so we might as well see it through. And I would cling to that thought like it was the last gift of the Emperor.

"Gods help us," she added with a chuckle.

CHAPTER EIGHT

The next day, Kaelyn and I got up bright and early to meet with Anne down at the docks. It wasn't a part of town I would normally expect to find a governor's daughter loitering in, but then again, there were a lot of things about this particular governor's daughter that were unusual.

It was mid-morning, and the air had a bit of a lingering chill to it, but dazzling sunlight spread across the bay as the sun rose over the city. Light reflecting off the water made the ships glow, dancing and sparkling from the reflections off the water.

Anne waited for us between two short buildings, framed against the backdrop of the bay. Her green silk dress shirt hugged her shoulders and waist in a flattering way, and she had it tucked into a smart pair of linen trousers that were gathered at the cuff in a pair of low boots.

I was relieved to see that she had dressed more sensibly than the night before. Embroidered silk was fine for the parlor but hell for the alley. The air about her was more relaxed as well, more like it was when we had first met, which put me at ease.

"Ah, good. You made it," Anne said when she spotted us.

"Are you sure about this craftsman of yours?" I asked.

"Of course," she said.

She turned with a smile and gave a quick nod to the guardsman standing nearby, then started off down the road.

He took up a position behind her and slightly to the right, following us at a discreet, but useful, distance as we walked toward the shipwrights.

Kaelyn looked dubious, but her expression screamed most articulately. *If this fancy lady thinks she can run around making backstreet deals and mingle with shady rogues, we might all be in trouble,* it seemed to say.

I smiled with as much reassurance as I could, reveling in the camaraderie of displeasure, and shrugged. We both followed Anne.

We turned down a side street, too large to be called an alley, then skirted an empty cart that was half-blocking the road. As we moved further off the main dock row, I wondered if she knew where she was going. Our current surroundings were dirty and cluttered, with myriad smells that were just incongruous enough to be unsettling.

"Are you sure about this carpenter?" I asked again. "This seems an unlikely place for a government contractor."

Anne paused long enough to spear me with an imperious look. "I assure you, I have done my due diligence," she said. "This family is well-respected in the area."

"Of course. I'm sorry. Didn't mean to imply anything. I just…" I looked around the alleyway at the dark and rundown buildings all around us. "Wasn't sure."

Anne pursed her lips as if contemplating whether or not to engage further, then spun without speaking. She stepped up to a tall building with a commanding view of the harbor. It had freshly patched shingles on a roof over the doorway, and bright red shutters.

It was, I noticed, the only building on this side of the road that was well lit, both from the natural light between its neighbors, and by a row of short lanterns than hung from the rafters.

It would have been quite inviting except for the large sign propped up in the window. In heavy lettering. it said,

CLOSED FOR ALL NON-ESSENTIAL BUSINESS

In a smaller script written in a daintier hand, there was a further note.

All business is essential, and we welcome your patronage. Please ask inside for Isaboe.

Anne rapped smartly on the door twice before a thin, sour-looking man appeared.

"We are here to speak with the Meister's youngest daughter, please. We have an appointment."

"Miss Rosemont is not in at the moment. If you care to come back–"

"Oh, Anne! You're here early," said a voice from behind us.

I barely had time to step aside as a small ball of energy pushed her way past us into the room. Her arms were full of baskets and bags of various shapes and sizes. She thrust them into the doorman's arms. "Father needs these right away. And remind him that Liam won't be back for another week, so he really needs to look over those contracts."

"Yes, Miss." With a slight bow and a sideways glance at us, he turned and left.

The young woman ushered us all into the front room of their tidy office. "Come in. Come in," she said as she swiftly moved around the bright room, clearing papers and books off chairs to make room for us. "We don't have tea or anything I can offer, since I just got in myself. Shall I put the kettle on?"

Her upturned nose and proud chin should have given her the appearance of arrogance, but her brown eyes danced in a merry way that only those possessed of a good humor could manage.

Anne shook her head politely as she took the seat nearest her. "I don't believe we will stay that long. We just came to discuss the refitting that I wrote to you about yesterday."

"Of course," the other girl said. She flumped down into a chair behind a large desk. Her light brown curls refused to be contained by the leather strap and kerchief she wore, and they sprang about with her swift movements.

The desk was so massive that she nearly disappeared behind it. She wasn't what I would call tiny–she came nearly to my nose when standing–but she seemed compact rather than slight.

This woman filled her space well, with a confident presence that knew where each and every pen, nib, and piece of paper in the room was without having to look for them. She was capable and businesslike and oh-so-efficient.

"So," she said, turning to us, "These are the people you told me about? I'm Isaboe." She offered a hand, which I gladly shook before taking a seat of my own.

"I'm Tianna. This is Kaelyn."

Kaelyn nodded in acknowledgment. It was hard to tell what she made of this new girl. She looked as if she didn't quite trust her, but she could just as easily have been wondering where she put her other shoes. I decided to wait and ask her about it later.

"This everyone? Anne said there were three of you."

"Oh, Merrik? He comes and goes." I waved my hand nonchalantly.

"He's probably at the blacksmiths," Kaelyn added. "We'll meet up with him later, though. He's always good at finding us when he's done with whatever it is he does."

"Whatever works for you is good enough for me." Isaboe said with a distracted shrug. "So, where is this Lovely Lady that needs my attention? At the marina, I suppose?"

Anne nodded. "The Siren. Yes, that is correct. The ship awaits in the end slip of the third lower secondary dock. We thought you might like to accompany us as we assessed her this morning."

"Quite right," Isaboe replied. "Third dock, you said?" Isaboe took a moment, trying to picture the exact location in her mind's eye. After a moment, her eyes lit up, and she clapped her hands together once excitedly, or perhaps decisively. "Excellent. Let's not waste time then." She jumped to her feet and led the way out of the house.

"I guess we're going again," I muttered to Kaelyn as we all filed back out into the street.

It wasn't far to the marina. The Siren sat just as we had left her, bobbing sadly on the waves, her derelict countenance gazing forlornly at the open waters.

In good time, my lady, that ocean will be yours again, I told her silently.

As we neared the docks, I noticed a flag that hadn't been there before. The large white paw print of a dog sat upon a solid green field. One or two other ships in the area carried the same emblem, and I remember I had seen it both on the guard's uniforms and carved into the door at the Governor's mansion as well. This was Anne's ship, then. Or was meant to appear so.

"Are these our official colors, then?" I asked, trying not to sound bitter.

Anne looked at where I was pointing. "Oh, I see. No. The Governor's ships are marked here in the bay so that the dock wardens can keep count. Once we're underway, I will not be able to afford us such protections." She looked at me carefully, reading something in my placid expression. "I hope that will not cause difficulties," she said, almost as a question.

I shook my head numbly. It wasn't like I knew what to expect outside of the bay any better than she did. Speculation alone wouldn't help us in a foreign dock on the other side of the atoll. All we could do was go and find out for ourselves.

We all climbed aboard and Isaboe began a methodical assessment of my one and only treasure.

Looking at her with fresh eyes. She wasn't in as good a shape as I remembered. In fact, she was in much worse repair than I would have liked, given that we had to pay to have it fixed. I shrank under this stranger's gaze, feeling that we had trouble measuring up.

Sour feelings reflected on my face as Isaboe paced and ducked, poked and prodded everywhere she could reach as she explored the ship. Anne smiled at me reassuringly.

"I am aware that it might not look like much," Anne told me. "But with the proper care and a little updating, I am sure she will be the pride of the Mervast."

"What are we doing with her, then?" I grumbled.

"We're her crew. I suppose that would make us the pride of the Mervast as well," she reasoned.

I opened my mouth to respond. I wanted to tell her that she was crazy. We were none of us sailors. What I knew about boats and the ocean could fill maybe one volume of nautical history and lore. She needed practical experience for an endeavor like this, yet she came to us.

I wanted to tell her that it was everything and more than I could have imagined. That I never thought we would have access to any ship, let alone one of this size and class. Did she need some work done? Sure. But we were all a little rough around the edges. Given enough time, we could grow together and maybe become something truly amazing. Anne's trust in us awed me, and I wanted her to know.

But words failed me.

I shook my head and shrugged. "Let's see what Isaboe has to say," I managed. *Practical as ever, Tianna.* Not exactly poetry there, despite my flow'ry thoughts.

"Lovely." Isaboe said breathlessly, running her hands over the railing. "Just lovely. She'll do just nicely."

I blinked in confusion. I wasn't used to hearing an expert agree with me.

Isaboe must have seen, and quickly added, "Oh, she'll have to be outfitted of course, but she's a grand lady. Been through some years, and probably been re-rigged at least once. I can see that from here. But she is lovely. How did you come to keep her, anyway?"

"Ah. That is, she's not…" I looked to Anne for a rescue, not knowing how to answer that question.

"That is a very long story. Best left to a quiet night and a hot cup of tea," Anne said sweetly.

Isaboe didn't seem to mind the brush off, and turned to walk the length of the ship. "Well, we'll have plenty of time for stories. This may take a few weeks."

She bent to examine something near the base of the mainmast, though I couldn't see what she was looking for. After a moment, she stood and nodded. Resting her hands on her hips, she nodded encouragingly. "Yes, indeed. You treat this grand tub well, and you'll never find a better boat to love."

"What do you need from us, then?" I asked. "Can we have an estimate of the work that needs done, and the cost, by the end of the week?"

"Well, it won't be the easiest job. And many things need to be replaced altogether. She's square rigged now—which you want to keep, yes?—so, we'll need new sheets for all twelve–"

"Twelve?" Kaelyn asked.

"Sails," Isaboe paused and explained simply. "Three each for the main and mizzen masts, plus the crossbacks. Two staysails, and two jib sails. Oh, and the spanker. So, that's thirteen." Her hands flew all around as she pointed. I tried to keep up, but ultimately dropped back into my deeply held belief that this woman knew what she was talking about.

"Right," Kaelyn said. She spun away from Isaboe and gave me a look. "Thirteen *sails*," she whispered in a near panic.

I gave her a reassuring smile. "The Naked Chicken had like twenty-four," I said as Isaboe continued poking into the decaying corners of my last hope.

"A couple yardarms to replace those missing up there," she muttered. "Braces, cleats… rope, of course."

"Of course," I agreed under my breath, as if any of that made sense.

"The main brace is a mess but I'll want to get a better look at the mizzen before I promise anything," Isaboe continued. "You'll need new stays for sure." She kicked out a piece of the stairs leading down into the galley and it broke off with a clatter as it tripped into the hold. "And a few boards besides. Plus, I'll want to take a look at the galley and hold, but…"

She trailed off, and Kaelyn looked worried. I choked on a laugh, turning it into a polite cough. Keeping my own worries at bay. "How much?" I asked.

Isaboe looked confused. "How much for what? Materials I have covered, labor is no problem. Cost shouldn't be an issue."

I looked at Anne. She didn't look worried, so I took my cue from her. I suppose it was her money, after all. If she wanted to pay out the nose for whatever this girl wanted to do to our ship, that was her choice. After a moment's consideration, I decided I would enjoy having a patron.

I returned my gaze to Isaboe and said, "Alright then. What do you need from us?"

Isaboe shrugged. "Like I said, I can handle most of the work, though if you could find one or two more deckhands, I wouldn't turn away the help. As for the rest," she shrugged again. "I'm sure I'll be more than happy with whatever is normal in these situations."

I paused, growing more confused again. "You mean, you don't know what's normal?"

She furrowed her brow. "Of course not, at least not the sailing part. I'm a carpenter and a merchant. Been around boats all my life but not really ever sailed one. So, whatever your normal boatswain's pay is, I'll gladly take it."

"Uh." I couldn't help but feel like I'd been tricked into something. Again. "What was that?"

"Don't expect to cheat me, either." She spun, using her smaller stature to look as tough as a granite statue. "I may not have experience as a boatswain, but I assure you, you will not find a better carpenter anywhere on this island. And good luck getting anywhere without me."

"Uhh…" I tried. "Without you? You're coming with us?"

The petite merchant's daughter looked at me assessing. I was getting sick of people looking at me as if I were lacking. "It's my ship. Where she goes, I go."

Oh, hells no. I glanced at Kaelyn, who should still have all the papers Anne had given us. If we were being double crossed, I wanted as much assurance on my end as I could get. Whatever Anne had promised Isaboe, I'd be damned before I let it ruin me and Kaelyn.

I rocked back on my heels and shifted into a fighting stance in case this case to blows. "Excuse me." I said in a clipped but polite tone. I quickly threw a glance at Anne, then back to Isaboe. "She's *your* ship?"

Isaboe sighed, exasperated. "I mean, I'm the person who can take care of her. I will fit her up, restore her to working order, and keep her that way on the voyage."

"You mean to join us, then?" I asked. *Not steal our ship*, I added silently, reassuring myself.

"Of course," Isaboe replied earnestly. "Why else would I be here?"

Kaelyn looked Isaboe over, circling her with purpose.

I took a breath and mentally stood down, feeling guilty for jumping to the wrong conclusion. I rubbed the bridge of my nose between my eyes. The more time went on, the more I was realizing how much patience it would take to ever get us off this island. I mean, how hard was it supposed to be to re-outfit a ship, forge some ownership papers, get a crew together, and sail for parts unknown? It sounded simple enough.

Kaelyn slowed to a stop with the potential crew member between us. She looked past Isaboe and locked eyes with me. If she was trying to pass me some kind of nonverbal message, I had no idea what it was. "Fine with me," she said eventually.

Isaboe grinned at me expectantly and Anne just smiled.

If the last few days had taught me anything, it was to know when to give up a losing battle. I didn't argue further. I shook my head, folded my arms, and sighed. "Welcome aboard, I guess."

Isaboe jumped and clapped again, before settling back into a professional mask. "Great!" she said. "Just give me two weeks and we'll be ready to take her to Don'Munoil and back if you've a mind to."

Without another word, she disappeared down the plank and onto the dock to set about the insane task of trying to get the Siren seaworthy.

I tried to tell myself that it was fine. Things weren't moving far too fast for my comfort. I mean, wasn't I only just complaining about not having a plan?

Our newest companion seemed to know her way around a boat. And we did need a boatswain, even if I wasn't sure what skills one would need to do the job. Isaboe seemed confident. Maybe I should just be glad it was that easy.

I grabbed Kaelyn's arm as she started past me. "How much is a regular boatswain's pay?"

She shrugged. "It doesn't matter, right? Anne's paying for it."

I smirked and followed her down the gangplank. This was either going to be the greatest adventure of my life, or a very painful life lesson. I just hoped it wouldn't be both.

A few days later found us aboard the Siren, me with a heavy sanding block and Merrik with a brush and a bucket of fresh paint. The sun was beating down on us, making me think fondly of the large shade trees outside Albert's bookstore. I halfheartedly pulled the block along the top railing of the afterdeck and sighed wistfully.

"You're never going to make progress like that," Merrik said, waving his brush at my lackadaisical sanding job.

I sighed again, more dramatically this time.

He swiped his paintbrush right up to where my elbow was resting. "Come along, miss. You're slowing me down."

I screwed up my face in faux annoyance. "Trade with me then. My arms aren't cut out for this anyway." I flexed my arms wide, flapping them back and forth, and then rotated my shoulders a few times to stretch them out.

Merrik laughed and handed over his paintbrush and bucket. "Works for me. You get to take credit for my lousy job. I'll make sure Isaboe knows you asked for this."

I stuck my tongue out at him and laughed. "Where is Isaboe, anyway?" I asked as I began going back over the part of the railing he had already painted.

He nodded toward the port side longboat. "She's got the crew replacing winch lines," he said. "Glad it's not us."

I nodded and watched them for a bit. Isaboe certainly seemed to know her business. She was shaking her head and waggling her finger in the face of a tall, broad-shouldered sailor. Every inch of her slight frame squared off against a man twice her size. And he looked cowed.

Not that I blamed him. I'd already been on the receiving end of her temper twice in as many days. I was glad of her skills, but it was one thing to know I knew nothing, and another to be shown exactly how incompetent I was when it came to ship maintenance.

That's why we hired her, I reminded myself for not the first time.

The general crew seemed to know their business, too. They were all experienced sailors. Anne had found us a dozen capable men and women that made me feel even more out of my depth. I wasn't sure where she had found them, but they showed up not long after we'd inked our contract with our new boatswain, and Isaboe put them to work immediately.

In just two days, we had already stripped the Siren down to her bones and were quickly patching things back up. Whatever else I thought of Isaboe personally, I couldn't find fault with her efficiency. The pace at which we worked made me wonder if—even if I couldn't keep up yet—I could maybe learn how to do this whole sailing thing.

I tried to turn my full attention to my task. While painting may not have been the most mentally stimulating job, I must have done good work of focusing on it. Before I knew it, the sun was sinking into the water and shone directly into my eyes.

I quickly scanned back to review my work. The railing around the afterdeck and halfway down the starboard side, nearly back around to the beam, was smoothly sanded and curing with an even coat of paint. I smiled proudly. *Not too bad,* I thought.

"What the hells is this?" Isaboe shouted a few feet away.

I looked up. She was standing near the starboard swivel gun, examining the detailed craftsmanship holding it in place. "Something wrong?"

She spun, glaring at me. "This paint job is totally uneven!"

I took a deep breath to keep the wind from being knocked out of me. "Does it matter?" I asked patiently.

"Of course it matters! The care put into the ship shows how we present ourselves, and how we present ourselves shows the world what to expect of us. We must be shipshape!"

This was not the first time we'd had this fight, so I already knew my next line. "Our first priority should be getting safely asea. How we present ourselves isn't as important as being able to get anywhere," I growled.

Kaelyn must have sensed we were winding up for yet another round of the form over function argument, and appeared at my shoulder. I nearly jumped when she piped in. "This is lovely and all, ladies, but it's getting on toward suppertime, and the crew is getting hungry and restless."

"Oh," I said.

"Of course." Isaboe said at the same time. She glanced at the crew, looking like she just remembered they were there.

"Tell them to go home for the day," I said.

The small boatswain glared at me, then swiftly wiped the look off her face. "Make sure they know to be back first thing in the morning."

Kaelyn looked at me. I nodded, adding a slight shrug. She nodded in return, then hurried off.

Isaboe turned to look at me. She had something else she wanted to say. I could see it lurking at the edges of her doe-brown eyes, but instead she spun and stalked off.

I shrugged and looked at Merrik. "Time for dinner?"

He instantly tossed the rag in his hands to the deck and made his way onto the dock, chatting happily with one of the departing crewmen.

A few minutes later, Kaelyn was back at my side and the three of us started up the street back toward what was quickly becoming our favorite tavern. "I don't know why she's making this so hard," I commented.

The light was starting to fade, and the sky was looking ominous. It suited my mood. As soon as the rain started, I would have a reason to feel so gloomy.

"Because it's her job," Kaelyn said matter-of-factly. "She knows that work needs to be done to get the Siren sailing again. You saw it right, Tianna? It's looking really good."

"Yeah, except for the parts I did," I muttered.

Merrik laughed. "We all have to be bad at something."

"I'm apparently bad at everything," I grumbled in reply. His teasing did nothing to make me feel any better. I scowled up at the sky as the first of the fat, heavy raindrops began to fall. "Ugh, whatever. Let's just get to dinner. Maybe this stupid rain will wash away the paint."

I turned my heels up the street and followed it down a covered alley. Blaming the weather was safer than being irritated at Isaboe, but I actually didn't want to be caught in the rain.

After dinner, we all went our separate ways to tend to other things. Merrik was still finishing up a job, and the more I thought of it, the less I knew what he did. He had a master? Or a former master? Who occasionally tossed side jobs his way. Building things? Fixing things? Was he a tinkerer or crafter?

Whatever it was he did, it kept him at the forge for long hours, returning sometimes only just before midnight, smudged with soot and sweat, and beaming like a man who knew his place in the world.

Kaelyn often returned a little less sure of herself, but just as contented from her day's work. She spent most of her time onboard the Siren right alongside Isaboe, setting things to rights. She still worked at the grocery when she could, to keep us fed, but I could see the subtle shifts in her. Every day she got up and went to work with a little more of her focus on the ship, and less on everything else.

I had no such drive. Isaboe's comments jabbed at me. I really didn't know what I was doing here. The ship may be in my name but so far I'd done little more than find those who were doing the real work. I needed to contribute something—be useful in some way—before I gave up and fled back to Wellsmith, where at least life was what I expected.

What was that old adage? You can't win if you don't gamble. I figured the opposite must be true as well. You can't fail if you don't try. That thought stayed with me for exactly one day and one night until I woke from dreams of open oceans and wind on my face.

I had only ever been good at reading and talking, but somewhere in that I could find a way to help. I had to. I was determined not to be a weight dragging this crew down. The ship already had an anchor. It didn't need the useless me getting in the way.

And so I began spending as much time as I could holed up in the governor's library researching the isles, or locked away in the warehouse pouring over charts, or picking up sailing tips and tricks from sailors around the docks.

By Isaboe's latest estimate, we had roughly nine more days of work before The Siren was ready to put to sea, at which time I planned to know at least the mechanics of sailing, navigating, and maintaining a ship. Experience would come with time. I just needed to know a little more, do a little more, be a little better prepared.

It was late one evening, and I was curled up in the corner of Anne's small study, copying notes from Athelard's *The Lost Art of Seamanship*. I vaguely heard the door creek open, but didn't look up from what I was doing.

"Tianna?" Merrik asked after me. When I didn't register his presence, he drew nearer and lightly tapped the desk in front of me. "You still with us?"

I jumped at the movement. I looked up and blinked, then blinked again. My eyes watered as they tried to focus on something more than a foot in front of my face.

Merrik sighed and reached past me. He picked up my candle, walked over to the hearth, and rekindled the fire that had gone cold. I watched him, still trying to pull my thoughts back to the present moment.

"You've been in here a long time. It's near sunset."

"Oh," I said, sheepishly. "I guess I was engrossed in what I was doing."

He turned to look at me, a worried expression creasing his brow. "What are you doing?"

I looked at the piles of books surrounding me, my pages of scribbled notes, and my ink-stained hands. "I'm... learning?"

"Mhmm."

I expected a look that would chastise me for ignoring my duties, or tease me for fussing over things that are better learned first-hand, or even confusion over how I could lose track of everything so easily. Instead, I saw only concern.

"Right," he said decisively. He stood up and wiped the ash from his hands. "Come along, miss. This is no good."

"What?" I stared at him for a minute, trying to make sense of his words.

He gestured, taking in the dark, cold study. "This. You've been at this for days. You need some fresh air." I stay where I sat, still looking at my books. "I will carry you out if I need to," he added.

I laughed at the image that conjured. I had no doubt that Merrik was one of the few who would be willing to sling me over his shoulder and drag me away. Luckily, I wasn't sure he *could*. He was strong, but I'm not sure he was that strong. Still, this was Merrik, and he wouldn't threaten without reason. So, I sighed, closed my book, and stood. "Lead on, then."

Every one of my muscles all screamed their objections to my suddenly changing position. I groaned out loud and wondered how long I had actually been sitting there. I shook it off, stretched, and followed Merrik outside.

We didn't speak. I had nothing to say and feared that if I did start talking, I would only spiral in self-pity again. So awash in chaotic thoughts, I followed him through the growing dusk.

Our path led us up the hill away from town, toward the ridgeline above the bay. Tall palm trees swayed in the swift breeze. Sea birds called to each other in the dusk. We crested a rise and followed the path toward the lighthouse.

"So, why are you pushing yourself so hard?" Merrik eventually asked as we walked side-by-side.

I started to shrug, then stopped myself and gave his question serious thought. "I don't know. It's a compulsion. I *need* to. I just feel so godsdamned useless. Isaboe is so good at what she does. And Kaelyn is good with the crew. You have the kind of natural gift for logistics that exporters and generals would kill for. Even Anne seems comfortable navigating the bureaucracy and paperwork side of things. It's like everyone has a place here, and I'm not even an able crewman."

"You own the ship, right?" he said casually.

I shook my head, frustrated. "Technically. But plenty of people own and finance voyages without having to go on one. You didn't see me on the way here, Merrik. I'm not good at anything. The me that I am now can't offer anything of value to this crew."

We fell silent again as I wallowed in the truth of that statement. I wanted to change the world, but I couldn't even tie a bend without looking at a drawing. I wasn't the smartest, or the fastest, or the strongest. I was no fighter. Every fight I was in, I found a way to avoid conflict or escape as soon as possible. There were, and always would be, better people suited for the task at hand. I would only burden the crew with my ineptitude. And worse, no one seemed to notice it but me.

We drew near the bluff, and I stopped, heart in my throat. The tide roared as it crashed against the cliff below us. The wind whipped up and past us, taking my breath with it. There before us, wide open, honest, and clear, was the crystalline waters of the Mervast. There were no words, or thoughts, or actions that could adequately capture that moment. I was, quite simply, stunned. The ocean spread out before me, unending in either direction, and promising more beyond.

I felt its call. I needed to be out there–a part of whatever lay beyond that fading line. It damn near brought tears to my eyes.

"That," Merrik whispered somewhere behind me.

I couldn't tear my gaze away from the ocean, but I heard him step up behind me. He placed his hands on my shoulders, steadying me.

"That is what you have to offer. While Isaboe focuses on the task at hand, and Kaelyn sees what the day will bring her, you are looking forward. A good ship and good crew are one thing, but they are useless without something to drive them. From what I've seen, you're the only one who's ever had a plan."

A plan? Me? I turned to look at him, ready to share a laugh at the ludicrous nature of his comment, but he wasn't smiling.

"But, Anne…" I started.

He shook his head. "Anne has an idea, maybe a goal, but that's not a plan."

I looked at him blankly again.

He sighed, dropping his hands and stepping back. "If we were doing a trade run around the Outer Isles, where would we start?"

"We are doing a–"

"It's a hypothetical. Play along, would you? I have a point, I promise. Where would you start?"

I thought about it for a moment. A map was forming in my mind as I charted a fictitious course.

"We'd go Northwest, right? Toward Angle Bay first, stopping at the larger ports along the way. Birdbeak maybe. There's bound to be good timber on some of the western islands, but they'll be starved for luxuries and the more exotic spices."

My mind began to spin up again, thinking of all the possible considerations for a journey of this magnitude.

"We'd probably travel reverse sunwise to take advantage of the atoll's currents around the reef. Skirt the islands for good anchor points in the late evenings. We don't have a big crew, so stopping each night and keeping a minimum watch would keep everyone well-rested. I guess we'd need enough rations for... two months?"

He nodded. "Two and a half by my guess, but yeah. Siren's got room to store twice that for a crew of ten, and a dozen passengers besides."

"Wow, that's really good to know. How much does that leave for general cargo and trade goods?"

He grinned, beaming proudly. "That," he said.

I scrunched my brow and cocked my head. "What?"

Merrik just kept smiling. "That's why we need you. You ask the right questions, you think of the possibilities well before they become a problem, and you already have a rough idea of a route planned. You've thought out the whole trip, and we haven't even left port."

"That's just common sense stuff. Everyone considers those kinds of things."

"Not everyone. I promise. I'm counting sacks of grain and you're thinking about how and when to dole them out to the crew, or trade them for something better. Or whether or not grain is even wise aboard a ship."

"It wouldn't be," I said. "Oats, or better yet, dried corn or seed meal. Wouldn't be as prone to the damp."

He grinned again, then turned away from me to look out to sea. "Exactly."

Was it really that odd to be thinking of these things? We were starting a journey and we were going to need to have most of the details worked out before we leave.

It was just common sense. What did he mean I was the only one looking at it? I couldn't be. Gods, I hoped I wasn't the only one thinking about it. We were in serious trouble if I was.

I closed my eyes for a second, letting the sound of the waves below me calm my nerves. I took a few deep breaths of fresh salt-air.

"Why do you want to do this?" Merrik asked.

"Do what? Sail?"

"Sail, trade, leave the island. What are you even trying to do?" he said.

I thought about it for a moment. "I have lived my whole life in one tiny part of one small town run by people who didn't care about those around them. I guess, I need to see if that's true everywhere."

"You want to see if there's some good out there in this world before you decide to change it all?"

I matched his smirk. "Something like that."

I grew sober again, pausing to fully consider his question. "Maybe I just want to see what else is out there, and I know the Siren is the surest way to make sure I can go where I want, when I want, on my terms."

I looked out at where the darkening sky met the deeper blue waters. I was trusting that there were answers beneath the waves. If I just looked long enough, searched hard enough...

"I keep asking myself questions about the word. What are the other islands like? Are there other people out there like me, looking for something more? Are there people out there different from me? How can I learn more about them? How can I help them?"

He made an approving noise in his throat. "Those sound like the right questions to me."

I scoffed at myself. "It seems pretty egotistical when I say it out loud, actually. Who am I to help anybody? I didn't change a damn thing in my hometown. If it wasn't for Kaelyn, I'd still be running from Krellen's men. Or dead already. I can't even help myself, never mind people I've never met."

"Eh, don't worry about it so much, Chief. Everyone needs help. Not always at first, sometimes at a mid-point. A pick me up to keep you on track, or just a reminder that it's not for nothing." He looked at me again. "You're good at that."

"Am I? I just see what needs to be done and try to do it, if I can." I looked down past the cliff's edge, shaking my head. "Sometimes, the risks seem too much and I can't do anything but hope."

He patted my shoulder and turned back toward town. His gray-green eyes met my blue ones, and he smiled wryly. "That."

I wanted to hit him. "You keep saying 'that', like I should know what you mean! Oh, Wise Sage, would you kindly tell me what the hells you're getting at?"

He laughed. "You look at the big picture?"

I nodded.

"But also at all the tiny details that go into making the big picture?"

I nodded again, a little slower this time, trying to see what he was getting at.

"You identify people's strengths and see where they can do the most good?"

I pursed my lips and nodded again.

"You assess the risks and rewards of a given situation and decide what actions are needed?"

"Yes. What's your point?"

"I'm not sure I can explain it any better than that," he said. He sighed deeply, almost sadly, then turned and started walking away. "Come along, Captain. Maybe Kaelyn can help sort you out."

I resisted the urge to stomp my foot. "Damn it, Merrik! What do you—wait. What?" I sputtered, unable to see the humor in his joke. I chased after him. "What do you mean, 'Captain'?"

CHAPTER NINE

These damn charts would be the death of me, I was sure of it. I had been studying hard to understand the math involved, and I the basics down now, but it was more difficult to put into practice than I'd thought it would be. I needed to master this, and quickly. It was only a matter of time before I let everyone down.

I mean, really, how did one best plan a course through unknown waters when they barely knew how to sail? There was only so much faking it I could get away with before someone noticed.

The others seemed to believe in me for some reason. Although I couldn't see what that reason was, I could at least trust that they believed it. It may not have been much, but it was somewhere to start, and it gave me a boost to dig in to my research more.

Merrik's pep talk hadn't made the problem go away all on its own, but it had revitalized some part of my spirit I'd given up on. As much as I hated to admit it—especially where he could hear me—his words had helped. Even if I still didn't understand his joke about calling me Captain.

But he always did that. Called me boss, chief, *primaé*… this was just more of that. I liked our inside jokes, but I'd have to get him to stop. It was fine for now, but it would be weird when we actually had a captain.

With these complex thoughts racing through my mind, I headed down to the Siren to find Anne. Since she was the only person on the crew who had even seen a real chart before, I hoped that between the two of us, we could figure out how to set a course before we left the harbor.

My arms were loaded down with scroll cases and watertight courier's pouches, and I juggled to keep them contained while I hurried along the rough stone road.

The day was hot, and the sun was merciless. I conceded to better judgment and wore a hat today, even though I generally preferred a scarf or hair wrap. I was glad of it too. It shaded my eyes enough to keep me from squinting. Which is why, when I came to the intersection where the main road meets the dock row, I was able to clearly see what lay before me.

I stopped, and stared.

Nearly one month to the day after I set foot in Anvilcove, I found myself standing on the dock, agape. What faced me was not the same broken down pile of planks that Merrik had dropped in our laps. This brig was… well, she was *beautiful*.

The deck was polished and shining in the early afternoon sunlight. The rails had all been painted—repainted by the looks of it—the soft red-brown color of old rust. Two masts of equal height jutted skyward, straight and clean, adorned with fresh, white canvas sails which were reefed and secured.

The twin masts stood on the deck, reaching up into the clear sky. The mainmast boasted four yardarms, while the mizzen had three. Each was consecutively smaller than the one below it. Atop each mast was a small platform where the stays all came together with pulleys and winches, and above that, flapping merrily in the breeze, was the flag of House Jenness.

Staysails were braced between the masts on booms to help direct wind into the sails while we were underway. The spanker—a smaller, square sail that looked like a fin off the back of the ship—was similarly attached from the mizzen to a swinging boom that jutted out behind the ship to direct the air, much as the rudder would in the water.

Finally, at the very front, attached to a boom line, were the jib sails, which would direct the forward wind up into the sails once we were underway.

I counted, starting from the bottom. Mainsail, topsail, topgallant,... thirteen sails. As promised. I didn't hide the smile as I thought about what Kaelyn's reaction must have been.

The mizzen topsail was lug-rigged, which I had learned from my work on the Naked Chicken, but the mainsail and main topsail were what Isaboe called "island rigged". I had mostly been listening when she had described her plan to me, but seeing it laid out, I could see how it all came together.

It wasn't anything like what I had been reading, but this wasn't the kind of ship most scholars wrote about, either. And it certainly was nothing like the Chicken. I couldn't have found any fault in it, even if I had spent the entire day searching for error. Someone far more proficient than I had rigged these sails, and thank goodness, too.

The figurehead was the only part of this ship untouched by the renovations. That is to say, un*changed*. She, too, had been cleaned up a bit, and now her previously scarred and weathered face now shone like a freshly powdered Lugaian debutante. She was ready to take on the world, and so was I.

One of the scroll cases slipped from my hand, threatening to topple the pile in my arms. I snapped myself out of my adoration and readjusted my load before hurrying aboard.

A half-dozen or so men were hauling crates onto the deck, and I tried to stay out of their way. They nodded politely as I passed, and one stepped aside and offered me a hand up the gangway. I smiled gratefully and stepped onto the deck, surveying the area once again.

The Siren was arrayed for any kind of outing. I skirted a few coils of rope, some barrels, boxes, and neatly stacked cannonballs. I did a quick double-take, making sure I saw that correctly. There were guns on my ship.

Whoever had stripped the ship before she came to us hadn't left us with a single cannon, rifle, or musket to be found. Now, we had four large, heavy cannons anchored to thick wooden wheels, and held in place on the main deck by sturdy chains. Two smaller swivel guns were carefully mounted on the foredeck railing. A rack of muskets, and another matching one of boarding blades were bolted to the outer wall of the aftcastle. It all seemed so imminent and deadly.

As I passed the newly refinished wheel, I reached out and brushed a hand over the spokes, luxuriating in the feel of it. I let my wonderment flow into the sun-warmed wood. This is where it began. We were bonding, the Siren and I. We would be very good to each other.

The jolt of reality hit me out of nowhere, and I laughed. This was simply amazing. In the hands of Isaboe Rosemont, merchant's daughter, The Siren had transformed from a dull, sea-worn raft with bad rigging into a brightly painted, freshly sanded, and sparkling six-gun brigantine that any Consortium merchant would go to war to have.

I looked around. Kaelyn was at mid-deck, directing the dockworkers as they loaded and stored our cargo. As I approached, I could hear Isaboe below, badgering the poor shipwright's apprentice who was trying to finish his work on the galley doors.

Poor lad, I thought. Better him than me.

"Ay, Tianna!" Kaelyn called, catching sight of me.

I waved back, then struggled to keep from dropping my armful of charts and papers. "How goes?"

She practically bounced over to me excitedly. "It couldn't be better. This crew's a dream. Good mix of experienced sailors and excited fresh blood."

"Well, that's great," I drawled. "They do know *we're* not experienced sailors, right? I would hate to disillusion them."

Kaelyn laughed. "I think they know. Several of them probably figured it out from watching us work the last few days, but we're paying them well, so I don't think they care. There's about fourteen hands, not counting our command staff, and they seem content to keep each other in check. Even saw the older ones showing the newbies a few things."

"That's sounds great. Especially so long as they don't mind teaching us, too." I offered the joke weakly, hoping Kaelyn wouldn't notice how unsure I still was about my position here.

She smiled warmly, as if she knew exactly how I was feeling. "We're nearly loaded with base provisions," she went on. "Merrik could tell you more about that, though. And we just got started on stowing the trade goods this morning."

That surprised me. "Anne already secured trade goods?"

"Yesterday. She was looking for you, too. Something about receipts."

"Where is she?" I asked.

Kaelyn pointed up.

My gaze trailed upward, following her direction. Up the mainmast, along the topgallant yard, I caught sight of what I guess was a human figure. It was a dark spot against a brilliant blue sky, and it moved with swift determination.

"Oyah, Anne!" Kaelyn called. "I found her!"

The figure paused, double checked the stays on the sheet, then scurried down the line, landing safely on the deck.

It was all quite expertly done, and I stood, gaping at Anne, who stood in front of me. "Where did you learn to do all that?" I squeaked out.

She grinned. "I've been sailing since I was five," she said nonchalantly. "This rigging differs completely from my father's yacht, though. It really is quite fascinating."

Her cheeks glowed from the sharp breeze and what I could only think was her joy at being aloft. Then her words sunk in. She could sail. She knew how to sail. My eyes grew wide, and I grinned. "Oh, you don't know how happy I am to hear that." I was almost crying with relief but laughed instead.

Anne looked momentarily confused, then shook it off. "I'm glad you're here. I wanted to go over a few notes in the ledger. Do you have time now?"

"Of course. Let me drop these things somewhere first." I lifted my arms, gesturing with the cases I still clung to.

She waved me off. "Let's put those in the cabin. That's where the logs are, anyway."

"Oh," I said. "That actually makes sense. Lead the way."

Kaelyn, noticing that she was no longer needed, turned back to her work directing cargo, and I followed Anne toward the aftcastle.

"I have been negotiating with the spice merchants for–"

A loud clattering from the far end of the deck made us both jump. It was followed by angry shouts, and I turned just in time to see Kaelyn running toward the commotion.

"What in the–" I stepped sideways around Anne, trying to get a better look at what was going on.

Two of the sailors—brothers, if my memory is correct— stood shoulder to shoulder in a bulwark of obstinacy.

One was red-faced and shouting at the top of his lungs, while the other was simply red-faced. They squared off against our smaller, curly-haired boatswain who was having none of it.

"Oh, shit." I dropped my papers and pouches to the deck before sprinting in that direction.

I arrived a hair too late. Just as I rounded the mast, about five solid paces from the group, the man who was shouting drew back a fist and swung at Isaboe. Before it could connect, one of the other sailors grabbed the man's forearm in mid-swing.

"Let's take a breath," the man said. I had seen him around before, though I couldn't recall his name. He was a tall, broad-shouldered man, with long, shaggy hair and an amiable smile buried in his thick beard. He towered over the angry sailor with a sort of calm menace, and I saw confusion flicker over the smaller man's face the longer their stare-off continued.

"Stay out of this, anglewinder. This is a sailor's business!" he shouted at the man still holding his arm.

"Giuseppe..." his brother said hesitantly.

The man called Giuseppe ripped his arm violently from the bigger man's grasp and glared at his brother.

"See? Even Alejandro knows you're overreacting," Isaboe growled at him.

They both turned to look at her. Giuseppe glared and sputtered again, and his brother Alejandro's eyes went wide.

Isaboe pressed her advantage. "If you'd just follow my orders, then–"

"Your orders make no sense! You untried, untrained merchant's daughter!" Giuseppe shouted, his rough southern Lugaian accent growing stronger with each angry word. He took a threatening step forward. "I should just–!"

"*ENOUGH!*" I shouted. I wasn't sure where the volume or tone came from, but I dug deep, bringing every ounce of unreproachable authority I could muster into the word. Everyone fell silent as I stepped forward. "What the hells is going on here?" I demanded as I stepped in. I wanted to put some distance between them before any blows actually connected with their target.

Voices all around me we shouting at once, each trying to be heard above the others. I couldn't understand any of them and I held up my hands for silence. When I didn't get it, I shouted again. "Hey! Quiet!"

"I don't need sailors who think they're above the master's order!" Isaboe yelled, ignoring me.

"We need no Red Swine for a Master!" Alejandro yelled back. His accent was even thicker than his brother's.

"Only 'ere, we have a self-important boatswain whose title is bigger than her brain!" Giuseppe added.

"You motherfu–" Isaboe tried to push past me, but I held my arms out. "I'm doing the job I was hired for, you Lugaian fishegg! Which, last I checked, is corralling idiot sailors with shit for sense!"

"A Tirican who can't tell her ass from a stovepipe has no place on a ship!" Giuseppe shouted, and then spat. Before I could step in again, Alejandro lunged forward, dipping past me and grabbing for Isaboe.

Within a heartbeat, chaos had broken out. Giuseppe grabbed the man who had stopped him before and pulled him down to the deck, using his stockier frame to wrestle rather than punch.

I grabbed for Alejandro, trying to pry him off Isaboe as two other sailors jumped into the fray. One swung a fist at me. I tried to dodge but was locked in place by my struggle with Alejandro.

His fist connected with my jaw, knocking my head backward. My vision went black for a second, before I came back, angry. I threw myself off him and into the bulk of another sailor who was trying to pry us apart. My weight upset his balance, and he stumbled backward into his friend, who pushed us both back upright.

The one who had hit me reared back again for another blow. Before it landed, Kaelyn brought up a short plank of wood, blocking his punch. She pushed him backward, and I stepped up, leaning my weight into the board as well. We pushed both sailors back against the railing. Kaelyn lashed out with an elbow, striking one, while I stomped and kicked the other. Both crumpled in pain before surging back against the board.

A pair of hands grabbed my shirt collar, pulling it tight. He reached a free hand out and plucked my hat off my head. I choked for a second and then wiggled, trying to get loose of his grip, as he placed it on his head.

I was struggling to find purchase when a small, lithe figure jumped from somewhere above. It landed on all four of us, pushing the group to the deck. As I tried to make sense of what had happened, I saw booted feet kick out and up, and the sailor I'd been fighting went flying backward.

My vision now clearer, I caught a glimpse of red hair and a cheeky grin on a young man's face. The smile was new, but I instantly recognized the young guard from a few weeks earlier. His blue eyes caught mine, and he winked before charging off after the other sailor again.

I would have laughed, but another pair of arms wrapped around my waist, pulling me to my feet and holding me still. I tried to spin around, bringing my elbow up to gut check whoever was holding me.

"Hold, damn you!" someone bellowed from somewhere behind me. I heard several pairs of boots come running across the deck. "By order of the city watch, we order you to stand down!"

Guards stormed the deck, taking each of us in hand. Slower than it probably should have, the commotion died down. Giuseppe, Alejandro, and their two companions glared daggers of death at Isaboe and Kaelyn, who were both spitting fiery curses of their own.

I tried to shake off the adrenaline of the battle and calmly address the guards. My voice croaked when I tried to speak.

"What is the meaning of all this?" The same voice from before called again. The deep and irritated tone from mid-deck was confident and commanding and I took that as a good sign, hoping sanity would win the day.

"*Vasta*," I muttered the Epirsan epithet under my breath without thinking. It was mostly a show of relief, but it didn't sound that way, and I instantly bit it back.

"What was that?" he demanded, spinning to face me.

"Nothing," I said. "Sorry."

"Hmm." He frowned. "You should be sorry. This is quite a mess." He turned and began pacing the deck, staring down at each of us in turn. "I wouldn't normally involve myself in shipboard disputes like these, but your ruckus is spilling onto my dock."

I whipped my head around, looking where he indicated, and saw several longshoremen, fisherman, sailors, and general passersby also being detained by green-and-silver uniformed guards.

"Oh, shit," I said again, in Tirican this time, because I wanted to share my feelings with everyone.

He turned to glare at me again. "Indeed."

My mind raced, looking for a solution. I knew there was a way out of this, even with a guardsman pinning my arms behind me. I just hadn't found it yet.

I saw movement out of the corner of my eye and turned to look. Anne, standing tall, imperious, and freshly attired in a clean velvet gown, stepped into the middle of the deck. I did a double-take and looked again. When had she changed clothes? For that matter, where was she while we were trading blows with her chosen crew?

"Patrolman, a word, if you please," she said placidly.

"Lady Annelia," the guard looked startled, then bowed deeply. "Forgive me, I didn't know this was one of your family's ships."

She affected a bored and slightly haughty look before tilting her chin upward to where the banner of her house was still flying off the top of the mainmast.

Looking down at the guard again, she audibly sighed. "It is quite all right. You were just doing your duty in protecting the harbor. In fact, I commend you on your diligence."

"Thank you, my lady," he said, blushing slightly.

"I believe treatment of the crew will be left to me, but if you wouldn't mind, perhaps we can adjourn to the ship's office to deal with the rest of this affair." Her eyes never wavered in their certainty as she spoke.

"Oh, of course," the guard said. He was still at attention and seemed unable to move while she watched him.

Anne held a soft leather glove in one hand, like she had been putting them on when she had been interrupted. She used it to wave toward the main road to town.

"We can always take this matter before Harbor Master Dennet, if you prefer?" she offered kindly.

"N-n-no, ma'am," the guard stammered.

Anne offered a tight smile. "Come along, then. Let us resolve this matter apace, shall we?"

"Y-yes, my lady." The patrolman scurried after her. A few moments later, I noticed all the guards looking at each other, unsure what to do until their commander returned.

"I think it would probably be alright if you let us go. We won't leave the ship or anything, just," I tried to pull my arms free and felt his grip loosen, "Maybe don't hold on so tight in the meantime."

The guard holding me hesitated, then let go. The others followed suit, and soon we were all standing around.

An uneasy wariness fell over the deck. The tension was just as close as it was before, only now there were more of us. The sailors still glared at us. We watched the guards closely, and the guards seemed unsure of what to do.

I turned toward Giuseppe. "I don't know what this was all about, but–"

"That pompous little bitc–"

"But," I said again pointedly. "I think it's best if you find another ship to crew."

"Damn right we will," he spat. "And you'll be damned lucky if anyone will sail with you. I'll make sure they know what kind of feckless officers you keep."

"I keep? What does that mean?" I asked, startled.

My earnest question deflated his anger for a moment. He looked confused. "You are Captain. These *sciosi* are your problem, no?"

My breath caught. That was the second time this week someone had made that joke. It wasn't very funny the first time. "I–"

Giuseppe shook his head. "No matters. You will still be blacklisted. No right sailor will set foot aboard this *epitto* while you sail her." He sneered again.

"Excuse me!?" Had he not seen the work we put into her? It was one thing to insult me or the crew, but this ship was a masterpiece, and he was lucky to have worked on her even as long as he had.

Before I could respond further, the patrolman came back looking pleased. "Let them go. Let's clean up the mess on the docks and get back to work. This day is already too long."

The other patrolmen looked smugly self-satisfied as they cheerily followed him back down to the dock.

"Come on, Alejandro, Loge," Giuseppe barked to his friends. "We have better things to do than hang out with Tirican pigs."

"Hold up," I ordered them. They hesitated long enough for me to march over. I stared down the one he'd called Loge and snatched my hat back. I placed it pointedly back on my head and sneered without breaking eye contact.

They scoffed and stalked off.

"Good riddance," Isaboe uttered under her breath.

I spun to face her before I even knew I had moved. "What the hells was that?" I demanded.

She sputtered for a moment before snapping her jaw shut. I could see her fight against all the righteous fury she wanted to turn on me. I spoke before she could.

I kept my voice low and steady, as hard as a crossbeam on a stone bridge. "There is no room for small-minded bigotry on this ship. Lugaian, Tirican, Epirsan, Isler—*all* are welcome and safe, so long as I have any say in it. Is that clear?"

The fight faded from her, turning into embarrassment. "Sorry, Tianna. I didn't mean anything by it. Just got carried away," she said. "Besides, they–"

"I know they started it," I said, "But if we want the world to ever be better, then we need to change it. And that means we do better."

She nodded silently. The pause stretched between us, until finally she said, "I really am sorry. I don't mean that shit. I know better. It's just hard to remember when it's being thrown at you."

"Truth and a half, my friend." I reached out a hand and rested it on her shoulder, giving her a gentle squeeze. "Thank you for trying."

She nodded once more in acknowledgment, then looked away. After just long enough to be sure the conversation was over, she turned and walked off to the rail to watch our former crew depart.

I followed her gaze and watched the sailors laughing with each other as they made their way up the road. I gave a sigh of relief, followed instantly by a flash of panic.

"What the hells are we going to do about a crew?" I asked quietly as Kaelyn stepped up next to me.

"Giuseppe's right," she said with a nervous shrug. "No right sailor in Tirica Denisi will fly our colors. His union will see to it, just as soon as he starts trashing us to 'em."

"Then we'll have to figure something else out," I said.

Lost in my thoughts, I didn't notice the shadow fall across the deck behind me. "What about unright sailors?" A warm, deep voice asked from over my shoulder.

I turned to look at the big man who had stepped in before. "What?"

"No right sailor that is will sail with ye once he's through. So what about freemen? There're plenty of crewmen to be found in the Outer Isles."

"Pirates, you mean," Kaelyn said.

He glanced around the deck, as if pointing out how empty it was. I regarded him carefully, but nodded when the red-headed man who had helped me in the fight came over to stand next to him.

"What about you two?" I asked. "Will you be leaving with the others?"

They both shook their heads. "No need. We like it here."

I regarded him thoughtfully. "I know you, don't I?"

The smaller, lithe frame stepped up next to him and grinned, showing fine, white teeth.

"Both of you," I added. "Aren't you two guards?"

The taller man shook his head. "No miss. Eh, that is, not specifically." The big man grinned and offered his hand. "I'm Eric Scobbie. This is Iain Swift. We've done a bit of everything. Guards, dockworkers, warehouse rats…"

"Lob'd th' boxy bits and stood th' fancy door a time or two…" Iain added.

Eric nodded. "Yep. We've acted as couriers, too. Builders, smelters, let's see, what else…"

I laughed. "I get it. You've a wide variety of experience."

He shared my smile. "That we do."

I nodded, turning to the girl at my side. "Kaelyn, how many people do you think we'd need to actually crew this ship effectively?"

She looked puzzled for a moment, then said, "I think Merrik said a full company of ten to twelve, so we can probably make do with half that."

"Good. That's settled then. By my count, we're already there. No need to take on new crew at all."

"What?" Isaboe said. There was still a tinge of anger in her voice, but I could tell she was trying to let it go. "Just because we can crew the Siren with six doesn't mean we should! If we can take on more crew, we should start–"

"Seven," I corrected her.

"What?"

"There are seven of us, if we're including these two fine gentlemen." I nodded, indicating Eric and Iain.

"We're no sailors," Eric said almost apologetically. "We're longshoremen by trade, dockworkers, or warehousemen, or day guards—whatever we need do, really."

"Day laborers."

They both nodded.

"Well, now you're sailors," I took his hand in a warm grip and shook it, as if sealing the deal.

Isaboe smacked her hand down on the railing. "Damnit, Tianna. We still can't sail with half a crew!"

"We can and we will," I replied, "But leaving that aside for now, there's still work to do. We need to get the rest of these crates stowed, Anne and I need to go over those receipts. And where the hells is Merrik, anyway?"

Right on cue, the sound of heavy footsteps bounding up the gangplank made us all turn. Merrik was whistling a jovial tune, hands in his pockets, as he came striding up to the group.

"What a look you all have," he said. "What did I miss?"

CHAPTER TEN

I remember that the cabin was cold. I couldn't tell you what time of day it was, but I felt like I had been staring at the same three charts for hours or days with no end and no answers. After three days of struggling with it while the crew saw to the last of the loading, I knew I was close. I just wasn't sure how close to finding a route from Anvilcove around the Outer Isles.

My mind was still somewhere between Hook Island and Ormede when Kaelyn found me. She entered with a tentative determination, unobtrusive but firm. I felt her walk over, and I pointed to a spot on my map.

"I think it will be about here," I told her before she spoke.

"What will?" She stepped around the desk to look over my shoulder.

I pointed again. "If the wind stays fair between Oster and Ormede, we should be able to re-provision in Sunset. If I'm wrong, I suppose we can try our luck in Farwind, but that seems–"

"Tianna!" Kaelyn said, snapping me out of my thoughts. I stopped and look up at her, blinking the map from my mind's eye to better see the room I was standing in.

The flame from my lanterns was low, but they were still burning. Foggy moisture was clinging to the small window beside me, and through it I could make out a dim light trying to illuminate the dark cabin.

"*Vasta*," I said, shaking my head to clear it further. "What time is it?"

"Just before dawn," Kaelyn stated. She stood back and examined me. "You look like shit."

"Thanks."

"Have you slept at all?"

I shrugged and looked down at the papers and books scattered around the desk.

Kaelyn reached down and picked one up. "'*Mathon's Guide to Navigation and Logbooks*'?" She set it down and picked up another. "'*Master's Standing Orders — A Primer*,' '*A Complete Fool's Guide To Sailing*,' What is all this stuff?"

"I'm..." I looked down at the piles of reference books. There was scattered notes and journals from local captains, some charts, maps, markers, and pages upon pages of my own scribblings. "Preparing," I finished weakly.

"For what?" She scoffed. "We're not going to war, Tianna."

I caught her gaze and returned it. "We might be. We don't know what's out there. What if we run into pirates or a slaver ship? What if–"

She grabbed my shoulders and jostled me. "Enough," she hissed. "You are exhausted. I came in here to give you a report on the preparations, but you are in no position to hear it."

"But, I–"

"No 'buts'." She hauled me bodily around until I was facing the bunk and pushed. "Sleep. I will come find you in a few hours and we can talk then."

"But–" I started, but then faltered when I saw the look on her face. I sighed and nodded. As I laid my head on the too-soft, lumpy pillow, I thought of a dozen other things I needed to ask her about, and then thought of nothing as I fell instantly asleep.

I must have been out for a few hours. I awoke slowly, blinking back into life and seeing the small room for the first time in what felt like weeks.

The sun was streaming through the open window on the far side of my desk, casting a warm ray of sunlight across my bunk. I sighed deeply and burrowed deeper into my pillow.

"Careful there!" A shout from outside drew my attention. It sounded like a male voice, but it was hard to tell clearly. Merrik maybe? I hauled myself from my sunlit cocoon and trudged over to the door.

My legs and back screamed in pain, reminding me that standing in one position all night was just as bad as working constantly. I stretched carefully, then headed out to see what all the hubbub was about.

I stifled a yawn as I stepped out onto the deck, still tired from the long nights before. Merrik and Kaelyn were tossing playful punches while Iain lounged restfully on the aftcastle wall, watching them. Isaboe was staring out over the harbor lost in thought, while Anne looked as if she were considering speaking with her. Eric stood nearby, seemingly disinterested in all of it.

I frowned at them. "What is all this?" I asked.

They turned, one after the other. Without speaking, they lined up in front of me and soon, six bright, sunny faces met my gaze, all grinning like jesters at a Lugaian carnivale. I looked them over from left to right; Kaelyn, Merrik, Isaboe, then Eric, Iain, and finally Anne.

Kaelyn took a step forward. "Crew are all present and accounted for," she said.

"Is everything ready? Are we really leaving?" A small spark lit up my heart. I was awash in quiet realization. Perhaps this hadn't all just been a fever dream.

Now standing just to my left, Kaelyn nodded. "The last of the cargo was loaded last night. We have provisions for ten for two months—three with easy rationing—and Isaboe and Merrik just finished their final checks on fittings and gear." Her grin nearly split her jaw in two. "We're as ready as we will ever be."

I nodded slowly, then again a little more surely. I watched each of the crew. They didn't move. I looked at Kaelyn, uncertain. She looked at me expectantly. "Uh…" They were waiting for something, and they were all staring at me. "What are we waiting for?"

Kaelyn chuckled. "We are awaiting your order, Captain."

"Oh, sure that makes sens—wait! Why my order?"

I will never forget the look she gave. Her eyes widened and her lips twitched. Though her smile didn't fade, it did lose a bit of its luster. Her gaze darted toward Merrik, then back to me.

It was as if up to that moment she had honestly thought that I was just playing dumb, and now I had revealed myself. Worry flickered across her face. *Am I following a moron?* her expression asked.

"No, of course. I mean, right," I stammered out quickly before she jumped ship. "Because I'm the… um, captain?" *I'm the captain. Right. How in the seven bloody hells did that happen?*

The small part of my brain that always likes to be right immediately reminded me that I had spent the last two weeks overseeing the refitting of the ship, the training of the crew, and charting our course for the next several months. Right. Captain. Well, then. "Uh… cast off the port line, and haul out the oars, I guess? Let's get underway."

Kaelyn nodded once sharply and turned to the crew. "You heard the captain, kids. Let's put her out to sea!"

A jubilant cheer rose from the deck of the Siren, loud enough to shake the windows of the ships nearest us and echo off the waters of the bay. No doubt every soul in Anvilcove now knew we were leaving her shores.

Isaboe and Iain hurried to untie the docking lines while Eric, Merrik, and Kaelyn all grabbed long, stout wooden poles. I watched them brace against the pier and push us off.

Slowly, so, so slowly, we started to move. Erik, standing furthest aft, used his pole to push us forward while Merrik and Kaelyn steered us away from the dock and kept us clear of the neighboring ships.

I walked to the top of the foredeck, watching it happen. I'd read about this so many times, drilled the motions and procedures with the crew, but watching it really happen was too much. A childish squeal escaped me and I clapped my hands over my mouth, unable to contain my glee.

A few of the crew grinned in response and continued their work. They were an efficient team. They worked well together, coordinated and adjusted as a unit. It was as if they'd been working together for years, not simply weeks. And I had the honor of sailing with them. My crew. My friends. I was higher than the icy peaks of the Worldspire Mountains, and my euphoria was just as hard to get over.

As we cleared the end of the dock, Kaelyn reappeared at my shoulder. "The Siren is away," she said formally.

I nodded and turned to look toward the mouth of the bay. It was mid-morning and only a few other ships were near the harbor wall. I nodded again, pleased. "Give it a few more yards, then let's see about letting out the sail."

Kaelyn hesitated. "I've haven't done sails since we left the Naked Chicken," she said. "You were working on that with Merrik and Anne."

I cocked my head curiously, and frowned. "Of course, I didn't mean you specifically."

She blinked. "Oh, then… why did you tell me?"

I cocked my head to the side and rested my hand on her shoulder. "It's the captain's job to give the orders, but it's your job to see the crew carries them out."

She paused, trying to decipher the meaning in my words. All of a sudden, her eyes lit up as if the words 'First Mate' had actually been written on my face.

"Oh!" she said, then spun on her heel and marched off determinedly. "Lay aloft and loose mainsails! Eric, Anne! Remember to coil the end stays. We don't need to foul the rigging before we see what she can do. Merrik, standby the main topsail! This isn't a game, children!"

I grinned, watching her. She was made for this. If I had to be Captain, at least I knew I had her to back me up.

I shook my head and walked over to the braces at the base of the mainmast and waited for Isaboe and Eric to finish loosing the ties holding the sails in place. As soon as their boots hit the deck, I looked at Kaelyn and told her, "Sheet home topsails."

"Sheet home topsails!" she bellowed out to the crew.

My pulse quickened as my commands became her orders. Shouts of "aye" from above and around us couldn't have been more perfect if they'd staged all this for my benefit. As one, Merrik and Iain began hauling the topsail sheets on the mainmast. Anne and Eric mirroring their movements on the mizzen.

I ran through the checklist in my head, making sure I wasn't missing anything. I had planned this over and over again, memorizing every detail, and I didn't want to fail now that we were actually doing it. "Uh…" I took a breath. "Hoist topgallant sails."

Kaelyn nodded and turned quickly, "Hoist topgallant sails!" she shouted, but Anne was already making her way aloft to join Iain along the topgallant yard. I watched in rapt fascination as everything I'd studied and read came to life in front of me.

I noticed a tightening along one of the topgallant sheets before it had been fully cast, and I shouted without thinking. "Ease the braces!" Merrik rushed to do just that, and Kaelyn grinned at me and winked before running off to help him.

We repeated the process for each of the sails in turn until full white sheets of canvas were stretched out along the yards and straining against the pull of the anchor.

Oh Gods, this is real, I thought. Another moment passed before I reminded myself to breathe. When Kaelyn gave me one last grin that nearly split her face in two, I had to bite back a laugh. I nearly whispered my command. "Weigh anchor."

She gave a loud ear-piercing whistle, then shouted, "Weigh anchor!"

Every free hand, including myself, converged on the anchor winch. It took all six of us pushing along the large horizontal wheel, spinning it round and round to raise the anchor home. I was so grateful Kaelyn and I weren't trying to do this alone. This was not a two-man job.

As the anchor slid into place, I felt the Siren shift under my feet. It was subtle at first, but with every creak and groan of the hull beneath me, it became clearer. We were moving.

Backward.

Panic washed over me as I watched the dock, which should have been getting further and further behind us, actually draw closer. My eyes flew open wide, and I saw the same confused worry on Kaelyn's face.

Anne ran past me and began hauling on the starboard rail braces. That's when I heard an unfiltered, mocking laugh from the helm. I looked over at the smug expression on Isaboe's face and she turned the wheel into the wind.

"Falling off to starboard," she said, watching me with a smirk. The ship drifted sideways into the current.

Of course, I thought, now remembering the part of my book that had talked about this. In the excitement, I had forgotten every wind resistance calculation and sail chart I'd studied so closely the week before.

A fought back my blush at my obvious mistake and turned to watch the Siren drifting into her new pattern. "Brace fore and aft!"

The wind blew sideways across the bow, pushing us back and aside as it went. My mind worked overtime, remembering every detail. *About thirty-degrees, stern momentum, then...* "Hoist out the jib!" I called.

The ship continued to move sternways, and then to the side. Slowly, the sails shifted into the wind, turning to catch just what I needed. *Sixty-five degrees... a little more, and...* Just as I was wondering if I'd miscalculated, the sails snapped taut. I caught my breath, unable to do anything but watch the full canvas as we shifted direction.

A cheer erupted from me before I could squash it, and it spread through the crew as grins as they continued to work. "Haul out the spanker," I ordered. I was giggling, not even bothering to hide my excitement as the final piece of the intricate canvas puzzle was pulled into place.

Finally, the moment I had been anticipating for far too long came. "Brace round forward," I called out. Moments later, the mainmast yards swung around until the sails came in line, the wind filling them.

"Set the courses!"

As we launched forward. The roar of the wind echoed through my ears, making my whole body thrum. I turned. The roar I was hearing was actually my crew, raising a cheer just like I had moments before.

Isaboe turn the wheel, setting us on course for the mouth of the bay. This was it. It was really happening.

As I watched Anvilcove sink further and further into the distance, I felt myself grow calmer. Sturdier. Rightness washed over me and I didn't feel like I'd ever come down from this high.

"That's that, then." I turned to my crew. Carefully steeling my face into a mask of resolute pride, I said, "The Siren is underway. Good work, crew."

I wore a grin that birds could have nested in, but I didn't care one bit. This was it. It was really happening.

The short coastal trip from Wellsmith to Anvilcove had done nothing to prepare me for sailing into the open ocean. Out past the edge of the seashore, where the breaking waves calm into a steady rocking and the wind becomes a constant force, your perception of time and space changes. There's no other way to describe the sheer limitlessness of it all.

I knew it would be different. An open, unfathomable expanse. I'd always dreamed of how I would feel beyond the reef where the world disappeared into an endless horizon. It was the magic of potential and it was all mine.

At least, that's what I thought it would be.

No book, no fishtale, no seaman's gossip could account for the emptiness of it. Pure, clear waves stretched forever in every direction.

Sunlight reflected off the water. The occasional fish, dolphin, or rock would breach the surface and break up the monotony, and by the morning of your third day, with no solid point of reference, you were lucky if you could remember what solid even meant.

The open ocean is boring.

"You good, Cap'n?" I lifted my head a fraction of an inch to glare at the towering giant who was strolling over calmly. He had his hands in his pockets and a hint of a smile peeking through his beard. His rolling gait was easy as he strolled over to where I was draped listlessly along the port side railing.

"Eric," I greeted him with what I hoped was a welcoming sound and not the bitter restlessness I was feeling. "Why did I think this was a good idea?" I asked. I followed it up with a hollow chuckle, hopefully tipping him off to the idea that I wasn't annoyed with him.

He stopped a few paces away from me, and I watched him squint his eyes and grin even wider. He pondered my lethargic form before shaking his head. With a soft chuckle, he turned and slid down beside me, resting his back against the inner wall of the hull, just below the railing.

"Nice day, isn't it?"

From anyone else I would have thought his tone was carefully calculated to pull my attention, distract me from my melancholy, or, I don't know, make me ponder the deep philosophical meaning behind my mood. But from Eric it just felt like a simple remark. His mood was unfettered by the dark clouds hanging over me, and he wanted me to know that.

It was a nice day. The sun was warm, but not scorching. There was a stiff breeze that kept us moving along at a steady pace, and the seas were calm. It was me that was stormy.

"I was in Irongate about, oh, ten years ago," he said.

I sat up, curious to see where this little non sequitur was going.

"Barely more'n a boy, and not far from where I grew up, but ready to take on the world. Or at least the island." He laughed, shook his head, and continued.

I didn't interrupt.

"There was this group of kids, not much older'n me causing trouble down at th' docks. Now, I was practically raised in a warehouse, and I knew a thing or two about scrapping with street rats, but I didn't account for the number of 'em and found myself high-tailing through back alleys trying not to get a fist in the eye or a boot in the gut."

"Gods," I scoffed, "Been there." Images of running from Krellen's boys or hiding from Mitsuni's guards flashed through my mind. I pushed the memories away and focused on Eric's story.

"Dunno if you know Irongate, but it's not a small place. Lot like Anvilcove, but built atop itself haphazard like. No city planning," he said. "It's far easy t'lose a tail you don' want when you're surrounded by all types. There's ships in and out of port every day from just 'bout everywhere, and one scrawny lad amongst them wasn't worth noting."

I raised an eyebrow at the use of the word '*scrawny*' to describe the behemoth in front of me, but didn't comment. I waved for him to continue.

"Turns out, the faceless crowd was good fer gettin' lost in, but it was also bad for finding yourself in. By the time I caught my breath, I was so turned around I couldn't have found the roof of the building next to me."

"You got lost in your own hometown?" I asked before I could stop myself.

"Well, Irongate is where I spent most of my time. It's not my home, though. I'm originally from Scova, south side of th' island." He chuckled, then nodded. "But, aye, that I did. Lost, I wandered through the streets until dusk, too, lookin' for any familiar sign that would lead me somewhere I knew would lead me back."

"And?" I prompted when he paused.

"And I found none." He shrugged as if it was inevitable. "It was like I was on a totally different island. I'd just about given up, and was looking for a safe corner of some alley to sleep in when I tripped over somat, and went flying face-first into a pile of millet-bags 'longside a shop stall."

I laughed out loud, easily picturing that moment. That was exactly the kind of thing I would do. It was nice to know I wasn't the only fumbling one aboard.

"Well," he went on. "When I was able to shake my head loose of the stars I was seein' and actually look around, I spotted a shock of bright red hair hangin' over me, and bright face grinning down at me like I was the best clown in the circus."

I grinned and glanced across the deck. "Iain?"

Eric nodded. "Aye, Iain."

He followed my gaze to where Iain sat on the deck with Merrik, with a set of dice spread out between them. His hands gestured wildly as he gave the most animated instruction I've ever seen.

"Not sure exactly when he blew into town, but Iain and I have been mates since the second we met. There I was, sprawled out in a pile of moldy grain, lost in a part of the city I've never seen, and there he was. I'd never been so glad to see his freckled Tirican face. Course, he gave me no end of grief for it. Still talks about it when he can, but I wouldn't be here without 'im."

I sat back against the railing, soaking in his story. Eric and Iain certainly seemed attached at the hip. I hadn't realized when Kaelyn hired them that they were a package deal, but now it seemed so natural that I couldn't imagine one without the other. They looked an unlikely pair, but they complemented each other well, and I was glad they were part of my crew.

I felt a niggling feeling of doubt creep in. Who was I to claim them as 'my crew'? Either one of them had more experience in and around ships than I did. Until a month ago, everything I knew was theoretical. I booked bets on whether ships would make it into port, or what kind of cargo they'd be hauling. I never expected to be commanding one. In fact, I still wasn't sure what being in command meant.

"Eric, what…" I started, unsure what I was trying to ask.

"I don't know how he found me that day. He was just there when I needed him most." He stood and brushed off his trousers, then looked down at me. "Guess sometimes we don't get to know why people are in our lives, we just get to be glad they are."

I chuckled dryly and looked down at my hands resting in my lap. "Who knew I hired a philosopher?"

His broad smile was back in full force. "Everyone's a philosopher, Cap'n. Just a matter of perspective."

As he walked off, I lifted my gaze out over the ocean. The calm waves rolled along, seemingly still. It was too much like me—still on the surface, but the currents underneath were pulling everything along toward an unknown and undecided end.

Life was easier in Wellsmith. I knew what was expected of me there, even if, yes, I admit, this was better. I was safer now, at least ostensibly. My work fascinated me and this group of people were quickly becoming very important to me.

For a moment, I spared a thought for my younger self. It was possible that I had more friends now than I'd had all through my childhood. In fact, I wondered if I'd ever had a real friend before Kaelyn woke me up. Well, aside from... *No,* I told myself. *He doesn't need to be a part of this.* I wasn't about to waste my time thinking of people that weren't around.

I sighed, deeply. There was still another full day of sailing before we were scheduled to come in sight of Birdbeak Island, the first stop on our tour. Another full day of open ocean, endless skies, and boredom.

I leaned back against the rail again and watched my crew. Eric had joined in the dice game that Merrik now seemed to be winning. Isaboe was scolding a firmly placid Anne as she manned the helm. They both stood relaxed, as if the lecture were more perfunctory than necessary. Without bothering to look up, I knew Kaelyn would be aloft, either in the mainmast crow's or resting along one of the yards. And I, silly, confused Captain that I was, loved every second of what I was seeing.

Camaraderie, seamanship, friendship.

This was my crew. And it was time I joined them.

CHAPTER ELEVEN

The first stop on our grand adventure was Nestford, a small port town on the Northeast cape of Birdbeak Island. As I stepped off the ship onto the quiet dock, I took a deep breath. The smell of brine and sea foam mixed with fresh fish, stale bread, warm tar, and burned leather to create that distinctive port town aroma.

The noonday sun was warm, and I turned my face into it. Whether my smile was for the sun, the scene, or simply the solid ground under my feet, I wasn't sure. And I really didn't care. All the parts intermingled to make a perfect moment.

I don't know what I was expecting from a new island, but in nearly every way that mattered, it was just like where I grew up. Aside from a few cosmetic differences, and the fact that it was maybe half the size, I could very well have stepped off the boat back where I started. There was nothing new or exotic about Nestford at all.

I grinned a little wider as Kaelyn came to stand next to me. "This is it, huh?"

"Problem?"

She shook her head slowly. "No, I just expected it to be…"

"Different?" I supplied. "You've been lots of places, right? Are they usually more exotic?"

She shrugged. "It's not like I expected Bird Beak to be anything like Calipi or Ilakata, but I feel like we could be back where I found you. I thought it would be… different."

"Let's be glad it's not," I added, patting her back. "Means we can find the market with no problem."

I turned back to the Siren and my waiting crew. "Where should we start?"

They all stared at me, not a single answer forthcoming.

All right… "Kaelyn," I said, turning to my first mate, "Why don't you and Eric go find some decent lodging for the night while Merrik and I scout out the market. We need to see what we're dealing with before we deal."

My command sounded more like a suggestion to my own ears, but I was met with nods all around. They seemed to accept it as orders, so I nodded once and turned away.

"And us?" Isaboe asked. She sounded half annoyed, half hopeful, and all impatient. I barely kept myself from shrugging. "Enjoy the town."

Isaboe, Anne, and Iain each looked thoughtful or excited as per their natures, and I fought to keep the mischievous gleam out of my eye. "One of you has to stay with the ship, but I'll let you decide who," I added, barely turning before they could see my smirk morph into a grin. I gestured to Merrik and walked up the road, leaving them all eyeing each other suspiciously.

I know, I know. Pitting my crew against each other over something as simple as shore leave shouldn't be fun, but I'm a bad, bad woman. I told myself they needed to work these things out themselves, that it would foster bonds between them or some other plausible excuse. I even almost believed it.

"Oh, actually," Anne said sweetly. "I was hoping to meet with a friend of mine while we were here. It won't take long. An hour or two, at the most."

I heard Isaboe grumble something under her breath as I turned to leave them to their own devices.

"So," I said, as Merrik joined in my casual stroll.

He raised an eyebrow, waiting for me to continue.

"The market." It wasn't stunning repartee, but not every conversation was.

"I have a few ideas, but I won't know what to expect until we get there. I'm hoping for a straight trade, but failing that, we'll take coin."

"As sound a plan as any," I told him. "I was hoping you'd take lead on this one."

"Not to worry, boss. I can handle it." He grinned that stupid infectious grin that made people instantly love him and suddenly, just as he'd said, I wasn't worried.

"Thanks, *kashi*. You know I'm not much of a trader."

He cocked his head, looking at me. "You called me that before. '*Kashi*'. What's that mean?"

I felt a tiny flush rush across my cheeks. "Oh, I didn't even think. It's Loaominese. Some formal dialect, I think. Jun taught me. It means 'little brother.'" I paused and thought about it. "Is that okay?"

He shrugged, brushing it off. "Good as anything else you might call me. What should I call you then?"

I grinned cheekily, knowing the answer that would make him laugh. "Captain."

He rewarded me with a chuckle and a shake of his head. "Sure thing, boss," he said facetiously, but I caught a definite smile as we made our way toward the center of town.

The market, as I kept calling it, really wasn't much more than a short row of storefronts with maybe a half-dozen stalls lining the road. Twelve, or maybe as many as fourteen people wandered between the shops. Some hurrying, some dallying, and two just stopped in the middle of the roadway talking. It was small-town domesticity at its finest, and I couldn't help the grin on my face from seeing something come to life that I'd only ever read about in books.

It had me so enchanted, in fact, that I failed to notice when Merrik disappeared. One moment he was simply no longer by my side, and as I scanned the street for signs of him, I knew it was hopeless. *I really need to talk to my crew about running off on me,* I thought as I headed into the nearest building.

The scent of dust overlaid wood and oil as I entered the large room. I quickly glanced around. Boxes and barrels were spread out around the room, lining walls and forming displays boasting a wide variety of goods. There didn't seem to be any rhyme or reason to the order of things.

A crate that held a mix of cutlery, wooden pegs, and paintbrushes sat proudly between a display of hand-carved masks and a chest filled with bundles of rope and twine. The longer I looked, the less this shop made sense, yet the more deliberate it all seemed.

"That sounds perfect, thank you." I looked to the back corner of the shop where Merrik was shaking hands with an older woman. She was short, the top of her head barely coming up to his shoulder, but her thin frame suggested an ironrod strength that casually tossed aside any notion of frailty.

As I stepped up to join them, Merrik turned toward me. I'd only been separated from him for a few minutes, but the smug smile gracing his lips was telling.

"Perfect timing, Captain," he said warmly. "It's done."

I blinked and grabbed at his sleeve, surprised. I took a step back to one side, pulling him along with me. "What do you mean 'done'?" I dropped my voice, trying to keep this conversation at least a little private in case it was going where I thought it was going.

Merrik nodded. "All done. Deal made." He smiled again, twice as smug this time.

I frowned at him. "We've been here less than five minutes. Are you sure it's wise to accept the first offer? We haven't even talked to anyone else."

His sea-green eyes were soft, like they were trying to read past my immediate apprehension. Eventually, he shrugged. "She seems nice."

"She hasn't even seen the cargo!" I whispered harshly and glanced back over my shoulder at the woman, who was now straightening the assorted items on her desk, carefully not listening in on us. Her smile was warm, and the line of her chin held a touch of stubbornness that appealed to me. I slowly turned my gaze back to my friend.

When I sighed, he knew he had won, and I let him have it. Deal was done anyway, there was no point in arguing. Instead, I turned and made my way back out into the street.

I paused at the door, suddenly remembering myself, and poked my head back inside. "Thank you," I called out as I waved. The shopkeeper's smile widened and her eyes sparkled with kindness. "I'll send some of my crew with the boxes this afternoon."

Merrik stretched his shoulders and shook out his arms as if he was getting ready for a fight or some heavy lifting. He grinned at me and walked away. The people loitering in the street continued to go about their business, ignoring us completely. This completely normal day seemed entirely unaware that something momentous had just happened.

It was one thing to load up a ship and sail away to parts unknown. It was another to actually be successful at anything after that. We had just conducted our first trade, and in record time. We were merchants now. No longer the weird orphan who loved books more than people, nor the smart-mouthed bookie dodging blows from her gang. Now I was a sailor and a sea trader, and I quite liked the sound of that.

A joy I hadn't felt in a very long time came bubbling up out of me, and I laughed. It was small and tentative at first, but before long it had overtaken me and I was giggling like a jackdaw in the morning sun. The markets patrons turned to gawk at the odd girl, and I shook my head, still laughing, and then ran off to catch up with Merrik.

This was turning out to be a very good day.

Merrik only glanced sideways at me as I slowed to match his pace, still chuckling. The smirk he was suppressing turned into a full grin, and we made our way down the road back to the ship.

Isaboe came out on deck as we started up the gangplank. Her expression turned from confused to worried to curious in rapid succession as she watched us. When I reached her, I nodded with a smile.

She eyed me suspiciously.

"Got stuck on watch, huh?" I asked casually.

She grit her teeth against whatever snappy remark she had brewing inside, and I watched her consciously switch over to a witty rejoinder. "Watching is easier than working, so I don't mind."

There it was, that glint in her eye that I saw the first time we met. If Kaelyn was raw burning fire, then Isaboe was a carefully tempered forge, her fire trained to work for her benefit. So long as she used it to my benefit as well, I didn't mind. Gods help me if she ever decided that I was her enemy.

"Afraid of a little hard work?" I couldn't help rising to the challenge in her gaze.

She cocked her head to one side slightly. "More afraid of not working."

I tsked. "That won't do. Sailors need to be familiar with knot-working."

Her lips twitched at my stupid pun. "Oh, I can be very naughty, but not when knots are not called for." She gave a solemn nod. "I don't like to be tied down."

A surprised laugh slipped from me. It was so loud I was surprised it didn't echo off the water. "When you're not working?"

"Knot ever." When she finally grinned, I shook my head.

From behind me, I heard Merrik sigh heavily. "Are you two done flirting? We have a trade to wrap up."

Isaboe and I glanced at each other and shared a look that I will never forget. In the space of a heartbeat we looked each other over, considering the possibilities and both came to the conclusion that we were, in fact, not flirting. It had been an exchange of wit, not want, and that mutual recognition instantly transformed uncertainty into a solid friendship.

"How was the market?" she asked, turning to Merrik. "Done already?"

"Done and done," he said with a quick nod. "Got us a straight trade at the general store. Once we bring the goods to her shop this evening, we'll haggle rates and then..." he clapped his hands and rubbed them together gleefully. "We go shopping."

Isaboe and I laughed at his avaricious expression. There was nothing greedy about Merrik and the absurdity of his dramatic gesture made me break out in laughter all over again.

Which is exactly how Kaelyn and Eric found us a few minutes later.

"Rooms secured, Cap'n," Eric stated as he joined our merry little group.

"They weren't cheap, but they'll do the job and not beggar us," Kaelyn added.

"Good, it's worth it." I nodded and smiled at both of them. "I'll take Watch for now. You've all been pushing your stamina this last week and deserve at least one night ashore." I darted a glance over at Isaboe. "Not working."

She bit back a laugh, and I grinned. Kaelyn looked between us, seeing an inside joke taking place that she was not in on, and not fully enjoying it. "What about the trade?" she asked instead of what she clearly wanted to know.

"Done," Merrik said once more.

Before he could explain again, I made a shooing motion with my arms. "All of you, get. Go find somewhere else to be. Explore the city. Have fun, whatever. Just go. I've earned some peace and quiet."

They all laughed and started back up the dock toward the city. I watched them walk off with a lightness in my heart that was spreading to my face again. I couldn't have contained my smile even if I'd cannon aimed at my belly. Right then, I felt damn lucky to be me.

I stepped onto the Siren and that feeling intensified. This was going to work. This was real. This was home.

Home...

It wasn't a concept I was familiar with, but just then, it hit me like the kind of truth they preach in churches. I was exactly where I was supposed to be.

I heard footsteps behind me and turned to see Kaelyn had ditched the group and circled back around.

"So," she said as she joined me, mirroring my pose. "That went well."

"The trade or the trip?" I asked, keeping my tone even.

"Both, I guess."

"It did. I wasn't sure when we left Anvilcove, but now, seeing how everyone came together this week, I just... Gods, Kaelyn, I think we can do this!"

When she didn't move or respond, I turned to look at her. My smile slipped a little when I saw her worrying the inside of her cheek. She refused to meet my eye, and my shoulders tensed as I waited.

"What?" I finally asked, afraid to hear her answer.

"That went well," she said, warily this time. She drew her brows together in a frown as she looked back down at the dock. "Nothing ever goes well."

I shook my head to keep myself from saying or doing something that would start a fight. He cynicism often served well to temper my idealistic musings, but sometimes it was just frustrating.

With what I hoped was a teasing smile, I reached up and clapped a hand on her slumped shoulder. "Kaelyn, m'dear. That's a *good* thing."

She shook her head stubbornly, her frown deepening. "It was too easy." She held my gaze for a long moment, pausing in thought. "You don't ever worry when things are too easy? Like there's bad waiting to follow it?"

I had nothing to add, so I just waited with a patient smile on my face.

She softened a little as I watched until uncertainty crept into her eyes. "Fine," she said eventually. "But if the next one goes just as smoothly, I'm jumping ship."

I laughed again as she started to walk away. "What's wrong? You don't trust me anymore?" I called after her.

She shook her head, still walking. "You're fine. It's the calm I don't trust."

I shook my head, still laughing at my pessimistic first mate. "Hey, wait! Are you saying I'm not calm?"

She kept walking.

"Wait up!" I started off after her. "What do you mean, I'm not calm?"

"You're as calm as a thunderstorm, Tianna."

My answering laugh echoed across the bay as I watched my friend make her way down the road.

This was home.

After spending a day resting and restocking in Nestford, we set out to Windway Island. I gave us lots of time, deciding to err in favor of not dashing us upon the shoals on our first attempt at navigating the reef. Instead, we headed due north and swung wide around the treacherous waters. It added a day to our trip, but well worth it. Four days after leaving the island of Birdbeak, we docked safely in Helm's Point, a solid, hale, and hearty crew.

"Tianna?"

I glanced around, snapping back into the present. Only when I looked at Kaelyn's face did I realize she had been trying to talk to me. And that I had been standing on the deck, looking out over the docks blankly. "Um… yeah?"

Kaelyn looked half-annoyed, but chuckled. "You didn't hear anything I said, did you?"

"No, I…uhh," I scrunched up my nose, glancing around for inspiration. She had said something about supplies? The crew? The weather? Damn. I shrugged. "Nope, wasn't listening. Sorry."

"Merrik says that even though it's a bigger town, the market here is smaller than in Nestford. Something to do with land space and shipping routes. But he still thinks we can find something worthwhile. Should we send him?"

I pondered the man in question. I wasn't sure how many days now he had stayed up past the midnight watch, taking inventory of our stocks and supplies. Enough that I noticed.

"Let him rest. You and I can go. Get the manifest from him, though. I'm sure he has ideas on what we need."

"Aye, Captain," she said simply and walked off.

I turned to address whoever else was nearby. Anne and Isaboe both paused long enough to meet my gaze. "The rest of you square things away here and start hauling the trades. I know we had a bit of fun in Nestford, but let's try to be a little more organized about things this time, aye?"

They chuckled and issued their own rounds of 'aye Captain' before I turned. "Iain has the deck," I called out over my shoulder, resisting the urge to find the grinning redhead just to see the surprise on his face. With a smile and a lightness in my step, I started down the walkway, knowing Kaelyn would catch up.

Helm's Point was a cute little town. Actually, calling it a town was probably being generous. I knew that the city stretched out into the hills, but down near the water, the population was less than a thousand people living in small houses tucked in near a road up the cliff. From one of the captain's log's I'd read, it was actually closer to the size of Wellsmith. But here, the streets were basically empty, and I had trouble reconciling that knowledge with the sleepy village around me.

The ambient sounds as I walked up the street were muffled, like the whole village was wrapped in cotton or trying not to disturb each other's rest. I could hear birds, for goodness' sake. Birds! People still called out to each other, and carts and wagons rattled along the cobblestones, but it was different, slower.

I strolled up the streets with my hands in my pockets, just enjoying the relaxing walk. *Maybe I should have sent Merrik after all*, I thought, but then a selfish part of me stamped out that voice and I gave myself permission to enjoy this for myself.

It was not long after that, as I turned onto the main roadway through town, when Kaelyn caught up. "So, official talk, First Mate," I said as she drew even with me.

She raised an eyebrow, but otherwise said nothing, only matching my pace and falling in step with me.

"How is the crew doing?" I asked. "Merrik can't be the only one who's tired. I know he's an overachiever, but I'm working them too hard, right?"

She made a small noise that might have been a sigh. After a pause that threatened to grow into a hesitation, she nodded slightly. "Maybe. But you're working just as hard."

I tried not to shrug too noticeably. "If you haven't noticed, I'm pretty new to this. Usually, captains have a lifetime of experience under their belt before they're given a ship. I have a lot of catching up to do."

"Not disagreeing, but again, we all do," she countered. "None of us had experience before joining the crew. You know that. I think everyone is busting themselves to prove they can do this."

"At this point, I'm just happy we can get from port to port without killing ourselves. I'm not expecting them to be experts."

"But you expect yourself to be an expert?"

This time I hesitated. "Well, yes," I said. That answer felt too obvious, so I paused, giving it a little more thought. "I guess… I guess I'm just trying to be the kind of captain we need. Show everyone that they can trust me to live up to the title."

Mixed emotions warred on her face as we walked. "You don't really have anything to live up to," she told me. "You said so yourself. You're new to this. One of the good things about none of us knowing what we're doing is that it doesn't take much to be the best at it."

I chuckled.

"Besides," she went on. "You don't really need to know everything about everything. You just have to know enough more than the crew does so that we can follow your lead."

I nodded. "I just need to be a page ahead of you in the text, as Albert would say."

She smiled. "That's a scholar's answer if ever I heard one."

I couldn't disagree and only smiled in return. It was nice to just chat like this with her. We hadn't had much opportunity since setting out from Anvilcove.

"Kaelyn, thank you."

"What?" She stopped walking and looked at me. Then seemed to find her feet again and caught up with me.

I shrugged, passing off my sentimentality as nothing. "You keep being here for me and saying the right things while pushing me to do better. You all but literally dragged me out of my comfort zone back in Wellsmith, and I, well, I appreciate it."

"And that was your comfort zone? Working for scraps, sleeping in storehouses, dodging violent criminals?"

Ouch. I could hear the teasing note in her voice, and the incredulous look she gave me should have had me at least cracking a smirk, but her observation was a little too on the mark.

I didn't hide the wince that came over me, because she was right. Comfort zone or not, I'd been complacent. It was easy to hide when you had no expectations for yourself. You just had to fit in, not make waves, let the world carry on.

These last few weeks, I'd allowed myself to do something different, be something different. Something more like I was when I was at Three Brothers. More like I was when I read all of the books about daring adventures and travels across the empire. In books, I was free to learn, and play, and connect with foreign lives and ideologies in ways I never could with Krellen, or even just at the orphanage.

Now, I was doing it again. Connecting with people. It was great. Now that I was on the other side of it, I could see that my life in Wellsmith was anything but comfortable. It was just all I had known.

The orphanage had been comfortable enough, but those memories were dull and grayscale. Muted like a faded sketch rather than an oil painting. It was like I had just been incubating, biding my time until I could live my own life. And when I had? I chose a life of clawing up from the bottom until I was just barely safer than a rat in a dog kennel. Had that really been a choice?

I had always known why Albert hadn't adopted me. A single man running a business simply wasn't able to care for a small girl. Adwin and Jun offered a bit more stability, but in that small house? I wouldn't have put that on them, no matter the cost to me. It was enough that they cared to look out for me however they could.

Working for Krellen wasn't something they approved of, and Adwin at least made no secret of it, but I never made that their problem. I kept that life separate from the bookstore, save only for the few times that Tavers had gotten a bit too enthusiastic in his games. Jun would treat my wounds, Albert would lecture me, and I would go back and do it all again.

I shuddered briefly at the memory of Tavers. I wasn't proud of all of my choices, but his cold ruthlessness had been the darkest spot in my otherwise... well, miserable life. I sighed. It was true. Kaelyn was right. Wellsmith hadn't been comfortable, it had just been my home.

"No," I finally said, answering her rhetorical question. "I suppose there was always more to it than that. But, my sentiment remains, Kaelyn, I'm grateful that you-" I stopped short, forgetting what I was about to say.

The figure in front of me chased away any thought I'd been about to have. Lean muscles pulled on the slim frame as he moved, like a jungle cat that thought he was a bear. For a moment, I thought I was seeing things. Surely, my train of thought had been unsettling enough to play mindtricks. But as I looked again, I knew there was no way I could be wrong about what I was seeing.

The thin, angular face was scruffier than I remembered, covered now with a light dusting of an unkempt beard, but I would know that profile—and sneer—anywhere.

"What the fuck is he doing here?" I whispered on a ragged breath.

Memories assaulted me. Images of too many nights hiding in the dark corner of some taproom somewhere before it was safe to sneak off to my bunk for a few hours of sleep.

I swallowed down the fear before it could choke me and I clenched my fists several times and blinked, willing the apparition to disappear.

"What is it?" Kaelyn asked, turning to see what had me so agitated. She stopped beside me and followed my gaze, landing on the man in the street. "Oh, shit. Is that–"

He turned to look down each street and alley as he walked, pausing now and then to peer around the people gathered nearby. He was looking for someone. Looking for... me?

That couldn't be right. Why would he even bother tracking me down? I was nobody. He wanted me gone, remember? This had to be a coincidence. A shitty, bizarre, worst-case scenario coincidence, but there was just no way he was here for me. Right?

"Darl Tavers," I said under my breath. I knew it came out as little more than a frightened whisper, but just as if a snake sensed a rabbit trembling in the bushes, he turned. His icy gaze locked onto mine.

My stomach rolled in a way that it never did at sea. My knees threatened to give out on me. His right eye was covered by a heavy patch, and his one good eye was empty of everything except me. I would have been flattered if his expression held anything other than murderous rage.

"What is he doing here?" Kaelyn repeated my question.

I clenched and unclenched my hands several times, digging my nails into my palms to wake myself from this stupor. I don't know how long I stood transfixed, but with every heartbeat I knew I was losing any advantage I had.

"Run," I breathed out the command.

"What?" Kaelyn stared at me, confused for a moment.

"The Siren," I snapped, urgently. "Run!" Without waiting for her to understand, I spun around and raced back to the dock with everything I had left in me.

My feet carried me past the city I'd barely had time to explore, faster than I would have thought possible. I wasn't much of a runner, never had been, but I couldn't stop to think about that as I wove in between the people on the street. I had only one goal screaming in my mind. Safety. Get away. Get safe. It was an old mantra borne on instinct that I thought I'd left behind in Wellsmith.

We passed Anne, who was just stepping onto the pier. "Ah, Captain," she called with a smile. "I was just about to-"

"No time," I shouted. "Get aboard. Now!" I raced past her and up the gangplank onto the familiar deck of my ship. Isaboe and Merrik ran over to see what the commotion was. I bent over nearly in half, wheezing from the exertion.

"Captain?" Isaboe asked. When I didn't answer, her tone turned demanding. "What's going on?"

I tried to stand and answer her, but I couldn't stop myself from shaking. Isaboe opened her mouth to ask again, just as Kaelyn came bounding up behind me.

"All hands, cast off! Lay aloft and loose sails! Prepare to weigh anchor!" She shouted her commands almost before her boots had hit the deck. "Move people, move! Don't make me say it twice!"

A heavy line landed on the deck a moment before Anne hurried aboard and started pulling in the wooden plank behind her. Merrik hurried to coil the line that had tied us to the dock, not stopping to question what was happening. Isaboe spared another glance at me, laced with a bit of worry, before running off to do as Kaelyn ordered.

For a brief moment, I wondered if everyone was already on board. I certainly hoped so. It would be kind of ridiculous to have to stop and turn around once we noticed someone was missing.

Oh, don't mind me, Mr. Violent Thug. I know you're here to kill me, but I just need to pick up my friend. The thought came unbidden, floating in on a sea of adrenaline.

The only thing I had ever wanted for myself was to leave Wellsmith and find a place to belong—to have friends, and a purpose. Now I did, and here was the last person I ever wanted to think about again, practically tripping over my path on a far-flung island in the middle of nowhere.

Fate really had it out for me.

I heard a startled laugh echoing across the deck. It took far too long before I realized it was coming from me. "Guess it's true what they say," I said to no one. I was still resting with my hands braced on my knees, and Kaelyn paused long enough to catch my eyes, deep worry etched into her brown ones. "You don't ever really leave home."

She shook her head without responding and ran off. I don't know if I was shirking my duties or putting too much on her, but right then I hoped she would tell the crew what was going on. I didn't want to explain. I couldn't.

Instead, I turned to watch over my shoulder as the ship drew further and further away from the shore. I shook my head as yet another city sank into the distance behind me, and I couldn't help but wonder why he was here.

We were safely underway, about ten leagues off shore and running with the wind toward Hook Island, when I felt the crew gather behind me. I could practically feel their worried and curious stares.

"Captain?" Isaboe asked in a firm, but imploring tone.

I shook my head. "No."

I knew I wasn't being right, but *vasta*, I needed a minute to process everything. Even at the time, I knew that wasn't entirely fair, either. I'd had the time everyone else was launching the ship and getting us out to sea to think it over, but I had no answers for them.

"Cap'n…" Eric said hesitantly.

"Someone get aloft. I need an eagle up there to keep an eye astern. Raise the call immediately if you spot a ship on our tail."

The mixed emotions on their faces met me like a punch to the gut as I glanced around, but I couldn't spare them any supportive words. I knew they needed something from me. They needed direction and purpose, even just an explanation just then, but I couldn't. I couldn't face them, and I couldn't think of anything to say that would make sense. I tried to shake the frustration from my head, and marched off to my cabin, berating myself for being such a terrible captain.

It didn't take long before the door opened and pounding footsteps followed me inside. "Care to tell me what that was about?" Isaboe asked.

"Not particularly, no." I didn't want to meet her gaze because I knew that when I did, I would have to answer her.

When I looked up, her dark eyes were serious. "I can't face him. I just… can't," I said.

"Face who?"

I let out a noise that was half-sigh, half-growl, clenching and unclenching my fist as I tried to calm myself. I looked at the floor, at the walls, at the piles of books–anywhere but at Isaboe–as I began pacing the small room.

"Captain," Isaboe said, her patience with me wearing thin. "You need to start talking. We can't just start turning away from every port just because you… I don't know what! We need more than silence from you."

I stopped and spun, wheeling on her like I was ready to pick a fight. Maybe I was. "It doesn't matter."

She took a step forward, clearly not intimidated by me. "Except that it does matter. At least enough for you to come charging back to the ship without doing what we set out to do. Did you even make it to the market?"

I clenched my jaw and turned away, still shaking. She didn't know what she was talking about, and she was only trying to rile me up. I needed to stay calm. I needed to stay in control. Facing Tavers again was bad enough.

"Helm's Point isn't the only port in the Outer Isles. We can make a trade when we get to Angle Bay," I said.

"And what if we run out of supplies before then?" she snapped back. "Did you talk to Merrik? Have you looked at the manifests? Or the conditions reports I gave you? It's another half-week to Hook Island!"

I knew she was mad and needed to have her say, so I would just let her get it out, then we could move on. It was the best plan. I knew it was right. It's what I should do.

"You only give me those reports so that I can assess the situation and make a call. You made me captain, so let me do my job!"

"Then do your job!" she shouted. "Do what's best for the crew and the Siren, not just for your own self-interest."

I reeled back as if she'd slapped me. "My what?"

She rested her hands on her hips and glared at me. "I don't know who or what we were running from back there, and I sure don't know why. But if you run into a problem that affects the crew, then it most definitely is my problem. You made it everyone's problem, *Captain*." She sneered the last word, tossing it back in my face.

I felt my face heating. I wanted to stay angry. Anger was clean and offered a clear direction. But as she spun and marched out of my cabin, the only thing I felt as the door slammed was shame. She was right.

Damn it.

I tore open the door and chased out after her. "You're right!" I shouted at her retreating back, trying not to notice how the rest of the crew had stopped and were watching us intently.

She stopped where she was and turned slowly back to face me. Disbelief flashed across her expression before her anger flared up again.

"I know I'm right," she snapped. "But that doesn't give you permission to make unilateral decisions without at least giving us a reason for it! We support you, but this isn't a dictatorship. Let us have a voice, too. At least then we can help you make the tough calls. Let us support you a little."

"I'm your Captain," I said firmly. "You need to let me lead. That means trusting me, even when you don't agree with my orders."

Isaboe took three large steps, coming back to within an arm's length of me. Quiet as cold steel, she said, "You're our captain? Start acting like it."

The shame flared up again. I tried to take a deep breath before I started crying. I was intensely aware of the six sets of eyes trained in my direction. Complicated emotions welled up in me, all fighting for supremacy. Shame, anger, fear, frustration, but also relief and gratitude. I didn't have to do this all alone.

We were a small crew, but the strength of that would always lie in our ability to support and trust one another. I had failed that test the very first time it had come up. That was clear.

I wasn't expecting any kind of validation from being wrong, but somehow knowing that she was angry because I hadn't trusted her made me want to trust her more. But even if she was right, she shouldn't have been yelling at me, and definitely not in front of the crew.

The longer I stood there under their collective gazes, the tighter I felt my shoulders bunch. Right at that moment, it didn't matter if she was right. I screwed up, and they were all judging me for it. I couldn't be wrong. I couldn't let them see how badly I had failed. I was their captain. They needed me to take charge of the situation. So I did, the only way I knew how.

"Everyone get back to work," I bellowed across the deck. I didn't wait to hear any agreement or argument. I turned and headed back into my cabin, forcing myself not to run, but racing to get there before the tears could fall.

As soon as I was safely inside, I threw myself on my bunk and cried like the lost little girl I was.

CHAPTER TWELVE

I didn't see the crew the rest of the day, or all of that night. Or most of the next day, either. I had stuck to my cabin, distracting myself with ledgers, or charts, or I don't know what. It didn't matter. I wasn't looking at it, anyway. My mind was still firmly back in Helm's Point.

The image of Tavers' hateful eyes replayed over and over in my mind against a soundtrack of Isaboe's words.

Do what's best for the crew, she'd said.

Wasn't that what I was doing? As soon as I knew it wasn't safe on Windway, I'd gotten us out of there. I'd protected my crew. Hadn't I?

Of course, I had. I couldn't and wouldn't sacrifice my crew's safety because my past wouldn't let me go. Just because I was too weak to face him before, doesn't mean that they need to suffer for it now. I should have… I should have…

And that's where it always fell apart. There wasn't anything else I could have done back in Wellsmith. I left that life behind precisely so that this wouldn't happen. I'd done everything I could, and still failed my crew.

And now every weakness I'd ever felt was unearthed, open and exposed to the world. I didn't want them to see me like this. I needed to be strong for them. I needed to stay in control so that they could do their jobs. Tavers was my problem and I would deal with it.

You made it everyone's problem, Captain.

He'd followed me. I didn't drag him here, and I didn't drag the crew into this mess either. It just happened, the way things always seem to happen. I should have been better prepared for the worst, but I hadn't foreseen this. I anticipated bad weather and unscrupulous merchants, not an aspiring crime boss with a vendetta.

I hadn't expected pirates either, or to get a ship out of some shady deal, or to be working alongside the governor's daughter. How could I have seen any of that coming? I still wasn't entirely sure how it had all happened.

The thought of running into pirates again, of being on the wrong side of them, and putting this crew at risk sent an icy chill down my spine. I was their captain. I needed to keep them safe. I just had no idea how to do that.

We need more than silence from you.

I dropped my head into my hands, no longer pretending to read the book in front of me. Every moment of the last month suddenly felt like a lie. It was a farce dreamed up by a bored and deranged child with more imagination than sense. I was playacting. I should never have been allowed onboard a ship, let alone leading the crew of one.

The walls of my cabin felt oppressive. I couldn't breathe through the musky scent of damp wood and lantern oil. I needed to get out. The urgent need for fresh air propelled me back from the desk and I all but raced out into the early morning chill.

The breeze along the coastline whipped across the deck. It lifted my worries like whispers in the night, uttered, then instantly forgotten. I breathed deeply for a few moments, giving myself the space to not think about the past week at all. I strode from one end of the ship to the other, keeping myself in this moment and no other. Exactly where I wanted to be.

I nodded at the sleepy-eyed Iain on the early watch. His eyes followed me with as much wariness as I've ever seen on his face. He still smiled, though, which did more to lighten my heart than anything. Maybe the crew didn't completely hate me.

I pushed the thought—and the ones that would surely follow it—away and continued my lap of the Siren's planks. For the first time in days, I felt a bit of peace, and I wanted to hang onto it.

Which is naturally why, as I was mounting the steps to the stern deck above the castle, that I saw it. A small, dark spot on the waves, slowly, but steadily, growing larger as I watched.

A ship.

The realization hit me like a salt bath in Northbay at midwinter, freezing my body where I stood, one foot raised to the next step in front of me. I should have expected it. I had been watching for it all night, waiting for him to catch up. Why was I surprised now?

No, not surprised. Scared.

I was scared. A ship was following us. He was following us. Tavers had found me, and no matter how far I ran from Wellsmith and the rotting confines of the Rat's Nest, he always would.

No. Vasta! I can't face him. Not like this. Not… ever. No… no, no…

I stared at the ship as if I could see his face sneering at me in triumph of his final victory over me. "Kaelyn," I whispered on a broken gasp of air.

I shook away the ghosts in my mind. Bounding back down the stairs, I called out frantically. "Kaelyn!" I threw myself toward the hatch down to the berthing, where most of the crew still slept.

I flung the door open, not caring about its hinges nor the clattering noise my ears almost registered. "All hands!" I roared into the darkness below me. "Ship astern, moving fast! Everyone to quarters!"

Merrik was the first to my side, looking sober but alert. Together we hurried back to the afterdeck, where I pointed nearly straight behind us.

The ship still trailed far out of our wake, but it was noticeably closer than it had been when I'd first spotted it. I gripped the railing until my fingers ached, forcing deep breaths into my lungs.

Merrik stepped around me to get a better view. He grunted once, nodded, and then raced off to the mainmast topsail yard for a better view.

Tavers appeared in my mind's eye again. His sickening laughter rang in my ears. His hand pressed around my throat. I couldn't breathe. I shuddered, gasping in quick breaths, unable to shake the phantom.

I startled, then slumped to my knees when Kaelyn placed a hand on my shoulder. After a few more shaking breaths, I noticed she was speaking.

"Captain!" she all but shouted in my ear.

I blinked and shook my head, forcing my thoughts to clear. She shoved a spyglass into my hands. I looked at it dumbly, trying to remember what it was for.

"Captain!" Kaelyn called again. Her eyes flashed with annoyance tinged with alarm.

"Oh," I said aloud, and raised the glass to my eye. Sure enough, a coastal barc was easily navigating the shoals near the reef. And it was headed our way.

I swallowed down the panic that was rising again, long enough to pass the spyglass back to her.

"Confirm?" My voice and hands were still shaking.

Kaelyn looked through the glass toward the ship for several long heartbeats. Too long. I gripped the railing with both hands until my knuckles turned white. Sweat broke out across my brow, even in the chill wind.

No...no...no... The litany continued. *Not this. Not him. Not now.*

Kaelyn stepped back and collapsed the glass before slipping it back into her pocket. "No confirmation."

"What?" I straightened and stared at her. "What do you mean? It's right there!" I pointed, as if it wasn't obvious.

She shook her head again, and I noticed the rest of the crew was gathering around us. "I see the ship, Tianna. It's not a threat."

"What?" I shouted. I sounded frantic, even to my own ears, but I had no control over it. "Of course he's a threat! He's... he's..."

"Flying a Tirican flag!" Kaelyn countered. "Would Tavers run the Scarlet Boar?"

"What? No," I said. "I mean, maybe? This is technically Tirica Denisi. Maybe he wanted to avoid the navy."

She cocked an eyebrow and leveled her stare at me. "Really? The navy?" she said, dryly. "Out here?"

"Confirmed! Ship astern!" Merrik called from above us before shimmying back down the lines to rejoin us.

I turned to him and nodded, just as Kaelyn glared in his direction.

"See? Confirmed. Ship astern. Get those sails up!" I called to no one in particular. "We need speed and they've got the advantage."

No one moved.

"Get us out of here!" I cried again. The trembling in my voice was starting to match the shaking in my limbs and I knew I wasn't hiding it from them.

Kaelyn and Merrik exchanged a look that I couldn't decipher. Neither of them moved.

"What are you waiting for?" I shouted. They didn't know him like I did. They couldn't know. They didn't see the promise of murder in his eyes every time he looked at me. They didn't remember the poison of his touch. "We need to run." I choked on a half-sob.

With more patience than I've ever seen from her, Kaelyn passed the spyglass back over to me. "Look again, Tianna."

I peered through. The detailed mermaid carving on the bow came into view, winking at us. Taunting us. The oak planking of the deck was cracked and weathered. All along the deck, its crew rushed about in a flurry, all coming up from wherever they were hiding below decks.

By ones and twos, I watched them line up along the railing. They were waiting until they were alongside us before rushing over. I saw the promise of bloodshed etched into every face, staring back at us.

The barc drew closer, evening out and slowing. I gulped around a dry throat, trying to find my breath, my heartbeat, anything to let me know I was still alive. At least for now. This was it? After everything I faced on Wellsmith, this was my end? How... pointless.

I blinked. Then blinked again. I squinted to be sure I was seeing correctly. The faces staring back at us suddenly didn't look murderous, they looked joyful? Warm smiles stretched across the expanse between ships. Several crewmen waved, and two of them held something above their heads, showing it off like a trophy.

I adjusted the glass to get a better view, and sure enough, the pair holding their prize aloft were grinning and dancing, much like the rest of the crew. It was a shark. A fat, freshly caught dogfish.

I closed my eyes as I lowered the spyglass, shaking now for an entirely different reason. "Fish," I blurted out around my choked laughter. "They're fishermen."

Slowly, deliberately, I exhaled the panic that was fleeing just as quickly as it had come. The truth smacked me in the face and left me numb.

I slumped to the deck, my legs finally giving out from under me. My crew greeted the passing fishermen with cheerful waves. The fight was gone from me, and I suddenly wanted to weep, though I wasn't sure if it was relief, lingering fear, or simple exhaustion. Maybe all three.

"Captain," Kaelyn said quietly. She kneeled down next to me to meet my gaze.

Her dark eyes held worry, stubbornness, and fear, but something else as well. Resolve, and perhaps a bit of anger.

I close my eyes and sighed, letting out the last of the breath in my lungs before inhaling deeply. Then, stable and safe in my own thoughts once more, I met her stare again.

"We need to talk," she said.

The galley was dark, lit by only a single lantern swinging from a beam overhead. I was grateful for the deep shadows on my crew's face. Maybe it would hide their disdain when I told them all about who I used to be, and if the Gods were kind, maybe it would hide my embarrassment as well.

I sat at the head of the small wooden table, where we had been gathering for communal meals. Eric, Iain, and Anne had taken seats as well, but Kaelyn was pacing the back wall. Merrik, I noticed, was leaning up against the doorway leading to the storeroom with his arms comfortably crossed. Isaboe stood directly opposite me, eyes locked with mine.

She opened her mouth to start the conversation, then snapped her jaw shut and shook her head. I knew what she was going to say, anyway. Her words from earlier still trailed behind me as persistent as an evening shadow. *We need more than silence from you.*

I took a deep breath and placed both hands on the table, grounding myself with the feel of the wood under my palms.

"I am very smart." Isaboe opened her mouth again, but I shook my head. "No, you wanted me to talk, so right now, you get to listen."

She nodded and slowly took a seat next to Iain.

"Words, numbers, language, *learning* has always come easily to me. Growing up, I read anything and everything I could get my hands on. The only place I ever felt safe was a bookstore. But there's only so much you can learn about the world from reading about it, and I knew the tiny orphanage where I grew up wasn't going to offer me more than what I had. So I left.

"I didn't go far. There's nowhere that's far from anything in Wellsmith. Jassec Krellen found me swapping stories for coin and offered me a job. I didn't need much money, but he offered me what I needed most—a place to stay, new people, and new experiences."

I paused, glancing around. Iain nodded his support while Eric looked thoughtful. Kaelyn stopped pacing and joined Merrik, folding her arms and settling next to him.

"What does any of that have to do with…" Isaboe waved her hand vaguely toward the hatch, somehow encompassing everything between landing in Helm's Point up through my panic attack over the fishermen.

"Krellen was a good boss, as these things go," I continued, ignoring her half-vocalized question. "A ruthless, nasty thug, but ultimately a businessman. I learned a lot from him.

After almost two years of running confidence schemes and booking bets for him, he let me take over the tracking and accounting for his private funds."

"He trusted you," Anne said. Her posture was closed and emotionless. I could only imagine what she thought about the criminal she'd hired on with.

"He did. Which would have been fine, but not everyone supported Krellen's attentions to me. His nephew was jealous, threatened by me or something. When I first joined, his petty bullying was an annoyance, but nothing I couldn't ignore. But over time, he became more and more vicious."

"Tavers," Kaelyn said, almost a question.

"Darl Tavers," I confirmed with a nod. "He's Krellen's nephew. His right-hand man. Even before I joined them, Krellen was grooming him to take over the family business someday, if you could call it a business. Everyone knew the sway he had with his uncle, but it wasn't enough for him. He took every chance he could to hold his successes and my failures against me."

Slowly, while I spoke, Kaelyn and then Merrik joined us at the table. Looking around now, I could see everyone clearly.

"He wasn't the most subtle or intelligent of bullies, and it wasn't long before he stopped trying to hide it. Harsh words turned into shit job assignments, shoves and sneers turned into bruises and broken bones. He never caused me any permanent harm, though. His uncle would have gutted him if I'd been unable to work.

"I wasn't sure how long I would carry on like that, but it didn't matter. Krellen was a rat, and working for him made me learn to shut off the part of my brain that cared. I knew if I dodged Tavers long enough, and made Krellen enough money, I'd be fine."

I sighed. "It wasn't a good life, and it definitely wasn't a comfortable life, but it was what I had. I made the choice to join them and I had to follow through." I offered a weak smile, but pressed on before their looks of discomfort could turn into looks of pity. "It's amazing what people will do when they don't have any other choice, huh?"

Isaboe shook her head slightly, as if looking for her thoughts. "What does that have to do with…" she asked again, quietly confused.

"I saw Darl Tavers in Helm's Point."

I heard a small gasp, but I wasn't sure who it came from. My gaze locked on Isaboe, watching for her reaction. She shook her head again.

"I get that he hurt you, but… Look, Tianna, your reaction up there was not that of someone who was bullied a little while they were younger." Her dark eyes bore into me, searching for the part of my story I was holding back from her. "What happened?"

My gaze dropped back down to the table as more words spilled from me. "Last winter I was working the low docks when me and a few of the guys I was with ran into Mitsuni's boys—that's the rival gang from across the river. We had to run for it. Tavers was with us, and not one to miss an opportunity. He tripped me and left me to Mitsuni's men."

"Shit," Eric muttered under his breath.

I choked out a short laugh. "I managed to knock over a street lantern, which started a small fire. It made enough of a commotion that people poured into the street and I got away, but it was a close call. They nearly…well it doesn't matter." I shuddered. I would not focus on what could have happened. "I made it back to the Rat's Nest just after midnight where Tavers was waiting for me. Before I could report back in, he knocked me out and dragged me into the cellar."

My voice was emotionless as I fought to keep my memories in the past. "When I woke, my hands and feet were bound and I had an old mildewed rag in my mouth. He and two of his bigger cronies took turns kicking, cutting, and groping me. I was never... violated, exactly, but it nearly broke me. Eventually, I was turned loose and when I reported back to Krellen, they blamed it all on Mitsuni."

Silence sat heavily in the room. No one moved, afraid to even breathe too loudly. Anne was the first to speak. "There was nothing you could do? Krellen took their word over yours?"

"What could I have said?" I asked. "'Your golden boy heir tried to kill me and framed your worst enemy for it'? That's almost not even a crime in their world."

"What..." Kaelyn started, then screwed up her face as if her words tasted bad. "What did you do?"

I looked over her shoulder into the shadowy corner of the room rather than at any of them. "I played by the rules. Kept to myself. Kept quiet. I was the perfect little cog in their machine, only giving Krellen reason to praise me, and avoiding Tavers as much as possible. It worked, and life went back to how it was. For about six months, anyway."

I laughed a little to myself, humorless and exhausted.

"I mentioned how Krellen let me take over his personal accounting? That was last spring, a month or so before I met Kaelyn. Mostly, I didn't mind when he was scamming loose change from sailors and extorting the city guard, but I found out he was into far more than I'd ever seen."

I let a wry smile tug at my lips. "Krellen was paying off Epirsan slavers to focus on Mitsuni's side of the river and supplying them with detailed charts of the eastern reef. He even commissioned a Tirican-style warship to smuggle people off the island. I... let's say I reached my limit."

I looked around at the anticipation on the surrounding faces. For the briefest flicker of a moment, I felt pride wash through me. I had them completely caught up in my story. But while I loved knowing I could spin a yarn, I wished that this was wholly fiction, and not my life.

"He hadn't been using his money to do it," I told them. "So, I made copies of the books and sent them to the men Krellen had been 'borrowing' from. Including several wealthy merchants, magistrate's men, even a couple of Mitsuni's lieutenants. They were less than pleased when they found out he was stealing from them.

"It all would have been fine. I wasn't going back to Krellen's compound, and I had a couple of ideas of how to avoid them in the future. But, well, it wasn't a fully thought-out plan."

I took a deep breath and settled into the last bit of my story. "I was making my way to the market row when Tavers caught up to me. His boys took me up to the bluff and knocked me around. I got away, but the only way past them was into the ocean. So I jumped."

There were a couple of gasps this time. Kaelyn just nodded. "Which is where I met you."

I nodded, "Indeed."

"Gods," she muttered.

"And so, when you saw Tavers again…" Isaboe started.

"I panicked."

"Clearly." She huffed out a soft breath and leaned back in her chair, a stunned expression on her face. "Clearly." She breathed out the word again, and this time I got the impression she was referring to something other than my reaction from earlier.

"They tried again," Kaelyn told the rest of the crew. "When we were in Wellsmith, we ran into them."

"That was different. I wasn't expecting to see him here, or anywhere, ever again. I wasn't ready. I... panicked."

"Are you ready now?" Kaelyn asked. "The ship following us this time wasn't Tavers, but the next time? Or the next? If you're right, he will catch up to us again. And then what? Will you fight or panic?"

I shook my head and shrugged. How did I even begin to answer that question? "I don't know."

"You didn't panic when they cornered us outside the tavern," she said, pressing forward. "You fought them then. Why not now?"

"That was different," I said again. A cold, slow-moving fear crept into my consciousness as I remembered that day. I fought to keep myself from shaking again. "W-we had no choice, and we... we..." I closed my eyes and shook my head, reliving the feeling of my blade sinking into the soft flesh of the man I killed.

When I opened my eyes again, the only gaze I could meet, the only question I could answer, was Kaelyn's. "I still have nightmares about that fight. I wasn't ready for– I didn't know it would be like– I didn't..."

"Me either," Kaelyn said quietly. "I was terrified. I'd never been in that kind of fight before."

I blinked at her, surprise washing away my nightmares. "You– but, you... in the fight, your knives–"

She shrugged and looked away. "Street brawls are nothing like dagger fighting in a training yard."

The room fell silent, and I looked around. Each one of my crew was staring down at their laps, or the table, or looking out the tiny porthole window. Anywhere but at each other. As I watched them absorb all the information I'd dumped on them, a sinking feeling hit me.

"Do any of you have combat experience?" I asked.

More silence.

I pushed back from the table and turned to pace the back wall. *What are we even doing out here?*

"I do." The deep voice was quiet, but strong. I turned back to face Merrik as he pushed himself off the wall and stood upright. "Sort of."

"Sort of?" I said, half question, half disbelief.

He gave a curt nod. "I spent time training with the Tirican Navy boys when I was in Boarstown."

"You were in the navy?" I asked at the same time Eric said, "Boarstown?"

"It was before I moved to Anvilcove." Merrik waved off Eric and turned back to me. "And I never said I was in the navy. I said I trained with some of the locals who were. But yes. Never crewed a ship until I met you, but I do know my way around a sword and pistol."

Everyone sat, staring at him. It was probably the most any of us had learned about his past. Although, I can't say I was surprised by the revelation that my adopted brother knew how to fight.

Iain cleared his throat. "Well's all good now. I used t' know a man-o-oars n' sheets back in Tir'Elesa. Day t'dawn, he'd spin yarns round about the trouble on the salt they saw. Didn't pay him much mind til I marked he made more sense than didn't."

I took a moment to parse what he'd just said. "You knew a Tirican sailor who taught you about open-seas combat?"

"Right 'nough, that's th' glib. I knew as a Cap'n read as you wouldn't have a stonewall against parsing the Mother's lingo, aye?" He winked and grinned. "Ship's lad told me more'n ought I'd need or want to know about all things tween th' wales."

"Hmm…" I chewed my bottom lip thoughtfully. Before long, I caught myself breaking into a smile. "I can't say it will help us, but it's better than nothing," I said eventually and turned to the rest of the crew. "I mean, knowledge without experience is kind of our signature move, right?"

Eric and Iain both chuckled. Kaelyn smiled weakly, but I noticed Anne looked pensive. But most alarming of all, Isaboe looked worried. I think I preferred her irritated. This was unsettling.

"Isaboe?" I ventured. "What's got you frowning?"

She pursed her lips and examined me before speaking. "We need to know how to defend ourselves."

Everyone nodded.

"That's a given," I said. "No one wants to die needlessly."

"We're getting pretty good at running, though," Eric said with a dry chuckle. I didn't laugh. Isaboe, damn her, smirked, and I thawed a bit. If they were teasing me, maybe it meant I was forgiven.

"That is my point though," Isaboe continued almost talking over top of everyone else. "We can't keep running from every threat, and we can't pretend we know what we're doing. We need… I don't know." She threw her hands up, wholly impatient. "We need to do better."

"Well," Merrik said when everyone grew silent again. "I don't know a thing about ship-to-ship fighting, but I can teach you how to handle a blade."

The conversation turned to each person's experience and skills with fighting, but I was only half-listening. I stepped back and let Merrik lead the conversation.

Could this work? They were talking about turning us into a fighting force. A combat-ready crew. What would that even mean for us? It sounded good in theory, but we were just merchants, right?

There was an undercurrent here that I couldn't quite pinpoint. The closer I tried to look at it, the less sure I became. Did some of them seem too eager? Or was I too timid?

The questions swirled in my mind as I listened to Merrik catalogue each crewman's strengths and weaknesses.

"What do you think, Captain?" he asked.

I stared at him, trying to catch up with the conversation. I must have had a dumb look on my face because he gave me a half-smile and repeated himself.

"I asked what you thought about us starting up daily weapon's training."

I nodded, fighting back that surge in my gut. "Yes. We need to know how to defend ourselves."

Merrik nodded, and Eric and Kaelyn exchanged grins. It seemed we were doing this then. I just needed to keep my worries out of it. And keep us out of danger until we were ready to test ourselves.

The room fell quiet once more, the meeting seemingly over. As people rose to go back to their duties, Anne spoke.

"Are we just going to ignore the primary issue, then?" She sat up straight in her chair and speared each of us with a glance before settling her gaze on me.

No one answered her. I watched her silently until she sighed. She shook her head, both irritated and pitying, as if we had forgotten our own names.

"This ship and this crew were hired by my father and myself to conduct a trade mission around the Outer Isles." Everyone nodded. We hadn't forgotten that part.

"While I am not opposed to us defending ourselves from pirates, slavers, or even old enemies, it seems that I am in position of reminding you that such aggressions were not part of the agreement. I cannot sit by and let anyone make the unilateral decision to turn the Siren into a warship."

I crossed my arms. It was a self-comforting move, but in hindsight, it might have come across as combative.

Anne arched an aggressive eyebrow at me, daring me to argue with her.

"No one is turning this into a warship," I said. "We are simply trying to do the best we can do to survive. Protecting you is part of the job as well, isn't it?"

Anne nodded sagely. "It most certainly is. But that doesn't address the concern."

"Which is?"

Anne stood. "Your actions, and subsequent inactions, your reticence and even communication with us, has not been in line with the actions of a leader."

"What?" I pushed to my feet, stunned by her accusation.

"She said you haven't been talking to us and that's not leadership," Eric helpfully supplied.

"Yes, I got that. Thank you." I glared at him, then turning to the whole crew. "Is that what you all think?"

No one answered, but I could see by their uncomfortable grimaces that more than a few of them were in agreement. "I see."

"Look, Tianna," Kaelyn spoke up. "We're not saying you can't do the job, only that you haven't been. We named you Captain for a reason, and we plan to stick by it. We just want you to include us in the decision-making process."

"The decision-making process? And how do I do that? Start asking permission before I issue orders?" I asked letting sarcasm drip into my tone.

"Yes," Isaboe answered me.

I blinked and turned to face her. "You want to run the ship by democracy? Majority vote on where we go, what we trade, who takes what duty? Are we going to draw lots for watch rotations?"

She glared at me, clearly over my petulance. "You need to make the calls on 'how', 'where', and 'when'. We just want a voice in the 'why'," she said. "No one is better at logistics than you, but let us in on the plan."

That made more sense than I wanted it to. I leaned forward, gripping the back of the chair I was standing behind. Was that what I had been doing? Making plans and keeping them to myself? Gods, what would they think if they realized I didn't have any plans at all? Maybe... maybe if I opened up to them and started a conversation about 'why', maybe we could all come up with a plan. Maybe I–maybe *we* wouldn't be flying blind any more.

I looked around the room again, trying to read each person before me. With a jolt that nearly knocked me off my feet, I realized there was not a single person at this table that I didn't trust. We'd fought alongside each other, we'd fought with each other, argued and reconciled. We'd bonded. They knew how I think. They knew what I was capable of. My strengths, my quirks. Now they knew about my past as well. And somehow, miraculously, they still wanted to follow me. They trusted me to lead them, and I trusted them to back me up.

"Alright," I said. "I can't promise that I won't make unilateral decision in the heat of the moment, but if you all can follow my orders when needed, I will do my best to let you know what I'm thinking and why I'm making the calls I do."

I was answered by nods all around.

"Kaelyn, as First Mate, your job is to make sure those orders are followed, even when you don't necessarily agree with them. If you have any, you come to me separately with your concerns. Can you do that?"

"Aye, Captain," she answered with a grin.

"Isaboe." She looked at me. "As boatswain, I need you to tell me when there's something wrong with the Siren herself. I don't know how to keep her up or what goes into maintenance, so you'll need to explain it to me, not just hand me reports."

"Aye, Captain," she answered.

I turned to the person now standing at her side. "Merrik, honestly, your job is the hardest. On top of tracking our stores and making sure we are well-supplied, it's now your duty to train the crew to fight. Which means building and maintaining our armory as well. Can you handle it?"

His grin practically was wolfish as he replied, "Aye aye, Chief. Though what does that make me? 'Quartermaster in Charge of Fighting' doesn't roll off the tongue, does it?"

I laughed and shook my head, matching his grin. "What do you think of 'Quartermaster at Arms?'"

His eyes glinted, and he nodded. "Aye, Captain. It'll do." He turned and eyed Eric and Iain. "Little help with the guns and ammunition?"

"Happily," Eric agreed. Iain nodded.

"What do the rest of you think?" I glanced around the room again. The answering grins told me everything I needed to know. Step by tiny, hesitant step, we were slowly becoming a real crew.

Now I just needed to make sure I was a worthy captain, or this was all going to blow up in my face.

CHAPTER THIRTEEN

There are only three cities in the Outer Isles large enough to rightly be called a city. Most were small or moderate-sized towns with a few thousand inhabitants. There were villages, townships, and even just places where a few families found a flat piece of land and built some houses near each other.

Hook Island probably had dozens of these little hamlets along the coast between Angle Bay and Castaway, and that didn't include the uncounted homesteads, farms, and villages further inland.

Angle Bay, however, boasted a population more like to rival Sunset or even Anvilcove. It had more land area to spread out over, though, and happily took advantage of this fact with sprawling farms and orchards just outside the city walls. Since their chief exports were fresh produce, livestock, and dyes, I still had a sliver of hope that we would be able to get a decent trade here.

Six days since my abrupt flight from Helm's Point, and Isaboe hadn't let me forget we were still carrying the textiles meant for the fishermen there.

Five days of me explaining myself and grovelling for the crew's forgiveness. Silently, of course. I still had to prove to them they could trust me to lead, and I couldn't do that if I was apologizing for every little thing. I had to trust in my decisions or they never would.

Four days of me pretending I could handle this.

THE PIRATE HORDE   225

Iain must have heard the deep sigh that escaped from me as we tied off at the inner harbor. He looked at me with a crooked smile.

"Oyi, Cap. Ya bellyin' for a snakebite in th' afternoon, or this more a natty gambol?"

"Neither?" I said, then shrugged. "Or maybe both. I'm just thinking."

"A nastier way'n th' pigseye," he replied with a laugh.

I was growing used to his colorful turns of phrase, and it was taking me less and less time to dissect his sentences. "Yeah, yeah, I know." Assuming I was right that he meant to tease me about my 'bad habit' of thinking, I waved him off. "Don't mind me. We've much to do, and it's a lovely day. I'll save my nasty habits for another time."

He laughed heartily and walked off to finish settling us in to port.

"Alright, folks and fellows," I said as everyone gathered around. I was starting to enjoy the way we would have these mini-meetings before splitting up. "Merrik, you'll be in charge of this trade. We'll be able to find cheap foodstuffs here, so try to resupply what we need most. But keep it budget-friendly. We need the best deal you can manage on trade goods too if we hope to turn a profit when we finally hit Farwind."

"Sure thing, Chief. Anything specific you want me to keep an eye to?"

I shrugged. "Anyone know what's best here? I only have passing knowledge of the regular exports of each island, so you might have to sniff around a bit. Chat up some locals. Think you can handle that?"

Merrik broke out in an esurient grin. "Sounds like fun." With a musing purse to his lips, he turned to Isaboe. "Feel like a hunting trip?"

Her grin matched Merrik's for intensity. "Oh, yes." She clapped her hands together gleefully.

"You do know this is just a trade, right?" I asked them nervously. "I mean, you won't actually be… hunting."

Everyone laughed, which I admit was a pleasant sound after the last several days of tension amongst the crew.

"Aye, Captain," Isaboe said. "I promise, no hunting people. Only good deals."

I chuckled nervously. "Alright, good."

"Anne," I turned to the next in line. "Why don't you–"

She shuffled self-consciously before meeting my gaze. "If it's no problem to you, Captain, I would like to get away for a bit. See the sights. Maybe just… be elsewhere.

I nodded, my gaze dropping down to examine the sanded boards under our feet. She was right to ask. I know she was. In fact, it surprised me that more of the crew wasn't asking to get away from me.

"That's fine. In fact, why don't the rest of you take off, too? Enjoy a day of liberty. I'll stay aboard."

Silence fell in our little corner of the dock. When it carried on longer than a simple conversational pause, I looked up. Six friendly faces shifted, not meeting my gaze.

Eric cleared his throat. "Actually, Cap'n, why don't you take off for a bit? See the island, meet some people who aren't just us. Iain and I will stay aboard."

I hesitated. "Are you… kicking me off my own ship?"

"Our ship," Isaboe corrected me.

I was about to argue that wasn't technically true since I held the deed, but a tiny voice in my head that I really should listen to more often told me that would just lead to a fight we didn't need right now. Instead, I ignored her comment and glanced at each of the others.

"Right. Well, good. Okay. Thank you."

Kaelyn offered me a supportive smile. "Why don't I go with you? I'm sure we can find a good way to kill some time."

"Alright then, shoo. Off with you. Let's go enjoy what it is that Angle Bay has to offer." I waved, pushing everyone toward the gangplank before following at my own pace.

The streets of Angle Bay were aptly eponymous with the town itself. Three main roads divided the main parts of the city into neat little districts. The road from the docks up into the center of town ran west, inland toward the market square, where it bisected another major thoroughfare that headed north and south into the center of town and down along the beach to the industrial district.

The market itself was a wide intersection where all the main roads and several of the side streets met. There was a wide open plaza, lined on all sides by two- and three-story buildings with brightly colored signs and placards hanging whereever they could be seen. Carts, tents, and stalls found places to wedge themselves in near the busy streets where merchants could hawk all manner of wares. And in the center of it all was a large, covered well. One of two which the city of Angle Bay boasted.

We aren't omniscient—all of this information was available thanks to a post-board at the eastern edge of the market square. It was nearly half-again as tall as me, with an intricate and detailed map showing us everything we might need to know, from the location of the second well, the best route to city hall, and several smaller notices posted about, announcing sales and exchanging gossip.

It was quite efficient.

"Wow," I said as we stood there examining it. "Hmm, where shall we go?"

Kaelyn glanced up and down both streets and around the square. "Want to just go for a walk?"

I let out a sigh of relief, surprising us both. The last few days had left me so wound up. I hadn't noticed how badly I needed the time off until the promise of nothing dangled in front of me. There were no duties to attend, no crew to supervise, no decisions to make or second-guess. I only had to enjoy the afternoon and get back to the ship this evening to regroup with the crew.

I smiled at Kaelyn. My first proper smile in what felt like months, even though I knew that wasn't true. "Let's go."

We walked north, following the main road into a smaller town square, similar to the one that housed the market. Instead of the patched plaster and paint that covered the much-used buildings, these here were larger and made of kept stone and wood. I would call it the 'upper district', or 'nice part of town' if not for the utilitarian feel of it.

The second well stood proudly in front of the largest of the buildings. It was a stone edifice that rose four stories above street level and took most of the length of the plaza. Guards in matching blue and gray uniforms stood a bored but attentive watch over the door.

I tapped Kaelyn on the shoulder and nodded her down a side street. "Let's avoid city hall. We've nothing to worry over, but I'm not sure I want the guard's attention on us for any reason. Even just passing through."

"Expecting trouble?" she asked.

"No, but even if all they do is mire us in paperwork, I don't want to go asking for it. Let's head this way."

She followed down the way I'd indicated, and we walked in silence a little longer.

"You've been tense," she said, out of the blue.

"I suppose." I eyed her. "You know why, though."

"Of course I do, but this is more… I don't know. You've been pulling back from the crew."

I sighed again. Until this moment I hadn't realized that's what I was doing, but of course she was right. Kaelyn was always right. Eventually, I would remember that. "I don't mean to be," I admitted quietly.

She shrugged one shoulder, still looking ahead. "Then don't," she said, as if it were the simplest thing in the world. As if opening up to another person—let alone six other people—was as easy as trying on a new pair of boots.

It wasn't enough for me to know that she was right. For all my grand speeches about trusting the crew more and bringing them in on discussions and the decision-making process, I had yet to actually do that.

"I'm just feeling unsettled," I admitted finally. "This is all happening so fast, and yet at the same time, not fast at all, you know?"

Kaelyn nodded, but let me continue.

"Two months ago, I was a nobody orphan living in a rotting carriage house doing odd jobs and running with lowlifes in the bottom end of nowhere. Literally a forgotten child of the forgotten city of Tirica Denisi.

"And now I'm what? A sea captain? Leader of a crew? I've never had to decide anything more complicated than when to eat, and now I have so much responsibility." I let out another heavy sigh, noticing that every time I did, I felt a little lighter.

"You're up for it, though," Kaelyn said firmly.

We reached the end of the road at a t-intersection. The road to our right ran up around the back of city hall and out of the towering gates to the mainland homesteads of Hook Island. Left, wound back down past the market and toward the docks. We paused, looking both directions. Inland, to a staid, simple life, or back to the Siren and the open ocean. The metaphor of this crossroads was not lost on me.

"Yes, I'm up for it. But I've been Captain only a few weeks and I've already led us into trouble once. I just don't know what I'd do if I let you all down again." I looked up toward the city gates. "What if I make the wrong choice?"

Kaelyn turned to me and placed a reassuring and firm hand on my shoulder. She made sure she caught my eye before she said, "Then you stick with it, and see it through. You can't lead by standing still."

I closed my eyes for a moment, letting that sink in. The only way forward was to move. With a thin laugh, I turned left, and we started off again.

"Think the crew will forgive me for hesitating?" I asked, more casually than I felt.

"Just give them a little time. We're all as new to this as you are, remember?"

"Right. I keep forgetting that, don't I?"

Kaelyn laughed. "There are worse things to forget. Like, who we are, where we come from, what we love."

I paused again. "You are really philosophical today. Is there something on your mind?"

She shrugged lightly, trying to brush it off. "Not really. Maybe I just needed to get out and away from the ship as much as anyone."

"Well, not anyone," I said lightly. "Anne couldn't get away from me fast enough."

Kaelyn rolled her eyes. "I'm sure that wasn't personal. She hasn't really bonded with anyone on the crew. This isn't even the first time she went off on her own, remember? You were busy in Nestford, but she practically bullied Isaboe into taking the first watch so she could go out."

I shook my head and came to a stop. "Then I hope she learns to trust us a bit more, too. I like her, and it would be great if she came to like us."

Something caught my eye, and we came to a stop. A painted door led to a thin building that was sandwiched between its neighbors. I would have missed it, or dismissed it as someone's house, if it hadn't been for the neatly carved book painted bright red on the green door.

"Is this a bookshop?" My eyes and smile opened wide, doing nothing to contain my glee.

Kaelyn lit up at the adventure. "Shall we find out?"

As soon as I stepped inside, I felt my muscles unclench. Tightness that I'd been carrying for weeks flowed away from me like a leaf in a heavy rain. The smell of treated linen paper, dyed leather and cloth, and just the faintest hint of dust and wheat paste...

I sighed with pleasure. "Thank the god of scribes that some things never change."

The room wasn't large, and it was deeper than it was wide. A large stone hearth sat directly opposite the door with a cheery fire burning in it. A pair of tall-backed chairs sat on either side, offering a welcome place to sit and read. The soft mellow tones of a guitar was playing somewhere beyond a door in the back.

I reverently trailed my fingers over leather and cloth-covered spines, scanning titles as I walked. *Travels Through Irsa*, *The Native Habits of Kurkurani Wilders*, and *The Last Winters of Vindanlund* stood out, but it didn't take long for me to notice a trend.

"Excuse me," I called out, looking for an attendant or shopkeeper. The music stopped and a moment later, a young man popped his head out of the door. Light brown hair hung loose and shaggy across his brow, just barely staying out of his eyes. He wore a clean linen shirt, and definitely looked like a bookstore was his native habitat. Then again, it was mine too, and I hardly looked the part these days.

He blinked at us twice before seeming to realize he was actually looking at customers. "Oh!" He rushed over to us, looking excitedly disheveled. "Welcome to Bann's Books!" he glanced at Kaelyn with a lingering smile. "Let me know if I can help you with anything at all."

She stifled a laugh and pretended to be looking over a book of Tirican maps.

"These all seem to be travel guides," I said.

"That's right," the man replied with a widening grin. "Best selection of travel guides, travelogues, histories, politicies, and atlas...es available."

"I don't see anything here on the Outer Isles," Kaelyn commented.

He scoffed. "No, you wouldn't, though, would you? As soon as someone writes a halfway decent one, I'll be sure t' stock it. In the meantime, you might try just askin' the locals whatever it is you want to know."

I pursed my lips, trying not to smirk at his sarcastic tone. Kaelyn grumbled and turned back to browsing.

"Do you have any novels?" I asked.

His eyes went wide as if I'd asked for the sacred Book of Kings from off the throne of Meket itself. He sputtered several times before finding his words.

"No! What? No! Why would we– what would– why would we even…" He trailed off, eyeing me suspiciously. "Oh," he said with a great sigh of relief. "You're joking, aren't you? Lida always tells me I have no sense of humor. I should have seen that." He laughed awkwardly. "Good one."

I didn't know whether to raise my eyebrows, scrunch my nose, or bite my lip so ended up doing all three. All I could hope was that it came across as if I was trying not to laugh at him. To be fair, I was trying not to laugh at him, though probably not for the reasons he would think.

"Yes, well." I turned back to the bookshelf nearest to where I was standing. "I was actually wondering if you have anything on ancient Anaxian architecture? Something by Memnirnus or the poet Usid, maybe?"

His eyes lit up. "Oh, a real fan of the classics!" He squealed excitedly before spinning around and running off. "I have a rare selection on classical antiquities and the evolution of column structures. You're just going t' love it!"

I stifled another laugh and followed him across the room. He quickly shoved three books into my open arms, happily chatting away about the merits of imperial stone roads versus modern cobblestone.

I picked one of the three at random and smiled at him. "This looks great. How much do you want for it?"

He waved me off. "For a fellow scholar, I'm sure I can come up with a great discount. Hold on." He fled back the way he came through the door in the back wall before I had a chance to say anything further.

As soon as he was out of earshot, Kaelyn let out a full-throated laugh. "You find the best people," she said to me. "I'll never get sick of traveling with you."

I turned and winked at her. "You'd better not. I happen to like your company."

The excitable shopkeeper returned in short order. He sidled up to me with a conspiratorial little smile and said, "I can let it go for five, but don't you dare come back here an' tell me it's no good."

I lifted a hand to my chest and mimicked a shocked gasp. "I know you wouldn't be asking me to give anything but an honest review!"

The poor man looked like I had kicked his puppy. "Oh, no! No, no, no. I would never suggest that, would I? Oh, th' nibs end. Never that!"

The laugh finally escaped me, and I smiled at him.

"Oh," he said. "You're teasing me again."

I smiled warmly. "I am. No hard feelings, friend. I promise to do right by you and, uh..." I glanced down at the cover of the book in my hand. "Master G.P. Blake, whoever he is."

The shopkeeper smiled so widely that I thought for sure his jaw was about to fall off. I'm not sure how I did it, but I seemed to have made this man's day. With another smile, I fished five pieces out of my pocket and counted them out to him.

With one last smile and a wave, Kaelyn and I left the store, poorer but lighter of spirit than we were before.

"What now?" Kaelyn asked, not bothering to keep the mirth from her voice.

I glanced around quickly, looking for inspiration. We were not far off the market square, and my stomach was beginning to make its emptiness felt.

"Lunch?" I suggested. "There's a tavern or inn nearby, for sure."

She laughed. "Sounds great, though I hope you aren't too hungry. You just spent your stipend on a book you don't plan to read."

"Oh, I have every intention of reading it," I told her earnestly. "I just make no promises about a review."

Laughing, we made our way up the road to see if we could find somewhere to eat. The tavern was not far and was, in fact, just off the main square of the market. It was a little early in the day yet for lunch. A few people sat in chairs, scattered around rows of round tables, mostly nursing mugs of something sour or bowed over bowls of something thick. No one made eye contact, or even bothered to look up when we came in.

Kaelyn and I found a table and even before we'd sat, an older woman came up to us. "Happy day fellows, and welcome to th' Bear Cub Tavern. What can I get for ye?" She sounded like she was fighting to stay positive and I thought I saw her stifle a yawn.

I looked around the room at the morose patrons, still minding their own business. Now, normally, I wouldn't take to heart people enjoying a bit of solitude, but it was quieter than a holy minister's tomb.

"We just came in for a quick something to fill our empty bellies, but now I'm wondering if we missed some tragic announcement. Did something happen?"

The waitress shook her head, strawberry blonde hair flying loosely around her tired face. "Not so far as they've told me. Jus', no one seems in th' mood t' be chatting much."

"Is that normal?" Kaelyn asked. Then quickly added, "We're not from around here, but most everyone seems really friendly. It's surprising to find it so... sober."

That nearly had the older woman cracking a smile. "Aye, sober in a tavern don't sit right, does it?"

I smiled with her, adding a mischievous twinkle that I hoped she would find charming.

"Maybe we can help?" I offered.

The waitress cocked a brow at us, looking both curious and measuring. "What do you have in mind?"

I glanced at Kaelyn with a grin edging its way onto my face. I whistled a couple of notes under my breath, and she caught on before I could get past the first measure of the song. Her wink was all the encouragement I needed.

I leaned back in my chair and propped my leg up on the table. I slid my hand into the cuff of my boot, and pulled out a small flute, then nodded to a raised dais across the room. "That a stage, there?"

The woman's eyes lit up, then almost as quickly grew dark and suspicious again. "You any good?"

"Good enough for a meal, I hope." The smile I gave her was meant to be friendly and reassuring but when I think back on it, it might have come across as a tad cocky and flirtatious. I blame my posture and the way I was still spread out across the table.

She raised her eyebrow again, giving me time to back down. Then she smiled and nodded. "Guess we'll find out." She waved us over to the stage and retreated to the kitchen.

The patrons continued to ignore our presence even as Kaelyn and I pulled chairs up on stage.

"Wishing Merrik were here," I whispered to her. "Think you can manage some percussion without him?"

Kaelyn shrugged, much the same way the waitress had. "Guess we'll find out," she said, then gave a wink.

She sat back in the chair, looking for all the world like she was settling in to watch me perform. I tried to take my cue off of her casual attitude, hoping we would look like we'd done this before.

I spun my chair around so that the back was facing the audience, and sat facing outward with my legs on either side. I rested my arms on the back of the chair and brought the flute to my lips.

The first few notes were long and sweet, moving from one low pitch to another major step away. It was just enough to draw the attention of the room, but nothing too sudden. I held the fifth piercing high note for two beats, three, four… then I winked at Kaelyn and gave her a quick nod before launching into a faster reel.

Alternating beats of straight quarter notes interspersed with playful eighths lit up the room. As if reading my mind, Kaelyn jumped in with the rhythm.

She started with a simple foot stomp, tapping her boot on the downbeat as I played. I moved into the next stanza and she followed right along, adding in body percussion where she could. She clapped, stomped, patted her thighs, and even snapped as the beat moved her.

We were riding the same melody. When I moved into the last turning, she let out a whistling tune that countered the notes from my flute. I swear, if I'd had any way to preserve what we were doing, I would have. Magic happened in music, and always when I was without a pen to write it down for later.

At first, the customers continued to ignore us, but as we got into it, our enthusiasm found its way out into the dining room. On our third song, I passed the flute to Kaelyn, and took my turn with percussion, tapping out a beat with the chair as more people filtered into the room.

"At least enough for a meal," our hostess said when we paused for a break. I grinned, and we ate a few bites before launching into another set.

I'm not sure how long we carried on that way, trading instruments back and forth, following whatever whim carried us. Kaelyn sang out one of our favorite ballads while I played counter-melody. I led the crowd in a round of rowdy drinking songs, and soon every fear, anxiety, and doubt of the last few days fell away until there was only us and the smiling, cheerful tavern guests.

Looking at the matching smile on Kaelyn's face, I knew she needed this at least as much as I did. And for the first time since I'd left Anvilcove, I felt like myself again. Not Tianna, Krellen's bookie, not Tianna, Taver's whipping post, not Tianna the orphan, not even Captain Blackboot, but something that was somehow all of those things, and none of them.

For those few hours in a small, empty tavern in Angle Bay, I got to be the Tianna the storyteller, musician, and friend. I got to be the Tianna Blackboot I wanted to be, and feel a bit of what my life could be like, if I let it.

For the first time, just for a little while, I got to be me.

CHAPTER FOURTEEN

We stayed in Angle Bay for two days and nights. I rotated the crew out on shifts so that everyone got a chance to sleep on solid ground again. By the time we left, everyone—myself included—seemed to be in much better spirits.

Heading south along the coast of Hook Island was a pleasure cruise at this time of year. The winds were favorable, and the weather held steady. It remained dry and cool until long after the cape was fading from view.

I was just outside my cabin, enjoying a breather, when a shadow fell across the deck at my feet. I looked up to see Merrik standing there, waiting for me to notice him. His curly hair was loose in the wind, and he wore his vest open over a plain shirt. He looked determined, rather than annoyed, so at least I knew I wasn't in trouble.

"Heya, boss," he said as he drew nearer.

"Heya, *kashi*," I replied, matching his tone.

"Still with that? You do know I'm not that much younger than you, yeah?"

"Of course, I know that," I said. "You do know that 'little brother' is a term of endearment, yeah?"

He shook his head, but I notice the small smile he tried to hide. He held up a gray slate with chalk marks all over it, effectively changing the subject. "I've worked out a training schedule."

I took the tablet and looked over his plans.

"I thought we could start simple, with a two on-two off rotating shift, hand-to-hand, close-quarters, and basic sword skills. If that goes well, we can talk to Eric about adding in some marksmanship. Course, then we'd have to see about finding guns for everyone, and that might get expensive."

I nodded, pretending I knew what most of that meant. "Why two on-off?"

"Training in shifts will give everyone time to train and time to rest without wasting much time. Also, then we can still have some crew working the ship, unless you want to find somewhere to anchor and go all in."

"That's not the worst idea. Port would be distracting, but what if we found sheltered moorage..." I scanned the horizon as if I could see all the way across the Mervast. "There, amongst the shoals?"

He looked as if he was torn between a nod and a shrug and ended up doing both. "That could work. We can drill as a group and do three on-off training, then. I want you and Kaelyn on different teams, though."

"Oh, I see," I said, catching the glint in his eye. "Trying to draw out our competitive sides. Betting we'll train harder if we're going head-to-head?"

"Well." He dragged out the word slowly then grinned. "That, and it will be more fun for me watching you two go head-to-head."

I punched him in the shoulder, which only made him laugh even harder.

"That's all you've got?" he said. "We definitely need to get started on the hand-to-hand training."

"Brat," I muttered, not fully under my breath. "Alright then, do whatever you need to. I'm trusting you handle the details with this. Let me know when you see improvement, though. I think I want to add in some sailing drills if we're going to be at anchor, anyway."

"Works for me. Not sure how long we'll be out here then. I'll have to retake stock of our supplies if we plan out being away more'n a month."

"A month?" I squeaked. I blinked several times, trying to get my eyes to stop being the size of dinner plates. "Why so long?"

"Uhh, because I'm instilling new skills in six untrained baby fighters?" He said, as if I was missing the entire lesson. He paused, then shook his head and continued.

"Tianna, you know this isn't just a matter of showing you how to hold a sword, right? There's balance, technique, how to think and move under pressure, how and where to hit someone to disable as opposed to kill. Not to mention basic conditioning before you're even in shape to handle any of that."

"We're in great shape!" I protested. "Everyone here pulls their weight and more."

He gave me that look again. The one that said I was being far-too naïve for my seventeen years.

"It's not like we're sitting idle on some Lugaian pleasure beach," I muttered.

"This is a different kind of skill," he said simply, then eyed me mischievously. "Want to make a bet on it?"

"Not really? I think it's safe to say you know more than I do here. I'm just choosing to have more faith in our crew's abilities than you seem to have."

He laughed and started walking off.

"It's just a few wind sprints, right?" I called after him. "How hard can it be?"

The next day, I had my answer to that question along with four hateful glares.

"Did you really have to challenge him?" Kaelyn asked between panting breaths. We stopped jogging on our fifth lap of the upper deck, halfway through our so-called 'warm up.' She bent over at the hips and rested her hands on her knees, trying to catch her breath.

It turns out Merrik may have known what he was talking about. We were all winded, red, and sweating, even in the early summer breeze. All of us except Iain, who looked as if he'd just woken from a long refreshing nap.

Iain bounced on his toes, shaking out some spare energy. "Just th' thing to get th' inner workings goin', ya? Get th' fire flowing in th' blood somehow," he said.

"What are you made of?" Isaboe whined.

"Eh, sheepskins, sallow ale, and bunker biscuits, mostly," Iain replied with a cheeky grin.

Eric shook his head. "Farm boys," he muttered under his breath. He laughed, but it soon turned into a raking cough as he fought to breathe.

"Alright, mateys!" Merrik called our attention back to where he stood. "We ready for more?"

"Oh, what now!? You were right, okay? Conditioning is important, but for the love of all human gods, give us a damn minute!" I cried, and I do mean cried. Real tears mixed with the sweat on my face.

"Sorry, Captain," he said. "You let me lead this dance, so just do your best to follow along, aye?" He gave me an evil grin that made me regret ever giving him any authority at all. Of course, it also calmed my fears at the same time.

Merrik may have been a mean bastard when he was in charge, but I knew he wouldn't do anything to harm this ship or crew. Just then, that trust was all that was keeping me going.

"Team up," he said. "Time for group training."

With a general grumble from the lot of us, we did just that. Eric, Anne, and Kaelyn walked off to the far side of the deck, while Isaboe and Iain joined me where I was standing. Merrik turned to Kaelyn's group first, giving us a brief respite, which I was happy to take.

I bent and grabbed the canteen that I'd left near the base of the mizzenmast and took a healthy drink of water, then passed another to Isaboe. I watched and listened as Merrik showed them a simple step and punch move, then set them to work practicing.

"You three," he said, turning to point at us. "I hope you were watching, because you'll be on the receiving end of those punches in a few minutes."

Isaboe squared her shoulders at the implied challenge and I smiled faintly. If I'd learned anything at all from my years in Wellsmith, it was how to take a punch.

As if sensing my thought, Merrik locked eyes with me and raised one eyebrow. "Keep in mind, I will teach you how to minimize the damage of any hit you do take, but the goal of this exercise is to avoid being hit in the first place. Like this."

He executed a quick ducking and shifting move a few times before he set us to trying it. It was a little awkward at first, but I soon got the hang of shifting my weight around the way he wanted. After a quarter-hour of practicing that move and a few others he showed us, he called us all back together.

"Alright, pair off. I want to see where we're at with this."

I wasn't kidding about that competitive streak. As soon as we had separated into two teams of three, Kaelyn and I had become unofficial team leads, and we both stepped up first. The rest of them made a semicircle around us as we faced off.

At first, I just watched her footwork, waiting for her to strike. She hesitated, unsure of throwing the first punch, but I could almost see the moment she remembered that was the point of this exercise. She feinted left, and then swung in close with her right fist, aiming for center mass.

Just like Merrik had shown us, I tried to duck but I was too slow and dove into her oncoming punch. I grunted and stumbled back, and Kaelyn's fist connected solidly with my jaw. I dropped backward on the deck, stunned.

"Oh, shit, Tianna." She gasped and ran over to me. "Are you alright?"

I made some kind of groan in the affirmative and tried to sit up. Merrik walked over wearing his ever-present smirk and looked down at me. "And that, folks, is why we practice. If this were real combat, we'd be short one captain now."

The crew all offered jokes and gentle ribbing at how easily I was taken down, but I felt a shift in them. Merrik's point rang true. As much as we wanted to play at this being a grand lark, none of us were ready to face the realities of combat. This wasn't a game, and it was time we stopped acting like it was.

Training became our all-consuming routine. For the first time, we ate, slept, and moved together. Running and bodyweight training in the mornings followed up another short warm up run and combat skills after lunch. The only break we took was after meals, when the crew separated long enough to attend regular ship's duties. It was a hard and intense pace that we weren't used to, but this was also a chance to slow down and connect as a group.

Merrik had insisted we stay close enough to civilization that we could seek help in case of training accidents, but I didn't feel right leaving the ship floating unattended where we were most likely to be found. And so we compromised.

We had found a small fishing village tucked away deep in the reef on a patch of land barely large enough to be called an island, and dropped anchor not far from there.

Daily training was hard work. We broke ourselves every day then woke up and did it again, but in many ways, it was everything I'd ever wanted. Companionship, shared toil, a chance to form bonds—for those three weeks aboard the Siren, life was perfect.

On the morning of the first week of the last month of summer, I decided to mix things up a bit.

"Good morning, friends! How are we on this lovely day?"

Five pairs of eyes turned and looked at me suspiciously, and one pair of blue-green eyes watched me in amusement. We had all gathered on the main deck as we have been for our morning run.

"We're fine, Cap'n, same as always," Eric said slowly.

I grinned at the note of hesitation in his voice, then clapped my hands together and walked over to Merrik. "Sorry, QMA, I'm taking over training this morning."

The crew erupted, trying to talk over top of each other.

"But you can't fight," Isaboe said.

"QMA?" Eric asked.

Merrik scoffed. "You're taking over?"

"Quarter Master at Arms. I shortened it. Easier, right?" I said, answering Eric. I ignored Isaboe and turned back to Merrik. "It's been a month. As we discussed, I think it's time for a drill."

I looked around at my crew, who were still all eyeing me with varying levels of suspicion.

Sighing, I shook my head. "Alright, let me explain. The skills we have been learning with Merrik are good—helpful and beneficial to be sure—but we won't know how much we've learned until we try to put it all together, aye?"

A couple of them softened and a few others nodded.

"Up until now, we have been learning the finer points of sailing as we go, and while we all seem to have the basics down, I have noticed we all gravitate toward the roles and jobs we are most comfortable with, aye?"

A few more nods met my pause this time. I loved it when I could see them coming around. I felt mighty—like I could actually do this.

"Well, it's time for some cross-training. Merrik." I turned back to him with what I hoped was a supportive smile. "I want you to man the helm."

He sputtered, looking for words, before turning it into a cough. "Sure thing, Captain. Whatever you say." As I turned to meet Kaelyn's gaze, I heard him mutter, "Not my fault if we need a new ship after this."

I pretended I didn't hear it and moved on. "Kaelyn, Iain, I'd like you both on the main sails. Eric, Isaboe, on the mizzen."

An unenthusiastic round of agreement circled the space as I turned to Anne. "You'll be on the deck with me. Since you have the most sailing experience, I want you watching everyone. Take note of everything so we can see where we still need improvement."

I took a step back so I could address at the group as a whole. "I know this is not what we're used to, and I don't expect perfection from any of us. Yes, 'us'. I know my rope handling leaves a lot to be desired."

Kaelyn and Iain both snickered, no doubt recalling too many times they've had to unravel my attempts at sailor's bend knots.

"We are all here to learn and grow together. We will rely on each other's strengths, and shore up each other's weaknesses. Stronger together, aye?"

'Aye!' and 'Aye, Captain' came almost at once from all six of them. I smiled and clapped my hands, rubbing them together gleefully.

"Excellent. Then, let's get that anchor up, then see what we see."

I turned and started walking toward center deck when a loud, piercing sound rang out behind me. I wheeled around to see Isaboe holding a tiny whistle to her lips. She emitted a series of short, sharp notes, before lowering her hand to grin at me.

"What is that?" I asked her.

She held up something small and thin, with a rounded bulb at the end. It's silver finish glinted in the sun as it hung from a brained rope around her wrist. "It's a boatswains pipe. I picked it up in Angle Bay."

"A what?"

"A boatswain's pipe," she repeated slowly. "It's used for signaling basic orders to the crew so Kaelyn doesn't have to shout all the time."

I shook my head, seeing a fight coming I didn't want to have just then. Or possibly ever. "Okay, yes. Well… let's leave that for now. We'll, uh, find some time to learn the signals. But, sailing drills first."

She shrugged, tucked the pipe into a small vest pocket, and ran off to her station. I made a mental note to find time for a crash course in whistle calls and returned to the task at hand.

It was only the work of moments for the seven of us to raise the anchor and stow the cable. The tide here was slow, little current to fight, and with the sails still fully reefed, we barely drifted. We had learned a lot since Kaelyn and I huddled together aboard the Naked Chicken, learning to splice lines.

I waved to Merrik and he nodded, running off to take the wheel. I could see the consternation cross his face as he tried to decide where best to place his hands, and I forced myself to look away so as not to laugh.

"Kaelyn," I said, meeting her gaze. "I'll be letting Anne lead this one." I hoped she would see my intention in this, and not take it as any kind of slight. The last thing I wanted was an angry first mate.

She nodded, swallowing the temporary demotion without comment, and I breathed a little easier.

"Crew to general quarters!" Anne called out, even though they were all standing within a few feet of her. They wasted no time scampering off to their new stations.

I stayed on the deck, handling the mast cables along with Anne. I watched Kaelyn and Iain climb the mainmast rig to the first yard, knowing Eric and Isaboe would be doing the same behind me on the mizzen.

"Prepare to set the lower topsails!" Anne called from her place on the deck.

Despite their hesitation, everyone aboard seemed to know their duties and worked well together. They exectuted their tasks—while not necessarily with precision—with passion and moderate skill.

Before long, we were moving along slowly. Small islands dotted the landscape on either side of the ship as we sailed forward, further into the shoals. There was one deep channel that ran the length of the reef, but Merrik should have already been aware of it. Despite his protestations, I knew he could handle the Siren through her courses. Imagine my surprise when he proved me right.

As we carried on, dodging heavy rocks and dangerous detritus, I notice a lessening tension throughout the ship. I knew that changing things up would be good for them, but I don't think I realized the full extent of their previous complacency. A noticeable change fell over each member of the crew as they each tested their mostly unused skills.

For most of an hour, the crew worked as one, in a couple of places even showing more competency than they did in their normal positions. I made a mental note to rotate duties more often. I hadn't had this much hope since our maiden departure from Anvilcove.

And then we exited the reef.

At first, the elation we all felt carried us forward. Relief mixed with joy as we reefed sails and prepared to stop. Rocks and coral reefs bracketed us on either side. It was beautiful, but a few taller rocks limited visibility off our starboard side, and as we rounded a tall, jagged rock, my heart nearly stopped.

A ship, roughly the same size and class as the Siren, waited just around the bend. They were tucked out of sight, but were clearly lying in wait. They were far closer than any sailor would have been comfortable with if they were just passing, and every instinct inside me screamed they were not, in fact, passing anything.

"Drop the sails! Hard to port!" I shouted, too late.

The ship was already moving and gaining speed, and there was nowhere for us to run.

"*Vasta!*" I cried in frustration laced with fear. "Siren! To arms!" I dropped the rope I'd been tying off and ran to grab a weapon.

I ran to the box built into the wall near my cabin. Inside were the swords and knives that we had been gathering for us to use in live training exercises. They weren't high-quality blades, but they were what we had.

I snatched up the sword belt that Merrik had chosen for me. It draped over one shoulder and rested against my hip.

The twin sheaths held a pair of blades—one short, the other longer and heavier—and there was a massive brass plate buckle on the front. The thing was gaudy as hells and I loved it.

Once it was in place, I spun to rally the crew. No one was there. I blinked and glanced around. Merrik was still at the wheel, and Isaboe had joined Anne on deck, but no one seemed to be running to my aid.

"To arms!" I shouted again frantically. "Damn it all, this isn't another fishing boat!"

I looked at Anne but her eyes were not on me. Everyone was watching the ship that was bearing down on us.

Far more slowly than I ever thought anyone could move, the crew came to join me, one by one, lining up to choose their arms.

Kaelyn pulled me aside. "How did you do this?"

"Do what?" I glanced over her shoulder as the ship drew closer. When I looked back at her, her eyes were wide and confused. "Wait. Do you think I planned this?"

"You didn't?"

"Damn it. No!" I turned and raised my voice to make sure everyone was very clear. "This is not part of the exercise, folks! Get your gear and get ready to test out what Merrik taught you because those are real pirates."

Another heartbeat, two, then three before anyone moved. I could see the moment reality hit them. Surprise gave way to bleak resolve.

"Move!" I roared. "Now!"

Moving with determination mixed with fear, each member of my crew took up places around the deck as the first of the grapple lines landed on the deck.

CHAPTER FIFTEEN

I fought down a surge of panic. *This isn't like last time,* I told myself. *This isn't a street brawl, you aren't alone. You know the terrain. You trained for this. You know what you're doing.*

So do it. Do it. Do anything. Now.

Move your damn feet, Tianna!

The heavy thud of iron grappling hooks landed nearby, snapping me from my paralysis.

"Anne," I called to her. "Take the helm and try to steer us out of here. I'll get us loose." She nodded and ran off to relive Merrik, freeing him to fight.

"Get those lines clear!" I ordered as I ran off to do just that. My left blade came down hard on the starboard side railing, neatly cutting the line in two. I blinked in surprise, knowing I wasn't that strong, then realized Merrik must have sharpened them after all.

Relief swept through me. Maybe we weren't entirely outmatched. Merrik knew what he was doing, and he's been training us. We could get through this.

I heard a few more lines snap and watched them fall away as Iain and Kaelyn hacked away at the hooks that were biting into the Siren's hull.

I looked up, across the expanse between the two ships. The other crew was full of burly sailors boasting enough scars and tattoos to would make a branding artist look twice.

They were throwing more ropes and pulling the ships still closer together. We cut as many as we could, but I knew we wouldn't be able to cut free.

Several men were maneuvering a heavy plank into position as a makeshift bridge between the decks. I braced myself, readying, waiting for the first attacker to cross over. I flinched as a loud shot rang out, about twelve feet to my left. One of the sailors holding the board dropped to the deck with a scream.

I glanced over at Eric. He wore a hard, determined look and was deftly reloading his pistol. "Keep doing that," I told him.

He half-smiled without looking at me. "Aye, Cap'n."

"We definitely need more guns," I muttered to myself as I turned back to see what was happening on the other ship. As if my looking summoned them, the first of the attackers crossed over.

Like something out of an adventure tale, two men swung down from a mainmast yard and used the leverage to launch themselves onto our deck. The first flew out over the water in an impressive arc, making himself an easy target. Another shot rang out, and he dropped.

The second man landed on next to me and growled. I spun and brought both blades up, blocking his downward strike. Without thinking, I let Merrik's training take over. While my blades distracted him, I brought my knee up into his gut and then kicked down at his knee.

He grunted and stumbled sideways. Pushing forward, I used his momentum to shove him over the rail. He splashed into the ocean and I quickly turned.

Isaboe was facing off against someone almost twice her size. She was holding her own, but barely, and I wasn't sure how long she would be able to hold out.

Merrik spotted it the same moment I did. He took three running steps before leaping in the air and twisting in a half spin. Using the force of this momentum, he brought his leg down in a flying kick to the pirate's throat. The man emitted a gurgling sound that would have made me laugh if I didn't see him turn red and fight for breath.

I swallowed hard and turned away from Merrik. It seemed there were some things he hadn't taught us yet. Stunned by his performance, I missed the two attackers who had come up behind me. The first one took a wide swing at my head and I just had time to duck.

Before I stood back up, he screamed. Two small blades blossomed in his chest, one near his armpit, the other just below the base of his throat. I nodded at Kaelyn, grateful for the assist. The pirate scrambled backward in pain, and tumbled into the man behind him.

As they fought to right themselves, Iain dropped from the afterdeck above them. A glint of light flashed off his thin blade as he pointed it downward into his leap, spearing the uninjured man in the shoulder.

Before he landed on the deck, Iain withdrew his rapier and sliced at the other man. All three dropped to the deck, and Iain stood, looking for his next target.

Somewhere over my shoulder, another shot rang out, this one lower and louder than the other. I looked up to see Isaboe standing halfway up the stairs with a rifle braced against a heavy barrel.

Behind me, from across the deck of the other ship, a horn sounded their retreat. Several answering calls echoed around their ship, calling the sailors back aboard.

Isaboe and Eric each got off one more shot, taking down a pair of retreating pirates. I stood, panting as the adrenaline faded, and watched as Merrik and Kaelyn cut the rest of the ropes away.

"Stand down," I told my crew as the other ship hurried to flee. There was no sense in chasing them, and even less profit. Everyone gathered on the main deck and we dropped anchor right where we were.

"Everyone alright?" We finally had a moment to exhale, and I took the time to assess. Kaelyn was bleeding from a shallow gash in her upper arm, but had already tied it off with one of her least favorite scarves, and Merrik was sporting a couple of new bruises on his jaw from a wild punch, but in all, we were whole and healthy.

"Well," Anne said. "That was quite bracing." There was a slight tremble in her voice, and I made a note to check on her once we were away from the rest of the crew.

She was correct, though. I felt so alive. The battle lasted less than ten minutes—well, no. The fighting lasted ten minutes. Ship maneuvering was considerably longer than that. I laughed weakly, brushing away the last of the strain of hostility.

"Great job, Merrik," I said. "I didn't think we would get to test out our new skills so soon."

Once we had all taken some time to calm down, catch our breaths and process what had just happened, we returned to duty stations and sailed out of the reef. We didn't discuss it in so many words, but none of us really wanted to stick around for whoever should come along next.

One ship, it turned out, we could manage just fine, but accidentally stumbling upon a whole nest of pirates would be something else altogether. We turned tail and got back along our original route as fast as the wind and tide allowed. Further training could wait.

We were less than a day outside of Farwind when Kaelyn approached me. I had propped the door to my cabin open to enjoy the breeze. She tapped gently on the door frame and let herself in.

"Hey," she said.

I looked up from the papers on my desk and smiled at her. "Hey. How's it going?"

"Well and good," she said. "Crew's in fine shape, and we'll be in port before nightfall."

"Excellent." I turned back to collect my loose pages into a pile when I noticed she hadn't moved. I looked up. She was standing just where she had been, watching me.

"Something up?"

She walked the few steps across the room and perched on the edge of the bed, facing me. "I… well, I was thinking. Actually, I…" she blew out a frustrated breath and looked me in the eye. "There is easy start to this conversation, so I'm just going to lean into blunt, alright?"

I bit my lip to keep from laughing and nodded.

"Are you okay?" she asked.

I cocked my head with a wrinkled brow, thinking. "Yes?"

"It's just that the last time we had to fight, you kind of fell apart. I just wanted to make sure you were handling this."

"Ah," I said, finally realizing what she was trying to say. "Right. Thank you."

She was right. I'd been doing a good job of hiding it, but I hadn't really been weathering the emotional storm well. Suddenly facing the life-or-deathness of our grand adventure was a lot to take in. But that was early days. Since then, I'd seen more, done more, learned more. I'd like to think I was a better version of myself at this point.

I turned to her. "You know, I really am," I answered her question with a surprised smile.

"Well, I guess I worried for nothing." She rapped her knuckles on my desk, then stood to go.

"Are *you* okay?" I asked as she walked to the door.

She paused and looked back at me. "Yeah, I think so. This whole thing is a lot more... more than I expected, you know?"

"But you're up for it?"

She nodded. "Yeah, I think so. It's just..."

"You're wondering what's next." It was a statement, not a question, and she nodded. "You know what? Hold on." I quickly stood and marched out onto the deck, hollering for my crew. "Heya! Everyone come here a minute! If you're on essential duties, wrap up your task and come here. It won't take long."

It took about five minutes before everyone gathered on the deck, looking at me with wild curiosity. Granted, this was far from protocol, but that's exactly what this meeting was about.

"The last few days have been eye opening." I started sternly, letting my gaze drift from person to person. I tried to read their body language while I held my shoulders back, trying to impart what little authority I had.

"We, none of us, have been giving it our all since we left the reef. And it has some to my attention..." I paused for dramatic effect, then let out a chuckle. I finished with a bright smile and a laugh in a much lighter tone. "We're really going about this all wrong."

I followed Kaelyn's example and decided to take the blunt approach. "Since forming this crew, we have been trying our damnedest to follow protocol and procedure. We based our standing orders on the examples at hand, and for weeks now we have been trying to act like an official navy, merchant, or cruise-chartered ship.

"Now, if this is anyone's fault, it's mine. But I'm not here to lay blame, I'm here to address the problem. The problem, folks, is that none of us have any navy, merchant, or cruise experience. We are not them. We never have been. And it's time we stopped acting like it."

I paused for effect, then continued.

"We are a group of children playing at something none of us fully understand. But we are on the cusp of something great. These last few weeks showed us that. I watched each one of you start out the day nervous that you wouldn't have the skills to succeed in your new positions. Hells, me too. I hate running deck, I'm no good at it. Yet somehow, we not only made it through the reef without running aground, we made better time that we would have at our usual tasks.

"When the pirates tried to turn our practice run into an ambush, we didn't panic, and we didn't shirk or shrink from the battle. We protected ourselves, our ship, and each other." I paused long enough to let that sink in, then turned to Kaelyn. "You were the most hurt in that fight. Was it worth it?"

"Hells yes," she said with a fierce grin. "No way would I let those bastards steal our ship."

"What about the rest of you? Was it worth it?" I saw nods all around, though Isaboe and Eric both hesitated a little at first.

"Will it still be worth it if we have to do it again—when we have to do it again? Because make no mistake, if we continue to sail the Outer Isles, it will happen again. There are still unforeseen dangers out here."

Merrik broke out of his stony facade long enough to meet my grin with one of his own. "Hard to expect otherwise. This is the Pirate Isles, Captain."

"What do you propose we do about it?" Isaboe asked.

Again, I looked around at the crew, meeting each of their gazes before answering. "We fight when necessary. We protect what's ours. We sail. We trade. Whatever fate of fortune awaits us, we seek our own glory. And we do it on our terms."

I turned to Anne to make sure she understood the full weight of my words. "Not pirates." I turned to Iain. "Not merchants." Finally, I turned to Merrik, "Not explorers. But maybe something like all three."

Interest began to spark and linger at the edges of their expressions. I gathered myself before speaking again.

"We don't know what we're doing out here. We are making it up as we go. We have no Kingdom, no flag, no master who can command us from afar. We have a contract with the Governor but it was not exclusive to what we can do while we finish this trade run. So I propose we stay open to whatever it is we can find."

"You want us to be freelance... what?" Isaboe asked. "Scavengers? Mercenaries? Taking on whatever jobs we can find? Maybe finding a wreck or two and collecting some salvage? Tell me again how we're not pirates."

"We saw it in the men who tried to take us. Pirates are thieves, murderers preying on weaker ships to take what isn't theirs. Do any of you want that?"

Muttering came with the shaking of heads.

"Then we don't. We'll write our own code, our own ship's articles, and stick to that. We don't seek or pursue other ships for the intention of taking a prize. We harm none in pursuit of our goals, save those that seek to harm us first. And above all, we agree to support each other, and continue to grow as a crew."

At some point while I was speaking, a fire had been lit in them, and I intended to fan those flames.

"We're inexperienced? So what? Experience comes from doing. We're untrained? We can learn. We have no goals? Then we will follow wherever the whimsical winds will lead us. To glory! To our future!"

"Aye!" the crew cheered together. I'm not sure I had ever given a rousing speech before, and it felt... actually kind of nice. I let the bubble of elation grow and spread throughout me until it busted out in a hearty laugh.

"We are the Siren!" I shouted.

"Siren!" they all echoed.

"There is nothing we can't accomplish if we do it as a crew. We do this together!"

"Aye!" they called, louder than before.

"We are more than a crew! We are a mighty horde!"

More cheers mixed with laughter this time.

"Now, get back to work! I'd like to have a hot meal on dry land tonight!"

With one last shout the crew went back to whatever they had been doing before my unexpected muster.

Kaelyn turned to me with a sly grin once the last of them were out of earshot.

"Scavengers, mercenaries, and explorers sailing under our own colors," she said. "We're pirates, right?"

"Oh, totally pirates," I said. "A mighty Pirate Horde."

"You know, if we're going to do this, we need our own colors. Can't be sailing under Anne's family flag forever."

I laughed at that. "Any ideas?"

"Not a one, but I'll let you know if that changes."

"Just not a jolly roger, alright?" I said. "Every pirate flies the same skull and crossbones. We need something better suited to us."

"Better suited to a mighty horde?"

"Yes! Exactly!"

She chuckled. "Can seven even be a horde?"

"Of course we can. Weren't you listening? We can do anything we want." I matched her smirk for smirk.

"Yarr," she growled under her breath. It was a low and amusing sound, but somehow carried the weight of all that we were trying to become and all the possibilities of what we might do.

I nodded, in full agreement of everything she didn't say with that one word.

"Yo ho ho," I said.

The excitement of our success followed us for the next two weeks. We stayed a few days in the quiet little town of Farwind, simply relaxing and taking time to think about what we might want to do with ourselves.

Merrik traded our stock of dyes and the remaining textiles for coin, and we happily spent part of it on a room in an old boarding house near the docks. It looked barely more than habitable, but it was clean and dry, and we were still riding too high to care about the setting.

After that, we hit up the smaller ports along the western coasts of Oster and Ormede, making small, barely profitable trades to keep us afloat. All the while, I locked myself in my cabin and met with the members of my crew.

Everyone had their own ideas and opinions about where we could be literally and figuratively headed. I listened carefully and took enough notes to fill the basement of Meket's Great University. And so by the time we landed in Sunset on the western tip of Coral Island, I had a freshly penned and complete list of ship's articles. Or our version of them, anyway.

I'd never seen ships' articles in person, but I had read a couple of history books with snips and cuts of examples used by the Lugaian and Epirsan Navies. I will never turn down valuable reference material, even when forging my own path.

Among the cities of the Outer Isles, Sunset is probably the most unique. It's large enough to support a thriving agriculture, busy enough to maintain a steady industry, and diverse enough to be a fertile ground for the arts, yet somehow it is none of those things. Sunset is, in a word, rich.

I had no real experience with the sort of people who inhabited the upper tiers of Sunseter society, but the varied and bustling population of lower classes who congregated at sea level—and thus literally below the upper echelons perched atop the steep hill—were much more what I was used to. These were your everyday riffraff, your run-of-the-mill tradesfolk, and your usual minstrels, drunkards, and barmen. Knowing what awaited me here, I felt solid again as soon as my boots hit dirt.

"This is familiar," I said as Eric and Iain came up and flanked me. "All I need now is a good old-fashioned tavern brawl and I'll be right at home. Anyone want to come and find a den of iniquity with me?"

"Iniquity?" Eric asked with a smirk.

"Th' wicked spirit o' th' dice callin'?" Iain chimed in. "Nothin' to a sallybye with a bonny lass, ale, and a tale, ya?"

"Yeah," I replied. "Although I wouldn't turn down a bonny lad either." I winked, and he laughed.

"Not my flavor, Captain," Eric said. "But you're welcome to whatever fruits you're craving."

"Too bad for selfsames. Somat needs t' tend th' Fair Lady, elsewhile I'd be after a twist or several m'self."

Eric stared at him in surprise. "You mean with a lass, right? I didn't think you... I mean, it's fine either way, but I didn't know that you..."

"Like t' dally with the lads in th' buckskin?" Iain waggled his eyebrows lasciviously, then let out a hearty laugh from the shock still written on Eric's face. "Hardly, tallboy. Yer not a fish I'd shoot at, no matter th' size o' th' barrel. Rest easy, ya?"

"I wasn't—uhh... I mean, I didn't-" Eric stammered out something like a reply.

I was laughing so hard I nearly missed Anne slipping quietly up the road away from our little group.

"Oh, Anne!" I called after her.

She stopped and turned to face me. Her expression was the same careful mask of polite indifference she wore when we'd met at her home in Anvilcove. It was one I was beginning to recognize she wore when she wanted to keep her thoughts and motivations to herself.

"Our contract," I said as I caught up to her. "The only stipulation was this delivery here, right? Where do we need to go and what do we need to bring?"

She smiled courteously. "Not to worry, Tianna. I have it under control."

"You're sure you don't want company? I can have Isaboe go with you."

She shook her head. "That's quite all right. I am just going to catch up with an old friend and deliver a letter from my father. It will likely be before midnight when I return."

I frowned. "At least take Merrik. He's the best mannered of all of us, and there isn't anyone around here better to play personal guard."

Anne forced another smile, and that was my cue to back off. "Thank you, but I really am fine."

"Alright." I conceded with a quick nod and a literal step back. "If you're sure. I'll mostly be sticking around the docks if you need anything. Just send a runner."

She nodded without a word and turned up the street. As she lifted her clean, layered skirts out of the cobblestone muck, I saw she was still wearing a pair of tight trousers underneath. I still didn't understand that girl, but the more I saw of her, the more she intrigued me.

"That lady has secrets," Kaelyn said softly from right next to me. She kept her voice low enough that the others couldn't hear her.

I turned to her. "That's funny. I was just thinking that same thing."

Kaelyn pursed her lips like she did when she didn't like what she was about to say. "Have you noticed she keeps slipping off by herself?"

"I thought we talked about this back in Angle Bay, She just hasn't bonded with the crew yet."

"And she won't, so long as she keeps refusing to spend any time with us." Kaelyn looked at me. "I think she's up to something."

My frown returned. "What do you mean?"

"I don't know. Wild thoughts and conjectures, maybe. I've been following her."

I tried to read her face. "Report?"

A burning street lamp behind her cast her silhouette with a faint glow. I watched her shadow shrug before she murmured. "Nothing to report, Captain."

"What do you mean?"

"Everywhere she stops, it's easy. Innocuous. She meets with friends for tea, or sits and reads a book for an hour. It really just looks like she's enjoying her own company, as she claims."

"I see." I didn't, really. "Isn't that a good thing? She isn't plotting against us or engaging in anything nefarious, so we should be at ease. I mean, right?"

Kaelyn frowned, unconvinced.

I chewed on my lip and I thought it over. "I guess it does mean that she still doesn't fully trust us, but that's something we can fix. We'll just have to put in a little more effort to get to know her."

Kaelyn hesitated, and I heard her shuffle. "I suppose..."

"What is it? I'd like to know everything, even if it's just your gut feeling on this."

"Our last day in Angle Bay, I followed her to a little cafe near City Hall, where she met with two middle-aged women. Sisters, twins I think. After twenty minutes or so of chitchat, Anne gave them a letter, which they read there at the table. It made them smile and the three of them chatted some more. Eventually, they left, and Anne stayed. It was exactly as she told us it would be."

"Right, so as I said, there's nothing to—"

"No, I mean, there was absolutely nothing suspicious about it. It feels too easy, doesn't it? Too... clean." I could almost feel the weight of her gaze on my face. "Look, if you were trying to cover up something, how would you go about it? Make up some lie or—"

"I would tell just enough of the truth that no one would question it." I sighed. "Well, damn it. Will you—"

"I'll follow her again today, see where she goes," she agreed quickly. Her tone was still hushed, but I felt the energy behind it. She nodded up the hill at the retreating back of our lonesome crew member. "It still might be nothing. It's possible she is just meeting with her father's contacts in the larger cities. Or her own friends. Or just sight-seeing, I don't know. But unless we find out what it is..."

"It could be a problem that comes back to bite us when we're not looking," I finished for her.

I reached up and rubbed my face with both hands. The rough calluses on my palms pulled on my salt-dried skin and I suddenly realized how desperately I wanted a bath.

"Do what you think you need to. I'm going to find some dinner and relax a bit. Hopefully, this is nothing we need to worry over."

Kaelyn gave me a half-smile. "I suppose it's odd to be hoping she just doesn't like us, right?"

I chuckled darkly. "Yet, here we are. Right now, that's exactly what I hope."

She took a step back and offered me a too-bright smile and her tone returned to normal as she addressed me more conversationally. "Enjoy your gallivanting, Captain. I think I'm going to take a stroll and enjoy the night air."

"What?" I replied in the same tone. "We're not good enough company for you anymore?"

"Good, yes. But loud. You're all so very, very loud. And I am going to find a nice patch of peace and quiet and hide myself in it until morning."

I laughed and then tipped my head to one side, thinking. "Actually, that sounds great. I'll come with you." I took a step to follow her, and she pushed me back.

"Like hells you will." She laughed and swatted at me like I was an irritating bug.

I let my carefree laughter cover the subtle nod I gave her. As she started up the road after Anne, I turned back to the rest of the crew with a grin. "Alright," I asked, rubbing my hands together gleefully. "Who's ready to go find some trouble?"

CHAPTER SIXTEEN

I'd been only half-joking about trouble. I loved mischief as much as the next open-minded, pseudo-repressed, budding adventurer out on her own for the first time could be. It just didn't seem to happen when I wanted it to.

Still, a quiet dinner in good company seemed just what we all needed. Eric, Merrik and I wandered the streets of Sunset, laughing and joking as the lamplighters set about their work. After an hour of meandering, peeking in shop windows, and debating over every tavern, inn, and eating house we passed, we settled outside a small taproom.

The short building stood out against its tall neighbors, not just for its full-brick facade next to the slat and tiled ones we'd seen all over town, but also for the large, open spit out front. A stout woman and a thin young man who might have been her son were arguing over hot coals as a hock of meat slowly turned.

The scent enchanted me like sprites in the old tales, luring unsuspecting children away to their magical realms. If one appeared now and offered me a piece of that meat in exchange, I would gladly go.

I glanced hopefully at my companions. Merrik looked bored, but I caught a spark of interest in the way his gaze lingered on the sizzling roast.

Eric pointed. "That looks good," he said. "Think they'll have enough for us?"

"Head on in, luvs," the woman shouted over to us. "Th' knock'll be ready t' eat in a tic."

Inside, the pub was just as homey as the outside. Clay tiles in varied reds and browns lined the entire wall behind the bar to our left. The other walls were all light wood paneling and covered in amateur art. Sketches, drawings, paintings, whatever could be slapped in a frame or pinned behind glass was hung and pasted on every spare bit of wall space.

Small round tables scattered about wherever they fit, and several extra chairs lined one wall in case they were needed. The room wasn't bustling, but it was far from empty. I guessed it was nearing the busy point of the night, and I was grateful that this bar was far enough off the beaten path we could still find a table.

Merrik disappeared and then reappeared almost as quickly with three hot mugs.

I quirked an eyebrow at him as he set the steaming liquid in front of me. "Tea?"

He shrugged and dropped his satchel onto the seat next to him. "Seemed like a good night for it."

I smiled, secretly agreeing. I wrapped my hands around the warm mug and let my mind wander. We sat quietly for a time, sifting through our own thoughts. I was grateful to have these two with me tonight, as they were just as content to lapse into comfortable silence as they were to chat about whatever came up. It took pressure off trying to socialize.

I wasn't sure what was on the minds of my fellows, but with the anticipation of a good meal to distract us, I was free to puzzle over something that had been at the back of my mind for weeks.

What do we do next?

Anne had contracted us for this first trip around the Outer Isles. From here, we were scheduled to stop in Tiraea, maybe a few of the smaller fishing villages in between, and then it was back to Anvilcove. We neared the end of our maiden voyage, and while it wasn't as momentous as starting out, the end weighed on me.

In case you haven't caught on yet, I generally don't enjoy being aimless.

There was nothing in the contract about renewal, but there wasn't anything explicitly stating that this was a one time trip either. Anne certainly hadn't discussed the possibility of an extension with us, and with her still holding separate from the group, I had no way of knowing where she stood on the subject.

"How would you guys feel about heading north after this?" I asked, staring at my tea.

Eric looked at me quizzically. "Back to Ormede?"

I looked up, addressing them properly. "I mean, after this circuit. We could head up to the Reefs, or east to the Inner Isles…"

"We don't really have a direction, do we?" Merrik stated, rather than asked.

"Just looking at the options." I dropped my gaze back into my tea, as if a course was waiting to be charted in its inky depths.

"I suppose we could," Merrik agreed. He had an almost imploring quality in his tone as he stared at me.

"Oh, quit trying to read my mind," I chided him. "I'm just thinking ahead. Once we're back in Anvilcove, that's it for this trip. Then what?"

"Whatever we want, I suppose," he replied.

And therein lay the crux of my problem. It seemed we had too many possibilities to decide on one.

"We could go just about anywhere, I suppose," Merrik said. "Keep taking odd jobs around the circuit, head east and take up with the Lugaian islers there. I'd be happy to introduce you to my family in Boarstown, but we'd be stuck there forever. Once I go home, I don't think they'll let me go again so easily."

I cocked my head, curious. There was still so little I knew about my enigmatic friend. I filed the tidbit away for later.

"Or, hells," Merrik continued. "We could find a local Market contact around here and focus on specialized trade if we wanted."

Eric perked up, like he was about to say something, but I shook my head. "I don't think that's a good idea," I blurted out. "We'd have to be damn desperate before I want to work with the Shadow Market."

Merrik shrugged again. "Just saying, we have options."

"Look," I said. "I'm all for jumping in and learning how to be a merchanteer as I go, but there's no reason to start out with chum tied to our feet in shark-infested waters just because we want a proving ground. Dealing with the Market would be a good way to wind up dead."

"Would the Guild be safer, ya think?" Eric asked.

"Possibly worse," I told him. "Wellsmith isn't a regular stop for Consortium ships, but what I know I know from working with people who know people who owe money and favors to people connected to the Consortium... it's a mess out here. The Guild Consortium, the Shadow Market, even the pirates, it's all the same game. Control the supply chain in the Mervast, and reap whatever the isles have to give."

I paused and shook my head, setting my teacup down. I looked up at my companions with a laugh bubbling out of me. "Why are we doing this again?"

"What the hells else are we gonna do?" Eric replied.

A weak chuckle floated around our table before we slowly tapered off into mirrored expressions of uncertainty. After a few minutes, I spoke up again.

"Well, we aren't alone. Not really. Whatever else happens, if we do decide to give this merchant thing an honest try, I still have some contacts from when I was working for Krellen. And I know you two have been in and around the merchants and the iron trade long enough to know people who know people. Or at least know people who know people who have connections. I think if we wanted to, we really could make a go of it."

"Mercenaries," Eric said dubiously.

"Mercenaries?" Merrik asked intrigued.

I nodded slowly. "Yes, but not fighting work necessarily. More something like a jack-of-all-trades for hire. Unload some cargo here, transport someone's wealthy sister there. Sort of a 'we go, they pay' kind of deal. Is that a thing? We could make that a thing."

"Hmmhm," Merrik said as noncommittally as possible.

I stared them down. "Well, what would you do?"

Neither man had a ready answer, and both suddenly found their mostly empty cups fascinating. The question hung over us like an albatross. I may not know what's next for us, but they didn't either. And it weighed on them as much as it did me.

Why couldn't someone just make these decisions for us? It would be so much easier if we had someone to work for who told us where to go and what to do. Or at the very least, someone to guide and direct us as... we... sailed. Oh. That was me. I was that person. Captain of the Siren and her currently worried crew.

Well, shit.

What did I want for us then? If I was going to make this choice and expect them to back me up, I needed to know what my options are. I needed to be sure I wasn't dragging them into ruin.

Thus far, we had carried on with luck on our side. We went where the whims and winds of fate sent us, with no guiding plan or structure. At least not one of my making. Did I even want to build this into more? Maybe I just wanted to keep wandering.

That's honestly all I ever wanted. Room to breathe. Security in knowing that I had a bed and enough food. Good friends to lift me up when I needed it. Freedom from everything I knew I didn't want.

But the absence of a plan wasn't a plan. I was sure of that much at least. What the hells did I want to do? What was I going to tell my crew? The silence stretched on for several long moments, our collective mood dipping lower and lower into the ditches of melancholy.

"Screw this," I said, pushing away from the table. "I need a proper drink. And something to eat."

I made my way to the bar, noticing that the crowd had grown considerably while we'd been talking. The patrons crammed in wherever they could stand.

A group of rowdy men with tanned skin and dark hair crowded at the bar, laughing and pushing each other around jovially. Their accents were the hodgepodge mix of languages that was unique to the diverse crews of the isles closest to Meket. I guessed them to be locals by the sound of it.

Two of them had their backs turned to me. They were chatting with the tall man, who seemed to be the leader of their little group. I pushed behind them, trying to make space at the bar so I could get the barkeep's attention.

"Can I get a couple plates of something?" I asked and tossed a few pieces down on the bar top, hoping he would understand that I was looking for whatever was in my price range, and not anything too elaborate.

The barkeep nodded at me and slid the coins into his palm before turning to duck his head through a small window into what I could only assume was the kitchen.

Left on my own again, wondering if I was going to get any food at all, I tried to make myself blend into the general ambiance of the room. I scooted as far to my left as I could get, away from the crowd, until I was tucked with one arm up against the wall.

"And then she says t' me, 'not likely, big man.'" The leader guffawed. "Y'know how she likes t' play games."

His friends laughed uproariously. "What 'appened next?" the one nearest me asked. He was smaller in build, but they were all taller, heavier, and meaner looking than me, so it was relative.

The leader puffed out his chest arrogantly. "What d'ya think? I dragged her back home to her pa. You know how much th' old man takes t' me. He thanked me, invited me for supper, an' by th' time they was serving up pie, she was making doe eyes at me like I'as all she's ever wanted."

The group all laughed again.

I choked on air and sneered. "Gross," I muttered quietly.

Apparently, not as quietly as I thought. They all turned to me. I noticed there were six of them, all men. Three were tall, broad-shouldered brawler types that looked like they lived in an arena. Two were shorter, stockier men that no doubt knew how to throw their weight around, and one slimmer, darker-skinned fellow who was close to my own height but with clearly defined biceps and forearms that there was no way he didn't know how to use.

The leader puffed out his chest and eyed me up and down. "What was that, girl?"

I looked up, blinking in feigned surprise. "Who? Me? Nothing."

He squinted as he watched me, like he was trying to decide if I was worth his time. Either he found me too thick to be attractive or too soft to be a threat, because he scoffed and turned away.

"Yeah, better you don't waste your time. I'm clearly out of your league," I muttered, because I'm incapable of keeping my mouth shut when I need to.

He spun back around. "Da'fuck? Who th'hells d'ya think you are?" It wasn't until he was shouting at me that I noticed how slurred his speech was.

Great, I thought. *Way to pick a fight with a drunk guy, Tianna.* I was in it now, though, and I was never known to back down once I'd committed to a path. Even—or perhaps especially—a foolish one.

I held up my hands placatingly. "I just meant you're barking up the wrong tallship, honey."

He sputtered again. "Who you callin' honey, street walker?"

I laughed at his weak insult. If he thought implying I was a prostitute would bother me, he clearly hadn't spent any time in Wellsmith. Some of the best people in the city were sex workers.

"I just meant, I'm clearly not your type. And since you're sure as anything not mine, let's just leave it as is and get back to our drinking."

I made to turn back to the bar, but someone grabbed my shoulder and shoved. I wasn't braced for it, so I careened into the wall, knocking the wind out of me. My vision blurred, and I was dizzy for a moment.

I heard a roar from somewhere behind me and thought I saw movement. My sight cleared just as a ceramic tea cup came flying at the face of the man who had grabbed me. It smashed into the side of his head, followed by a fist. I didn't even have to look to know it was Merrik.

A fist flew at my head, and I ducked sideways. My attacker grunted in pain as he punched the wall behind me. I gathered myself to launch onto him, but a pair of muscular arms wrapped around his chest and yanked him backward. As he fell, my gaze landed on the wiry man who had been at the bar. He was now standing over the one who had tried to hit me.

He grinned and then kicked the man before leaping over him and onto the back of another brawler. I thought he was with them, but it didn't seem that way now. He wouldn't be the first person I'd met that just enjoyed a good fight, regardless of who was taking the beating.

Someone else shouted nearby and the noise in the room rose to another level. The bartender hollered over the din, trying to break things up, but by then there were at least three pairs of people exchanging blows.

I kept backing up away from the commotion until I felt the tall, familiar presence of Eric next to me.

"What was that you said about a good old-fashioned tavern brawl?" He laughed as he dodged a flying mug.

A grin spread across my face. "Just like home."

I wheeled, ready to take on my next foe as the rush of adrenaline and excitement took hold of me. I had been joking before, but I really did feel more at home here than I had in any other town we'd been in yet.

I ducked under one man's wild swing and kicked a chair into his legs. While he was distracted, I grabbed a wooden mug off the table and cracked it over his head.

I barely had time to register that something was flying over the table toward me, and that that thing was a body. We collided, and both toppled over, landing on the sticky floor as the battle raged around us.

A naked torso and bare arms wrapped around me. That same small fighter that I couldn't figure out was laughing like a maniac as his weight crushed me to the floor. I'm not sure when he lost his shirt.

I tried to push the half-clothed barbarian off me, but he sat like dead weight. With a grunt, I pushed up, bracing against the floor for extra leverage, and rolled us both until I could sit up.

He froze with his arms still around me and cocked his head. He seemed enraptured by something near my feet.

I leaned in, trying to see what was so fascinating.

"My boots!" he shouted.

"What?" I pulled myself out from under him. Before he could react, I was back on my feet and kicking his legs out of my way.

I took a moment to appraise my would-be assailant. He had well-muscled but slender shoulders. Clearly made in the fashion of a street fighter. I had no doubt of his keen love of fighting, nor of his abilities. I'd gotten a sense for those already. But his motives still eluded me.

He was completely bald, but unwrinkled. Somehow, he looked older than sand and younger than raindrops at the same time. His pale eyes would mark him as Tirican, but his dark, sun-weathered tan was that of someone from much further south. He wore loose pants and a long vest that looked comfortable enough for a sailor, yet were as finely made as a nobleman's garb. The whole effect brought to mind wood carving prints of ancient Irsan mariners.

He was contradictory in every way possible.

I didn't have long to ponder, much as I wanted to. He pointed at my feet and shouted again. "Those! My boots!"

This time I heard a distinct Epirsan accent, which only added to my curiosity. But before I had time to question the cultural dichotomy this man presented, he dove forward.

I let out a howl as he knock me back to the floor and wrapped his arms around my legs so that I couldn't kick again. This time, he twisted his body around so that he was sitting on top of me. My right leg was pinned under his knee as he lifted my left.

"Hey!" I hit and punched at his back near the base of his neck, but he didn't seem to notice. "Damn it! Let go!"

With one graceful twist, he pulled my boot clean off my foot and stood. At first, I was too amazed to do anything. Both in shock at someone stealing my boot, but also because I knew entirely too-well how difficult it was to take off my knee-high, cuffed leather boots. I'd fallen asleep in them on more than one occasion simply because I was too tired to fight with them.

"Hey!" I shouted. "Give that back!"

Whether he couldn't hear me over the din, or didn't care to reply, he ignored me. With a triumphant grin, he spun and leaped over the table, heading to the door.

"*Vasta!*" I screamed and jumped to my feet, crawling over the table and using one of the loose chairs to make my way past the few people still brawling.

I spotted him as soon as I was outside, headed down a darkened side street. Lopsided from the one low heel I was now on, I took off sprinting down the alley.

Like a prized Epirsan horse, this man was built for speed. I was panting and aching before I rounded the next corner. I pushed forward, leaning into my glowing anger to spur me onward.

Suddenly, he stopped. He spun in place, and I stumbled over my feet, trying to keep from barreling into him. I didn't quite stop in time, and the both of us went over backward into a ditch with a wet splat. I didn't want to think about what we landed in. I hoped it was mud.

"Why you running, *olah*?"

I pushed up off him and scrambled back onto my knees beside him. "What?" I said. "You... but you..." I pointed at my shoe. "You have my boot," I finished lamely.

He got up and brushed himself off. To my surprise, he offered me a hand.

It took me a moment to understand, then finally I took it and hauled myself out of the street sludge.

"I... uh," I stammered. This man didn't seem to want to rob, murder, or otherwise despoil my good person, but I didn't know what to do with that knowledge. Although his actions made no sense, I didn't feel like I was in danger. "I thought you were trying to mug me."

He looked confused, but laughed. "What purpose in that, eh?" He shook his head, for all the world dismissing the foolish notions of the silly girl he had just accused me of being.

I pointed again. "You took my boot."

"Is my boot," he pointed out calmly.

"So you have said." I scrunched my nose. "I think you must be confused. If they were your boots, why would they be on my feet?"

I stared. Was I really having this conversation? As I tried to unravel my confusion, the boys came running up behind me.

The odd man standing in the street looked at us. We were disheveled from the fight, sweating from the run, and eyeing him suspiciously.

He grinned. His gaze drifted around, taking us all in before settling on me. With twinkling eyes, he nodded once, then pointed to himself. "Sinan."

"Uhh, Tianna," I said, imitating the gesture. Then I pointed at my companions in turn. "Merrik. Eric."

Sinan cocked his head to the side. "Brothers?" he asked, then pursed his lips, thinking. "Hmm, what is word... *effiye.* Rhyme match, yes?"

"*Asz fezlah,*" I answered in his language. *Close enough.* Or at least that's what I hoped it meant. My Epirsan was rusty and I was never as good speaking it as I was at reading.

Sinan's face lit up. He quickly jumbled off a complex sentence that me and my rough knowledge of language had no hope of following. I caught the words 'speak' and 'Empire' though, which was good enough for context.

I quickly waved my hands in front of my face. "No, no. Not really. I speak Tirican. I only know a little Epirsan."

"Oh." He looked crestfallen for a sliver of a moment before brightening again. "No harm. We speak Boar tongue."

"He's Epirsan?" Eric asked, catching on from the little he understood.

"Oh, uh. Yeah. Apparently," I told my friend.

"What's 'boar tongue'?" Merrik asked quietly, aside.

I turned to him. "I think he means Tirican. The language of the Scarlet Boar?"

Sinan nodded in big, heavy bobs. "Yes! I speak good. No harm."

"Right," I said. "Okay, well..." We established that we could all speak Tirican, but not what we would use it to discuss. And now my foot was getting cold. "May I have my boot back, please?"

"Oh!" Sinan said as if he'd forgotten he still held it. "I need... but, yes. Okay. Yes."

He handed it over reluctantly, and I yanked it from his grip. With a quick glare, I bent and reach inside. I pulled out my flute, two pens, and a small coin purse which were all, thankfully, still inside. With a quiet grumble, I yanked the boot back on, and shoved everything back inside.

"Come. I show you wife," Sinan said. He waved for us to follow him down the alley. No one made a move to follow him. We just stood there watching him and looking at each other for some kind of guidance.

After a moment, Merrik laughed. "You're the one who wanted an adventure, Tianna."

"That's true, I did." I hated it when he had a good point. "I guess we follow him?"

Sinan paused at the mouth of the alley and turned back to wave us over to him again. "Come. Come. We drink. We talk. I show you wife. I show you boots."

I was about to object again, since I was wearing the boots he wanted me to see, but that conversation was only going to lead us in circles. Something I quickly learning was our odd new friend's specialty.

After almost thirty minutes of wandering in circles—I'm sure we had to have passed that same apple cart six times—Sinan stopped in front of a drab, weathered door. We were just on the upper edge of the main road leading out of the middle-district, standing on a small side street. The road here was too narrow for wagon traffic, and so the stones were still comfortable and smooth beneath our boots. Two- and three-story townhomes lined the walk on either side, each one looking exactly like its neighbors.

He didn't bother to knock, and when he paused just inside the door to kick off his low ankle boots. The door opened on a narrow hallway with a door at the far end and a single small lantern hanging from a crossbeam.

The foyer was dim, but not dark, and I could easily see to the top of the next landing. There were stairs up to the second floor along the left-hand wall ending in another door. He bounded up these two at a time. After another moment's hesitation, we followed.

The room upstairs was everything the entry was not. A fire burned merrily in a hearth on the interior wall, casting the room in a warm yellow glow. There was a thick woven rug in the middle of the room, with a low table centered on top of it. A pair of mismatched armchairs sat on either side of a small window directly across from the doorway we were standing in, and I quickly noticed another door in the middle of the wall to our right.

The main attraction in the homey parlor room, however, was the graceful blonde woman standing over the fire. She stirred a large cauldron hanging in the stone arch of the hearth, Whatever it was, smelled delicious.

Her long limbs, and softly angled features, were lovely in a way that art rarely captures, and though her face was the pretty side of plain, I found her entirely captivating.

As I watched her turn toward the intrusion into her home, I felt myself smile. She smiled back, though I noticed, mostly at Sinan.

"Welcome back, *eşlah*," she said sweetly. Her voice was just as lilting and graceful as I would have guessed from the rest of her.

He walked over and wrapped her up in an enormous embrace, as if it has been months since their reunion. My smile grew wider and softer, even a touch astonished, as I took in all the ways the scene before me was a contrast in expectations.

Her skin was just as pale as his was dark, though both were sun-kissed and full of life. Her blond hair and wide, rosy lips spoke of a strong Tirican lineage, while he was classically Syarsian in every way except the eyes. Even the length of her braid, which hung past her hips, was directly opposite of his balding pate. But despite all their differences, they had one thing in common that you couldn't ignore. They clearly loved each other.

I had no idea why I was here.

Either I was shuffling too loudly or Eric cleared his throat pointedly enough, but the woman broke out of her husband's hold and smiled at us shyly. There was a merry twinkle in her eyes. She pushed Sinan away when he reached for her again, and neatly stepped between him and the fire.

"Forgive my husband," she said in the natural flowing Tirican of a native speaker. She reached out a soft hand in my direction. "I am Ember Vanni, and as you are friends of Sinan, you are welcome in my home."

I shook her hand, feeling bad about the rough calluses on my palm until I felt a similar roughness on her fingertips. She seemed to notice my surprise and gestured toward the chairs. On the seat was a heavy fold of dark linen. A spool of thread and a pincushion rested on it, and I moved it aside so I could sit.

She saw what had caught my attention and her smile turned brighter, excited even. "I am a seamstress by trade. Tailor and textiles merchant, actually."

"Ah," I said. "That's… nice."

"It is." She picked up her spoon and began stirring again. "What brings you to Sunset? I assume you are not locals."

Sinan walked over and plopped himself in the empty chair by the window, and stuck his feet out toward the fire. Ember kicked them out of her way as she walked back to her chair. She gestured at a small sofa, offering us a seat.

"Ah, well, I uh…" I said, eloquent as always.

She sat back, evaluating me with a smirk. "You seem nervous. You can relax, you know. As I said, if Sinan brought you here, then you are friends."

"Oh." I cleared my throat awkwardly and glanced around the room. "I guess this whole thing is just... even more unusual than I'm used to. And I have seen a lot of weird things."

Her eyes crinkled at the corners like she was trying not to laugh. "You haven't visited a friend at home before?"

"Actually, no. But it's more the 'friend' bit that's throwing me. I only met your husband less than an hour ago when his friends started a brawl in a tavern, and then he stole my boot."

She whipped around to glare at Sinan. "What's this?"

Sinan shook his head. "No, no. Not friend. I had drink at tavern, where Bull Mag was telling stories. Is asshole, lost in gossip train. Started with the wrong people and when fight begin, I fight."

"Bull Mag?" Eric asked.

Ember turned back to him with a dramatic roll of her eyes. "Bullworth Magnison," she answered him. "He's an entitled prick who spends his time and his parent's money chasing women all over town. Usually women that want no part of him."

I scoffed. From what little I'd seen of him, her story was entirely believable. "Yeah, well, who would?"

She offered me a sly half-smile, then turned back to Sinan sternly. "What's this about her boot?"

Catching his cue, he pointed at my feet. "My boots."

Ember frowned and looked at my feet. They were resting gently on her thick area rug. My boots were scuffed, but mostly clean. When she saw them, her eyes opened wide, and the laugh she had held back before broke out.

"Holy shit," she gasped between chortles. "What are the odds?"

I looked between them and shook my head. I'd had these boots for years. As soon as I realized I was actually getting paid—albeit not much—for the work I did for Krellen, I ran out and bought myself some warm trousers and a dry pair of boots. These boots.

How did some foreign man on an island I'd never been to become so sure that I had something of his? And why did it have to be the only thing I'd ever bought for myself? You could say they were my most prized possession. Hells, I'd even named myself for them. I was really sure, more than I'd ever been about anything before, these were *my* boots.

Ember met my incredulous gaze, her's still full of mirth. "We had a luggage mishap a few years ago, traveling the Inner Isles. All of his bags went missing somewhere en route between Ilakata and Sen Angelique. It was quite the thing," she explained. "Luckily, all of my bags made it, and none of our actual goods were lost, but still. It took us most of a month to replace his clothes."

Eric chuckled like he was imagining that, and Merrik raised an eyebrow. I frowned sympathetically. "That sounds terrible... I guess someone might have stolen them. It's possible these boots could have made their way around the isles until they ended up in Wellsmith, but they really have been mine for over two years."

"Do you mind if I take a look?" Ember asked. "Sinan's left boot had a distinctive mark near the heel."

"Uhh... oh, umm..." Something clicked inside me. Or maybe snapped. Generally speaking, my patience for the absurd is near legendary, but I wasn't about to part with one of the few things that was actually mine. At least not again, and not willingly.

"Look," I said firmly. "I'm not giving them up. They're my boots now. I walking out of here with them."

Both Ember and Sinan looked at me blankly. "Of course, you are!" Ember said the same time Sinan uttered a simple, "Yes."

"Okay then… Good." I hesitated another few seconds, and then—at a loss for anything else to do in this situation —I bent to remove my boot, again.

I deposited its contents onto the sofa next to me, then handed the troublesome boot to Ember. I wiggled my one again freed toes, trying not to feel self-conscious of the hole that I knew was starting to form on the bottom of my sock. Awkwardly, let my one stockinged-foot dig lightly into their plush rug, waiting for whatever it was they were looking for.

"There, see?" She leaned over toward Sinan and pointed to a barely visible mark near the heel. "It seems you were correct, my love."

I bit my tongue to keep from speaking. The snarky comments forming in my head needed to stay locked up. I wasn't sure how she could tell one scuff mark from another. I hadn't exactly been keeping them in a display case.

With a laugh, Sinan lunged forward and snatched the boot from his wife's grip. He shouted, gesturing with it like it was a prize trophy. "I am winner! I knew we not lose it! Now we see."

He fell silent, looking at all the seams, checking for… I don't know what.

"Can I have my–" I started to ask, but as I reached out to take it back from him, he laughed triumphantly again.

I watched in slow growing horror as he held the foot of the boot in front of him in a solid grip. With his other hand, he grasped the heel solidly, and twisted.

I held my breath, waiting for the inch-thick leather to snap, or give, or somehow break off. I had visions of hobbling around Sunset with one shoe, trying to figure out how I'd be able to afford new boots. Maybe I could just go barefoot until winter.

Only it didn't break. It didn't tear. It clicked.

My remonstration got lodged in my throat and I leaned forward, peering closely. I watched as Sinan deftly slid back part of the heel, not more than a sliver of an inch. He pressed his blunt thumbnail into the small opening, and I heard the click again. Then, simple as anything, I watched him twist once more, and the bottom of the heel slipped sideways, revealing a small, hidden compartment.

"Wh-what?" I stammered.

"What!?" Merrik cried, laughing. Eric only laughed, but the two of them exchanged excited glances.

Merrik leaned into my side and dropped his voice into a falsely hushed tone. "Did you know it could do that?"

I only shook my head.

With the tips of two fingers, Sinan reached in and withdrew a tiny scrap of parchment. It was tightly rolled and resembled a well-preserved scroll, but in miniature.

"I knew it still be here," Sinan said again. "Don't I tell you, wife? I know."

Ember patted him on his knee, both condescending and dismissive. She then rose and returned to her soup, putting the whole thing behind her.

"Goodness, is it getting so late already?" she commented, looking out the window into the dark night. "I don't mean to keep you. I'm sure you lot have better things to do than sit around with us."

"No matter. We weren't doing much." Eric offered her a disarming smile.

Rather than being disarmed though, Ember looked put out. "Oh no. Of course. I don't mean anything by it. Don't let me rush you off. It's only that I am expecting company soon. I wish I had a better idea of what the time is."

Ember stirred her soup absently, losing herself in thought. When she looked up again, it was with a wrinkled brow. "Love, go get the thing for me."

Sinan looked up from where he was still playing with my boot, momentarily confused. "What thing?"

She waved vaguely toward the other door, distracted by something outside. "The time... clock... thingy."

He looked at me as if I had an answer. When he saw I didn't, Sinan only shrugged, then stood to do as his wife bade him. He closed up the small compartment in the boot heel and tossed it in my lap on the way by.

I stared at it for a moment, unsure of what I was seeing. It was a common thing, one I looked at every day, but it had secrets. Boots shouldn't have secrets.

Ember cleared her throat, breaking my bemused daze. I slipped the boot back on, then lightly stomped to make sure the heel was still solid. It felt the same as it always did, and I wasn't sure I was disappointed or relieved.

"What is... how did... who-?" I couldn't seem to decide on a single question, instead relying on the tried and true jumbled mess of words. I paused, focused, and tried again. "What the... what?"

Ember diverted her gaze away from me, glancing at the door where Sinan had gone, out the window, back to her soup, anywhere but at the three people sitting on her couch.

"How odd this all must be for you," she commented, as if she was discussing the weather. "Not the night you were expecting, I'd wager."

I smiled at that. "You would win that bet," I told her.

She turned to look at me. "The night it wearing on. I'm sure you likely have more important things to be doing, or places to be. I don't want to keep you."

"It's really alright, Ember. But if we are disturbing you, we can go." I stood, Merrik rising not a moment later.

Ember waved us back down. "Oh, no. I'm being silly."

Sinan poked his head back into the room. "Psst, wife. Here." He waved her over to him. I'm not sure if he was aiming for subtlety, but I gave him the courtesy of looking distracted and paying them no mind.

Ember hurried over to him. "What is it?"

He quickly rattled off a string of Epirsan. I really needed to brush up my fluency, because I missed most of it. I perked up at his tone, though. He sounded hurried and strained, though he kept his voice low. Ember looked alarmed and glanced at the tiny scroll in his hand, then back to the front door. She said something back that I didn't understand, but through their murmurs, I made out three words.

Informant. Guild. Jenness.

What the hells? I thought. *Surely not…*

I looked at my crewmen, matching gazes with first one and then the other. Merrik looked at our hosts curiously, and Eric seemed focused on the soup over the fire.

I cleared my throat and went to stand again. Ember looked at me but didn't speak, and I smiled awkwardly. Before anyone else could move, the door to the stairwell opened. We all turned as a light rap accompanied a sweet—and familiar—voice.

"Hello? Sorry, I am later than planned, but I…"

As I turned to look at who had come to join this mad party, only one thing came to mind.

"What!?"

CHAPTER SEVENTEEN

Anne blinked, still standing in the open doorway at the top of the stairs. She looked at me, then Merrik, and opened her mouth to speak. When no words came, she snapped it shut with a click. "Well, this is most unexpected."

"I'll say," I muttered.

"Ah, Lady Anna. Please come in." Ember hurried over to welcome her latest guest. "Are you hungry? I have soup here, or I could perhaps find some bread?"

Eric perked up at the mention of soup, but didn't try to interrupt the flow of conversation. He ignored his stomach and turned back onto our newly arrived crew member.

"No, thank you, Mistress Vanni. Perhaps just some tea," Anne said to Ember before pasting a polite smile on her face.

She closed the door behind her and swept into the room. Taking a seat in an armchair near the window, she turned to address me. "This is quite a coincidence. Or did we not agreed I would manage the delivery myself?"

"We did." It wasn't lost on me that Anne and I found ourselves on opposite sides of a parlor again, just as we had been two months ago in Anvilcove. While I was just as surprised to see her as I had been then, there was a note of hesitation in the air around me. "This is, as you say, a coincidence. And I admit, quite a surprising one."

"How do you know these fine people?"

"An accident of fate, actually. We just met." I warily watched her. I hated feeling suspicious of my own crew, but I couldn't fight the flourishing seed of doubt that Kaelyn had planted.

"I see."

"There's no reason to hold court in someone else's home, my lady," I said, carefully emphasizing her title to make my point. I nodded in the blond woman's direction without taking my eyes off Anne. "Even with a host as gracious as Ember here."

She had the grace to blush as her gaze darted to the floor. She took a moment to compose herself and then returned to look at me. "Of course, I am sorry. I'm afraid I slipped into old habits of noblesse. I am here on my father's business, after all."

"Your father's business," I echoed her skeptically.

"Of course. Which reminds me." She reached into the small bag at her side and withdrew a letter and a small, unmarked package wrapped in simple paper. With a nod and a half-smile, she handed both to the other woman.

"Thank you, Anne." Ember accepted both, and handed the box to Sinan without looking at it. "How is your father?" she asked in a way that sounded forced.

"He is well," Anne replied in the same tone.

Ember opened the letter and proceeded to ignore the lot of us. After a moment, she looked up at Anne, eyes wide. "Is this–"

"It has been verified," Anne replied.

Ember nodded and pushed Sinan into the back room. Soon I heard low voices speaking in hurried whispers. They gradually grew more heated until I could make out Ember's voice. "We need to... this in... hands right away. He's the only one who can–"

The door clicked shut, putting and end to any further eavesdropping.

The four of us sat stiffly, not even able to make small talk. Eric conspicuously looked at nothing while Merrik picked dirt from his fingernails. After a few moments, Anne sighed.

"What's all that about?" I asked, nodding toward the closed door.

Anne nearly shrugged before realizing how undignified it would be and affected a polite smile instead. "Given that I was sent here to deliver it personally, I can only assume it is official business."

"From your father? What kind of official business would he have with a silk merchant way out here? Especially business that would leave her so flustered."

She looked away, gathering her thoughts.

A small thump came from the stairwell. It was faint, and I would have missed it, but for the uncomfortable silence. Anne's gaze skipped to me before she got up. She padded silently over to the door, then softly placed a hand on the knob and turned.

The door fell open, and Kaelyn stumbled into the room, landing at Anne's feet. "Oh, hi." With a quick twisting roll, she hopped to her feet and smiled anxiously. "Uhh…" she took in the situation, glancing around the room. "Sorry, I'm late?"

Anne snapped a glare first at Kaelyn, then at me. "Did you follow me?"

"Uhh… well, umm." Kaelyn's eyes found mine, pleading for help.

There had been times aboard the ship when patience had worn thin. Anne was from an upper-crust background and was used to a certain amount of decorum. Naturally, our uncouth natures had worn hard on her over time, and I had seen her grow frustrated to the point of obvious ire. But it wasn't until this moment that something became very clear to me.

I had never seen Anne angry before.

"How dare you!" She spun to stare me down. "Both of you! I have done naught to warrant this level of distrust. And, lest you forget, I am still your patron for this voyage. You have no call to question me nor have me followed!"

I stood and circled the sofa until I was standing a few feet from her. With no one else between us, I could look her in the eye.

"As Captain of the Siren and her crew, I am entrusted to do what I feel is necessary to ensure our safety. What else was I to do, Anne? You hold yourself apart from the rest of us, you disappear mysteriously at each port, and you refuse to be candid with me about what it is you do. So, yes, I had Kaelyn follow you."

"You have no right!"

"Yes, I do!" I shouted back. With a deep breath, I drew up my cloak of authority. I might be new to it, but I knew I was in the right and that surety bolstered my resolve. "When you keep secrets from the crew, you endanger us all."

"You... hypocrite." Anne growled, but seemed at a loss for other words. She shook her head and stepped over to the window, looking out into the night.

"You're right. But I have already been called out about my past behavior. By you, if memory serves. I'm working on opening up to the crew. Working on letting people in. We're all in this together, right? Are you?"

She spun back around and pointed at me. "You are a self-righteous, controlling, know-it-all! I put you into your position and I can remove you from it!"

"Actually, the ship is in my name, so the worst you can do is defund us and we're nearly out of money, anyway." I shook my head, frustrated and then hurried to backtrack. "That, however, isn't the point here."

"What is the point then, Captain?"

I glanced to my side and saw Merrik watching us, his hands resting casually on his knees. Kaelyn had moved over next to him, and at some point Eric had gotten up to stand in front of the door. His bulky frame blocked the only exit.

Turning back to Anne, I saw our hosts were also watching us from the doorway into the next room.

"'Your actions, reticence, and communication with the crew has not been in line with the actions of a leader.' That's what you said to me, isn't it?" I quoted back to her, hoping that if I couldn't get her to see sense, maybe she would see the truth in her own words.

"This is a specific situation. Different from what you–!"

"How so? I was keeping secrets that impacted this crew." I gestured around to the others. "Do they not deserve the same courtesy from you that you demanded of me? You call me a hypocrite, but from what I can see it's the same damn situation."

Anne glowered as her gaze darted around, unsure of where to look. "You... this is different! You have no right!"

"I have the right when you take up with spies and don't tell us!"

Stillness fell over the room—a quiet shock that forbade even the slightest breath. Then, laughter broke out in the other room. I glanced over as Sinan strolled out of the darkness, his deep tenor voice rolling with mirth.

"Clever, this one, *olah*," he said to Anne. "Wife, come. Hiding is no point now, yes?"

Ember hesitated at the threshold, but soon stepped up beside her husband. "Should we deny it? Try to hide what you seem so sure of?"

Anne stared, agape. "What is it you think you know?"

"Just what I said." The fight was gone from me, and with it fled the tense adrenaline that was coursing through my body. I sank into the sofa next to Merrik.

I gestured at Ember and Sinan. "These two are spies. Or smugglers. Or both, I suppose. Though spies seems more likely since they seem to trade in information. Information which you just supplied to them. If I'm wrong about your intended purpose here, then please correct me, but I am not wrong about who they are."

Sinan laughed again, and Anne looked dazed. She patted around until she found the chair and sat.

"Did you know?" I asked her firmly.

"W-what?"

"You arranged to meet with them. You hand-delivered a package that you refused to even let me see. And you kept all of this from us when you had ample opportunities to bring us in. Did you know?"

Anne hesitated. "I do not know the contents of the letter."

"That isn't what I asked." I watched her carefully, looking for any sign of deception.

"I…" she looked at Ember, and the other woman only smiled ruefully, then nodded. Anne sat up straighter and met my gaze. "I did. They are one of my contacts here in Sunset and Tiraea. And before you ask, my father has no part in this. As far as he is concerned, the truth is as I told it to you in Anvilcove."

I sat back, letting it all sink in. It cast light into many of the shadows I'd been chasing. This wasn't something I could answer alone, though.

"We will need you to talk to the crew," I said, glancing around. "The entire crew. Isaboe and Iain should be in on this conversation, too. No more secrets, Anne."

She met my gaze, faintly discomfited. "That is more than equitable after I forced you into a similar position. I am sorry. For before. I should not have raised my voice."

She caught me off guard, and I laughed. "Anne, you are a treasure. All is forgiven. Or at least the argument is, anyway. Let's head back to the ship, have a nice long chat, and then decide where to go from here, okay?" That last, I addressed to the room at large, and waited for their nods.

I turned to our hosts. "I would like you to come, too. Your part in this isn't over yet, and if it's all the same, I'd like to keep an eye on you until it's settled."

"Of course," Ember answered immediately, not even bothering to check with her husband.

With a sharp nod, I rose and began ushering people to the door. We all filed out into the hall and down the stairs. A low grumble reverberated off the walls and Eric clutched his empty stomach.

He offered everyone a sheepish grin. "Umm, any chance we can get a little of that soup to take with us?"

I'm not sure what Isaboe must have thought when she saw the lot of us trundling up the roadway at a little past midnight. We had left separately and were now returning not only as one group, but with two additions as well.

With a quick word for Iain to join us, we were soon all gathered once more around the heavy table in the galley.

"So, what's all this about, then? Are we having another intervention for Tianna?" Isaboe asked—I hoped jokingly.

When no one laughed, Isaboe glanced around the room. Eric and Iain were having a whispered conversation in the corner while Merrik lit another lantern to give the room a little more light.

Kaelyn fiddled with the scarf at her wrist absently, lost in thought. Our two guests, had taken seats and looked like they were trying to appear open and friendly while still watching us all cautiously.

I gestured for everyone else to sit until only Anne and I were standing. Then, I turned and answered Isaboe.

"As a matter of fact, it is. But not for me." I turned and nodded to Anne before taking my chair just to her right. "Maybe you should start talking."

To her credit, Anne didn't hesitate or prevaricate. She squared her shoulders and met the gazes of her fellows.

"Three months ago, I brought an idea to my father about sending scout ships to the other islands. They were to be crewed by skilled diplomats and traders from among the common citizenry of Anvilcove. The intention being that they would foster our connections around Tirican Denisi and become a welcome part of inter-island trade, perhaps even establishing more common routes through some of the more unpatrolled parts of the Outer Isles.

"He, of course, loved the idea. Or, that is to say, he loved the idea of the idea. There were too many complications and complex factors, which he claimed I did not understand. And so, the project halted before it ever began."

She paused with a half-smile on her face, as she recalled something almost fondly. "Over time, I wore him down to my way of thinking, and got him to agree to let me launch a pilot program. One crew, one ship—at my expense, of course—to prove that such an endeavor would prove worthwhile to his governance of the isles."

"Tippy up th' ladder 'round th' docks 'n all, ya? Bound t' work least a proof or two. There ya are," Iain said.

"Us, you mean?" Isaboe asked.

Anne nodded. "Yes, exactly. The hiring of your ship was not by design, but it was an opportunity I would have been foolish to pass up. And so I struck a bargain with Tianna."

"Only that wasn't the entire story, was it?" I wanted to give her a chance to explain herself. I had my suspicions about why she didn't tell us and what her plans were, but I needed to hear it from her. And she owed it to the crew.

"No," she admitted softly. Her shoulders slumped slightly, bowing in before she steeled herself again. "I have not been entirely forthcoming with any of you."

Isaboe's gaze narrowed on Anne, sizing her up in a way she never had before. She sat back in her chair, arms folded, and pursed her lips, but made no comment.

Anne swept a hand to her left, indicating the two people sitting there. "This is Ember Vanni and her husband, Sinan bit Sarin of the Endless Sands. They are friends of mine, and my primary contacts across the southern isles from Bryne Silée to Sunset."

"Contacts?" Isaboe asked gruffly. "Merchants? Traders? Not likely military. Then, what?"

"We are confidential informants. We trade in essential intelligence," Ember said.

When she was met with the confused and thoughtful expression on Isaboe's face, she added, "We are spies. Anne is our local nexus."

Before anyone reacted, Anne pressed on.

"The plan that I put to my father was as simple as I could make it appear on paper. We would be growing and strengthening ties to the furthest points of the Outer Isles.

However, my goal was also to use these points and contacts as a means of acquiring and passing information."

"What kinds of information?" Merrik wore a carefully placid expression while he analyzed her.

"All kind. We have uncovered the locations of Epirsan slave hubs. Charted the numbers and strength of navy movements where the navy shouldn't be. Uprooted dissent and collusion among what's left of the nobility. Anything that might offer insight into threats to the isles is of interest."

"And you contracted us to... what?" Isaboe asked. "Be your mules? Smuggle you back-and-forth unawares while you played out your spy games?" Her rising irritation mirrored my own. While I didn't want to see this devolve into a fight like Anne and I had earlier, I wanted to know the answer to that question. So I let Isaboe loose and turned my gaze back on Anne.

She frowned, looking inwardly for an answer. Finally, she settled on a simple, "Yes."

Fire flashed in Isaboe's eyes and Merrik lifted his chin defiantly.

"My father knew nothing of my actual plans. His interest had always been in running the isles with the least possible of disruption to the status quo. I, however, can see the winds shifting. There are others of like mind as well. The Isles, the Mervast—all of Arret really—is on the brink of change. There are forces at work in every direction, and for the first time in nearly a hundred years, the eyes of every nation are looking West."

"Or if in Meket, perhaps North, yes?" Sinan added. It was a joke, we all knew it was a joke, but it fell flat. He slumped in his chair, grumbling to himself, when no one so much as looked his direction.

"So, who do you work for?" Kaelyn asked.

"The short answer to that question could potentially be misleading, but I ask that you hear me out before you make assumptions."

Some around the table nodded, but I hesitated. I hated agreeing to things before I know the details. I still do. Call me mistrustful, but it's always safer to know what you're getting into. When I nodded as well, she continued.

"Lugaia."

Matching gasps came from Isaboe and Iain. Kaelyn's eyes bulged out of her head. I swear Merrik made a choking sound, and I think I stopped breathing.

"You work for the Consortium!?" I croaked out around a suddenly dry throat.

Her gaze snapped to me. "Did I not just ask you to refrain from making assumptions?"

"That was before I knew you were working for the people, causing most of the misery for people like us!"

Anne turned her dark eyes on me, pinning me to my seat. "I will explain this once, because I do not enjoy having my loyalties called into question. I am not, have not, and will never aid the Consortium's efforts. Here or anywhere in Arret. I am, foremost, a Tirican citizen as well as a citizen of the isles, and I will do what I must to protect my home."

The room was silent while everyone adjusted into the sudden tension.

Her words hit me deeply. Didn't I feel much the same? Not about Bann Tirica, maybe. The Crown had never done anything for me, but what wouldn't I do to protect Wellsmith? If a few bits of well-timed intelligence made the difference in a never-ending war, wouldn't I make sure it got into the right hands?

Right now, I wish I knew whose hands those were. This was heavier than anything Krellen and Mitsuni could dream up. What Anne was talking about was a hells of a lot bigger than a local turf war.

Ember cleared her throat, and all eyes turned to her. "The Consortium of Merchants began as an official trading company recognized by the Kingdom of Lugaia," she said quietly. "Over time, they grew and gained power from the unchecked wealth they amassed. For decades, they operated as the official overseers of Lugaia's economic power in Denisi. Of course, such power, unchecked..."

"Will corrupt anything it touches." The fight drained from me as her words sunk in. I slumped back in my chair and ran my hands over my face.

Ember nodded. "Exactly so. Without the Lugaian crown nearby to sanction and control the Consortium, they began to take liberties. Minor offenses at first—usurious pricing, unnecessary tariffs, and the like—but it soon escalated into more disagreeable acts."

I snorted, an unladylike sound of agreement. "So I have seen. Pay the guildies with your coin or your body. It makes no difference to them."

Ember nodded, wearily. "And even those transgressions went unchecked for so long that it is now commonplace. Simply a reality of life in Lugaia Denisi and Denisi Tirica."

"It's even worse out here," I said. "I haven't been the Lugaia Denisi, but the Outer Isles live by whatever they can scrape out from under the Consortium's boot."

Everyone around the table nodded and muttered in agreement. This wasn't just something I'd had to live with. We'd all seen it.

"Make no mistake," Ember said. "This corruption is everywhere. It's something all the isles have in common."

Eric tapped his fingers on the table, a thoughtful look on his face. "Why doesn't the navy do something?"

I unclenched my jaw before finding my words. "The Lugaian Navy patrols Lugaia Denisi but the bulk of its forces stay near the bases in Sen Belia and Irongate. Lugaia can't extend this far or they would already have annexed the Outer Isles."

"But what about—"

"Bann Tirica has no stake in the Outer Isles anymore," Anne explained, rightly guessing at his next question. "The navy has never been large enough to maintain a presence this far away from the capitol at Don'Munoil, and the Army's land forces must hold the borders."

"But why work for Lugaia?" Kaelyn asked again.

Anne sighed and shuffled as if embarrassed by the answer. "Bann Tirica is not best known for its nuanced approach to intelligence."

"Boar spies know rocks," Sinan said, his playful tone at odds with the rest of the room.

Ember reached over and patted his shoulder lovingly. "Politics in Bann Tirica do not tend to travel much further than its borders. There is a reason we are still seen as a kingdom of barbarians."

"But vital intelligence has no borders." I was finally starting to understanding what they were saying. "What you learn from Lugaia will serve Bann Tirica just as well."

Ember gave a nod and a smile. "If not better."

"It is not limited to Bann Tirica," Anne said. "What we learn here can help the Outer Isles grow and stabilize. With information about ship movements, we can root out slave strongholds before they become a problem. The names of emerging warlords will help us stop the armada before it claims our people or land. The work we are doing is for the betterment of all the isles, not just Lugaian or Tirican interests. It is for all of us."

We all fell silent again, mulling over everything. This certainly wasn't how I saw my night going, but then again, you'd think I'd be used to surprises by now.

It wasn't hard to see the righteousness in their cause. Or at least, I could see how they would think it right. Anne, Ember, and Sinan seemed comfortable with what they were doing, and I had heard nothing to convince me that they were doing wrong, but...

"What information did we come here for?" I asked.

Anne looked at me with a soft smile, as if humoring a pupil who had finally asked the right question. "We have had word of a growing rebellion somewhere in the Outer Isles. It is just rumblings now, street gossip and speculation. If they are right, dissidents are trying to wrest power away from the governor. We need to know why, and what they intend to do with that power should they succeed."

"The rumors are vague as of now, but we have a meeting with a friend in Tiraea who can tell us more. Our meeting with Anne was only to compare notes." Ember added a sly smile in my direction. "But that was before we met you."

"Me?" I asked, bewildered.

Sinan sat back and propped his foot on the table. He reached into the shaft of his boot and pulled out the tiny scroll from before and handed it to Anne. "You bring us list."

She quickly unrolled it and scanned the contents. Her face morphed from stoic to excited to contemplative in quick succession. "This is out of date?"

Sinan shrugged. "We lose, but find again."

"Should we be concerned over who may have seen it while it was out of your hands?"

Ember chuckled and I said, "Actually, I had it."

Anne raised an eyebrow in question.

"It was... uh, in my boot."

"It's possible some part of it may still be useful," Ember said before the conversation could veer too far off track.

Anne nodded distractedly, still reading. "Some of this I know. Lord Templeton had his holdings seized ten months ago, and this one… this commander was killed last year." She looked up at Ember and explained, "That is how I met my handler in Lugaia. He was assigned to the commander's post." She continued to mull over the list.

I pushed down my growing impatience and cleared my throat pointedly. "Care to share?"

When Anne turned to look at me, a grin erupted on her face, but she schooled her expression again. "This is a list of known Consortium sympathizers. Part of our work has been rooting them out before the Guild can establish a foothold here."

Ember cleared her throat, then handed over the letter Anne had delivered earlier. "This is its other half. A list of local nobility ready and willing to work with us. Our information network is growing, thanks to the work we have been doing."

Anne nodded eagerly. Then looked at me, her face a mask of earnest determination. "I have no intention of stopping my work, Tianna. I need to get this into the hands of my primary agent as soon as possible. If the rumors of a budding rebellion are true, I'm certain the Consortium is involved. We might very well need the help of Lugaia to shut it down."

"If the rumors I've been hearing are true, I worry that a rebellion may have already begun," Ember said.

"Well, then." Isaboe smacked her hands down on the table and leveraged herself out of her chair. "I suppose that means we need to get you there."

I fought a mix of emotions at Isaboe's assertion. "Do we?"

Anne turned to look at me. "Tianna," she said softly. "Captain, I feel that this is of the utmost importance. It would mean everything to me for you to sail by my side in this, but I will not hold you to it. I contracted you only for a trade run around the Outer Isles. This falls outside that purview, and I will understand if you would rather leave me here to deal with this on my own."

I drew a picture of everything I knew about her with everything I had learned tonight. Lady Annelia Jenness might be the governor's daughter with a wild streak, but Anne was a proud, stalwart girl who was unafraid of hard work. She had yet to turn her back on us, even when she likely should have. As I pondered it, I found there was only one answer that felt even close to right.

"It is not my decision alone to make." I turned to the group. "What say you all?"

No one immediately spoke up.

"Isaboe, you seem all in. What are your thoughts?"

She answered with a sharp nod. "I say we go. Anne needs our support, and for the time being at least, we are her crew."

I nodded and turned to the man next to me. "Merrik?"

He shrugged, letting me know he had an opinion, but there was no point in trying to pry it from him. "As you will, Captain. I'll support your choice."

"Eric? Iain?"

"We wanted a direction, aye? Nothing like a good cause," Eric said, and Iain grinned, bobbing his head in enthusiastic support.

I fought a smile and turned to the last member of my crew. I told myself her's wasn't the opinion that held the most weight, but I was lying. We started this journey together, and whatever Kaelyn said next would influence my decision.

She chewed on her bottom lip, eyes glued to the table in front of her. For a few long moments, the only sound was that of the creaking hull and the gentle lapping of waves outside. Ultimately, those deep brown eyes, expressive and so full of worry, met mine.

"I won't go against the crew," she said. "But I really don't know about this. We are islers. We are all really good at taking care of ourselves and getting by when we need to, but I can't see the sense of getting involved in someone else's war."

I had no answer for that. The reasoning was too like my own used to be.

Ember did, though.

"You are not alone," she said. "Not in your beliefs, and not in this fight. This is everybody's war. Few know it. Fewer still act upon it. Forces from all sides are gathering, and right now, the spies and assassins are the only ones fighting for us."

"That's a chilling thought." Kaelyn uttered a small, almost nonexistent laugh. She took a deep breath in and locked gazes with me once more. Words passed unspoken between us, but I knew what she was trying to say. *This is probably a mistake, but we have to take a chance, right?*

I gave a small, subtle nod. She sighed, nodding along.

I turned to Anne. "I'm afraid to ask, but where did we just agree to take you?"

Her lips tilted up in a small but warm and grateful smile. "Sen Tagna."

"Sen Tagna?" My voice came out more shrill than I'd intended. "In the Inner Isles?"

It may have only been the next archipelago to the east, but the Inner Isles could very well be an alien world for all I knew of it. The last two months had taught me so much about how different and the same the world outside my front door was. Would Lugaia Denisi be the same, or yet somehow unexpected? It might be exactly the adventure I'd asked for.

"It should be an easy matter to chart a course East to the island of Tagnagine," Anne explained.

"I've never made that trip. How long do you estimate?"

She paused a moment, doing the calculations in her mind. "It is eight days' sailing to Anvilcove from here. Then just under a week from Anvilcove to Sen Tagna. Stopping for provisions, we could arrive at Tagnagine in fourteen or fifteen days.

"If we go around the horn of Hammersmith Island, we could make the trip in twelve days," Isaboe jumped in.

Anne shook her head. "That's a terrible idea. Those waters aren't fully charted. It's too dangerous. If we route to Anvilcove for supplies, it would take longer to then head south again."

"Not if we skip Anvilcove," Isaboe said. "Sail straight from here."

"That would be a long haul," Merrik said. "We could do it, but we'd most like be stir crazy once we made landfall again. We haven't been aship for more than a week straight."

"Twelve days around the horn…" I grinned, realizing where that route would take us. "What if we stopped three days east of Tiraea?"

"That would indeed be ideal," Anne scoffed. "But as I have already said, those waters are still uncharted. It's not a viable route. Disregarding any conversation about pirate activity, you are still talking about sailing through uncertain waters at the change of seasons. The risks aren't worth the extra time. Not even to mention that if we did manage to get through unscathed, there is no where to resupply."

"Oh, yes, there is." I assured her.

Everyone turned to look at me, varying flavors of the same question on their faces.

Kaelyn chuckled and shook her head. "Looks like you're going home, Tianna."

CHAPTER EIGHTEEN

I'm not stupid. I was fully aware that heading back to Wellsmith came with a colossal risk, what with that whole influential gang leader wanting me dead thing hanging over my head. But I'm not the same girl I was when I left, and I was excited to show my crew the world I grew up in. I was sure they would have my back if it came down to a fight, so I was able to shove the nerves aside. And once I did, I found I wanted nothing more than to see Albert, Adwin, and Jun again.

Since travel by sea is not instant, I got to sit with that excitement for six days as we sailed south out of Sunset and east past what would have been our next stop if we had continued on our earlier plan.

As the days and islands passed, I found my thoughts frequently drifting back to Albert and the bookstore. I had done a remarkable job keeping my worries at bay, but that morning was indelibly etched in my mind. When Kaelyn and I fled from whoever it was that had breached the fragile peace of the marketplace, too many questions to wonder at arose, with no answers as to any of it.

Who were those men? Why had they attacked Albert? What had happened to the bookstore? Did Jun have a chance to heal, or... I couldn't let myself dwell on that last question. As soon as we made it safely into port, The Three Brothers Bookshop was my first stop. Then I would know.

With the coastal shores of Coral Island behind me and a tenuous excitement of homecoming in front, I could only try to focus on my crew and live in the moment. Which I failed at rather spectacularly.

Through the day, Kaelyn would snap at me, drawing my attention back to the rope I was working, or Isaboe would stomp her foot and glare at me as I asked her to repeat what she'd just said.

In my defense, this was the longest stretch we had gone without putting into port or stopping for training and sailing drills. I had nothing to do but daydream, so I did. My mind was elsewhere, and it wasn't until we passed Tiraea into the open ocean that it returned.

"Eh, Cap'n?" Eric called from the other end of the ship somewhere astern. I dragged myself out of my latest daze and headed over to see what my master gunner required of me.

He was standing at the railing of the aftdeck, watching behind us. I glanced that way, trying to see what had caught his attention. The setting sun made it hard to see much of anything. The golden light caught the highlights in his loose hair in a rather dashing way, though, which did nothing but fuel my poetic brain.

"Cap'n?" he said again as I stood there, watching him.

I blinked and shook myself. Right. "What can I do for you, Master Scobbie?"

He smirked at my formal address and pointed aft. "I spotted something off our wake. It's far off, and possibly nothing, what with the sun, where it is and all. Too good a chance I was mistaken, but I wanted you to know. You know, in case I was right."

"Right." I turned to look where he had pointed, but could only make out the shifting of the glittering light off the water. "I will keep an eye to it, but... No, wait."

A dark shadow moved through the brilliant glow. I squinted, trying to track it with my eyes. "You're right. There might be something." I called up to the yards where I knew she would be obsessively double-checking yard arm stays. "Kaelyn! Unknown, spotted aft, near terminal visibility. Can you confirm?"

"Confirming!" she called back as she scurried around above the sheets.

I took a moment of pride in watching her lithe form dancing through the wind-swept upper reaches of the mizzenmast. We'd come a long way since where we started two months ago.

After another moment of waiting, she called down, "Aye, Captain. Confirmed! Ship following aft. Distance uncertain."

"Thank you!" I told her and turned back to Eric just as Isaboe and Anne joined us.

"Something up?" Isaboe asked.

I shrugged. "Not sure. Possible ship sighted tailing us, but we can't get a clear visual with the sun's position."

Both women nodded, and Anne raised a hand to shield her eyes as she tried to get a better look.

"Are you worried?" Anne asked me.

"Should I be?" I wasn't, but now I was wondering.

Isaboe elbowed me playfully. "There is no reason to, as far as I am aware. Does anyone here have a price on their head that they forgot to mention?"

I swallowed back a nervous laugh as Eric snorted.

"We'll keep a watchful eye, but it's probably nothing," she said, sounding more cheerful than I think I'd ever heard her before. "This isn't the most-traveled route, but it is the fastest way from Tiraea to Anvilcove."

"That's true." I turned to Anne. "How far are we from Wellsmith now?"

She got that calculating look on her face again. "Perhaps another day. It's been several hours since I last recalculated our position. Of course, with Iain at the helm there is no telling where we might have drifted off to," she added the last, just loud enough for the man in question to hear her.

He shot her a cheeky grin.

I knew she was joking, but I didn't love the sentiment. I had heard too many horror stories about the rocks around here to leave it to chance and guessing. "Alright," I said. "Sooner rather than later, yeah? I don't want to wait until we've run aground to start with the should've's."

Anne and Isaboe both chuckled as they wandered back off to their duties.

The approach to Wellsmith was no joke. There was a reason that my hometown didn't appear on many official maps, and it wasn't just the warm welcome that guards and navy men could expect from the drawn blades of Krellen and Mitsuni.

The rocky cliffs to the north made for unpredictable wind and the shoals to the south were death on any hull. To even sail into port, one needed to sail due east, head-on toward land. I had, obviously, already been over all this with Anne when we charted our course, but I needed to know my crew was at peak performance if we were going to do this safely.

I turned to the remaining crewman standing nearby. "Keep an eye behind us? I know it might be nothing, but I also know that The Pirate Isles is more than just a cute nickname. If we do trip up on the rocks, I don't want to be food for scavengers."

Eric smiled supportively. "Aye, Cap'n. Not sure that sounds like a good day for any of us."

"Nervous?"

"Me? Never."

"Good man," I said with a laugh. "Still, the sooner we get to port, the happier I'll be."

He readily agreed, and I headed back to the fore.

I wasn't even halfway back when the call came from the mainmast crow's nest. "Ship spotted!"

I paused and looked up, barely making out Merrik perched high above me. "I know!"

"No, port bow! Ship spotted, not local." He called down to me. "Two, wait… three ships!"

"What?" I didn't utter it loud enough for any answer. It was really just for my own edification. I hurried the rest of the way to the bow, ducking under the jib boom to lean out against the figurehead. "Seriously?"

Only a moment or two later, Isaboe and Merrik both joined me.

"Popular route," Isaboe muttered.

"Uh… no, it really isn't. Not usually."

Merrik handed over a spyglass, no doubt taken off Kaelyn on his was down to the deck. "Port side, near that ridge line."

I raised the glass and looked to where he had pointed. "Oh, hells."

Somehow, I think I should have known that a change of plan, growing darkness, a ship trailing us, and new and dangerous waters wouldn't be enough all at once.

I scanned the ships, taking in their foreign hull design. They were long and sleek, with heavy braces for two rows of dozens of oars, guaranteeing maneuverability even without wind. Flying near the top of the main beam was a bright red flag bearing no blazon or symbol I recognized. Whoever these people were, they weren't local.

I lowered the glass and met Merrik's fixed gaze.

"Meketian, right?" he asked, more seeking confirmation than asking a question.

A frown creased my brow. "Meketian ships, but I don't know that flag. I've never seen it."

"They're all the same banner, though, right?" Isaboe asked. "Those ships are together?"

I hesitated, double-checking what I was looking at before I answered. "They're seem to be anchored in formation. We're looking at a convoy, and I'd bet anything that's a choke point they're guarding."

"Well, hells," she echoed my earlier statement. "Since when do slavers travel in convoys?"

"We don't actually know that they're slavers," I said. "Those aren't Epirsan colors. At least I don't think so."

"Consortium?" Merrik asked, taking the spyglass back from me and looking outward again.

"How did the Consortium get their hands on Meketian biremes?" Isaboe asked.

Action plans and escape routes spun through my mind as I tried to come up with a genius way out of this trap we had stumbled into. As I weight risk factors, the rest of the crew, except for Iain, who was still at the helm, joined us.

Merrik muttered something and drew my attention back out to sea. "Unless they've gotten an upgrade, those aren't biremes, boss. Those are warships. And new ones, by the look of it."

I hesitated. "I don't know... We don't know that they are Consortium. They might just be independents."

"Pirates, you mean," Anne said distastefully.

"Let's hope so," I snapped. "If they are Consortium, we're as good as dead already."

Everyone fell silent as my words sank in.

Kaelyn cleared her throat. "Is there any way through?"

"Potentially," Anne said. "But it would be difficult to navigate these shoals our first time through without the threat of attack. Under these circumstances…"

"Let's not risk it," I said. "Turn us about and see if we can't get some space between us and whatever they're up to. And Anne, you take the wheel. I don't want to risk any mistakes on this."

Anne nodded sharply and ran off to relieve Iain.

"I'll sheet monkey. I don't know if we'll need it, but I don't want to waste time climbing the rigging if we need to trim the sails," Isaboe offered.

"Thank you."

She looked up at the sky before running off. "Thank every god that the wind is with us."

I turned to Eric. "Are our guns in fighting condition? If this turns into anything other than us running away, I want to be ready for it."

"Aye, Cap'n. I just finished my routine check an hour ago."

"I hope we won't need them, but I'm glad we have the option. Go snag Iain and be ready to help Isaboe."

With everyone else off to ready us for what was to come, Kaelyn, Merrik and I stood, keeping a watchful eye on the convoy.

"They're anchored, right?" Kaelyn asked. "Are they even interested in us?"

I let out a shaky breath. "Let's hope not."

Merrik cracked his neck and rolled his shoulders. "We'll be ready if they do."

I slowly panned my head to look at him. He seemed serious, though that could only have been a joke. "You are messing with me, right? It's three to one. Three *ships* to one. Do you have any idea how many able crewmen, not to mention trained fighters, a ship that size can hold?"

He shrugged it off as if I was explaining the difference between conch shells and abalone. "We're faster."

Kaelyn squeaked something like an objection, her eyes wide. "Are we?"

I didn't have any reply to that, and neither did Merrik. We all knew that if any of those three ships moved, we would find out.

Slowly—so godsdamned slowly I thought the currents must have stopped—we started to turn. I was never more grateful for the spot training we'd done around the Hook Island reef as we made the wide turn without needing to reverse direction. It was tense, but this was a simple enough maneuver, and I trusted Anne with my ship.

While I would have liked to help the crew navigate this about-face, fear rooted my feet where I stood. I couldn't tear my gaze away from the warships until the growing twilight engulfed them completely.

Finally, after what felt like far too many hours without a full breath in my lungs, I sighed. "Alright, let's get headed north and see if we can–"

"Ship spotted, dead ahead!" Isaboe called from aloft.

"Are you kidding me?!" I cried.

Merrik, still standing next to me, raised his glass. It only took a moment before he confirmed. "Less than a league and headed toward us."

I spun to see where he was pointing and sure enough, there was a ship, sailing straight at us as if it were on a mission. "Is there a soiree we didn't know about?"

Kaelyn leaned across me to get a better look. "Are they a threat?"

Merrik ran to the chests of guns and blades he kept on deck for us. He was readying ammunition and supplies before I even took a breath to reply.

I turned to Kaelyn. "I have no way of knowing. It's not like they're about to announce themselves."

She smiled weakly and opened her mouth to reply when a heavy splash landed not more than a dozen yards to my left. "What the-"

A loud boom echoed across the water. I flinched and spun around in time to see the faint puff of smoke rising from their starboard rail gun.

"You were saying," Kaelyn growled.

"Seriously?!" I shouted to the universe.

Kaelyn and I both spun to chase after Merrik. It seemed our new friends wanted a fight, after all.

"Eric, Iain! I want you both on deck, powder-monkeys! This one isn't going to be as simple as chasing off some swill-wasted pirates!" I called out before going after Merrik. "Probably," I added under my breath.

Isaboe called again from somewhere above me. "The convoy is moving!"

"Seems we caught their attention." Merrik's outward calm was belied by the slight tremor in his hand as he handed me my swords.

I took a moment and swallowed down my fear. "Try to route around the lone ship," I shouted to Anne at the wheel. "See if we can get behind them. I don't want to face their broadsides, but I want to get caged in even less."

"Aye, Captain!" I heard from behind me as I spun to watch the encroaching ship again.

I brushed my hand across the brass plate buckle on my sword belt. The whole thing was about the size of my fist and had an intricate spiral design etched into its face. It would have been easy to let myself mediate in the twisting lines and ignore everything around me. Anything but face what was happening.

I shook the fear away, and draped the sword belt over my shoulder. The buckle hung just above my hip, weighted and reassuring.

"Where's that glass?"

Merrik handed it over without a word, and I raised it to my eye. "I want to know who laid this trap."

I need to take a moment here as an aside to explain a few things that might otherwise have been lost in the narrative of my little tale. I realize that a great many of you fine scholars who have chanced upon this book might not be well-versed in naval warfare, or indeed in sailing at all.

So, to that end, let me first clarify that, despite the swift pace of dialogue and the thrill of action, things happen at sea slowly. From our first spotting of the ship to the west until this moment where I have paused in relating these events to you, several hours had elapsed.

Second, the wind was coming out of the southwest, as it typically did at this time of year, and the current from the north was strong. This was the current we had intended to follow out around the cape of Hammersmith Island once we had stopped to resupply.

As much as I would love to tell you that we merely spun 'round at the first glimpse of the convoy, it was not so easily done. Ships simply don't turn that fast, especially under full sail. However, as we were not yet upon the rocks, and the setting sun was behind us aiding visibility for the last few moments before twilight, we had approximately a mile and a half—that's nautical miles, mind you—in which to maneuver. In other words, we got lucky.

Very lucky.

A port lean about brought us south, following the current. It also, however, brought us against the wind, which slowed us even further. But only long enough to point our nose west-northwest and pick up the crosswind we would need to pull us forward again. This would have been enough to see us safely to Tiraea, where we could regroup and try again in a day or two.

Of course, being full dark now, we had no hope of seeing the ship that had been trailing us until we were nearly upon it, well within moderate effective range of their long guns. Which is why, once we did spot them, I was so clearly able to see their flag.

And it was one I knew far, far too well.

As the ship appeared from out of the shadows, I instantly saw it's distinct style and form, so different from those now behind us. She was larger than the Siren, but not by more than a yard or two. What she did have was three masts to our two, and a full gun deck. I could only assume it also came with a full company trained and ready to fire those guns at us if we gave them the opportunity.

I wasn't able to convey that to my crew, as my throat seized up at the sight of the banner that still featured in my nightmares. The black and red check background framed the image of a dead rat, stabbed through by a short blade.

I coughed, trying to catch my breath, and caught Kaelyn's attention instead.

"What is it?" Her voice came out as shaky as I felt.

"Krellen."

She snatched the glass out of my hand to get a look at the ship that was now nearly a half-mile off our starboard bow. "He followed you out here?"

"I-I don't know." Another splash followed by a cannon's boom sounded, snapping me from whatever fear had been trying to immobilize me. "Shit."

I ran back toward Anne, shouting as I went. "Hard to port! Turn with them! Stay out of range of their guns!"

She only hesitated a moment, but followed my order, turning us so that we were sailing straight toward them. I breathed the moment we started to pull away and promised myself if we lived through this, I would learn everything I could about ship-to-ship combat tactics.

The agonizing nature of watching four ships descend on us all at once was the kind of torture I wouldn't wish on my worst enemy. Or so I thought. But since he was within sight, maybe I could wish it on him.

We circled Krellen's ship in a dance to see who would slip first and offer their soft belly to gunfire. And while we did, the warships drew inescapably within firing range.

"The first opportunity you have to break away, you take it, Anne! I want to live to tell this tale someday." The words had scarcely escaped my lips before the answering sound of cannon fire met my ears. One after the other— boom boom boom boom boom—in rapid succession.

"Down!" I shouted, gripping the rail and throwing myself to the deck, only to realize there was no impact.

"Did they miss?" I asked, bewildered as I popped by head up.

Shouts and screams erupted from Krellen's ship as splinters shot up everywhere. Rigging snapped, and the crew scattered, leaving me watching in wonder. I could only watch as all three warships turned to attack the lone pirate frigate.

Not about to question whatever good fortune had the convoy attacking my enemy for me, I started shouting orders to my crew to prepare muskets. "Focus fire on their crew. Every round counts. Anne, keep working your magic!"

The roar of cannon and gunfire was deafening. The surrounding chaos overwhelmed me and pushed against every instinct I had for self-preservation. I wanted to flee.

I wanted to fight. I wanted to cover my eyes and ears and block everything out until sanity returned and I woke up in Wellsmith.

And somewhere, deep within all of it, I wanted this. I chose this. This was my life now, and I didn't have time to stop and regret it. Krellen's ship was maneuvering into position.

"*Vasta!* We're out of time!" I shouted. "Eric! Where are we with the long guns?"

I barely gave voice to the words when the pirates got off their first volley. The deck under my feet shook with a crack as first one, then two, and three heavy cannonballs hit home.

The impact tossed me off my feet, and I landed a few feet from one of the long guns. Shouts and screams sounded around the Siren's deck. Splinters, dust, and debris erupted into the air, so thick it blocked the dim light. I cradled my head to protect myself from the worst of it, and a roar of pain cried out from mid-deck.

As soon as I could stand, I raced over to where Eric was bent over a now scattered pile of twelve-pound cannonballs. He clutched his left arm tightly with his right hand, but his sleeve was covered in blood.

"You alright?" I asked, knowing it was a stupid question.

"I–I'm…" he stuttered in shock. Even in the dusky lantern light, I could see how pale he was.

"Can you hold it together until we get out of here?"

He nodded sharply. "Aye, Cap'n. I'll… be fine." He gritted his teeth, but Iain tore off his shirt sleeves and quickly fashioned a bandage.

"Trip th' tub out th' deadzone, ya? I'll see t' th' tallboy," Iain told me earnestly as he picked a long piece of wood out of Eric's arm.

I nodded and stood, pushing aside phantom images of tiny splinters and gangrene. Grabbing up both the rifle and small musket near Eric's feet, I ran back to the rail and brought the heavier gun up. I took aim at the first moving body aboard the pirate ship and fired.

I didn't stop to see if I hit anything, I only dropped down to the deck again to reload.

The Siren shook as more cannonballs struck her hull. I rose into a standing crouch, looking for my next target, when I saw the third convoy ship break away from the pack, turning her broadsides to us.

"Incoming!" I shouted the warning too late. From among the thunder that roared all around us, I heard a sharp whistling sound. Two rounds of chain shot flew across the aft-deck. I watched in horror as it just missed Kaelyn, who was firing rounds at Krellen's ship.

The chains wrap around the starboard mizzen brace and ripped it loose from the stays. The mast wobbled, but stayed upright. I had almost breathed a sigh of relief when the second ball struck, tearing a massive hole in the sailcloth and setting the mizzen lower topsail yard rocking. It shook furiously from the direct hit before resettling.

The wild movement wasn't enough to tear down the mast, but it did knock loose its only inhabitant. I was helpless to do anything but watch as Isaboe fell. At the last minute, her safety line engaged. Rather than landing painfully on the deck, she dangled ten feet in the air, tangled up in loose rigging, unmoving.

"Tianna!" Kaelyn shouted from somewhere to my left.

I ran over to her. "What is it?"

When she answered me with a grimace and pointed across to Krellen's deck. I took up her glass once more and sighted through the darkness.

I scanned the pirate ship for whatever it was I was supposed to see.

With a twist of fate I could have lived three lifetimes without experiencing, I saw him. My stomach sank.

Darl Tavers stood on his deck in the same position that I was on mine. While the Meketian ships were trying to break us both apart, he stood watching me.

Bile rose in my throat and I spat it out, wishing it would travel the distance and hit him. The last time I saw him, he almost wrecked me simply by showing his face. I couldn't let myself get distracted by him again. This time, I was ready to face him.

Or flee, because as I previously mentioned, I'm not stupid. I could see what four-to-one odds were doing to us.

I ran to mid-deck where Eric and Iain were readying our long-guns. "Dump the cannons!"

Everyone within auditory range stopped to look at me like I was bleeding from my ears.

"You heard me! Toss them over board. We need to lose some weight. Quickly. They're the heaviest thing aboard."

They hesitated.

"Now damn it! We're not going to use them, anyway. They can fire twelve guns before you can fire a single shot. It won't matter even if we try to fire at them. Let's use what we can and lose the rest!"

The extra weight would have helped us maintain our speed on a long straightaway, but we needed to turn and dodge out of range of the heavier ships or it wouldn't matter. We only needed to get far enough ahead of them to slip away. And while I knew that, I didn't have time to explain. I could only hope that my crew trusted to me.

Eric swallowed. With a nod, he and Iain began loosing the ties that held the cannons in place.

"Anne, it's now or never! Get us out of here!"

"Aye, Captain!" she called back. The Siren groaned against the current as she hurried to comply.

"Kaelyn, Merrik, help me here." Together, the three of us placed a heavy board across the leeway on the deck, creating a little ramp. It took all five of us to push the half-ton behemoth overboard. Then we did it again. We only had four cannons aboard, but every ton counted as we turned and sped into the darkness.

I stood and watched the moment Tavers realized what was happening. A look overcame him as he saw his prize slipping away again. Like a man possessed with frantic malady, he shouted obscenities at me. I breathed easier, watching him reach for anything of use as the battle faded into the distance behind us.

My cheeky grin faded in the bare instant it took to notice him grab up a long-barrel musket. I barely registered what was happening before he pointed it in my direction and fired.

A flash of heat spread through my stomach and knocked the air from my lungs. I looked down to where the stain of red was seeping into my white shirt. I fought for breath. "Kaelyn..." My legs gave out from under me, and I gasped out before the world faded into darkness.

CHAPTER NINETEEN

Wood creaked, and waves crashed. Cannons boomed. No… not cannons. Thunder? Rain. Wind. A storm. Urgent voices shouted. Anger. Fear. I was warm. Was I dead?

No, being dead would be quiet. This was too loud.

Dark. It was dark. Where was I?

I opened my eyes but couldn't see anything. My vision blurred. Shadows moved…

…The scent of mildew mixed with old blood. Copper and musk. Stale ale and unwashed bodies. This was familiar. I knew this.

I needed to get up. Tavers would come find me soon. Kick me awake, or worse if he was in the mood.

Peeking through a crack in the door. A well-lit room. A full meal spread out on the table. Krellen chatted with a tall man with a dark tan. They shook hands. He turned to look at me, blue eyes nearly the same color as my own locked onto my hiding place.

I shivered in the cold. A bony hand clamped down on my shoulder. Sour breath on my neck. "There you are, little mouse. Time to play." I spun, staring into the cold, merciless eyes of Darl Tavers…

…Bright light. I squinted, trying to block the pain. I was warm. Too warm. I tried to push the quilt off. Quilt? Did I have a quilt like this?

"No. I told you before, you can't go in there. I will let you know when something changes." The voice was hard. No nonsense. It was reassuring somehow, even though I didn't know what they were talking about.

"But-"

"No, Kaelyn. Go." the voice said again.

More grumbling came as an answer before the voice faded away.

A door opened and closed again quietly. After a moment, a cool hand touched my forehead and a face came into view. "Hey, you're awake." A cool cloth wiped over my face, removing sweat I didn't realize was there.

I tried to speak, but words didn't form.

"It's okay. You're okay, Tianna. Get some more rest. You're safe here."

Here? Where was here? My eyelids grew heavy...

...The air was cool, with a gentle breeze that ruffled my hair. Laughter mingled with song through the night. Light from torches and lanterns cast dancing shadows on the tents and shelters outside of the town. Festival nights were always my favorite.

A warm hand held mine in the darkest alleyway. No light or stars reached us. "It's good to see you smile." He spoke softly, murmuring just above my ear. When his lips met mine, it wasn't even a surprise. This had been building for too long already. It was inevitable. We were inevitable...

...The bed in the orphanage was lumpy, and the other children muttered and cried in their sleep. It was another long night for me. Sleepless and empty. No light to read by, no music to listen to, no people to talk to. I was surrounded, but alone.

"Tianna, time to wake up. There's chores need doing"...

…Blond hair held back in a tight braid, and a concerned purse on her lips. Ember. She pressed a wet cloth to my brow. I blinked up at her, trying to speak.

"Where…?" I coughed. She patted my chest gently until I calmed again.

"Good to see you're still with us," she said.

"…trying," I almost smiled.

"We've been worried. Some more than others. Here, drink this." She helped me to sit up.

Pain lanced through my torso, stealing the air from my lungs. If I could get a whole breath I would have coughed.

"Careful," she said. "You're still healing."

No shit, I wanted to say, but settled for sipping from the glass she held to my lips.

"What…?" I eventually said, or tried to. Words still escaped me.

"You were shot trying to escape the battle with the convoy. Do you remember?"

I paused, remembering cannon fire, splintered wood, shredded rigging. "Isa–"

"She is fine. As are Eric and Kaelyn. They all got a little banged up, but you had it the worst. They brought you to Tiraea. Lucky Sinan and I were in port."

I licked my dry lips. "Sen Tagna," I muttered. "Anne…"

"Don't fret. Our mission isn't over, just delayed for a few days." She patted my hand gently. " Rest up. We'll take care of you until you're back on your feet."

I nodded slowly and sank back into my pillows…

…The fireplace warmed the cozy room. I curled up on the floor, listening to Jun bustling around in the kitchen downstairs. The room smelled of tea and sticky buns, and I sighed into it.

Albert sat in his chair, his slippered feet resting on a stool as he read aloud. "The Sun's bright palace, on high columns raised, with burnished gold and flaming jewels ablazed; the folding gates diffused a silver light, and with a milder gleam refreshed the sight... Tianna, are you even listening, child?"

The sound of his voice and the crackling fire lulled me into a drowsy haze. I didn't answer him. I wasn't even sure he'd spoken.

"Tianna?" He sighed. "Why do I bother?"

I watched the fire dance in the hearth, growing warmer, larger. It captured my mind, encompassed the room. Flames licked at the walls and across the windows. A high-pitched wail came from downstairs. A scream nearby. I scrambled to my feet, but it was too late. Shadows rose from everywhere, consuming everything.

I met Albert's terrified gaze as the darkness consumed him. I opened my mouth to scream...

My eyes were open. I wasn't sure when that happened, but as the dream slowly faded, I became more and more aware of the room I was in until I realized I was awake.

"Hey there, sleepyhead." Kaelyn's warm voice greeted me. I heard her rustle around from somewhere to my left. Footsteps sounded, and a door opened. Murmured voices held a bit of urgency out in the hall.

After a moment, Kaelyn's heavy-booted steps returned.

"Welcome back to the land of the living," she said, leaning over the bed to look at me. I must have grimaced because she chuckled. "Too soon for jokes?"

"Too close. Not fully sure I am alive yet." My voice came out weak. Throat was dry. Head hurt. I closed my eyes again.

"Fair enough." She carefully took a seat on the bed, near my feet.

I opened my eyes slowly. The room was blurry as I waited for my vision to clear and focus to return. I couldn't see much without moving. And I had very little incentive to try. After several minutes, I finally settled my gaze on Kaelyn's worried face.

She chewed on her bottom lip as she scanned my face for something. I couldn't tell if she was looking for reassurance or forgiveness but she took her time, choosing her words with care. "Are you... alright?"

If I thought I could have laughed without passing out, I would have. But even the sharp intake of breath felt like a too-small steel corset lined with spikes. "No."

She shook her head vehemently. "Of course not. Stupid question," she rambled. "I mean, you were shot. That isn't something you can just get over in two days."

Two days? Had I been out for two days? What had happened with the convoy? With Anne's meeting? I started to sit up. I needed to find some answers.

"It would be miraculous if someone were to recover from a gunshot so quickly," Ember said cheerily as she glided into the room. "And if that were her injury, I wouldn't be letting you in here now." She shooed Kaelyn off the bed and leaned over me to look in my face.

"I wasn't shot?" I said dully.

She smiled and held a small mirror in front of my face, reflecting the light from the window into my eyes. I squinted and tried to squirm away. After a moment of torture, she set it down and ran her hands down both of my arms and squeezed my fingers.

"Technically, no," she finally answered. "Has anyone ever told you that you are the luckiest person alive?"

Kaelyn laughed, and kept on laughing, even after I glared harmlessly in her direction.

With another smile, Ember explained. "You were shot *at*, and would have sustained a major injury, but somehow, the bullet managed to strike the buckle of your sword harness. It deflected off with only minor grazing."

"What–" I tried to sit up again and fell back to the bed with a cry, panting for breath that I couldn't find. "This doesn't feel minor."

"Oh, you've got some incredible bruises, maybe a cracked rib, and a rather deep gash where the buckle tore into you. You definitely won't be doing any heavy lifting for a while." Ember waved me off, but looked me dead in the eyes. "But what you *don't* have is a gaping hole in your torso. And you very nearly did."

I gaped at her, letting that reality sink in. He shot me. Tavers *shot* me. I almost gave that bastard the one thing he's always wanted from me. Rage washed through me, chased quickly by a kind of satori that only comes from cheating death.

"I… oh," I said.

Ember patted my shoulder. "As I said, lucky."

I laid in a stupor while she continued her examination of my wounds. She gently folded the quilt down and lifted my loose bedshirt. I couldn't see the bruises from my position, but I imagined them to be a glorious shade of blue and purple, mottled like a northern aurora at midwinter. At least, that seemed poetic enough to keep me from crying out when her soft fingers prodded into my side.

"You've missed quite a lot, Captain," Kaelyn said.

I knew she was trying to distract me, and I was grateful for it. I also needed to know whatever it was she had to tell me, so I tried to focus on her and not whatever Ember was doing with that sticky blue salve that smelled like the inside of a goat. "Report," I grunted through my teeth.

"When you fell, we were already underway." Her tone was even and relaxed, as if she was reciting a passage from a history book instead of reciting a first-hand battle account. "Tossing the cannons gave us enough extra speed that we were able to outmaneuver Tavers' ship with no problem. Especially Since the convoy was still blocking his way, we had unexpected help. I still think he could have caught us in a straight race, but last we saw, he was stuck. In the end, we suffered only cosmetic damage to the hull and sails. The rigging took the largest hit, but Isaboe swears it's fixable."

"Isab–" I started to say, but Kaelyn cut me off efficiently.

"The crew are alive and accounted for. Present company included... It could have been so much worse, Tianna."

I noted a small hitch in her voice, and suddenly I was reminded that she was even younger than I was. I tried to reach past Ember to grasp her hand. After fumbling for a few minutes, my friend caught on to what I wanted and took a step forward to where I could see her. She clasped her warm hand around mine and let out a small sigh.

"I'm still here, Kaelyn," I told her. "I'm fine."

"I know." She swallowed audibly and took a step back out of my field of vision again. When she continued, she was composed once more. "Most of the crew has recovered well. Eric and I both had some cuts from shrapnel, but nothing permanent. Eric might scar, but I don't think that will slow him down. Isaboe took a knock to the head and was grumpy about it for a while, but she's doing fine now."

"No concussion that I could find," Ember added. "But she did have some lovely bruises to her shoulders and ego. Not unlike yourself, Captain."

"When we fled, the convoy focused on Tavers. We aren't sure what happened to him, but there have been rumors of a small, unmarked fleet heading south. So we have reason to believe the convoy didn't stick around. We still have no idea who they are or what they were doing here. My best guess is still slavers. Merrik is betting on a Consortium plot."

"You're betting on this?" I asked incredulously.

Kaelyn snickered. "Not literally. Nothing to be gained from it, right?"

I grunted something like a laugh. "You'd be surprised. Taking bets on ships coming and going from Wellsmith was most of what I did for Krellen."

Both women hesitated. They looked at me then to each other, then nowhere.

"You don't think Krellen had anything to do with this, do you?" Kaelyn asked carefully.

I shook my head slightly on my pillow. "No. I wouldn't put it past Krellen to pay pirates to attack incoming ships to guarantee the outcome of some bets, but I don't think he had any part of this. There's no profit in blocking the best route into Wellsmith, and they wouldn't have attacked Tavers if they were in Krellen's employ."

"That's... true, I guess,. But that's what worries me," Kaelyn said slowly. "If this is bigger than Krellen, then what are we facing?" She fell silent, lost in thought.

After a moment, Ember picked up the conversation. "We sent a letter to Anne's contact in Sen Tagna. She explained that you were incapacitated and your ship was damaged, so you will land-bound for a while. I believe she will be wanting to arrange a meeting with him as soon as you can, but no one wants you on your feet before you're ready, Captain. It looks like you'll be stuck here for a while."

I huffed out a breath. "Where is here, exactly?"

"You are in my home in Tiraea," she answered sweetly. "And you're welcome."

I blinked. "Tiraea? I thought you lived in Sunset? Did you move in the week we were away?"

The older woman chuckled. "Hardly. Sinan and I left the day after you did, continuing our mission as well. Since we don't know how long we will stay in a port, we like to rent. It's one of the few pleasures the job affords."

"Ah," I said, trying to comprehend that kind of life. "So, Tiraea?"

Ember nodded and smiled. "I like Tiraea. And I hope you do too, since you'll be here for a while. You will recover, but not overnight." Satisfied I was healing well, she replaced my shirt and tucked the quilt back up around my chest, then sat back on the bed where Kaelyn had been earlier.

"I hardly know. This is my first time here."

The warmth of her chuckle spread out to fill the room. "You'd best settle in for a long recovery. You're welcome to stay here as long as you need."

She started to pack up her medical supplies, and Kaelyn stepped back into view.

"There is something else, Captain," she said, drawing my attention back to her. "There have been rumors circulating around town. While you've been out, we put the crew to work doing day labor and odd jobs. Mostly to keep busy, but also to earn a little coin and keep an ear to the ground."

I grunted my approval. "That's good."

Kaelyn coughed and waited a beat before continuing. "If the whispers hold any truth, there might be merit to your fears of a war between Epirsa and Lugaia. Epirsan ground troops have been attacking holdings along the border of the southern provinces. The city-state of Farré especially. So far, this is just happening on the continent but…"

"But you're worried that if Epirsa should gain a foothold over Lugaia, that could bleed over into the isles," I finished for her.

"Just so," she said quietly and fell silent again.

"I wonder if it hasn't already."

"What do you mean?" Ember looked at me sharply.

I met her stare for stare, reading as much from her as I could. She made no secret of working within the Lugaian spy network and was open about her political leanings. But I had to choose my words carefully, knowing that they could be given to whomever she reported to next.

"For the last several years, there have been stirrings in the Outer Isles. Small rumbles of displeasure aren't uncommon, but when the coup in Bann Tirica replaced King Marcus, loyalists were quick to secure what little power they had, and more alarmingly, those that weren't terribly loyal were happy to gain whatever power they could. It's largely how Wellsmith came to be what it is. Mitsuni and Krellen both were in a position to gain power through force, and King Frederick did nothing."

"I thought you didn't care for foreign politics?" Ember said with a hint of that signature smirk.

"I don't but Albert was incensed and believe me, I heard plenty when it happened. This affects us locally, trust me."

She sighed. "None of what you say is new, exactly. I wasn't sure about Wellsmith, but I've seen this elsewhere."

"Good, then you will understand when I say that a power vacuum can only lead to unrest among the people. It's hard enough to have faith in your government when it's in upheaval, but the further you get from the center of power, the less stable that power becomes. Unless–"

"Unless you exert that power by placing people you trust in overseer roles," Ember said. "What aren't you saying?"

I chewed on my lip as I thought over my words. "When King Frederick pulled back from Bann Tirica, we essentially became lawless. What will happen if King Antonie does the same? Lugaia still has a lot of resources tied up in Denisi, but if he consolidates his forces to fight back Epirsa on the border, then…"

We all fell silent because we all knew what that would mean. How much damage had Bann Tirica's indifference caused here in the Outer Isles? Lugaia Denisi held all the power and resources out here. Trade with the Inner Isles was the only reason we weren't completely cut off from the rest of the world. If they turned to a similar anarchy, where would that leave us?

"I guess they don't call this the Pirate Isles for nothing," Kaelyn said, echoing something Jasen had said on our first voyage together. It was far less funny this time.

"It's exactly what you were afraid of, Kaelyn," I said. "A war between Lugaia and Epirsa will draw attention from Meket and Bann Tirica and who knows who else. The Isles will land squarely in the middle of everyone's war."

We all sat with that for a few minutes. There wasn't more to add. The weight of it all would have been too much, even if I was in top physical shape. I let my mind wander until I felt the threads of sleep begin to pull me back under.

"We can't do nothing," Kaelyn's voice was barely more than a whisper.

"I know," I said. "We won't. Whatever politics are at play, innocent people are caught in the middle. They need help, even if they don't know it yet. And right now, we're all they have."

"What are you proposing, Captain?" Ember asked. "Is there a plan behind this grand idealism?"

"A plan?" I almost laughed. That damn word again.

"We find out as much as we can, and we stop the war from coming here."

"How?"

"Well…" I said as I lost the battle back into a hopefully dreamless sleep. "That is the question, isn't it?"

CHAPTER TWENTY

I tried not to skip as I walked through the park. Even with as much pain as I was still in after another three days of healing, I was giddy with excitement.

The night air was warm with the last lingering hints of summer, but the rich smell of fallen leaves and overripe fruit spoke of fall. It had been raining all week, but the storm had finally cleared that afternoon leaving everything fresher, cleaner, and renewed.

The park was bursting. Half the town—thousands of people—must have been there. They filled the green expanse in front of city hall, the surrounding buildings, and spilled out into every street nearby.

Several nearby theaters had even thrown open their doors, showing highlights from their most popular plays. Actors in bright paint and costumes danced in the streets to draw people in.

A small stage had been set up in a corner of the open space where one-acts and pantomimes were performed. Musicians, jugglers, and whoever else could claim the space jumped in to entertain the crowd. I had even seen a small band of drummers up there when we'd first arrived.

Now that night had fallen, bonfires had been lit on either end of the lawn with a smaller one near the park entrance. Benches and hay bales were set out for people to sit and relax, as well as chairs that people brought with them.

A temporary boardwalk made of spare planks was laid out side-by-side on the grass. The avenue circled the park, looping back to itself near the steps to city hall. Vendors hawking just about every type of ware lined both sides of it, and patrons meandered up and down the row, cavorting and laughing, while spending their coin.

Everything from gaudy trinkets to small weapons to hand-painted portraits was available for sale. And the food. My gods, the food. Meat smoked and sizzled above two spits in the center of everything. There was fresh bread and pastries, roasted potatoes, candied fruits, baked apples and pears, pies—so many pies!—and everything anyone might concoct from the bountiful harvest that Isla Tirae had to offer.

So, yes. I was giddy and trying not to skip. I was always a sucker for a good festival. And this was a great festival.

We had been here almost an hour and I couldn't stop my wide-eyed wonder. After several days of encroaching on her hospitality, Ember had suggested we all come down here for some much-needed fun. It had been a damned-fantastic idea that I eagerly jumped at.

Figuratively, of course. She would have tied me to the bed if I'd tried to move too fast before I was fully healed.

We had started out as one group. The nine of us coming down to the park around supper time to see what struck our fancies. As the evening turned into full night, we started to break into smaller groups to explore.

Ember and Sinan walked with me and Kaelyn for a time, but eventually found a seat near a bonfire, and settled in with a couple of drinks and a warm cloak. Anne, Iain, and Isaboe meandered ahead of us on the boardwalk, going from stall to stall, window shopping and laughing at the wares they found. Eric had gotten caught up in a conversation with a woodcarver and strayed behind. I hadn't seen Merrik almost since we arrived, but I knew he was around somewhere and would show up again soon.

That night is an amalgamation of near-perfect memories for me. Had I another hundred pages, I wouldn't be able to explain everything that happened that night, but I would be remiss if I left them out altogether. So, I will attempt to provide the highlights.

Kaelyn and I bought cups of hot cider from a booth and wandered over to the fire pit closest to the stage. A group of people in matching bright yellow kerchiefs stood in a smaller circle off the one side, readying props for something.

After a few minutes, one of them drew our attention. "Fine folk, if you could clear this space, please?"

Two of them then started ushering people away from the fire into a loose circle with a space in the middle.

Once the way was clear, a man in bright red pants that had to be too tight to move in walked out. He was carrying a long pole with braided cotton strips wrapped on either end. When he reached the fire, he thrust it into the flame, and lit the end of it. Then he tossed it up in the air, flipping it one handed lengthwise, and lit the other end.

Kaelyn's eyes were open wide as she watched. "What?" she gasped out on a laugh.

I laughed too, mostly too stunned to speak. The man with the fire pole had my full focus. He was bare-chested and, I noticed, clean-shaven. Probably smart, considering what I was watching.

Slowly, he took hold of the staff with both hands, holding it near the middle. Then he spun. He twirled the flaming staff in a circle. Slow at first, then faster, until the trailing ends of the light from the fire created a circle of flame. It wreathed him in yellow-orange light.

At some point, drums started pounding out a heavy rhythm. The cadence lifted the energy of the show and twirled through the crowd, perfectly matching his movements.

He twirled the staff around his body in a figure-eight pattern, then in a spiraling twister that wrapped around his body. Then he took a step. He leaned down to the right, and back up in a twirl, the fire never stopping its rapid pace around him.

He was dancing. With fire.

Kaelyn stood transfixed. Her eyes couldn't have gotten wider without her mindguts falling out. Her jaw hung open slightly as she took in the sinuous movements of the fire dancer in front of us.

I leaned in over her shoulder and whispered. "You could do that."

She started laughing again. Mechanically at first, then maniacally, then bordering on hysterics.

I turned back to watch the dazzling performance just in time for him to throw his arms up in a jerk. The staff flew up high into the air. It spun end over end before plummeting back down, caught and spun again.

Kaelyn laughed again and shook her head. "Nope."

Sometime later, Merrik found us.

We walked around until we came to a large open tent. Inside, dozens of people gathered around small tables, some in pairs, some in small groups. Each table had a game board built into its surface, and the clinking of coin and rattling of dice told me exactly what we'd found.

Despite my history, or perhaps because of it, I was never a huge fan of gambling. I enjoyed a good game, but it always lost its luster once money was on the line. We stuck around to watch some though, and soak in the general atmosphere.

"Eh, enough with the coin trade, ya?" someone shouted, throwing his now empty purse onto the table. "How do we liven this up?"

One of the two men standing guard near the entrance cleared his throat. "You are welcome to use drink instead of coin, but you have to play the table if yer sittin' at it."

The woman across the board from him grinned. "A'right, I'm in. Tiny glasses 'stead of coin? Move 'em th' same, ya? Seven line's a line e'en with drink 'stead of pieces."

I watched them haggle over the rules for several minutes, growing more and more excited before settling on terms. They easily found glasses but seemed perplexed about what to do next.

Suddenly, they turned to us, still just standing near the entryway. "You three! Yer no' playin', right? We need ale. Find us some?"

I chuckled and started to back away, but Merrik jumped in. "Not a problem, friends. What're you looking for?"

"Uh, ale?" the man said.

"Right away! Give me your tankards and I'll be back in a spiff."

They quickly complied and even gave us some coin for the drink.

Merrik spun and grabbed both Kaelyn and me on his way out. He dragged us down the boardwalk to the center of the park where the food stalls were.

"Are we doing this?" I asked, laughing.

He clapped his hands together, grinning. "Oh, yes. I love a good quest."

"Is this a quest? We're just fetching beer." I was still laughing. I think I spent most of that night laughing.

Kaelyn's tone was sullen, but her eyes sparkled with mischief. "Are we barmaids now?"

Merrik looked her over. "Well, you're not. But with a smile and a flat tray, we can work on it."

She reached over and smacked him.

"What's all this violence, then?" Eric came strolling up to us, full mug in hand and wearing a wide grin. As he drew into the lantern light, I also caught sight of a small bruise darkening the skin just under his jaw.

I grabbed his chin and tilted his head back to get a better look. "I'd ask the same of you, but I don't think that was a violent attack."

Kaelyn caught on to what I was looking at and chuckled. "Violent passion, maybe."

Eric wasn't the type to blush, otherwise I'm sure he would have. Instead, he grinned wider and nodded behind us to where a petite, dark-haired lass was eyeing him. "A burden, t'be sure. But one I plan t' get back to."

We all laughed as he started to walk away.

"Wait!" Merrik called. "We're on a mission to enable a drinking game. Join us!"

Eric looked at Merrik, then at the girl waiting for him, then back at Merrik. He shrugged. "Alright."

Merrik looked gleeful. "Yes! Party member acquired. On to the next objective…"

I shook my head, leaving the boys to their quest.

Isaboe came running up to me. "You've got to see this!"

I followed her out of the park and across the street to a small taphouse. It was a simple one-room affair with a few tables and kegs along one wall. Generic artwork was hung to remind patrons that decor wasn't the point, and a crush of people gathered around a bar-height counter near the back.

"Ain't no way little man c'n last 'ere!" some drunk man was shouting.

"Oh? I wouldn't be so sure. He seems scrappy to me."

I knew the second voice quite well. Sure enough, as we pushed our way through the crowd, I spotted Anne standing near the middle of the group, looking haughty and dispassionate. The man next to her, on the other hand, was drunk and eager. He stood a solid head and shoulders above her and was full muscle.

He scoffed and shook his head, gesturing at the table. "I's not 'bout t' crush th' poor lad!"

Anne lifted one shoulder and looked away. "Care to wager on that?" she said. "I've a purse that says you will be surprised."

That's when I pushed past the last patron between me and the scene. Iain leaned casually against the bar with an amused expression on his face. "No loss t' th' angley-bits, ya? Come n' go as ya please an' back t' yer sunup trade."

The other man squinted and then blinked at him.

"Oh, I'll gladly back that bet," I said, happy to jump in on this one. "I'm a sucker for an underdog, even one as scrawny as this."

Isaboe pulled me aside. "Do you even know what they're betting on?"

I shrugged. "No clue, but my money's on Iain. Or, more importantly, their money isn't on Iain."

"What will it be then, Champion?" Anne was goading the big man, and I saw the moment he gave in.

"I'm not 'bout t' be shown up in me own bar," he said. "Ain't no loser."

Soon, other patrons in the room were placing bets and arguing over who would be the winner. I happily took their money, wrote down their names, and chatted just enough to convince them they'd bought into a sure thing.

"Hey, Isaboe," I whispered as soon as we had a moment. "I don't have enough to back these should he lose."

I fell in love with the wicked twinkle in her eye. "Guess we'd better be ready to run, then."

"Bets are closed!" A few people grumbled, but most cheered as we got ready for whatever was about to go down.

Iain and the bigger man were staring each other down. They took up places on either side of the bar and leaned in, clasping hands, elbows resting on the counter.

"Arm wrestling? Really?" I looked at Isaboe, then at the Champion's bulging arms and wide shoulders. "Uhh…"

Anne winked at me and pulled a small, stoppered bottle from her pocket.

Someone started counting down. The tension built until I could barely breathe. I glanced at the door to make sure my exit was clear.

"Go!"

It happened so fast I almost missed it. The big man leaned in, pressing his weight into the bend of his arm. Iain's grin never faltered.

The man strained.

Iain didn't move.

Anne leaned forward and uncapped the bottle. She silently applied a few generous drops of something to the inside of her wrists.

Iain's arm didn't budge for one heartbeat, two, then all at once, the big man sneezed and he fell to the side as Iain slammed their hands onto the bar.

Cheers and groans rose up around the room. "Agh! No fair!" the newly unseated champion shouted.

Anne patted him on the shoulder. "That is a tough break. I am sure you almost had him."

"Hap' t' dance with a day fish, ya? Yer true scrap in a stall barn, lad." Iain clasped hands with the man and offered him another perfect smile.

I quickly paid out anyone who had bet on Iain and collected my winnings.

Anne blinked innocently at me and pocketed her phial. "I had no idea he was allergic to perfume," she said.

Back outside, we all gathered around the fire. Ember and Sinan huddled together, and we pulled up seats near them. Most of the chairs were taken. I drew my coat around my shoulders, ready to flop down on the damp ground, but hesitated, still favoring my right side.

"Heya, Cap. Take th' bountybale. I'm tip t' fiddlin' in m'boots anyhap." Iain stood and gently guided me down onto the seat he'd abandoned, then flopped down on the ground next to Eric.

This was a quieter lot than around the other fire. Rather than one group of chatting carousers, the folk here took turns, one at a time telling stories, singing songs, or otherwise entertaining the circle.

Kaelyn and I each took turns play my flute or singing as the mood struck. Merrik had found a drum somewhere and tapped out a lively beat while Isaboe danced a jig.

Iain and Isaboe traded off parts of a terrible joke that I wish I could remember well enough to share here. It was an elaborate parable ending in an unfortunate play on words. By the end, they had the whole fire groaning.

When Sinan rose to tell a story, Ember tried to pull him back down. He patted her on the head and slipped out of her arms. She hid her face while he told everyone about tricking a Baron into spilling bear all over himself. I had trouble following it, but it seemed amusing.

Many long hours slipped by this way. I sang a few songs, told a few stories, and mostly floated by on a sea of merriment. Slowly, as the night wore on, the members of my crew drifted away until only I was left.

"Last one by th' embers, hmm?"

I turned to look for the voice over my shoulder. A man with an open, if somewhat blurry, smile sat down next to me. I had seen him around the fire most of the night, enjoying the stories and songs as much as the rest of us had. He had hair the color of wet sand, and a warm voice with just a hint of culture to it.

"Name's Theo. I'm not one for early nights either."

That's when I looked around and saw that it really was nowhere near early any more. Or rather, it was so early that morning was already upon us.

The sky was just starting to hint at lightening in the east and the park was empty of all but the heartiest of revelers.

"Oh, goodness. Guess I was having fun. I should get back." To punctuate my point, I yawned generously.

My new friend chuckled. "Can I walk you back? I'd hate for somewhat t' happen to you."

I eyed him carefully. He was thin and wiry, but slow and bleary. If he was trying to get me alone to hurt me, I could handle him. Of course, if he was just trying to chat me up, he would have to work harder. Either way, I deemed it safe enough and I stood.

He rose to his feet with me and wobbled a little bit. With a deep bow, he offered me an arm. I chuckled at his show of gallantry and took it.

We set off across the grass toward the road back to Sinan and Ember's house. Since I was holding on to him, I could experience firsthand the way he staggered and weaved while we walked. He would pull me first one way, then the other, as we wove our way across the park.

"Are you drunk, Theo?"

He looked at me, confused. "No. Not much anyway."

I knew that had to be a lie. The man couldn't walk a straight line. "Here. I seem to have the more stable feet, so I'll lead us to the road." I unhooked my arm from his, then offered my elbow for him to grab onto.

He chuckled. "Oh! I'm not drunk," he said again. "It's these damn boots." He pointed down at his feet. They were just a pair of low black leather boots. I'd seen similar footwear on half the townfolk tonight.

"Your boots are making you stagger?"

"No heels."

I paused and looked at him, waiting for him to continue or explain.

He laughed again as we started walking. "I'm used t' my deck boots that have a low heel. These land shoes are hard t' walk in."

Theo sounded so earnest it was hard not to laugh. I didn't want him to think I was laughing at him, though, so I refrained. But honestly, staggering from a lack of heeled boots? At the wrong side of dawn after a harvest festival? It was simpler to assume the man was just drunk.

We eventually made our way to the road in front of my temporary home, and I bade Theo goodnight with a quick kiss on his cheek. "Maybe we'll meet again, the next time I'm in Tiraea."

He smiled sweetly, but shook his head. "Unlikely. I don't stay in one place long. But mayhap we'll chance upon th' same port again someday."

"Another island, another festival?"

"It's a date." With that, he walked off, stumbling back up the road.

I made the rest of the journey on my own, smiling to myself. I was flying high from my amazing night and I was in no hurry to have it end. Even as tired as I was.

I rounded the last corner to home and paused. Merrik and Kaelyn were standing on the front step. Their heads were bent together, deep in conversation. I didn't want to interrupt them, but I was also surprised to see them both still awake.

Merrik spotted me first, and raised an eyebrow, then he and Kaelyn rushed over. They sandwiched me between them as they asked rapid-fire questions.

"You're just getting home?"

"Why were you out so late?"

"Who were you with?"

"What were you doing?"

I held up both hands, laughing so hard I couldn't speak. Not that they were giving me time to speak. "I was at the festival. What about you two? What are you doing awake and in the street?"

Merrik turned away, taking a step back. He stretched his arms wide and gave a big, showy yawn. "Wow, sun's coming up. I'd better get back to the ship and get some sleep. Night!"

He strolled away slowly, but somehow the effect was just as if he'd bolted and run down to the docks.

Kaelyn was staring at me.

"Want to tell me what's going on?" I asked slowly.

She shook her head. "Nope."

I laughed, and we headed inside. I couldn't stop the smile on my face as we crawled into bed.

We pulled the quilt up just as the birds started to chirp their morning song. Kaelyn hid under a pillow in protest. "Damn birds," she mumbled as we slipped off into warm and happy dreams. The respite I needed.

That was a perfect night.

CHAPTER TWENTY-ONE

I stared into the fire, watching the logs crackle and pop. The warmth pervaded my aching body. It carried away lingering tension, and any thoughts I might have been having. The deep hearth chair I sat in had a tall back, and gently sloping arms. The whole of it was large enough for me to curl up in. I wrapped myself in a blanket and became insensible of the world around me.

Or I would have done, but there was too much laughter and chatting for me to fade away completely.

Another raucous round of laughter came from the group standing by the windows. I glanced that way to see Sinan telling another elaborate story. The man talked with his hands in large, sweeping gestures which his audience seemed to find thrilling. Eric, Iain, and Isaboe seemed completely caught up in whatever yarn he was spinning.

Across the room, Anne, Merrik, and Ember stood around a sideboard table, quietly chatting and picking at a supply of finger foods. Ember was a gracious hostess. We never seemed to want for anything, and even after a week stuck in one place, everyone was wearing massive smiles. They were relaxed. Happy.

Kaelyn plopped down in front of me, wearing a smile of her own. "Heya, friend. How're you feeling?"

I offered a half smile in return, then sighed and settled deeper into the pillowy blankets surrounding me. "Cozy."

"Sure, sure, brag about it. But I meant the ribs? Still breathing okay?"

I shifted and let out a small groan. Her smile gave way to a wariness and I took the moment to check the state of my own well-being so I could answer her.

There was a tightness around my chest but the raw stabbing had subsided. The bruising had turned a deep purple color in the center and was fading to a patchy yellow around the edges. The deep gash was healing over, and I was glad I hadn't needed stitches. My legs ached from too many days of lying in bed, but overall I was just as I'd told Kaelyn—cozy.

Everyone had been kind, quiet, and supportive while I was convalescing, but their reports were sketchy. I was able to piece together what had happened that night, but I couldn't wait to get back aboard the Siren and see for myself what state she was in.

I still hadn't been down to the docks. In fact, in the four days since the festival, I'd barely been out of the house at all. I was itching to see open waters and feel fresh air on my skin. That horizon was calling my name, and it almost ached to deny that call.

"M'fine," I told her. "Breathing okay, just achy. Tired."

"I've got something I want to show you." She looked away, a slight flush staining her cheeks. Ember's been helping me with it, but I think you'll like it."

"Hmm…" I uttered drowsily. "Later, yeah? Sleepy."

Her face lit in a warm, patient smile, and she patted my blanket-clad shoulder. "Sure. I'm glad you're feeling better. You deserve a rest."

She cursed me. In the great grand scheme of the universe, *you deserve a rest* had to be almost as bad as *at least it's not raining*. Never challenge worse.

The dim parlor lit up in a flash of light as an echoing boom sounded from somewhere outside. Sinan tore open the window and leaned out. Screams and shouts wafted in from the street below, followed by the smell of smoke.

"*Anlakahs*," Sinan hissed, all sense of playfulness gone. "Slavers." He translated for those who didn't speak Epirsan, but it hardly mattered. Not a moment after he spoke, more cries rose from below.

"Guards, help! Slavers attacking! To arms! To arms!"

I rolled to my feet, more temerity than I felt, blankets falling all around me. "Kaelyn, stay with Anne and Ember. Barricade the house. The rest of you with me."

Kaelyn must have seen me wobble slightly and gripped my elbow. "You shouldn't be out there."

I shook my head, pulling out of her grasp. "I'm fine. This isn't up for debate. They need us now." I turned away from her and disappeared into the guest room where I had been staying. I pulled on my boots and grabbed my swords, noticing the massive dent in the buckle.

I traced my finger over it, saying a silent thank you to whichever god had made that possible. I was very lucky.

The front door opened and footsteps pound down the steps. I quickly followed them into the street. Sinan and Merrik immediately broke away, heading north along the main road toward the docks, where the fighting would be heaviest. I could trust Merrik to try and flank them, maybe even block their retreat. The more people we kept off their ships, the better.

A pair of older women huddled in the doorway of a nearby house, clutching to each other and shaking. Eric took a protective stance over them, pushing the combatants back into the main road. Iain, Isaboe, and I headed into the fray just outside the door.

I ran toward a group of men who were trying to put out a fire. It was rapidly growing and threatening to erupt into a blaze that would consume several of the houses across the street. As I neared the firefighters, a large, dirty man who was definitely not with them blocked my path. He grinned at me, showing a jagged row of teeth in an unkempt beard.

I ducked low, throwing my weight behind a lunge with my long blade. I gasped as he parried, throwing me off balance. Pain lanced through my chest as I dodged out of the way of his downward swing.

Still low, I took my shorter blade and stabbed into the back of his thigh and dragged it upward as I stood, rending a gaping wound up the back of his leg. With a scream, he buckled and fell. I leaped over him, ignoring the wave of nausea that left me wanting to lose the contents of my stomach from the effort I'd exerted.

Down the road, Isaboe brought the flat of her heavy blade down on the back of one slaver's head. He turned to see who was attacking him and let go of the young boy held in his grasp. Isaboe moved until she was just in front of him, and he reached out with both hands, grasping her shoulders.

Solidly in his grip, she took a half-step back until his arms were fully extended and then brought her heavy blade up sharply. With a sickening crack, I watched as both of his elbows bent the wrong way. He howled and dropped her, his arms useless.

As he screamed, she easily ran him through and kicked him away from her.

"Run, or fight," she shouted to the boy who still stood there. "Don't be a target!"

He ran off.

Behind them, Iain deftly ran up a stack of barrels until he was more than twice a man's height. With a lightning fast, spinning kick that looked more like a dance move than an attack, he tumbled himself down onto the backs of two more slavers who were chasing a couple into an alley.

He wrapped his arms and legs around the torso of a leather-clad woman, clinging to her back. He produced a long, thin dagger he'd had hidden on his person and slit her throat. She fell in a spurt of blood that splashed across her companion. With a growl, the man grabbed hold of Iain and threw him into a wall.

Watching this, I hurried to my right, where a pile of new bricks lay piled near a bucket and wheelbarrow. I grabbed a smaller one and chucked it at the man who threw Iain. It hit him on the side of his head, and he fell like a stone. As Iain stood and dusted himself off, I turned back to the fire.

More screams echoed down the road. Another slaver grabbed a matronly woman by the hair and thrust his sword through her chest, tossing her lifeless body aside. I didn't wait to see more. I threw myself on top of him. I brought my shorter blade up and rammed it up through his chin into his skull.

The sounds of clashing swords and intermittent gunfire drowned out everything else. I whipped my head around, watching the road to the docks. A large group was moving toward us. Eight more slavers made their way to us.

Two broke off, disappearing into a house where more screams erupted. A gunshot rang out. One tossed an old man back through an open door. Another one kicked a fallen body that was lying in the street. When the form didn't stir, he stabbed it, making sure the villager was dead. The slaver sneered and spat before moving on.

"Everyone run!" I shouted as loud as I could. "Get out of here! Help the wounded and elderly! Get somewhere safe!"

"Where?" a scared woman called. She was clutching a crying babe to her chest, and I nearly broke into tears at the sight.

"I… I don't–"

"The old theater!" the man who had put out the fire called. "Brick building on the High Street! Won't burn and we can barricade the walls." He immediately turned, shouting orders to the men and women around him.

"Iain, Isaboe, to me!"

"Here, Cap'n. All'n good round," Iain said, running over to me. He turned to face down the approaching slavers and drew his blade again. "Let's give th' lot time t–ugh!"

The blast of a nearby pistol cut off whatever he was about to say. He shouted in pain and fell to the ground. His trousers were quickly stained red, and growing wetter with his blood as he clutched at a wound in his lower calf.

"Iain!" Isaboe cried and ran over to him. She wrapped her arms around his shoulders and hauled him over to the relative cover of a stone wall.

I glanced around. "Eric!" He was at my side before I finished turning. I just pointed at Iain, and he ran over. Without saying anything, he scooped up his friend and hauled him over to Ember's door.

"Set me aright, tallboy. I'm fine 'nough for runnin.'"

Eric glared. "Not a flaming chance, man. You're hurt."

"No," he said succinctly. "Hand up a firestick 'n let me knock a punch or two. Not lettin' em through. th' noisy fest, ya?" His speech slurred, and he looked pale in the wan light but Eric nodded.

"Fine. But you'll let me bind your leg first."

Eric handed Iain his gun, then took his knife and cut a piece off the smaller man's shirt.

"Notta use yer own weave, ya?"

Eric scoffed. "It's your leg. We'll use your shirt."

Iain started to protest again, but cried out instead as Eric drew the bandage tight. I turned and left them to it.

The slavers worked their way down the street, killing anyone foolish enough to get in their way.

Killing.

I looked around. Bodies littered the street, slaver and villager alike. I knew some of these people. I'd seen them at the festival. But why were there so many dead if…

"Isaboe!" I shouted. "Are they taking prisoners?"

She hurriedly looked around, horror spreading on her face as she saw what I did. "Why are there so many dead?"

"*Vasta*. They're not slavers! Form a line!" I shouted to whoever could still fight. "Give the evacuees enough time to get away."

Three men and an older woman with muscle definition that a bear-wrestler would kill to have joined me. Isaboe took up a spot on the line as well. I offered her a grim smile, and she laughed. "There are worse ways to go. It's been a damn pleasure, Tianna."

"Knock off that nonsense. You're not done with me yet." I wasn't sure how we were going to survive this, but I knew we would. We had to. This was not where my story ended.

Just as I was bracing myself to charge at the group of slavers, a wild shout echoed through the night. It was a chaotic and free sound, like something a wild animal would let loose before striking its prey. A more apt description I would never be able to devise, because that's exactly what I saw—two frantic and bestial forms moving with and through the shadows, picking off our foes.

One shade struck out with fists and knees, each punch and kick controlling and moving their target into position to be struck again and again, unable to fight back.

The other moved like a snake or a goose, slinking low to the ground. It struck out, quick and precise, with only a flash of a blade and then nothing. One enemy fell. Then another. A scream erupted from a third, who clawed at the bleeding stump where his hand used to be.

We watched Merrik and Sinan attack and withdraw in a dance of pain. They fought separately but together, as if they had trained to do exactly this. Their prey was no match, even six on two, and soon they broke away. With an unspoken order to abandon their quarry and retreat, they turned and ran back to the docks and whatever safety their ship offered.

I ran after them. The cloud of battle fogged my mind, narrowing my focus to one point. We needed to stop them. We had to press our advantage. If we let them go, they would regroup and bring reinforcements.

As I rushed past him, Merrik grabbed both my arms. He pulled me to him in a hug that was meant to incapacitate. "Don't even think of running off on your own, boss."

I struggled for a moment before I stopped. He let go, and I fell the inch back to my feet. I pulled up to my full height, brushing off the indignity of being restrained from my own foolishness. "They're not slavers," I told everyone. "I'm not sure who they are, but they're killing, not capturing. We need to go after them. Press our advantage before they regroup and find out why they're here."

I looked at the scorched walls, broken crates and barrels, bodies and blood in the street. "Are the locals safe?"

Isaboe nodded. "They should be. Some are still fighting a few streets over. Let's stick together."

I stared down the road, watching back the way the slavers had fled. My mind reeled, trying to piece together what little information I had. Who were these people? Why were they here? What did they want?

"Tianna?" Merrik said sharply.

"Huh?" I turned, realizing he had been speaking.

"I just said I was going to go let Kaelyn know what's happening. But now I think I shouldn't leave you alone. Are you alright?"

An eerie fog drifted slowly up from the bay. It mingled with lingering smoke, mixing the smell of gunpowder with the smell of brine.

"What?" I asked again.

"Are you alright?" Merrik reached out and grabbed my arm again.

The smoke started to clear and I stared down the road as a lone, bedraggled figure appeared in the mist.

Where his eyes were once cold and cruel, now a single orb shone in the darkness, wild and deranged. His clothes were ripped and torn and several day's worth of beard growth on his face made him almost unrecognizable. But like something out of a worsening nightmare, I would know him anywhere.

"Godsdamn it," I growled. "That bastard! He must have brought them."

"What is it?" Merrik and Isaboe both turned to see what had caught my attention.

I didn't answer. Without waiting around to explain or thinking of a better plan, I tore off down the street toward Darl Tavers.

It was time to end this.

CHAPTER TWENTY-TWO

"Tianna, wait!" someone called out behind me. The sounded almost frantic, I wasn't sure. I couldn't tell you who it was. I didn't care. This time, I wasn't running away.

The moment Tavers spotted me, filthy words spilled from his mouth. He uttered an endless litany of curses, slurs, and obscenities loosely strung together in a sentence. His clothes were torn, his skin dirty, cut, and bruised. He looked like he'd been caught on the wrong side of a kraken in a hurricane.

Or a pirate convoy.

"You filthy whore!" he shouted. "How many times do I have to kill you?"

"That's my damn question!" I shouted back, still running. "How are you still alive?"

I was close enough now to see the unhinged terror and hatred in his wide eyes. He screamed in rage and turned.

"He's running away!? Are you kidding me?" My scream of frustration nearly matched his own. I rounded the corner into the alley he had fled down. Up ahead, he was weaving between piles of refuse, scattering detritus to slow my path. I stumbled over a broken flower pot just as he rounded another corner.

I chased him down the dark alley to a thick, high wall. Tavers stood still, screaming his frustration at it. "Dead end, asshole. It's time you answered for your crimes."

He turned slowly, a look of incredulous bewilderment on his face. With his scraggly hair, too-long beard, and wild eyes, he looked like a caricature of himself. A caricature that looked like I'd just hit him over the head with a plank of wood.

"My crimes? What about you, murderer? Everything I did, I did for my family, for my uncle! What about you?"

"What the hells are you talking about?" I shouted. "I haven't done anything to you, except survive!"

He spat at me. Something wet and half-solid landed near my feet. "You killed him!"

I took a step back. Who was he talking about? Before tonight, I'd only ever killed one man. Back in Wellsmith, when... oh. "That man of yours? Nate, right? What was he to you, your lover?"

He recoiled in horror, looking like I'd just shoved a pile of horse muck in his mouth.

"Look, I didn't want to kill him. I was defending myself. I hate that he died, but–"

"I don't care about that idiot!" Tavers banged his fist on the stone wall behind him. "I mean Uncle Jassec!"

For a moment, his statement didn't even sound like words. "Krellen's dead?"

Tavers blinked, trying to see through this latest trick of mine. "Don't play with me, bitch! I know you killed him!"

For want of any better response, I shrugged. "Uh, no. I didn't. He was still alive when I left. Alive and well, as far as I know."

"Don't lie to me! You killed him!" He screamed and launched himself at me.

He rushed and drew a long, thin sword from a scabbard at his belt. I had just enough warning to bring my blades up, crossed in front of me to catch his downward swing.

Hatred colder and deeper than anything I'd ever read in any storybook oozed from him. "I'll kill you," he said with shocking calm.

"Not this time," I growled.

I pushed back against his bulk, leaning into his attack. While he was distracted by my counter, I brought my knee up into his groin.

He buckled and staggered back a couple of steps. Cursing at me again.

Hurried footsteps and jangling metal came from the mouth of the alley, and Tavers swung his hand up. "No, stay back. I'll kill her myself."

I was surrounded. While Tavers and I had fought, his men had found us, trapping me in this dead end with him. They watched in fascination, but did as he commanded and stood back.

I turned my attention fully back to Tavers, ignoring the new clutch of potential enemies gathering behind me. If this is how he wanted it, I would oblige. Resettling my grip on the blades still in my hands, I took a step forward and swung.

My aim went high, and he blocked with his sword, skipping easily out of the way.

I turned as he swung. My blade caught his, and I swept down into the counter Merrik had taught me, then swung again. And again before he had a chance to move.

Tavers moved too slowly, surprised by my trained attack. He jumped back just in time to avoid a deep slice to the chest. The tip of my blade cut into his shirt, leaving a thin line of blood beneath.

He cut down, aiming a similar blow at my torso. I brought the hilt of my sword up and knocked it aside, but he was relentless. He swung again, aiming for my head.

I ducked, but not fast enough. The flat of his blade skipped across my scalp before he spun to follow through. I didn't let him complete the turn, though. Before he was fully facing me again, I lashed out with the basket guard of my long blade, slamming it into his face.

He staggered back under the weight of my punch, but quickly righted himself.

"You fatherless insect! You think you're special. That you're smarter and better than me, but you're not! You are gutter trash and always will be!"

I stood, bringing my blade between us, watching him as I answered. "I am smarter than you, Tavers, because I knew when to leave that sinking ship you call home."

He screamed again. "You were never good enough to polish his boots!"

"Krellen respected me. I guess you'll never know what that's like."

"You ruined everything!" He shrieked and lunged at me again.

Despite being ready for him, the weight of his attack pushed me back into a wall. It took everything I had to avoid being skewered. I knocked his blade down away from my stomach, where the tip sank into my thigh.

I screamed in pain and lashed out wildly, pushing him back away from the uncontrolled edge of my swing. He took a step back to counter and swung high, aiming for my chest again.

I took a half-step to the side, dodging his attack, and checked his blade with my shorter one. Then, bringing my longer one up and around, I sliced into his shoulder.

He screamed more obscenities at me. Calling me every vile name he could think of as we continued to attack, block, counter, and attack again. Some blows landed, many did not.

Despite my training, I was terrified to learn that we were evenly matched. Within a few short minutes, we were both panting for breath and bleeding from light, shallow wounds.

The sound of clashing swords and angry shouts and cries of pain filtered down the alley. As Tavers took a step back to regroup, I spared a quick glance up. My crew was here. And they were engaging with Tavers' men. Our back alley duel had just become an all-out brawl.

Tavers never looked away from me. My momentary distraction gave him an opening and I missed him stepping in to swing again. I brought both my blades up at the last moment, catching his downward swing.

My arms burned as I pushed back against his heavier weight, bearing down on me. Just when I thought I could break free, he pulled back suddenly. I staggered forward, and he pushed me back the other way.

The force of the kick knocked the air from my lungs. As I fell backward, I swung out, uncrossing both blades in a sweeping attack, but Tavers wasn't there.

With nowhere to follow, though, I lowered my blades and tried to catch myself. Tavers was suddenly there, pressing into me again. He rocked low and then up, using all his weight behind his shoulder to push me backward.

I tripped and fell onto the hard packed dirt of the alley. My blades fell at my sides. I grabbed for my long blade just as he stepped on it, locking it in place.

He sneered down at me and booted the shorter blade out of reach, and kicked me with his free leg. He licked blood from his lip, then spit. Blood mixed with saliva dripped down the side of my face.

"Back in the dirt where you belong, bitch."

"Never again, Tavers," I snarled as I tried to pull free.

He dropped to his knee on my free arm. Sharp pain radiated to my shoulder. With both arms trapped beneath his bulk, I could do little more than struggle.

Gently, almost tenderly, he stroked his hand down my right arm to where it was still reaching for my sword. "Krellen always spoke of your skill with a pen. Such a fine, delicate hand," he crooned. "Pity he no longer needs your services."

His sweet words were belied by the malice in his eyes, and he took my forefinger in his meaty hands and cracked it backward.

The ugly popping sound hit me before I knew what had happened. At first, I didn't feel it at all, but as he laid it back on the cold ground, I felt all my blood rush to my finger. I would have fainted, but my attention was still on his sickening sweet smile.

"I don't suppose anyone will be needing your services now," he said, just as sweetly. There was a touch of pity this time, as if he were comforting a loved one. "But don't worry, I still have uses for you."

A second crack sounded in the alley as he grabbed my middle finger and yanked it backward.

I cried out, tears rolling freely down my face as I rocked, trying to pull free of him. His smile broadened, and he laughed.

"What happened to you killing me?" I asked through gritted teeth. "Wouldn't that be easier?"

He leaned down, bringing his face very close to mine, and whispered. "There's been a change of plans."

The moment his weight shifted forward, I rolled. Using my arm that was still pinned under his knee as a brace, I pushed myself toward my injured right hand, rolling my hips and swinging my legs over. We both toppled.

As we fell into the dirt in a pile of limbs, I reared back with my left hand and slugged him across the cheek. He rocked back and his head connected with the wall. He stared at me, dazed for a moment.

I took the chance I had and straddled his chest, pinning him to the ground the way he had me. I quickly grabbed my sword and held it across his throat. "Don't fucking move."

He smiled again, enjoying whatever jest he thought this was. "You can't stop what's coming, Tianna," he said. "Not even you are that lucky."

"I don't need luck," I told him, hoping the hubris was louder than the fear in my voice.

He started to say something, but stopped, gazing up at me. His face twisted into a wild mask. His eyes lit with fury and a bone-deep madness that I hadn't seen in him before. He was unhinged and, as of now, had nothing left to live for. And he knew it.

"No!" he screamed. "No! No! No!" He thrashed and banged his head back against the ground, over and over, while he shouted his denials to the universe. "This wasn't the plan! The Isles were supposed to be ours after he settles everything!"

I pressed a little harder into his wrists with my knees, bringing his attention back to me. "Who? What is this plan? You mean Krellen?"

His eyes locked on to mine. Every bit of perverted desire and deranged malice was gone. In their wake was left an ocean of pure hatred. "You bitch. This is your fault!"

Without warning, he kicked out, knocking me aside. He dove past me, reaching for the shorter sword where it had fallen in the dirt. I turned into a roll and popped up into a low crouch, trying to keep my face to him. With another brainsick cry, he threw himself forward, blade first.

I brought the tip of my sword up and braced myself as he careened artlessly into me. We both flew backward again. I punched with my free hand and screamed when the broken fingers met his rib-cage.

Agony swamped me. I slumped backward, unable to fight back against the dizzying pain. I struggled to move as he pinned under him, but I was pressed into the street by his heavy weight.

My head cleared, and he was still on top of me. Barely breathing. A wet, whimpering sound gurgled from his mouth next to my ear.

I rolled us over. My sword went with him, buried in his stomach.

His face was tight. With pain, with rage. With some terminal combination of the two. Blood stained his lips as he gasped for breath. His wandering eyes locked onto mine and slowly recognition bloomed. The tension faded from his face, and he smiled.

It was a sincere, heartfelt smile. The most sickening thing I'd ever seen. I felt my bile rising again.

He reached up with one shaking and bloodstained hand and reached out for my face.

I pulled away, horrified.

"Mine…" He coughed. "You are mine. You will… never be rid of me."

Eyes wide, I shook my head violently. "No. Never. I was never yours."

"Always… mine. I will… always come for you." He clutched at his vest pocket. Groping for something and holding onto it like a charm.

I shook my head again. "No," I told him.

"Until death…" he said as he reached for me again. "Mine…"

He meant it. I could see how true the words were for him. Had he really been so deranged? Is that what all his years of torture were? Some kind of love game? With the sickening clarity, I knew there was only one answer for me. I reached over and slid my short blade from his hand.

"You ruined everything. I don't care..." his eyes locked on mine, still aglow with that effervescent smile. "I lov–"

His confession dissolved into a gurgling gasp as I slit his throat.

I sat with him until his eyes glazed over and his face went slack. I don't know how long I sat there, just staring at him before Merrik approached.

"Tianna?" he said.

I started to raise my head to look at him, but the last few moments all caught up with me. Days of exhaustion. Exertion. Panic. Terror. Pain. I turned and heaved, retching what little was in my stomach into the street next to the body of the only man I'd ever wanted to kill.

After several minutes, I noticed a small clay jug hovering next to my shoulder. I looked up at Merrik. His face was an unreadable mask.

I took the offered jug, pleased to find it was citrus water. I took a long swig and swished the cool liquid in my mouth then spat it out before taking a proper drink. When I re-stoppered it and handed it back, I said the only thing that came to mind. "What the fuck?"

It was a weak, half-whispered declaration, but it was the only thought in my head for the last several minutes. *What the fuck?* For years, Darl Tavers had tortured and tormented me. He nearly killed me. Then he chased me all across the isles. Why? Because he fancied some kind of twisted courtship where there was only survival? How was that even possible?

I looked over at his lifeless form. He looked peaceful, the bastard. How dare he be peaceful in death? I stood, ready to beat his corpse until I felt more like myself, but I noticed he was still clutching at his vest.

Merrik reached for my shoulder as I bent over the body, then crouched next to me to see what I was doing.

I removed Tavers' fingers from their hold, and dug into his pocket, searching out his treasure.

In his grip, I found a neatly folded piece of paper wrapped around something. When I unfolded it, I cried out and tossed it aside.

Cautiously, Merrik leaned over to pick up the bundle. He pulled loose a small, silver coin. It was stamped on one side with the old Lugaian crest. The other side was filed away until it was nearly polished.

"What's this?" Merrik asked.

I reached for it with shaking fingers. "It was a gift from my… my father," I told him, not wanting to explain the complexities of my relationship with Albert just then. "Tavers stole it from me years ago, after he realized how important it was to me."

His eyes opened wide, and he swallowed hard, looking down into the paper again. He picked up something else gingerly, and said, "And this… this is…" He held out a soft, dark, braided lock about the length of his palm.

"My hair." Quickly turning, I lost the rest of what was in my stomach, not bothering to hide my shaking.

"Obsessive asshole," Merrik muttered.

The laugh that escaped me was not a joyful one. Quiet, unfiltered resignation weaved into every part of the sound coming from me. "Not anymore."

I carefully stood. There would be time later to process all of this, but for now, I was done. I was safe. It was time to go.

Merrik reached out and grabbed my wrist. I winced and pulled away, careful not to bump my hand.

"Wait." When I turned to him, he held up the paper. "There's something written here."

I took the letter from him with my good hand. I held it for a few moments before I stopped shaking enough to read it. It was a short missive in an ornate scrawling hand. Only one sentence. It said,

> Take your revenge if you must, but deal with them—G.R.

"Who is G.R?" Merrik asked, looking over my shoulder.

"No idea, but I assume we are the 'them' to be dealt with." I looked into Merrik's calm, gray-green eyes and found I could breathe a little easier.

He jerked his chin toward the entry of the alleyway. "Maybe they have answers."

I turned to look where he'd indicated and realized I'd forgotten all about Tavers crew.

Five men and three women sat on their knees. Their hands were behind their backs and their heads hung low in complete surrender to my crew. Kaelyn, Sinan, and Isaboe were pacing up and down the line, making sure they were staying put. Eric kneeled next to a younger man who sat fully on the ground, half-leaning against a wall, bleeding from a deep cut in his thigh.

As Merrik and I approached, Kaelyn walked over. She started to say something, then cried out when she looked at me. Cut, bruised, and bleeding in several places. I cradled my rapidly swelling hand against my chest.

"What the hells happened?" She reached for me, but stopped, not wanting to injure me further. She scanned me from top to toe, looking for mortal wounds.

"I'm fine, Kae. Promise." I cradled my right arm to my chest, then lifted my uninjured hand and waved it in front of her. "Idiot forgot I was left-handed."

I didn't wait for more than a smile from her before I marched past her to the line of subdued pirates.

"Which of you is in charge?"

One, the second to the end closest to me, lifted her head. "I... I suppose I am," she said reluctantly. "The mate's back aship, and th' young Lord there–" she nodded a gesture at Tavers' body, then shrugged.

I scoffed at the notion of him as a young lord, but turned to look at the woman without commenting on it. "Were you privy to his plans? Or do I need to track down your superior?"

She shook her head and shrugged again. "No one knew his plans," she said. "He'd get a letter, we'd get orders from the mate or Master, and we'd go. He paid well to mind our own."

"Well, shit," I muttered.

"These letters," Merrik asked. "They were his orders? Where did they come from?"

"Fr-from all over... I think? We would await in port, then jump when he called. 'Cept 'bout three months past when he started a grand tour. No one knew why, but the letters stopped."

I snapped my head back to look at Kaelyn, then back at the woman on the ground. "The letters stopped three months ago? When you left Wellsmith?"

The woman nodded. "Tha's right."

Kaelyn looked at me. "When *you* left Wellsmith. That's a hell of a coincidence."

I grunted in agreement, then held up the last note Tavers had clutched to. "And this one?"

The pirate shook her head, looking scared. "I... I don't–"

"Tha' one came when we was boarded," a small voice squeaked from the end of the row.

I turned and walked over to peer down at the older man who was kneeling, hunched over himself.

"Explain."

He looked up with clouded eyes and I marked a minor cut just below his brow that was clotting unevenly. "I think right, t'was yer ship we was chasin' tail outta Sunset," he said, half-questioning.

I nodded when he paused, and he continued.

"When we set upon ye, that group o'three big 'uns shows up and a mad firestorm breaks lose."

"I remember." I absently rubbed at my aching rib-cage.

"After yas all cut n' run, Young Master tells us t' follow but our rig's disabled from th' heavy cannon and we was caught, grappled easy. We was boarded by th' trained lot."

"The convoy caught and boarded you?" Kaelyn asked, astonished. "How did you get away?"

He met my gaze again, staring at me with a weight that I couldn't understand. "We didn't."

"What do you mean, you–" Kaelyn started.

"They let you go," I said.

The old man nodded. "Aye. Passed somat to Young Master, and turned us loose. Took a fancy bit o' sailing t' bring us back into port, but the slavers beat us here. Bad bit o' coincidence headed the sameways."

I was beginning to believe less and less in coincidence as time went on.

I blinked at him. "They weren't slavers, though."

He cocked his head to the side, confusion all over his face. "They wasn't?"

I shook my head. "They didn't come with you?"

He shrugged, still looking lost.

"Do any of you know who they were?"

No one answered, and everyone looked baffled.

"Tianna," Kaelyn said, pulling me aside. "If these letters were orders from whoever commanded that convoy, the southern isles could still be in trouble."

"She's right," Merrik added. "Tavers was nothing in their plan. We have to know what they were doing."

"Shit, you're right. And if those men weren't with Tavers, chances are they might have been here for him." I ran my hand through my hair and tugged on my braid, trying to shake loose a plan.

I looked at each member of my crew. We were every one of us battered, but we were standing. "Sinan, Eric, y'alright lads?" I asked, pasting on a cocky smile.

They both returned with answering grins. "Right enough, Cap'n," Eric said.

"Great. Let's get this lot trundled down to the docks, then. I think it's time we returned them to their ship."

Isaboe made a startled gasping sound. "We're just letting them go?"

I shook my head. "Of course not. This is a good old-fashioned hostage exchange."

"What about him?" Merrik asked, staring at the body at the end of the alley.

I suppressed a shudder and blew out a slow breath. "Bring the bodies. They have the right to bury their dead as they see fit."

"But Tavers–"

I speared Merrik with an unwavering look, hoping he could see the icy chill I felt all the way to the deepest parts of my heart.

"Darl Tavers is no longer my problem."

CHAPTER TWENTY-THREE

Our captives were happy to be trundled off down to the docks once we made it clear that we had no intention of keeping them for some kind of ransom scheme. Honestly, the idea sounded like way more trouble than it would be worth. Unbound and unarmed, we led them to the quay.

Merrik led the way while Isaboe kept watch along the column. Sinan and Eric organized a few of the crewmen to gather the bodies of their fellows, while Kaelyn stuck to my side like a starving barnacle. My energy was flagging, but we followed along behind the group, keeping apace as best I could.

"You alright?" Kaelyn asked in a low voice. "You're looking a little green around the edges."

I swayed a bit, but glared at her. "I'm fine. Few scratches, couple of broken bones, no big deal."

Her brown eyes bore into me, not the least bit amused by my attitude.

"I'm fine," I said more vehemently. "I've dealt with worse than this."

She shook her head, still frowning. "I don't doubt it. I only worry about how recently you've had to deal with it."

It was a waste of breath for either of us to argue, so I didn't. She seemed to share my sentiment, but never took her eyes off me. I felt my first mate's stubborn gaze all the way to the docks.

The cracked mainmast and splintered upper deck clearly marked our target. This ship had seen battle, and recently. A brass nameplate along the upper edge of the aftcastle proclaimed her "The Heartland". I noticed she wasn't flying any flag, but I knew this was the right ship.

Our arrival did not go unmarked. As we gathered on the walk near the Heartland, calls from aboard rang out. Soon, curious sailors were gathering along the rail.

"Ahoy, good fellows!" I called with a cracked and weary voice. "We would speak with your captain, if we may."

The group aboard the Heartland parted as a tall, thin man pushed his way forward. He stared down at me with judging eyes and a careful expression. "Our captain is away, but you can speak with me."

I nodded at Eric with a grim half-smile. Setting his jaw, he laid Tavers' body down along the walk. "Your captain is here," I said simply.

A few gasps and murmurs broke out among the gathered crew, and several made signs against evil, spitting at their feet when they saw the body.

"Dare I ask what befell th' man, that you drag his body here like some trophy?" the tall man said.

I grimaced. "No trophy. Tavers sought my death, but met his instead. I have no quarrel with you."

He stared at me, unmoving.

"Your crew here," I nodded to those still standing along the walk with us, "Have shown themselves to be honorable sailors and worthy fighters. By any measure you can see, they are not our captives. They stand here free, yet they hold themselves back as if held in chains. I take that as a testament to their training." I made sure to meet the man's gaze squarely, no hint of guile or trickery in my stance. "Something I'm guessing Tavers had no part in."

The man continued to watch me for a long moment. Only a slight ticking in his brow proved he wasn't a statue.

I took a deep breath, bracing my feet. Couldn't this just go simply? I wasn't sure I could stand up for another fight. And what if he turned these sailors away? I'd heard of some captains punishing those who were captured in battle with death or desertion. Would he do the same to these? Perhaps we could take them on. We had the room for a few more hands aboard the Siren.

Suddenly, a laugh broke out from him in a burst. It soon devolved until the entire crew was laughing with him. "You've done us a favor, friend. The world is well rid of him. Come aboard so we can talk."

I barely waited for him to wave us aboard before I moved up the gangplank, Kaelyn and Merrik close at my heels. The others rejoined their fellows, breaking off in tittering excitement to share the story of our encounter.

I stumbled slightly as I went to step down onto the deck and Merrik caught me with a firm hand on my elbow. I offered him a weak smile and shook him off, then made my way over to where the tall man was waiting.

"I am Elis Archer," he said, offering me a hand. "First Mate of th' Heartland."

I nodded and offered him a firm but friendly smile. "Captain Blackboot."

"Tianna Blackboot?" Surprise lit his face for a moment, followed by clarity. He shook his head in disgust and spit, as if he could chase the vile taste from his mouth. I nearly did the same. "He spoke of you."

"Do you sail out of Wellsmith?" I grimaced at the abrupt subject change, and hoped he would keep up anyway. I was running out of patience, so I pressed ahead. "Is it true, then? About Krellen?"

Elis met my eyes, searching for a moment. His warm gaze measured me, once again deciding whether or not to trust me. "Jassec Krellen is dead," he answered.

I breathed the last sigh of relief I didn't know I was holding onto. A sense of euphoria came over me then. I was floating.

For the first time since I could remember, I was free. Really free. No more watching over my shoulder. No more waiting for a knife in the dark. I could go home.

Just as quickly as it came, that euphoria washed away. I wasn't out of danger yet. If my fears were correct, none of us were. Who the hells was giving Tavers orders if not Krellen? I needed to know what was going on.

I snapped my gaze back up to meet Elis' dark eyes and gritted my teeth. "I need to see Tavers' cabin," I told him. "He had papers—evidence—of something... possibly everything. I need... I need–" My breath was ragged and uneven as I fought to find the right words.

"Calm yourself, Captain," Elis said. His smile this time was warm, patient even. He waved me off toward the cabin. "By all means, tear th' place apart. I'll have to burn most of th' furnishings to make it habitable again, anyway."

I smiled thinly at him as I walked away. "Merrik, Kaelyn, with me." I nodded over my shoulder and they appeared at my side.

The small room had little more than the basics. A table and a low dresser were bolted to the far wall. A narrow bed had been pushed into one corner, with a heavy silk brocade coverlet draped across it. Thick grime coated everything. The man clearly hadn't packed a wash rag when he left Wellsmith.

"What are we looking for, exactly?" Kaelyn asked, glancing around the dank room.

"Papers? Letters, plans, a journal maybe?" I shuddered at what one might contain. Gods alone knew what that bastard's innermost thoughts held. "Anything that tells us who Tavers was working for."

We split up and searched the room. I leafed through papers on the desk, finding a few charts and a crudely drawn sketch of a Mermaid but nothing remarkable. I pushed them away and leaned on the desk, both hands braced in front of me as I caught my breath.

"Here."

Three paces had me across the room to where Merrik kneeled in front of a heavy sea chest.

Books, scrolls, and loose papers filled the box nearly to the brim. I grunted. "Of course, he wouldn't make this easy," I muttered under my breath. I settled in front of the box. I handed a pile of papers each to Merrik and Kaelyn before sorting my own.

"We're looking for a clue to who was calling the shots, but I'll settle for anything useful," I said, then met their gazes. "Uhh, maybe if it's too... you know–"

"Vile?" Merrik supplied.

I nodded. "Maybe don't tell me about those ones?"

My friends both offered supportive smiles before settling in to read.

The first paper I picked up was a list of names, some of which I recognized from when I was working for Krellen. Most were crossed off, but a few weren't. A hit list, I supposed. Cleaning up Krellen's loose ends. One had a question mark next to it, which I noted with amusement. Captain Kurou was fun and quick with a joke, but not what I was looking for. While I was glad he might have escaped Tavers' clutches, I was after something specific.

I set it aside.

The next was a supply list dated two months ago. I tossed that away and reached for a small book. I only had it open for a moment before I saw it was full of sketches, all of them done in a crude hand, all of them of young women I knew from around Wellsmith. One of them was of me.

I nearly cried. "Gods, I hate him. Am I horrible?"

Kaelyn watched with a worried furrow in her brow.

I handed her the book. "I'm not glad he's dead, exactly, but I'm not sorry."

She shook her head and gestured with the book. "If this means what I think it does, you saved a lot of women a lot of pain. I'd say the world is better off without him."

Without a word, Merrik plucked the book from Kaelyn's hands and flung it away. We all watched with a sense of satisfaction as it spun neatly out of the small porthole window and ended its life with a wet splash.

I smiled gratefully and turned back to the pile.

Darl Tavers wasn't what I would call a great literarian, nor a halfway decent agent. He was sadistic, but he wasn't terribly conniving. There was nothing here that would lead me to thinking he was part of some great spy ring.

There were letters to Krellen discussing their expansion across the river into Mitsuni's territory, which was stupid, but not surprising. There was a brief note from Krellen sending Tavers to bring me home, which made me shudder, but revealed nothing new. A hastily scribbled note from Tavers caught my eye.

> They've killed him. We knew it would come to this someday, but I had always planned on being in control by the time it happened. Wellsmith is in chaos, and Mitsuni won't be able to hold it all. I'll come back and reclaim what I can, but until then, I'll just have to stick to the plan.

With a frustrated cry, I crumpled the page into a ball and threw it across the room. "But what is the plan!?"

"Mhmm, Tianna," Merrik said quietly, measuringly.

I looked up, but he said nothing else. He just handed me a thick stack of letters, all with carefully broken wax seals. They'd been tied together in a heavy bundle with a thin piece of twine. Pulling it into my lap, I snapped the string and picked up the first letter.

> We are happy to entertain you at such a time as you see fit to journey to the continent, Lord Krellen. It is always advantageous to foster new alliances in these trying times. Rest assured, you and yours will be honored guests of my House.
>
> —G.R.

"'G.R.' again. Who are you?" I muttered as I scanned the page again for clues. The only identifying marks were the stylizes calligraphy of those two letters, next to an image of a tall ship, stamped in red ink.

I set it aside and read the next letter in the bundle. It was more of the same. They were stilted—almost archaic in structure—but they read like love letters between Krellen and whoever this G.R. person was. The more I read, the more my mouth dried, the more my eyes widened, the more I shook. When I reached the last one, I nearly bit my tongue.

> It is more than acceptable, Master Redship. Once I am in control of the Harbor, you will have your Sea Port. Make no mistake, while I love Wellsmith dearly, I believe it will suit your cause far better than my own. I shall be happy to make the move to Anvilcove and see to the governance of the isles whilst you focus your forces wherever you see fit.

I must deal with a small matter of some rebels here in town, but it will be over quickly and then we will meet. The Armada will always have a home in Isla Piratica.

—J. Krellen

"What is Isla Piratica?" Kaelyn asked.

"I think he means the pirate isles," I guessed. "This… he means to give the armada a home port here."

"The Epirsan Armada? Here? In the Outer Isles? Is he mad?" Her alarm mirrored mine, though as usual she was more animated than me.

I shuddered, blinking away a fresh wave of revulsion. "He was."

I sat silently, staring at the letters in front of me. Clear evidence of an Epirsan invasion and collusion with a local citizen. If Krellen's vision came to pass, nowhere would be safe. Never mind being caught in the middle of a war, we would be on the front lines. It would become all out war.

"No," I said. "This isn't going to happen. I won't let it."

I launched myself to my feet, then braced myself on the wall, feeling light-headed. "We need to get to Wellsmith. And Sen Tagna. Send a letter to Bann Tirica, too. They need to know what's happening," I said while I waited for my vision to clear. "Anne needs to see those letters. Maybe one of her contacts will know more about G.R. and even if they don't, the navy needs to know that the armada has designs on the Outer Isles."

"Tian–" Kaelyn reached out to place a hand on my arm.

"I'm fine." I shook her off and pushed out into the crisp fall air. "Captain! Captain Archer!" I was vaguely aware of Kaelyn and Merrik following behind me. Blood rushed to my head and my focus narrowed to a single purpose.

Elis strolled over with a gentle smirk on his face. "While I do appreciate the thought, I'm only the mate. At least for the time being."

I slapped a wax-wrapped parchment against his chest. "This is your ship now. If your crew names you Captain, that's none of my concern."

He took the packet from me and opened it with a grin. "The deed? What a lucky find." He cackled, letting the possibilities race across his face. He met my grim gaze and his grin dropped as quickly as it has formed.

"What matters to me is what you know of this." I held the bundle of letters for him to see. "How much did Tavers tell you? Were you working with Krellen?"

As he read, his frown deepened. "No. Not precisely. I worked for Krellen, but I don't know what those are. Tavers rarely let me in on his plans."

"Who is G.R? Master Redship, who is he?" I demanded, crowding into his space.

The former first mate stepped back and held up his hands placatingly. "I don't know what you're talking about. I was not a part of whatever this is."

I growled, clenching my jaw so hard I was surprised I didn't break a tooth. "Do you have any loyalty at all to Wellsmith? To the isles and its people? Can I trust you?"

Elis drew up to his full height, towering over me. He held himself stiffly and with an air of assurance, not arrogance. "I would die to protect the people of the isles. This is my home, Miss Blackboot. Krellen was my employer, not my master. And I don't appreciate your tone."

His clipped words sent a wave of ease through me, and I let out a breath. "Thank you," I said on an exhale.

He took another step back, brow furrowed again, this time in confusion.

"We are going to war, Captain, and I may very well need your help. We need to warn everybody. Krellen was…" I trailed off as a wave of dizziness nearly knocked me over. I shook my head. "Krellen was–"

"Tianna!" Kaelyn's startled cry and Merrik's sturdy arms were the last thing I registered before I keeled over. I almost had time to curse myself for pushing past my own limits before I fell, again, into darkness.

CHAPTER TWENTY-FOUR

A familiar aroma greeted me as I slowly came back to consciousness. Damp wool, pine tar, and salt water. It nested gently against the backdrop of creaking oaken boards, and I knew I was home. In my cabin, back aboard the Siren.

"Eh ya, Cap'n. Mornin' right 'n sunlit sparkles 'bout yer eyes." The cheery voice nearly had me wishing for oblivion again but I smiled.

I cracked an eye open and eased my gaze across the way to where I'd heard him. "Iain," I croaked. "Where–" My throat was dry and my tongue felt three times too big for my mouth. I swallowed thickly and tried again. "Where's Kaelyn?"

Iain beamed at me from a cot near the foot of my bed. He was resting in a seated position with plenty of pillows and spare linens under him for support. His leg was stretched out in front of him, braced and wrapped tightly across his calf, and I noticed a darker patch seeping into the cloth that was most likely his blood.

"That looks like it hurts," I said, lifting a hand to gesture at his wound. My hand was heavy, bound and splinted to match Iain's dressings. I grimaced.

He grinned wider. "All trussed up n' a lily dam. Fit t' lolly a jig 'round a balefire." He shifted and winced. "Eh, 'hap a tad tender roasted. 'Round a camp stove, then."

I chuckled, enjoying his whimsy for the respite it was. "Where's Kaelyn?" I asked again as I pushed myself to my feet. I felt like an entire tree had fallen across my chest and crushed everything but my spirit. But that wasn't going to stop me.

Iain picked up a stout stick and rapped it twice on the wall next to him.

In less time than it took me to walk across the space, the door opened and Kaelyn, Isaboe, and Anne charged in.

I glared at Iain. "You a sentry then? And here I thought you were resting."

He only grinned.

"You! Back in bed!" Isaboe snapped before anyone could say anything else.

I raised an eyebrow at her imperious tone. "Who died and made you Captain?"

"Thankfully, not you. And you keep it. I'm quite happy with the job I have, thank you," she replied. "Bed. Now. You need rest."

I grumbled, but sat. The mattress sank comfortably beneath me, a soft counterpoint to the urgency I was feeling. "I can't stay in bed. We need to warn everyone."

Kaelyn crossed her arms in front of her chest and set her feet. She was standing directly between me and the door. "I told them. And I showed them the letters."

That was something, at least. "We can't wait around for me to recuperate. We have no way of knowing how old this information is, or what this Redship is even still planning without Krellen around to help." I speared each of them with a direct stare, making sure I was not in any way misunderstood. "I will not abandon the isles to some power hungry warlord."

Grave nods came from my crew.

"We are all aware of your wishes, Tianna," Anne said solemnly. "However, as I tried to tell you yesterday before the chaos erupted–"

"Yesterday!?" I cried and tried to stand again. Kaelyn pushed me back gently. "How long was I out?"

"Almost eighteen hours," she answered evenly. "It is nearing the evening tide."

"Where are we? We're still in Tiraea?"

She nodded. "The crew is gathered, but we didn't dare leave until we could all discuss what was going on."

"We need to go, now. We can't wait longer," I said.

"We know," Isaboe replied. She had one hand buried in her curls at the back of her head, tugging in frustration. "But we can't leave yet. We–"

"As I was saying," Anne spoke pointedly, raising her tone to be heard over the rest of us. "I had already reached out to some of my other contacts after our ill-fated encounter with the convoy. Your convalescence would not have allowed for a long sea voyage, and I still have that list of names to impart as well."

Abashed, I looked down at my stockinged feet. "I haven't forgotten. I just…" I looked up with pleading eyes and met her dark ones. She bore a similar expression. "I can't let more people die for this."

"I know."

"We all know," Isaboe added. "And we agree with you. We're all in here. We just can't do anything at the moment."

"Bullshit." I rose and brushed off Kaelyn's gentle hand this time. "There's always something that can be done."

"Here like as a pigeon-stye 'bout an alehouse grinder. Choices like water in a wheat cask, we have," Iain stated. He was not at all like his usual lilting, humor-filled self.

We all turned to him, listening.

"Bask in th' sandspit 'round local, or lark out th' crest and tail t' th' farrier's den." He stared at us for a moment as we took that in.

Isaboe spoke first. "I suppose you're right. We can head straight for Sen Tagna now, but we'd be limping along, Captain. Even if you were in shape to be sailing—which you're definitely not—there's still at least a week's work of patching I need to do to get our Siren shipshape again."

Of course there was. There was no part of this week that was going my way. I didn't even have time to bask in the bittersweet joy of finally breaking free of my old life.

"How much can you do underway?"

Her face ran through a variety of different expressions in rapid succession. Thoughtful, suspicious, and finally resigned. "All of it," she admitted with a sigh.

I nodded and gestured to the door. "Then we aren't going to wait. Kaelyn, get the crew assigned doing what they're best at. We need as much speed and accuracy as we can get. Lessons are over."

They all filed out into the evening air, leaving Iain and me to limp behind.

"You alright to join us?"

He pushed to his feet and grabbed the club-like staff he'd been playing with before. "Right as horses in th' galley bell," he said. "Bout as lis'm as a spring roast, though." He gestured with his makeshift cane and followed behind me.

It was calm on deck. Everything seemed peaceful. The weather was cool, the skies clear, and the bay restful. It was the sort of evening that was made for a stroll along the beach or to sit and have a cup of hot tea while watching the stars awake. But it wasn't any other night. No one knew what evils were plotting to destroy this cozy hamlet. Possibly even as I stood there.

Visions of a distant war bearing down on my horizon flooded my mind. The vision was so strong that for a brief flash I couldn't see anything else. I shook myself, breaking out of the too-real phantasm's grip, and turned to look again at the harbor.

With a moment of surprise, I noticed the Heartland was raising sails. Her hull was not in much better shape than I'd last seen her, yet she seemed to be leaving port.

"I thought they were still in dry dock?"

Merrik appeared at my elbow. "Captain Archer was concerned about you when you dropped near dead on his deck. Go figure."

I snorted. "Don't be dramatic. I'm fi–"

"Fine. Yes, you've told us."

I smirked at him, happy that the banter were normal between us at least. "Don't be cheeky."

He shrugged. "It's all I've got, boss."

"And the Heartland?" I nodded toward the other ship.

"Once he read the letters, he was incensed and agreed to sail direct to Wellsmith. I think he means to see what he could do to help. Though if Krellen is dead, I wonder at what kind of chaos he'll find there."

Even with his cynical words, I was relieved. I had worked with many captains and crewmen in my time with Krellen. Most of them were selfish, cruel types with more wanton desire than sense, but Archer seemed different. I wasn't sure if I could trust him long term, but for now at least, in this, I could count him an ally.

I turned my attention to my ship, seeing that Kaelyn had gathered the crew together. Everyone was accounted for, dressed in work clothes, and ready for whatever was to come. I wondered how many of them knew what we were headed into. I wondered if I did.

"Well, friends, we've landed in it now. For months, I've been looking for a purpose. A path and a plan that will lead us to the freedom and agency that we all crave. This isn't what I was looking for, but it's what we got."

I looked at their bleak faces. Kaelyn's normally tight braid was ragged, hanging loosely over her shoulder. Eric's normally winsome smile was weary and forced. Even Anne's impeccable skirt was speckled with mud around the hem. None of them looked like they'd gotten much sleep.

"You've all read the letters, I assume? Or at least know what's in them?" I waited for a few hesitant nods and murmured assent. "Then you know that this war isn't a vague threat any longer. It's here. Or will be very soon. Right now, we have to assume we are the only ones with proof. Proof which we need to get to the Lugaians as soon as possible."

"Why Lugaia?" Eric asked. "Anvilcove is closer. Shouldn't we tell the governor?"

Anne stood straighter. "No, that we cannot do. My father is…" She sighed heavily and shook herself as if forcing the truth past her own lips. "My father is a fine governor as things go, but he is getting older. He has spent much of his tenure securing his power and fighting against the leaders of the other islands. He has next to no ties left with Bann Tirica, and virtually nothing in the way of military might. Even if we laid this burden on him, it would do no good. He cannot help us."

Isaboe placed a gentle hand on the other girl's shoulder. "That's what you've been saying all along, isn't it? That's why you're working for Lugaia?"

Anne nodded, looking quietly sad. "It is."

"And that is why our first, and as of now, only priority is getting these letters to Sen Tagna. Nothing we want is more important now than warning the navy."

Nothing but silence from my crew. I knew I couldn't push. They needed to be on board with this.

"Aye, Captain," Merrik said. "We stand with you. We won't want it any other way. If you say this is how we help, how we save our folk, then this is what we do."

I blinked away a sudden tear. "Do any of you want to go? I wasn't going to hold it against you before when the stakes were low. I certainly won't begrudge you now."

"No, Cap'n," Eric said. "We're in it. As Merrik says, we stand with you."

I looked around to be sure that Eric spoke for everyone. I saw only one thing in their expression. Determination. Grim determination to be sure, but determination all the same.

"Then let's go save the isles." I nodded to Kaelyn, steeling myself for what was to come. "Company to stations, let's get underwa–"

Panicked cries from the Heartland interrupted my order. They were far enough away that I couldn't make out any words, but the tone was clear as a Northbay ice mirror. We all spun to see what the commotion was, just as the echoing boom rattled the deck under my feet.

"Ships! All aggro-red and hide-lipped off th' beam, Cap!" Iain shouted from his perch near the rail. A second cannon blast underlined his warning.

Another frantic shout came from the deck of the Heartland, and then a shot of their own followed. Three long guns in rapid succession fired off, one after the other after the other.

"What's happening? Who is it?" I pushed through my crew until I was standing at the balustrade. From where I stood, it was easy to make out four ships, but more than that were lost in a sea of masts and sails further out.

A mix of Epirsan, Meketian, even Lugaian warships were blockading the harbor, and opening fire on any ship trying to leave. Which, just then, was the Heartland.

"What the absolute hells is this?" I shouted.

Kaelyn braced a hand on my shoulder and brought her spyglass up so it was resting in the crook of my neck as she gazed out to the mouth of the bay. "Looks like the convoy brought friends."

"Why the hells would they be here? I thought they didn't follow us!"

I watched Captain Archer's crew scrambling around the deck, running out guns and trimming the sails with a skill that would have made me envious if I wasn't terrified.

With ruthless efficiency, they crossed the bow of the lead ship and fired again. "That's a fool's move," I said breathlessly. "He'll get one shot off before they pin him in!"

As if I made it so by speaking it, two other convoy ships broke off trying to hem in the Heartland between them.

"Damn it, Archer! I hope you've got something really stupid up your sleeve. We could use some hero tricks right about now."

"We need to help them!" Isaboe shouted.

Realizing I had been watching the theater of war for longer than I should have, I turned to look at Kaelyn and Merrik. "Can we get through?"

Kaelyn looked through her glass again. "I see six ships, Captain. Even with the Heartland drawing fire, we wouldn't be able to get through. I suspect he knows that, too."

I held back a sigh, biting the inside of my cheek. Nowhere to flee. All out of options. Situation hopelessly dire—it's like I was made for this.

"Anne?" I spun, trying to locate my navigator.

"Here." She rushed over to my side.

"Who has the letters?"

She hesitated a moment. "They are in your lockbox. Why would you think of that now?"

"Get them."

I rarely issued direct orders, but when I did, it was because I needed my crew to obey. Right then, I wasn't in the mood for debate.

She ran off to my cabin and returned presently, bundle in hand. When she went to hand them to me, I grabbed her wrist, firmly folding her arm against her chest.

"Go," I said. "Take them to Ember. Find another way off this island and get those to the navy."

"But-" It was the only time I had ever heard Anne start a sentence with a conjunction. That alone should have let me know how scared she was.

I squared off with her, pinning her terrified stare with my unwavering one. "You need to get these to Lugaia. Nothing else that happens here will matter if those don't get through."

I watched her swallow hard, then nod.

"Gods keep you, Tianna." She hurried to the gangway and into the street without stopping to look back.

I spun back to look at the other ships, and locked eyes with Kaelyn. "We run the blockade," I said.

She choked out a startled cry and stared at me, bug-eyed. "Seriously?! Are you *mad*?"

I turned to her, bringing up every bit of rage, and hurt, and injustice that I'd suffered because of men like this, and growled. "I'm godsdammed furious."

"Not what I meant, but okay..." Kaelyn grumbled.

Turning back to the rest of my crew, I smiled. I was aiming for firmly compassionate, but I think I managed relentless purpose, which would do just fine.

"We can't make it through, and we can't back down. If that convoy gets those letters, then we're lost. The isles are lost. Are we going to let that happen?"

"No, Cap'n!" Eric shouted.

My tone grew more stalwart with each word. "Are we going to stand aside and let our friends, our family, and our homes be destroyed by greedy corsairs?"

"No!" came the shout from multiple people.

"Are we going to bow to Epirsan rule and let them make slaves of us all?"

"NO!" everyone shouted.

I took a breath, dropping into a deadly calm. "And are we willing to lay down our lives to see that Anne makes it through?"

There was a collective pause, and for just the barest moment, I was afraid I was alone in my conviction, until Merrik said, "Aye, Captain."

"Aye," Isaboe echoed. Then Eric and Iain. When she didn't answer, I turned to Kaelyn.

"I know this isn't what you signed up for, but you did want an adventure," I said, offering a smirk just for her.

She chuckled weakly, then shook her head. The tail of her headscarf draped over her face, before she looked up at me again. "Aye, Tianna."

I clapped her on the shoulder and gave a gentle squeeze. "I told Tavers that I don't need luck, but the truth is I make my own luck. So, let's see what I can conjure."

One by one, they straightened, riling themselves up for a fight.

"Alright mates, listen up." Isaboe called for everyone's attention. "We aren't going to be doing a lot of fancy sailing this time. The goal is to get her going and going fast. Then we focus on fighting."

"Right." Merrik added. "We need medium-range shots at first—rifles, muskets, and swivel guns—until we're too close. Then, switch to close-quarters. Hand-to-hand and pistols. Whatever you're best at. This isn't about finesse, the only goal is to stay alive as long as possible."

"Iain," I added my piece. "I'd like you on the swivel gun since you can't sail. As soon as we're in range, aim for every bit of rigging you see. Disable first. Think you can manage that with your leg?"

"Right doin', Cap."

I glanced back over my shoulder to check the Heartland's progress. To my surprise, she was still sailing. And well at that. One of the convoy ships had stalled, masts down and sheets torn, in the middle of the bay as our allies turned their nose into the wind.

"Like that." I pointed out the incapacitated ship. "If we can flounder the convoy, the Heartland can help us pick off their crews." I stepped up onto a nearby box and hoped it would hold my weight. It wouldn't be a terribly inspiring moment if my foot broke through it. Luckily, it held.

"Now would be a great time for a speech about going down in a blaze of glory, about being remembered for our sacrifice, but I don't think that's our style, is it? Live, friends. However you have to, make sure you make it through this. And take as many of those bastards down as you can in the process!"

They cheered and rushed off to do that. I helped Iain take up position near one of the twelve-pound rail guns. He grinned at me, then bent to begin the loading process.

I handed him Kaelyn's spyglass. "Keep this. If the gun proves too much for your leg, drop back and keep watch. Call enemy positions and keep us on track."

"Ya got th' mutton in th' bale, Cap. Not a worry."

I patted his back and let him get ready to do as much damage as he could.

"Merrik, Eric, Isaboe, haul the hook!" I hurried over to give them a hand, and together we pulled up the anchor. I heard more than saw Kaelyn scamper up the rig to unfurl the sails. Merrik would join her after to set them while I managed the lines below. We had done this enough times now that I knew we could do it, and I sent up a prayer that we might get a chance to do it again.

Cannon fire continued to sound in the fading dusk, as a thick fog rolled in. "Fog? Really? Of course it's fog." I muttered something about poetic irony and facetious perfection, then took my position.

The Heartland was taking a heavy beating. I wasn't sure they could hold out much longer. Another ship had joined our side, coming off the south side of the quay. They were larger than either of our ships, and had a full gun battery, but they were still too far away to help the Heartland.

Still, three against six was better odds.

"Tianna!" Kaelyn shouted from above me. I looked up and saw her pointing. I spun, looking past the nearest ships, searching for whatever she had seen.

Flashes of light bloomed in the growing darkness. More cannons than could possibly be coming from the convoy ships. There were dozens of guns sounding in the dark—a rolling thunder with no end.

Shouts from the Heartland echoed Kaelyn's, and many of them were pointing in the same direction. I dropped my line in the confusion and raced over to Iain. I ripped the spyglass from his hand, nearly dropping it in the process.

I scanned the horizon, looking past the Heartland, past the convoy ships, through the smoke and fog, searching desperately for whatever was causing this onslaught.

Finally, amidst bright flashes of light that left trailing wisps of smoke behind, I saw it flying high atop the mast of a massive man-of-war. A silver banner bearing the crest of a blue dragon.

The Lugaian Navy had arrived.

For an endless moment, I didn't move. I didn't breathe. I couldn't even form a coherent thought. Then all at once the air rushed out of my lungs in a wild laugh. "Oh, thank every God," I said, drooping forward over the railing in relief. Three against six against a navy fleet was much better odds.

As soon as I could catch my breath enough to form words again, I shouted as loud as I could, "Change of plans, kiddos!"

Kaelyn's boots thumped on the deck behind me and then hurried over.

"Looks like the navy's come to play," I said, without turning to look at her as she stepped up beside me. She took the glass and searched the horizon, just as I had.

"How…" She turned to me, a look of pure amazement. "This that luck you were conjuring?"

"I'll gladly take credit, but no. I think this was just fate messing with me again."

Wonder colored her voice. "Messing with you? Or blessing you?"

"I'm not sure I know the difference." I looked out again, watching the Heartland pull back to regroup with the other local ship as the convoy turned their attention to the greater threat.

"Order the crew to drop anchor," I told Kaelyn at length. "We're sitting this one out."

"Oh, thank you," she said with a frantic laugh of her own. "We were so badly outgunned."

I laughed at her as she ran off to reassemble the crew. And I—standing on the deck of a ship that rightly should never have come to me, commanding a crew of misfits, and eking out success on the whimsical winds of fate— watched the horrific scene unfold, unable to help, unable to look away.

CHAPTER TWENTY-FIVE

It was long past midnight when the ships landed in the harbor. All night, they had fought, disabled, and ultimately seized the enemy ships. Their crews were either dead or captured. Even without knowing what the future held, I knew this night would go down as one of the longest in Tiraea's history.

I don't imagine anyone in town got much sleep. We sure didn't. For most of the night, we stood vigil aboard the Siren, watching impotently as the carnage unfolded half a league away.

I can't say what time it was when the cannon fire stopped, or exactly how long it took for the navy to board the disabled ships and start bringing prisoners ashore.

Merrik and Isaboe both disappeared for a while, helping organize and facilitate bringing the navy ashore however they could. I wasn't sure what they could do that the trained sailors of the Lugaian Navy couldn't, but I also didn't think to ask. They both returned separately some time later and rejoined our quiet watch.

Eventually, I looked up to reorient myself in the moment, looking at what had become of the harbor. The Heartland had safely docked, though I saw only a skeleton crew on her deck.

"Does anyone know what happened to Archer?" I asked, and then turned to look at my crew.

Isaboe and Kaelyn were holding a quiet conversation, their heads bowed together, speaking low. Iain sat nearby, resting on a barrel and Eric sat at his elbow, shuffling a deck of cards absently. Merrik stood, leaning back against the mainmast, looking out past all of us. He had a blanket thrown over his shoulders and appeared lost in thought.

At my question, Isaboe looked up. "I sent him and his wounded to Ember."

"Why Ember?"

"When we first came, we tried to bring you to the local doctor, but Ember wouldn't have it. Turns out she's a trained medic." Isaboe smirked. "Good thing, too. What passes for a hospital here couldn't house more than a half-dozen people. That lovely rented home of hers has become a field hospital."

That made sense in a way that I should have expected, but somehow hadn't. "Were there many wounded? Do we know how many died?"

Eric looked at me and smiled calmly. "A few. They're a'right, Cap'n. They knew the risks."

I sighed at his non-answer and tried to let it go. What Eric said was true, and I knew they weren't my responsibility, but sometime in the last thirty hours, I had grown fond of them. I turned back out to watch the torches and lamplight dancing across the water for a little while longer.

About two hours before dawn, a light, musical voice from the dock shouted up to us.

"Ahoy the Siren. Anyone aboard?"

I moved over so I could see down to the road. A young boy, maybe seven or eight years old, wearing the baldric of the city council over top of a ragged and dirty shirt stood looking up expectantly.

"Aye, child. What do you need?"

He reached into a small satchel at his side and drew out a folded letter. "I have a message from a Lady Anna for..." he looked at the front of the note, reading. "T. Blackboot." He over-enunciated every syllable, and I bit back a smile.

"I am Captain Blackboot." I hurried down the walk. Taking the missive, I pressed a coin into his hand and thanked him. I made my way back to the others before I unfolded it and read.

"From Anne?" Isaboe asked.

"What is it?" Kaelyn asked nearly at the same time.

I quickly reread to make sure my tired brain understood the words. "She wants me to meet her at the navy's temporary headquarters within the hour." I looked up at the group. "Suppose she means to present our evidence. I'm glad she decided not to wait."

Kaelyn and Eric murmured their agreement. "Want us to go with you?" I couldn't tell from Kaelyn's expression if she was hoping I would say yes or no.

I shook my head. "Best not. I think we're already pushing our luck, seeking out her contact while all this is going on." I gestured vaguely at everything around us.

"Good," was all Kaelyn said. She settled back down into her nest of blankets next to Isaboe.

I looked up at Merrik, who was still brooding in the corner. "What's on your mind, *kashi*?"

"Pieces. Threads. A puzzle without a picture," he said, muttering darkly without looking at us.

I stared for a moment, waiting for him to elaborate. "Well, that was cryptic. Alright then. I'll be off. You..." I trailed off, looking at the fatigued and weary faces of my friends. Each looked stubbornly ready to push through whatever I ordered them to next.

"Try to get some sleep," I said.

THE PIRATE HORDE391

It wasn't hard to find my way to the large stone building near the edge of the docks. The constant line of blue uniforms moving in and out of the building made it obvious. The large stone building was overflowing with people.

Officers with silver braiding on their coats were trying to organize prisoners, checking and double checking lists, and barking orders. Several bleary-eyed guards dressed in the simple red tunics of the local constabulary were offering backup where they could, but there was no part of this that looked clean and efficient.

I looked around for Anne, eventually spotting her across the main road from the doors. She was dressed in clean trousers with a knee-length wool overcoat. She looked warm, but just as tired as the rest of us. I noticed she had her large shoulder bag, which meant she had brought Krellen's letters with her.

Crossing over to her, I raised a hand in greeting.

"Tianna, darling, you look rather worn out. Have you been getting enough rest?"

I snorted a humorless laugh and pointed back over my shoulder toward the building. "Can you get us in to meet your contact?"

She nodded. "If these fellows came from Sen Tagna, then he should be leading the fleet. We just need to get into the building. He will see me."

I waved her onward. "Lead the way then, my lady."

Getting in was actually quite easy. No one stopped us at the door, or in the main entryway, or in the hallway leading to the office spaces. We weaved between clusters of frustrated officers and corsairs until we came to a small room, which was really more of a wide spot in the hallway. There, an older woman sitting behind a tiny, portable desk covered in papers stopped us.

"Can I help you, *misés*?" she said in a lightly accented, and completely weary voice.

She was dressed like the other officers, but with a silver pin at her lapel in the shape of a scroll and quill. I assumed that meant she was a secretary or scribe. Her hair was pulled back in a severe bun, and although she had laugh lines around her eyes, her mouth creased in a stern frown and she looked tired.

"I am Lady Anna of the Invisible Pen and this is my companion, Captain Blackboot. You can let the chevalier know we are here to see him."

The woman's frown deepened.

"I understand this is not the best timing," Anne said before the woman could object. "But this is most urgent, and has to do with that mess outside. Please let him know we are here. He should know who I am."

The woman exhaled through her nose sharply and set her pen down. "Wait here, please." She stood from behind the desk and moved down the hall to a large, carved door. She rapped on it twice before slipping inside.

We stood awkwardly for a few moments, waiting for her return. As I was looking around for a chair to rest in, the door opened and she ushered us over. "He will see you," she said. As I passed, she grabbed my sleeve. "It has been a very long day, yes? Try to keep it short."

I smiled at her and patted her hand. "A long night for all of us, madam," I replied in Lugaian.

She returned my smile and closed the door behind us.

The room wasn't overly large, but it was a well-lit, utilitarian space that had seen a lot of use. A gruff man stood behind a heavy desk in the middle of the room.

He was a sturdy gentleman in the uniform of a navy commander, complete with silver buckles and trim, and enough embroidery to make a needle dull. He had heavy bags under his dark eyes, and his chestnut-colored hair was tousled as if he'd run his hands through it several times. I wondered who he had displaced to claim this office for himself.

He looked up as we approached. I stood next to Anne and a little behind, trying to look like I belonged here. Which, I suppose in a way I did but having never met a chevalier before, I didn't really know the etiquette. Something I'm sure Albert would have chided me for, since I'm certain he tried to teach me at some point.

"*Sulté, misélles,*" he said passionlessly. "What is it I can do for you this morning?"

Anne seemed surprised. "I was expecting Sir Nicolas."

He sighed wearily. "My predecessor was relocated into a position better suited to his talents. I now command the naval base at Sen Tagna."

"I see. I was not aware that he had been replaced."

He waved his hand. A gesture that seemed more annoyed than flippant. "It is something that happens quite frequently these days. Where His Majesty commands, we go."

She nodded, looking down at her hands, which were now clasped in front of her. She pursed her lips, thinking. "I see," she said again.

After another look, the man stood upright and nodded politely at us. "I am Chevalier Marcos Seba d'Lugano. My assurances, Lady Anna, that although we have not met, I do know of you. I was briefed quite thoroughly when I took my position here."

Anne studied him for a moment and seemed to decide something. She nodded her head deeply, almost in a bow. "If that is the case, then our friends from Merlaeone send their greetings."

His gaze sharpened as she spoke and squared his shoulders. The corners of his mouth lifted in the ghost of a smile. "I have not been to Merlaeone in some time. Have you tried the meat pies from the Swallow's Inn?"

"I found them to my liking," she replied evenly.

I watched the two of them trade small talk like a game of battledore. It didn't take a sharp mind to make out what was happening here.

"I found them a little stale," I butted in. "Much like code words for establishing identity."

Anne looked horrified, and I knew I probably should have kept my thoughts to myself. But did we really have time for all this?

Sir Marcos nodded. "Indeed," he said laconically. "Such games are antiquated but tradition demands respect, no?"

"I prefer action, especially when it is called for," I said, matching his tone.

He raised an eyebrow. "And is it called for?"

"Yes, sir," Anne said. "We believe it is."

He watched, weighing our interaction before deciding on his next move. At length, he nodded. "I suspect you are correct." He lifted a folder from his desk. "Your letter is why we are here."

"What letter?" I asked.

Anne looked at me. "When we first arrived, I sent a letter through my other contacts, informing them we had vital information for the navy, but that your injuries made it impossible to reach out to them directly. I suppose it found its way to Sen Tagna."

"It did indeed," Sir Marcos said. He gestured toward the door and the chaos that lay just beyond. "I would say it arrived in good time, too."

I huffed something, almost like a laugh.

"Coming here to meet you was intended. Encountering a pirate convoy attacking the town was fortuitous. Though I do wonder how Bann Tirica will take our presence here." He muttered the last to himself, then shook his head before looking up at Anne again. "What is this vital information?"

Anne reached into her bag and pulled out the letters.

He reached for them, scanning the papers as he spoke. "What is this?"

"Plans for an Epirsan invasion," I said.

His head snapped up in alarm as he looked at me. He bent again and opened the first letter.

"These are personal correspondence between Jassec Krellen of Wellsmith and an unidentified Epirsan corsair," I continued. "We don't have an exact date for when this is to take place, but based on the evidence we've gathered, I'm sure it has to be within the next year. Krellen was poised to strike, but with his passing, the timeline became less clear."

"Who is this 'G.R.'?"

I shrugged. "He's referred to only as Master Redship in a later letter."

Sir Marcos nodded absently. "And this supposed base?"

I couldn't shake the feeling that we were going in circles. This was all in the letters he was holding.

"Wellsmith." I told him. "It's a port town on the southern edge tip of Hammersmith Island."

"Ah, a pirate haven. A barely-there landing site for unwelcome miscreants."

"There are a lot more unwelcome miscreants out here than you know," I said, biting back an even sharper tone.

He hummed, low in his chest and pursed his lips. "That makes a certain amount of sense, but it is an immaterial location. It is not even on most maps." He set down the letters and looked up at me. "Is that not correct?"

I clenched my fists and forced them open again, trying to keep myself calm as I continued to explain.

"Jassec Krellen was a criminal leader, one of two, in Wellsmith. He controlled the lower half of the city, including the docks. It has never been a secret that he wanted the whole of the town instead of part of it. What these letters tell us, is that he had bigger ambitions. He wanted all of the Outer Isles and was willing to hand over naval authority to the armada to get it."

Sir Marcos looked at me, his expression growing thoughtful. "Yet this Krellen is, by your own admission, dead, no? Is the threat not resolved?"

I shook my head. "No, sir. I don't think so."

"What is so special about this Wellsmith that the armada should desire it?"

His dismissive tone grated against what little patience I had. I wanted to slap the man and make him see reason. We were wasting time and breath arguing when we could be sailing off to fix this.

Violence wouldn't convince this man of anything, though. I knew pride when I saw it. It looked like I would have to rely on persuasion. I took a breath, silently thanking Adwin for his early lessons in military tactics.

"Don't be fooled by it's history, sir, Wellsmith is a self-contained, moderately wealthy, and secure port. The main approach lies just beyond a wide reef, and is blocked to the north by steep cliffs, making it highly defensible. It sits not far off the conjunction of three major shipping routes, as well as the main passages to Meket and Lugaia Denisi."

I paused to see if he caught where I was going with this. His expression remained implacable, so I continued. "It's a gateway to the Outer Isles. A perfect foothold for a military that is looking to launch a full-scale invasion."

He nodded, seeming to mull it over. "I do see the concern," he admitted. "Is there anything more?"

Anne leaned forward, as if she were about to speak, but stopped, eyeing him. I saw her thumb twitch over her bag, then she pulled back. She pursed her lips again, frowning, and shook her head. "No, sir."

"Is that not enough?"

"Thank you for bringing this to my attention," he said, as if I hadn't just asked a question. Granted, it was mostly rhetorical, but it was still rude. He walked over and opened the door, calling for the scribe to join us, then returned to the table and stacked the letters.

When the woman joined us, he handed them all over to her. "Mark these to be filed when we return to Sen Tagna."

"The official register?"

He shook his head. "The third catacomb archives should do. With the other Epirsan errata."

"Very good, sir." She collected the letters and walked out.

My shock was palpable. I thought I had made my point clearly enough. Was he really brushing this aside?

"Errata?" I practically shouted at him.

He breathed out a heavy sigh, his expression growing patiently bored, as if I were a toddler throwing a tantrum.

"*Misélle*," he said, meeting my icy glare with a weary expression. "We have been at war with Epirsa in one form or another since the foundation of our kingdom. We see reports such as this nearly every day. I cannot chase down every minor threat at the edge of the world. "We simply do not have the resources to commit to surges of paranoia."

"Paranoia!" That time I did shout. "How dare you?"

"Tianna," Anne whispered harshly. I knew she was trying to keep me silent for my own good, but mine wasn't the good I was concerned with.

"How dare you dismiss these people that way? The people of the Outer Isles—those who live at the 'edge of the world' as you say—are as much citizens of Denisi as you are. Probably more so since they live and work and die here. It's their sake we should fight for. Not some crown an ocean away!"

"Tianna!" Anne snapped. "That's enough." She reached for my arm to calm me, but I shook her off.

"No, it isn't." I turned and pointed an accusing finger at the high and mighty knight commander standing in front of me. "You are blind to what's happening here. And you are twice damned if you think it doesn't matter to Lugaia Denisi. If the armada establishes a presence here, they will overrun the Outer Isles, and if the isles fall, Lugaia Denisi will be flanked by enemy forces. I'm not even a military genius and I can see that much!"

He gave me another long-suffering look. "I can see your concern, but at the moment, we have more pressing matters to attend to. As you no doubt saw on your way in."

He turned away from me, figuratively stepping away from this conversation, and turned to Anne. "I understand that your previous handler was somewhat remiss in your treatment but I assure you, I would prefer to maintain our working relationship. From what I have been told, you have a keen mind and a sharp eye. You will be most beneficial to our cause."

"Thank you, sir," Anne replied slowly as if she wasn't sure how to respond to his sudden shift in topic.

"I understand you were not on the payroll, yes? We can remedy that as well. I prefer to see my agents compensated."

Anne nodded, watching him like a snake determining a threat. "I appreciate that, Sir, but I am not currently a lone agent. As part of Captain Blackboot's crew, I wonder if that offer will be extended to them as well? As long as I sail with them, I am not the only one to assume the risk for this cause."

A grimace, almost like a sneer, crossed his face and then was gone in a flash. "Yes, of course. You are both… quite able. I suppose something can be arranged to suit your needs."

I laughed bitterly. "High praise. Are you so effusive with all your spies, or just the ones who annoy you?"

He pierced me with his dark glare. "I assure you, I am never effusive."

That was easy to believe. I should have laughed it off. I should have walked away and thought over his surprisingly generous offer, but I couldn't hold my tongue.

"Stuff your bankroll. We don't need or want your help." I snapped. "I would never get involved with anyone who's too short-sighted to deal with the problems that are pressing down on their backs. Anyone–*anyone*–who would sacrifice their neighbors for an illusion of peace that won't last, is either fooling themselves or have lost what little compassion they might have had."

I threw my arm out behind me in a sweeping gesture, pointing toward the bay. "There were Lugaian ships in that convoy! The Consortium doesn't sell their vessels, and I sure hope the navy doesn't. So unless the corsairs have figured out how to capture and crew the supposed 'finest ships of the Mervast', then you've got a serious problem, *masérre*."

He gritted his teeth, obviously clenching his jaw as the lines around his eyes tightened. That didn't stop me from getting in one last jab.

"Maybe you need to clean up your own mess before it spreads to the rest of the world," I said coldly.

He held my snapping gaze for a moment before blinking and looking away. I watched his shoulders droop under the weight of it all. "You may be right," he breathed.

"And you–what?" I said, doing a mental double-take at his admission.

He looked at me again, and I saw sorrow in his eyes. "It is not my place to comment on the state of the world, especially in matters of State or military protocol, but I have standing orders which I must abide by. Which we all must abide by."

After a pause, he seemed to regroup. He stood upright and tapped twice on his desk with one stubby finger. "We can only work with the resources and intelligence that we have," he said. "I wonder if you would reconsider my offer of employment if we make a bargain? I will immediately dispatch your information to the continent for analysis, if you will lend me your skills again to keep this kind of thing from happening elsewhere."

I watched him, thinking it over. It was a good offer. It was what I had come in here for, actually. So, why was every alarm bell in my head warning me away from it?

I glanced over at Anne, whose expression was locked down tighter than a kitchen cellar on a high feast day. I had no way of knowing what she was thinking.

"What would you have us do, exactly?" I asked.

"Only that which you have been doing already. Make contacts among the locals and the nobility, gather rumor and gossip, and search for any information that may prove useful to the interests of our people and our cause. Then, share that information with us."

"Our people... The Lugaian people, you mean." I couldn't keep the resentment out of my voice.

"Naturally."

Suddenly, the bubble of boiling fury that was my anger burst. It all washed away, leaving a clear realization of what was happening. We were nothing to him. The isles were nothing to him. We were children playing at war while he had official military business to conduct, and we were wasting his time.

I laughed and his eyes widened as if I'd lost my mind quite suddenly. Perhaps I had. Or perhaps I was finally seeing what was there all along. There was no salvation for the isles. We were all just wayward children to these people. Well, this orphan knew one thing for damn sure—wayward children look out for each other.

"No."

He blinked, shook his head, and blinked again. "No?"

I shook my head and smiled a bit sadly. "Take yourself to whatever hell will have you. I have more pressing matters to attend to."

I didn't wait to hear his reply, or to see how Anne reacted. I stormed out into the hall. I nodded to the scribe on my way past and kept going, following my feet until I was outside in the chilly autumn air.

The street was quieter now. We had been in our meeting for maybe only twenty minutes, but things had settled down in that time. It was still far busier than it should have been at this time of morning, but at least there was evidence that things would return to normal soon.

It felt like a lie. We were a long was from normal. Life was going to be horribly disrupted for these people if no one did anything to stop the changes that were coming. Someone had to do something.

Determined footsteps behind me alerted me to Anne's presence before she spoke.

"Tianna," she called out. "Hold up a moment?"

I paused. With a deep breath, I slowly turned, readying myself to face whatever judgment was coming after my tirade in there. I offered her a tiny, chagrined smile.

"Sorry," I said, gesturing weakly at the barracks and the mess inside. "For all that."

"I understand why you did it. And…" She hesitated, but then met me squarely. "I agree with you."

"You do?"

She nodded. "I do, but I still believe in my cause. In their cause. How we uncovered Krellen's plot only proves that this works."

I shook my head, not able to believe what I was hearing. "But it doesn't work. What's the point of learning anything if the people with the power to change it do nothing?"

She looked displeased but spoke clearly. "I have to believe that it works."

I shook my head again, partly in frustration with her and partly because I knew what she was saying. Hadn't I thought much the same, not that long ago? Wasn't that what had spurred me on this whole damnable journey, anyway? We have to have hope. We have to believe it will work out for us, or we lose before we begin. Only, I wasn't ready to give in either.

"I have to believe it isn't the only thing that works."

"I know," she said.

We lapsed into silence as we both considered the weight of what was happening. "Why didn't you give him the list of spies that you got from Sinan?"

She smiled a secret little smile. "Well, let's call that a contingency. I may have decided to work with him, but that doesn't mean I fully trust him yet. I mean, it has already waited two years. His name wasn't on it, so it can wait until I'm a little more sure of who I'm working with."

Anne never failed to surprise and fascinate me. "Your contradictions are your best feature. Don't change that for the world, okay?"

"As long as we change the world, right?" She grinned a rare, unfiltered smile.

"Damn right."

After a moment, I sighed. It was deep, resonating, and final. "Is this it, then?"

Anne shrugged awkwardly and turned away, unable to look at me. "I didn't really expect that we would sail together forever, anyway. Sooner or later, our paths would necessarily part." She turned back to look at me. "It just turned out to be sooner."

I cleared my throat, suddenly feeling a little choked up. "It's been a fun ride, my friend. I hope we'll stay in touch."

"Of course, Captain."

I held out my hand, hoping to part on the best terms possible, and she pushed it aside, hugging me instead. As she pulled back, she blinked away what I could have sworn were unshed tears. She gave me a watery smile and said, "I will send a letter of credit to the bank in Anvilcove and it will cover the rest of your expenses."

"One trip around the isles," I mumbled.

She nodded. "That is what we agreed to, and I always hold to my promises. You've done a remarkable job, all things considered."

I laughed and hugged her again.

With no more words left to say, I put my hands in my pockets, nodded, and watched her walk away.

CHAPTER TWENTY-SIX

I headed back to the Siren full of conflicting emotions. Sad it turned out this way, tired in a way that went much deeper than just my body, vindicated for my righteous fury, and proud and a touch giddy at the way I had stood up for myself. But most notably, I was relieved.

The worries I'd always had from being directionless were gone. The burden of needing to know what I was doing, where I was going, and why, had faded as soon as I saw the truth. This whole time I had it wrong. I didn't need a plan. I needed a purpose.

Well, now I had one for sure. Or at least, it sure sounded like I did when I was yelling at the fancy Lugaian knight. Time would tell if I could live up to my grand speeches. But then again, Anne was right with that one—I had to believe this would work.

Fatigue was licking at my heels as I crawled my way up the gangplank and onto the deck of the Siren. I had fully expected to find every member of my crew in their bunks, dead to the world. Maybe not Merrik. Whatever had been on his mind seemed too weighty for sleep, but the rest of them, certainly.

I did not except to find them exactly where I had left them. They were more or less curled up in a cozy pile on the deck, talking quietly among themselves, and looking quite contented.

"Cap'n," Eric greeted me. "Welcome back."

The others offered quiet greetings as well, and Kaelyn lifted one corner of her blanket in offering. "Come join us, Tianna," she said.

I did so gladly. I curled up next to Kaelyn and dropped my head onto her shoulder.

For several long minutes no one said anything, and eventually, into the quiet, I told them, "Anne left."

No one said anything. There was still so much left unsaid, but in that quiet moment, I let it rest. So much had happened in such a relatively short period of time. None of us were who we had been when we set off, and right then, I couldn't have thought of a better way to begin.

Waves gently knocked against the hull and the occasional frog chirruped but otherwise, the night was quiet. I looked up, watching the stars, listening to nothing.

"Hell of a summer, huh?" Kaelyn asked, amusement lighting up her voice.

A laugh we all desperately needed broke out. First a chuckle, then growing into a full bellied amusement.

"'Bout n' round th' bend, me toddies," Iain commented with a chuckle. "We c'n call th' merry maid home with all th' fuss."

"No kidding," Eric added. "Am I the only one who feels like it's been years, not weeks?"

I snorted. "Seriously." As I considered that, I grew sober. "I know I haven't known any of you that long, But I'm glad I met each of you. I couldn't imagine a single step of this without you all by my side."

"Ugh, don't get sappy!" Isaboe grumbled and everyone laughed again.

After another moment of restful quiet, Merrik finally spoke. "So, what's next?"

Unlike every other time that question had been asked, I was filled with a sense of excitement, not dread. I didn't know all the details—or even most of the details—but I knew it would work out.

"Well, the Siren is ours. Anne is paying us for the work we completed," I told them. "We will go where we need to, and do what we must. And we'll do it together."

"That's not exactly a destination," Merrik said.

"No," Kaelyn agreed, "But it's exactly right." She wiggled around until she was able to look me in the face. "When we met, you told me you wanted to see more of the world. Meet people, learn, have an adventure."

Isaboe scoffed. "Well, we've certainly done that."

I smirked, but let Kaelyn continue.

"Let's do that," she said. "More of that."

I nodded and craned my neck to look at Merrik with a cheesy grin on my face. "Yes, that. More adventure."

He glared at me for a long moment. I saw the corner of his mouth twitch, stretching up into a smile, before he rolled his eyes. "More pirates? More scars and terrible lapses in judgment? How about more headaches from those jigs Iain's always playing?"

"Yes!" I said happily. "More music, like those jigs Iain is always playing." I turned and offered the man in question a wink. Then added, "More laughter, more travel, more things that excite and thrill us. More changes to learn, and more of us. Together."

A somewhat muted cheer worked its way sluggishly through the group.

"Well, that was less than thrilling," I told them dryly. Then seriously, I asked, "Is that not what you want?"

Isaboe laughed first and loudest. "Of course, that's what we want!"

"We also know that it comes at a cost," Merrik cut in. "Adventures are good, but they take a toll. Like this one did."

I sighed and dropped my head onto Kaelyn's shoulder again. "Fine," I muttered into her shirt.

I wasn't there more than a breath before I sat up again, urgency and certainty racing up my spine. "You know what? You're right. There will be danger. Nothing to be done about that except face it. Whether we like it or hate it or want to change it, the fact is that the rest of the world has abandoned the isles as a lost cause. We're nothing more than a mark on some map in their quest for power. But we can't let that be all there is. We can't let that be the end of the story. Too many people need us and we have to help however we can."

"But what can we–" Eric hesitated, and I cut him off.

"However we can," I said. "We will help whoever we can, however we can, because that's the only way to make the world better."

There were no cheers at my words, but I did see smiles, and that was pretty damn heartwarming.

"We could do worse," Merrik said, and I grinned at him again.

"As long as we're together, I'm happy 'nough," Eric said nonchalantly, which caused Iain to pipe in.

"Aye, long as th' icefall months tramp 'round, hap we c'n learn t' tie a better knot, ya?"

Soft laughter made its way around again, and I relished in the sound of joy, even—or perhaps especially—knowing that he meant more than just knots.

We were on our own now. We couldn't keep going, just surviving. It was time to start living this life we chose.

"Hey, Captain?" Kaelyn hemmed in a way I wasn't used to from her. "I uh… I have something for you."

She stood and walked off to a corner of the deck we'd been using mostly for storage. She rooted in some boxes, but after a moment returned with a heavy piece of dark sailcloth sewn and patched with a design of some kind.

She dropped the bundle in my lap and I looked at her, confused. I stood and unfurled it. The whole thing was the length of my arms outstretched, and hung to my knees when I held it up. I gasped.

It was a flag.

Our flag.

A white skull wearing a dark hat was stitched onto a black background. The hat looked suspiciously like mine, and the skull wore an eye patch over its right eye. I raised a brow at Kaelyn, wondering if she's intended the connection to Tavers. Crossed under it, instead of bones, was a pair of flutes representing music—the thing we all had in common. It was the most beautiful thing I had ever seen.

"A jolly roger?" I gasped out around a throat tights with tears.

Kaelyn shrugged. "Not exactly. We're not your normal band of pirates, are we? Said yourself that a jolly roger didn't seem appropriate. So, this is a jolly... Frederick."

"Frederick?"

"We'll call him Fred." Her grin lit up the morning brighter than the sunrise.

Actually, that was the sunrise. The sky is just starting to lighten, and the first soft trills of birdsong were floating in the air. It was calm, peaceful in a way we all needed, and despite the lack of sleep, I could tell we were all more rested after the last hour together than we would have been after hours in our beds.

"It's nearing high tide," I noted. "Since no one seems able to sleep, why don't we get some ocean under us?"

"Uhh… Tianna," Isaboe said. "You know how ships work, right? There's already ocean under us."

"Har har," I replied, standing.

Isaboe chuckled at her own joke, and I dragged her out of her blankets to her feet, eliciting a yelp from her. Once she was up, I brushed her off, and we shared a smile.

"Let's go," I said. "I'm so ready to be away from here."

"Aye, aye, Captain."

Everyone stood and stretched, shaking off some of the lingering aches from our long night.

"What's our heading, then?" Kaelyn asked.

After a pause, I told her the only thing that I could think of that made any sense at all. "Wellsmith?"

She looked smug and winked. "Somehow, I knew you were going to say that."

I laughed and pushed her playfully. "We'll go back to Wellsmith to get a better idea of what's happening there. There may still be more answers about whatever it was Krellen and Redship were planning." I turned and looked up out to the slowly lightening sky. "After that, who knows? Anywhere we want, right?"

"Right," she said with a full grin. With a newfound excitement, Kaelyn clapped her hands together once and shouted. "Alright, you lot. Let's get a move on. All crew to stations! Weigh anchor and loose the sails! Someone hoist Fred! He's about to make a grand debut!"

Chuckling to myself, I set off to do just that.

I made my way down the line, untying stays and getting ready to cast off, when a voice call out from behind and below me, on shore.

"Tianna! Captain! Wait there a moment!"

I turned to see Anne running up to the ship. She was actually running. I stood in wonder and waited for her.

"Permission to come aboard?" she gasped out between panting breaths.

"Get up here, you fool!" I called down to her.

She grinned and hurried up to join me.

"I changed my mind."

"You did?" I asked. I was going for a facetious brow lift, but I was surprised and happy to see her, and my face showed it.

She bobbed her head in a relaxed nod. Then she took a breath, steadying herself. "I may, on occasion, act hastily. And in this particular instance, I let fear and predetermined plans cloud my judgment."

I smiled at her. "I see. And?"

"I was thinking over everything that you said to Sir Marcos, and realized that while Lugaia will always have other spies, the Outer Isles need me here right now."

I eyed her carefully. "And?" I prompted again.

"And," she hesitated, then pressed forward. "And I don't particularly relish the thought of going back into that gilded cage my sisters live in, nor shipped off to Lugaia Denisi to make nice with the aristocracy and trade in open secrets."

I nodded solemnly, meeting her gaze, unwavering. "And?"

"And…" Worry flashed through her eyes. She swallowed hard. "And I'm sorry! Please? I would so much rather sail with you than…" she trailed off again, finally noting the teasing twitch of my lips.

She made a disgusted noise in the back of her throat and drew herself up to her full height, affecting that air of superiority she was born to. "I am a damn good navigator, and you would do well to welcome me back with open arms. You would like be lost asea within hours without me here to guide you."

I grinned and wrapped my arms around her. "Welcome back, Annie."

"Don't call me Annie," she grumbled with a smile.

No one missed her return, and they hurried over to welcome her back. Merrik squeezed her shoulder with a warm smile. Iain gave her a saucy wink and said, "Thought ya lost in th' fields, Annie-girl. Flow'rs don' seem a'sweet as a tip of yer lift."

Anne blushed and quickly let herself be pulled into a crushing hug from Isaboe. "Don't do that again! At least say goodbye next time!"

The morale of the crew was growing as steadily as the approaching dawn, and I couldn't fight off my cheer.

"That's enough! Everyone get back to work," I ordered. "We've got places to be!"

A cheer rose up from the crew. A real cheer this time, like the one I'd been looking for earlier. I coughed subtly, letting myself get swept away in emotion while everyone ran back to their stations.

Before she raced off to join everyone else, Anne turned back to me. "You know, I will go at some point. I meant what I said about needing to be out there."

"I know," I told her. "But I'll keep you around as long as you want to stay."

With one last smile, she nodded and went to work.

We cast off and began to depart. I worked my way up, checking the lines until I found myself standing at the bow of the ship.

I looked out over the bay where chaos had reigned just hours before. Men and women died out there, some of them good people. Not just in this battle, but in many more just like it, every day. I knew that it could have been us—should have been us.

This is the life we chose. Risks, reward, epic tales, and terrible battles. We knew all that going in. But what was is all for if not to chase that horizon?

And with these people beside me? I was the luckiest damn woman in all of Denisi.

We slowly picked up speed, moving away from the docks. Once we were away, Kaelyn joined me. We stood side-by-side quietly as we headed east, out of the bay into the open ocean.

I had no words. Nothing to say and nothing but the thrill of the unknown laid out before me. Our future awaited and I took my first deep breath in weeks as I stared out at the horizon, watching the sun rise.

Thank you for reading The Pirate Horde!

There is so much more planned for this series. Follow @tiannablackboot on facebook for updates, ARC opportunities, and special offers. Or for something a little more lighthearted, check me out on twitter and instagram. To contact me, visit http://www.tiannablackboot.com

Not done with the Horde? That's okay, I'm not either. Check out <u>The Tales From The Siren</u>, a series of standalone novellas are all about our favorite miscreants.

Follow their adventures as they run afoul of the law, damage public property, fall in love, fall out of love, attend fancy parties, accidentally move some merchandise and so much more.

The Pirates of the Whimsical Winds
will return in 2023

THE PIRATE KING

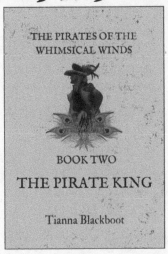

The isles always been a political wasteland. So why is there
a new banner flying above the Reefs?

War is still threatening in the east. Let it. I'm keeping
my focus right here in the Isles. Every day it seems like more
and more people need our help. Rebellions have been
cropping up all over and it doesn't take a prophet to read
the signs–big change is coming.

Do the pirate isles really need a king?